THE GOLDEN ANGEL

BOOKS BY GILBERT MORRIS

Through a Glass Darkly

THE HOUSE OF WINSLOW SERIES

1. *The Honorable Imposter*
2. *The Captive Bride*
3. *The Indentured Heart*
4. *The Gentle Rebel*
5. *The Saintly Buccaneer*
6. *The Holy Warrior*
7. *The Reluctant Bridegroom*
8. *The Last Confederate*
9. *The Dixie Widow*
10. *The Wounded Yankee*
11. *The Union Belle*
12. *The Final Adversary*
13. *The Crossed Sabres*
14. *The Valiant Gunman*
15. *The Gallant Outlaw*
16. *The Jeweled Spur*
17. *The Yukon Queen*
18. *The Rough Rider*
19. *The Iron Lady*
20. *The Silver Star*
21. *The Shadow Portrait*
22. *The White Hunter*
23. *The Flying Cavalier*
24. *The Glorious Prodigal*
25. *The Amazon Quest*
26. *The Golden Angel*
27. *The Heavenly Fugitive*
28. *The Fiery Ring*

THE LIBERTY BELL

1. *Sound the Trumpet*
2. *Song in a Strange Land*
3. *Tread Upon the Lion*
4. *Arrow of the Almighty*
5. *Wind From the Wilderness*
6. *The Right Hand of God*
7. *Command the Sun*

CHENEY DUVALL, M.D.[1]

1. *The Stars for a Light*
2. *Shadow of the Mountains*
3. *A City Not Forsaken*
4. *Toward the Sunrising*
5. *Secret Place of Thunder*
6. *In the Twilight, in the Evening*
7. *Island of the Innocent*
8. *Driven With the Wind*

CHENEY AND SHILOH: THE INHERITANCE[1]

1. *Where Two Seas Met*
2. *The Moon by Night*

THE SPIRIT OF APPALACHIA[2]

1. *Over the Misty Mountains*
2. *Beyond the Quiet Hills*
3. *Among the King's Soldiers*
4. *Beneath the Mockingbird's Wings*
5. *Around the River's Bend*

LIONS OF JUDAH

1. *Heart of a Lion*

[1]with Lynn Morris   [2]with Aaron McCarver

THE
GOLDEN ANGEL
GILBERT ★ MORRIS

BETHANYHOUSE
PUBLISHERS
MINNEAPOLIS, MINNESOTA

Published by Bethany House Publishers
A Ministry of Bethany Fellowship International
11400 Hampshire Avenue South
Bloomington, Minnesota 55438
www.bethanyhouse.com

Printed in the United States of America by
Bethany Press International, Bloomington, Minnesota 55438

Library of Congress Cataloging-in-Publication Data

Morris, Gilbert.
    The golden angel / by Gilbert Morris.
        p.   cm. — (The house of Winslow ; Bk. 26)
    ISBN 0-7642-2118-3
    1. Winslow family (Fictitious characters)—Fiction. 2. Women stunt performers—Fiction. 3. Women air pilots—Fiction. 4. Stunt flying—Fiction. I. Title.
    PS3563.O8742 G65   2001
813'.54—dc21   2001002516

To Paul and Shirley St. John

Johnnie and I are so grateful
that God has put us together.
You two have been a blessing to us.
The pilgrim way is sweeter
with companions like you!

GILBERT MORRIS spent ten years as a pastor before becoming Professor of English at Ouachita Baptist University in Arkansas and earning a Ph.D. at the University of Arkansas. During the summers of 1984 and 1985, he did postgraduate work at the University of London. A prolific writer, he has had over 25 scholarly articles and 200 poems published in various periodicals, and over the past years has had more than 70 novels published. His family includes three grown children, and he and his wife live in Alabama.

CONTENTS

PART FOUR
Illusions Fall 1922

THE HOUSE OF WINSLOW

★ ★ ★ ★

THE HOUSE OF WINSLOW

★ ★ ★ ★

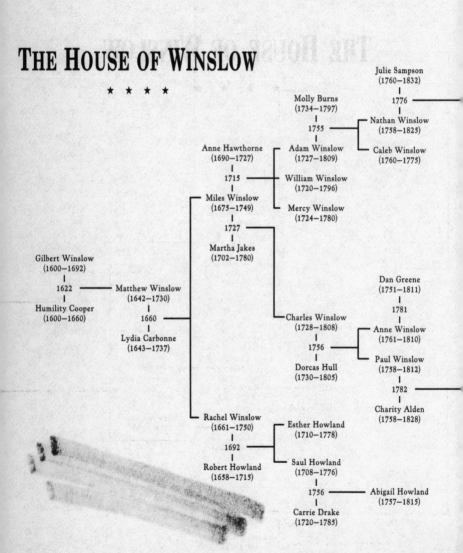

Julie Sampson
(1760–1832)

1776

Molly Burns
(1734–1797)

1755

Nathan Winslow
(1758–1825)

Anne Hawthorne
(1690–1727)

1715

Adam Winslow
(1727–1809)

Caleb Winslow
(1760–1775)

Miles Winslow
(1675–1749)

William Winslow
(1720–1796)

1727

Mercy Winslow
(1724–1780)

Martha Jakes
(1702–1780)

Dan Greene
(1751–1811)

Gilbert Winslow
(1600–1692)

1781

1622

Matthew Winslow
(1642–1730)

Anne Winslow
(1761–1810)

Humility Cooper
(1600–1660)

1660

Charles Winslow
(1728–1808)

Paul Winslow
(1758–1812)

Lydia Carbonne
(1643–1737)

1756

1782

Dorcas Hull
(1730–1805)

Charity Alden
(1758–1828)

Rachel Winslow
(1661–1750)

Esther Howland
(1710–1778)

1692

Saul Howland
(1708–1776)

Robert Howland
(1658–1715)

1756

Abigail Howland
(1757–1815)

Carrie Drake
(1720–1785)

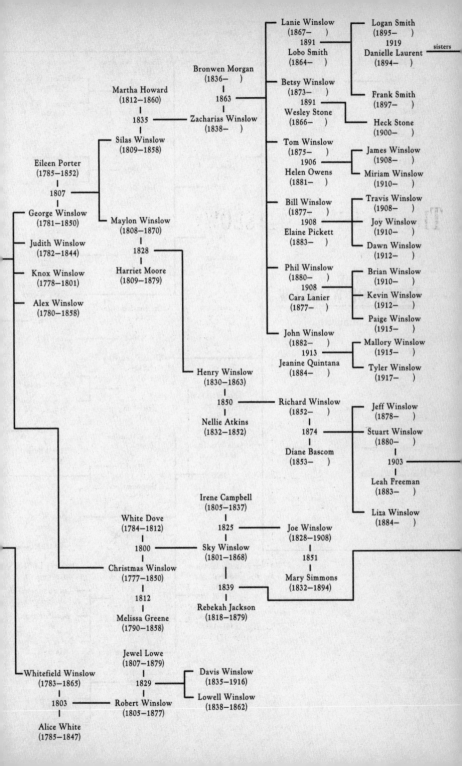

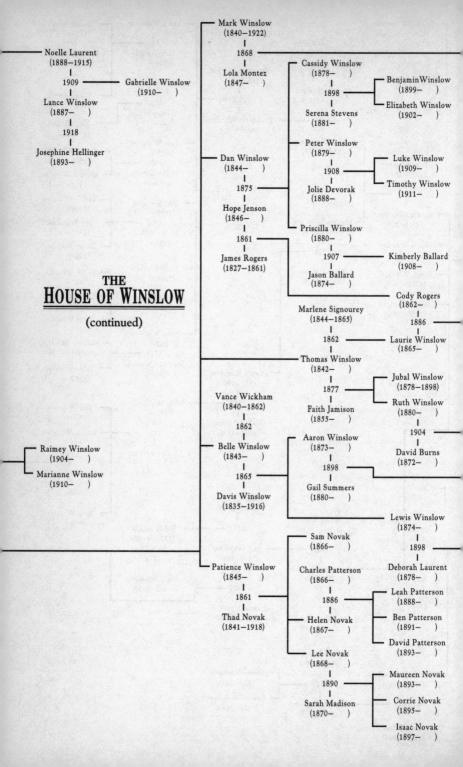

THE
HOUSE OF WINSLOW

(continued)

```
┌─ Barney Winslow
│   (1870–   )
│         │              ┌─ Patrick Winslow
│        1900 ───────────┤    (1902–   )
│         │              └─ Erin Winslow
│   Katie Sullivan            (1904–   )
│   (1875–   )
│
│
├─ Andrew Winslow
│   (1873–   )
│         │              ┌─ Amelia Winslow
│        1900 ───────────┤    (1902–   )
│         │              └─ Phillip Winslow
│   Dorothy Hansen            (1904–   )
│   (1875–   )
│
│
└─ Esther Winslow
    (1876–   )
          │
         1905 ───────────── Ross Kruger
          │                  (1906–   )
    Jan Kruger
    (1873–   )


    Kathleen O'Fallon
    (1890–   )
          │
         1913
          │
┌─ Bill Rogers
│   (1888–   )
│
│
│
│
│
│
│
└────────────────── Annie Rogers
                     (1890–   )
┌─ Aileen Burns          │
│   (1908–   )          1913
│                         │
└──────────── Jeb Winslow (adopted)
              (1886–   )
┌─ Jared Winslow
│   (1899–   )
├─ Emily Winslow
│   (1901–   )
└─ Wesley Winslow
    (1903–   )
┌─ Hannah Winslow
│   (1899–   )
└─ Joshua Winslow
    (1902–   )
```

PART ONE

THE MISFIT

★ ★ ★ ★

1913–1921

CHAPTER ONE

THE REBELLION

★ ★ ★ ★

1913

As soon as Erin Winslow awoke, the thought of facing another day at school oppressed her like a heavy weight settling on her spirits. As always she awoke in a sudden rush, not coming out of sleep slowly in stages but instantly at one moment of time, completely aware of where she was and of the circumstances around her. She lay there in the darkness of her room, her inner clock telling her that dawn was still at least half an hour away. It was a gift she had, even at the age of nine, of knowing time in a strange, intuitive fashion.

I won't go to that old school today—I won't!

She rolled off of her narrow bed and dressed quickly in the darkness. As always, she had put her clothes on the chair beside her bed, and now she slipped into them quickly. The air was hot and humid, and as she donned underwear and a khaki dress, then slipped on stockings and a pair of worn black leather shoes, the dread of facing another day in a classroom increased.

Not wanting her parents to see her, she would have exited out the window if she could have, but it was barred to keep out prowling leopards and other dangerous wildlife. She opened the door silently, not allowing it to squeak, and moved down the short hall through the living area of the house and carefully turned the front doorknob. She held her breath, waiting for a sound. None came, and she felt a quick satisfaction in making her escape.

Closing the door silently behind her, Erin paused only for an instant. The outbuildings were mere shadows in the ebony darkness just before the dawn, but she knew every inch of ground in this territory as well as she knew the layout of her own room. When she reached the fence, which was tall enough to keep out all but an agile leopard, she pushed up the bar, stepped outside, and pulled the gate closed after her. As soon as she was outside the gate, she moved through the predawn darkness, breathing in the warm air with its accompanying smells.

Traveling in the dark in the African veldt could be dangerous, but Erin had grown up with such dangers. Now she breathed in the scent of loamy earth and the green fragrance of the woodland as it closed in a hundred yards from her home. She took a well-beaten path and moved steadily away from her house, totally familiar with her surroundings.

She reached an opening in the thick brush. The land began to lighten as the sun peeked over the eastern hills, bringing with its warmth a sense of gladness that Erin always enjoyed at first light. She was a perceptive child, more aware of her environment than most white people. The native Masai, with whom Erin felt quite at home, were completely at one with this world and needed neither watches to tell time nor barometers to forecast a storm. Even at her youthful age, Erin had somehow soaked in some of this gift from her Masai friends.

The day before, Erin had endured great humiliation at school and had arrived home full of rebellious thoughts. Just before going to sleep, she had told herself, *I'll just go out in the morning and stay until it's too late to go to school!* The plan had seemed simple enough, but even as she watched the pale sun rise, touching the hills with glimmers of light, driving away the shadows from the African world, she understood that it would not do to skip school.

Slowing her pace as the sun turned orange in the tawny sky and illuminated the veldt, she slowed to a halt, then sat down on a fallen tree. Her heart was sad and discouraged, but at the same time an anger she could not explain gnawed at her insides.

She sat there motionless, listening to the sounds of chattering birds and monkeys screaming as they swung effortlessly through the trees to her left. Her eye caught the fluttering wings of a bird dropping down before her to perch in a thorn tree. Instantly she identified it as a black-throated honey guide. She knew the bird well, for her Masai friend Nbuta had taught her the strange habits of the honey guide two years ago. *"This bird,"* he had told her, *"will lead the honey badger and even a man to the hives of bees. He feasts on the leavings of the raid."* Erin suddenly remembered how Nbuta had smiled and added, *"If no honey is left for the honey guide, it will lead the next man to a snake or a lion. . . ."*

Even with the rebellious spirit that lay in Erin at that moment, she had to smile, for Nbuta had been teasing her. She had learned to trust the towering Masai warrior, but she had also discovered that the man's sense of humor often led him to make exaggerated statements. While she was enjoying the early-morning freshness and reflecting on these memories, time passed without her concern or awareness. Erin had absorbed the Masai attitude toward time. While other white people were enslaved to watches and schedules, Erin had learned simply to let time carry her along, to not let life hurry her.

Now as she arose from the fallen tree, knowing that she was being foolish and that she would have to go to the hated school, she turned and moved reluctantly back toward the house. The world about her seemed to be stretching awake in the morning stillness. As she crossed a grassy pasture, cabbage butterflies scattered at her footsteps and fluttered from flower to flower, and high above her a hawk soared ever upward on rising thermals. She was tempted to turn from the path and go to the river's edge to watch the white egrets as they dotted the darkness of the water, but she kept to her resolve to return home.

Close to her house a white-maned bush pig materialized out of the brush. He stared at her with red, malevolent eyes, but she wisely stood her ground and made no threatening moves. After scratching his raspy hide with a sharp hoof, he turned and disappeared. Erin saw the female dashing after him, leading a bunch of striped piglets, which squealed mightily as they dove into the lush vegetation.

Erin stiffened at the sound of her own name. Her mother was calling her, so she picked up her pace until she reached the fence enclosing their property. She saw her mother standing in front of the house, and with reluctance Erin opened the gate and made her way across the fenced-in enclosure until she stood in front of her.

"You're going to be late for school, Erin. Where have you been?"

"Just out looking at the sunrise, Mother."

Katie Winslow had the same blond hair at the age of thirty-eight she'd had as a girl. Even with her hair tied back and wearing a simple, shapeless housedress, she was still a striking woman, although the years in Africa had aged her somewhat. Her blue eyes searched Erin's face intently. "Were you outside the gate, Erin?"

"Yes, I was, Mama."

"Your father told you never to do that in the dark." She paused, awaiting an apology from her daughter that was not forthcoming. Her disappointment pulled her mouth taut. "All right, now go inside and get ready for school. Don't forget to wash your face and brush your teeth."

Erin moved inside with resignation, but she revealed her anger in the set of her back. She went at once to her room to make her brief preparations. After pouring some water from a pitcher into a porcelain basin on the washstand beside her bed, she gave her face a cursory scrubbing and brushed her teeth with some baking soda she kept in a pottery jar. Then standing before a small mirror on the wall, she pulled a brush through her luxurious blond hair. Staring back at her was a sturdy child with wide-set eyes, and she whispered to the image before her, "I hate that old school—I hate it!"

She picked up her books bound with a leather strap and stepped out of her bedroom. When she reached the large room that served as a kitchen, dining area, and living room, she found the rest of the family waiting. Her brother Patrick, two years older, snapped at her, "Why don't you hurry up! I'm starving to death!" Patrick was a stringy boy with dark brown hair and dark blue eyes.

"That's enough from you, Patrick," their father ordered. "Sit down, Erin." Barney Winslow had the same black hair he had brought to Africa with him years before. His features were somewhat battered, for he had been a prizefighter while a young man, and his struggle to survive on the dark continent had left lines around the corners of his eyes. He had a scar that ran down his right cheek in front of his ear and disappeared where his neck joined his jawbone. He was wearing a pair of worn khaki drill trousers and a light blue shirt unbuttoned at the neck. His hands were strong and square, and he wore a simple wedding band on the third finger of his left hand. "Your mother tells me you went outside the gate before dawn. I told you not to do that."

"I'm sorry, Daddy."

"Well, don't do it again." Barney bowed his head and asked a quick blessing. He spoke to God in an intimate fashion, as a man would speak to his friend, yet at the same time in a voice filled with respect and just a touch of awe. "Our Father, we ask that you help us to have grateful hearts for this food. Let us never take for granted all the daily blessings that come from your hand. In the name of Jesus, bless this food and keep us safe this day, and help us to be your representatives, declaring the gospel wherever we go. In Jesus' name. Amen."

Patrick speared a pancake and plopped it onto his plate even before his father had finished uttering the amen.

"You had your eyes open while Daddy was praying!" Erin accused.

"How would you know that unless you had your eyes open, too?"

"You always have your eyes open."

"That's enough, Erin," Katie said. "Now eat."

Erin was a light eater and lingered over her meal. The pancakes were soft and delicious, made especially so by the dark honey that Erin herself had gathered along with Nbuta.

"If you don't want that pancake, I'll eat it," Patrick offered.

Erin blinked her eyes, for she had been thinking of school and dreaded the moment when they would have to go. "No. I want it." She did not really want it, but her disagreeable thoughts about school caused her to deny her brother the pleasure of an extra pancake. She forced herself to eat half of it while her parents talked about the business of the mission field. Being the daughter of missionaries was the only life she knew, and meal-time conversations quite naturally tended to focus on the needs of the people they were called to serve. She heard her father speaking of the sick and those who were in trouble, and of the trips that he would make to hold evangelistic services deep in the interior. To Erin, this was his everyday business, and having heard it all before, she was only half listening now.

When the meal was over, Patrick ran off to get his books. Erin interrupted her father to say, "Daddy, I don't know why I have to go to that old school."

"You've got to go to school, sweetheart. Everyone has to. We all did."

"I'm just no good at it. Please don't make me go."

Barney Winslow shot a quick glance at his wife, who shook her head slightly and raised her shoulders in frustration. The two had talked of this often, and now he simply said, "If you'd try harder, you'd do better, Erin."

"I *do* try hard!" The rebellion in her reached a crescendo at her father's comment. Erin gritted her teeth and set her jaw. "You don't believe me, but I try hard!"

"No, you don't." Patrick had come back into the room. "You just give up."

"You shut up, Patrick!"

"That's enough, Erin, and you too, Patrick. I'm going to start the car. You come with me, Patrick."

Patrick stuck his tongue out at Erin and left with his father. At once Katie went over and put her hand on Erin's shoulder in an effort to reassure her. "It's all right. You'll do well today, I'm sure."

Erin stood suddenly and shook off her mother's hand. She loved her mother, but now she could no longer contain her anger, and she burst out, "No, I won't, Mama! I'm stupid! All the kids do better than I do—even the little ones."

Katie at once put her arms around the girl. Her heart grieved for her, and she said quietly, "It just takes you a little longer. You'll catch up. You'll see."

"I won't! I won't ever catch up! I'm just stupid!"

Erin snatched up her books and left the room. Katie followed her to the door and watched her daughter as she climbed into the car, which Barney had brought to the front door. The ancient automobile made a raucous noise, breaking the stillness of the morning air, and as the car chugged through the double gates, Katie watched them disappear in a cloud of dust.

Turning back inside, she went to the kitchen, where Pamela, a tall, lean woman in her midthirties, shook her head. "That Miss Erin, she is a problem." Pamela had served the Winslows for years as cook, housecleaner, and at least partially a mother to the two children. Now she said, "I feel sorry for Miss Erin. She's always behind. Why is that, Miss Katie?"

Katie shook her head. "I don't know. She says she's stupid, but that's not so."

"No, it's not so," Pamela nodded abruptly. "She's smart enough to know every animal and every bird in the world. It's just books that bothers her."

"She'll do better as she gets older." Katie began to help Pamela clean up the breakfast dishes, but her heart ached as she pondered her daughter's problems with school. Patrick had always loved books and study, but Erin never had. The only interest she had ever taken was when she was a mere baby and loved picture books. But when it came time for her to do her own reading, she had suddenly rebelled. Life had been one continual struggle since then.

As Katie Winslow moved about her work that morning, she prayed with all her heart for Erin and wondered what would happen to her. As was her custom, she asked for God's grace for the day ahead. "Oh, God, keep Erin in your hand this day, for she needs you!"

★　★　★　★

Mr. Franklin Simms was a small man of thirty-five with pale blue eyes and thinning blond hair. His thick glasses gave him an owlish look, and his high-pitched voice often came out rather shrill. The son of missionary parents, he had dedicated his own life to teaching in the mission school, instructing both missionary children and any native children who cared to attend. Now Mr. Simms looked over the class and saw that all were present. His eyes lingered on the four Winslow children. Amelia and Phillip Winslow sat together on the front row. Both of them had auburn hair, a common trait among the Winslows. Their father, Andrew, was the director of the mission station. Along with his wife, Dorothy, they lived in a large house ten miles away from the school, which had been located centrally for the missionaries. Mr. Simms was pleased enough with both Amelia and Phillip, for both of them were manageable and good at their work.

Shifting his eyes to the seats behind them, Mr. Simms took in their cousins Patrick and Erin Winslow. His eyes drew down into a squint as he saw that, as usual, Erin was staring out the window.

"The lesson is here, Erin, not in that tree outside." He waited until Erin looked around and faced him squarely. Mr. Simms felt he had never been able to get control of this child, for she had an independence that was rare even among missionary children. Now as their gazes locked, he made a vow again, *I'll teach this child if it kills us both!* Then aloud, he addressed the class. "All right. We will begin this morning with geometry."

A slight groan went up from part of the class, but he noted that Erin Winslow relaxed slightly. *She always does well at geometry*, Mr. Simms thought. *Why can't she do better with history and English and the other subjects?*

"Why do we have to study this old stuff—squares and triangles?" The speaker was Harry Long, the thirteen-year-old son of a missionary whose station was nearly thirty miles away. Harry stayed at Andrew Winslow's house during the school term. He was an athletic young man not particularly given to studies.

"We go through this every day on every subject!" Mr. Simms snapped impatiently. "It's part of the world that you'll have to live in, so stop arguing, Harry, and just do your work. Now we'll take the first problem, and, Harry, I'll let you go to the board and work it."

"Let me do it, Mr. Simms." Erin had her hand up, and Simms turned to her. "All right, Erin. You do it, then."

Erin loved to do geometry, for it was the one subject that came easily to her. She went to the board and went through the problem with obvious pleasure.

Amelia turned around and whispered to her cousin, "Hey,

Patrick, how come Erin does so good at geometry but can't do the other subjects?"

"I don't know. She just doesn't try, I think." Despite his criticism of her and his constant teasing, Patrick Winslow actually had a great affection for his sister and worried about her difficulties in school. He himself was excellent in all his subjects and suffered no small embarrassment that his sister did so poorly. He took it almost as a personal disappointment, and while he loved Erin, he wished heartily that she would try harder. Now he watched as her hand flew over the chalkboard, figuring the geometry problem quickly and efficiently. He shook his head in confusion. *Why in the world doesn't she work that hard on other stuff?* he thought.

★ ★ ★ ★

The morning passed surprisingly well for Erin—primarily because she had satisfied Mr. Simms with her ability in geometry. During the history lesson she was able to answer the one question he put to her because she remembered when he had discussed it in class. School went that way with her. She filed away everything the teacher *said*, but when she had to dig the material out of books for herself there was always some sort of breakdown.

After lunch the children all went outside and played a game of soccer. The Masai children were particularly good at this, and Harry Long prided himself on his ability. Once he shoved a younger boy down, and Erin yelled at him, "Why don't you pick on somebody your own size?"

Harry chafed at Erin's jab, remembering his humiliation earlier when he had followed her at the blackboard and his ignorance in geometry had been painfully exposed in front of the class. Now he flew at her and shoved her, yelling, "You keep your mouth shut, Erin Winslow, or I'll rub your face in the dirt!"

Instantly Patrick, who was two years younger than Harry but not in the least intimidated by him, forced himself between the two. "You mind your own business, Long, and leave my sister alone or I'll bloody your nose!"

Harry stared at the smaller boy and laughed. "Aw, come on, Patrick, it's just a game."

"Well, play the game and quit pushing little kids and girls around!"

Erin felt a warmness at Patrick's defense of her, and she stuck her tongue out at Harry. "Come on. Let's play, but don't act ugly anymore."

The game went on until Mr. Simms rang the bell outside the schoolroom door. The children piled back inside in a rush, and he had to call the class to order several times. When quiet was restored, he said more calmly, "Now we will continue with our history lesson. We're in the middle of the American Revolution. Let's see what you've learned."

He began pointing at various students and popping questions. Erin began to panic, knowing she was in trouble.

"All right, Erin," Mr. Simms said. "Who was the king of England during the American Revolution?"

Erin's mind went blank. She could feel her face blanch as she struggled to remember, but she finally mumbled in defeat, "I don't know, Mr. Simms."

"You don't know! How can that be? It's plain as day in the work you were assigned. Did you do your homework?"

"I did my best."

"Well, your best isn't very good. Really, Erin, I'm disappointed in you."

Erin gritted her teeth, overwhelmed by a sense of total humiliation. As the questions went on, she wanted nothing more than to jump up and run out of the room.

Somehow she endured the torture until afternoon recess, but as soon as she stepped outside and the children took up the soccer game they had begun at lunchtime, she ran directly at Harry Long and kicked the ball away from him.

Startled, Harry glared at her. "Well, if it ain't dummy Winslow! You kick a ball better than you do your homework. What makes you so dumb, Erin?"

Rage boiled up in Erin and spilled over. She ran straight toward the tall young man and butted her head into his stomach. He uttered an explosive *"Whoof!"* and fell backward. "Hey! Stop that!" he gasped, for Erin was pummeling him with her fists.

Harry Long had been taught never to fight a girl, but he was hard put to avoid all of her blows.

Patrick had been startled at the ferocity of Erin's attack and stood watching the fight, stunned, but regaining his wits, he ran over and grabbed her, pulling her back. "What's wrong with you, Erin? Have you gone crazy?"

Mr. Simms suddenly appeared and shouted, "Erin, stop that this instant!" His face pale, he said nervously, "Now you go inside and write on the board 'I will not lose my temper.' You keep writing that until I tell you to stop."

Harry turned to Patrick. "What's wrong with that sister of yours? She's crazy!"

"Well, if you'd stop calling her names, she wouldn't light into you. I'm warning you, Harry. Don't you ever call my sister a dummy again, or I'll for sure bloody your nose."

Harry saw that their schoolteacher was staring at him with displeasure, and he felt somewhat guilty. Yet he gave Mr. Simms a less-than-sincere apologetic look. "Oh, I didn't mean nothing by it!"

"Don't you ever call Erin dumb again. Do you hear me, Harry?" Mr. Simms demanded.

"Yes, Mr. Simms. I hear you." Embarrassed, he quickly turned back to the other children. "Come on. Let's get on with the game."

The game ended shortly, and Mr. Simms turned to lead the group back inside for the last hour of school for the day. He found only one student there, a tall Masai girl who hadn't gone out for recess. Simms looked at the board and saw that it was blank. He also saw that Erin was not there.

"Where's Erin, Matula?"

"She run out the back."

Patrick groaned and whispered to his cousin Amelia, "She's run away again. What's going to happen to that girl?"

★   ★   ★   ★

After recess Erin had not stopped for even an instant inside the school. Instead she had burst through the front door, crossed the classroom to the door at the rear, and shot outside. She had not stopped running until her breath began to come in short, hard bursts and she had to slow down to calm herself. A fierce anger was still burning in her as she traversed the wild country she knew so well. She crossed a plain that changed into woodland, passing native trees as she went—acacias, fig, baobab, and others that she readily recognized. On the other side of the woods, she emerged onto a dirt road and began to run again. Thick vegetation crowded the road, and as she put distance between herself and the schoolhouse, she slowed down again. Her running gave way to a trot and then to a fast walk.

She had no idea where she was going, but as always she paid close attention to her surroundings. As she passed a stream, she saw a reedbuck crouching at its edge. When it spotted her, it shot away like an arrow, releasing its tightly wound muscles. She watched the animal scattering the water with high, bounding silver splashes, and then she walked along the small creek, where goldenback weavers swayed and dangled from long stocks of purple amaranth. As she moved along the creek, a frog chorus rose, then died, then began again as she outdistanced it. Once she turned quickly to see a bush shrike, chestnut winged, watching her from the branches of a baobab.

She took a path that led through the lush part of the country and soon was out in the open plains. She walked slowly, dreading what was to come. It would be, Erin well knew, another embarrassing scene, for her parents would be hurt, and she would be unable to explain her behavior to them. The words of Harry Long kept ringing in her ears: *"Dummy! You're a dummy!"* and tears rose to her eyes, which she dashed away fiercely.

As she made her way across the plains, her eyes alert for danger, she suddenly thought of Nbuta. Just the thought of her friend made her walk faster. "I'll go see him," she spoke aloud and then broke into a trot as she made her way along. She knew she would have to go home eventually, but Nbuta's village was not far from the mission station, and always, since she had been very small, she had been his favorite. "*He* never called me dumb," Erin said and picked up her pace as she hurried across the grassland.

* * * *

Nbuta's house was like all other Masai houses. The women always built them, never the men, for men were the hunters. No Masai woman would ask a man to help her build the house.

The houses themselves looked like large, rounded, elongated lumps. The women made them by first putting saplings in the ground, then bending them over and tying them together with vines. They interwove those with grasses and sticks to form a firm foundation. Then they coated the entire structure with animal dung and mud. When the rain inevitably washed some away, there was always plenty of dung and mud to repair the damage.

As Nbuta gazed at the late-afternoon sky, he suddenly spotted movement in the distance. He narrowed his eyes. He was standing on one leg, the other leg crooked with the sole of his foot against his knee and leaning on a long spear that was his constant companion. He was alert and aware of any movement, but he relaxed somewhat when he recognized the individual who was coming at a fast trot.

"Something wrong," he shook his head. He was a very tall, lean man, as were almost all the Masai men. He wore a simple garment with one shoulder strap. The garment was died a dark red, and the only other colors he wore were red, blue, and white beads that hung from his ears and around his neck in a thick chain. He was thirty years old and had a penetrating gaze and phenomenal eyesight. He recognized Erin Winslow when she was merely a dot on the horizon, but he did not move until she came up to him. He noted the dusty face and the troubled blue-green eyes, but he smiled at her and spoke to her in Swahili. "Greetings, daughter. What brings you here?"

Erin answered in Nbuta's language. She had picked that up easily enough, not from books, but simply from spending so much time with the Masai people. "I have come," she said formally.

"You must be hungry. Are you, daughter?"

Erin suddenly realized she had eaten nothing since lunch, and it was late in the afternoon. Her long run from the schoolhouse had indeed left her hungry. "Yes, I am."

"Come. We will eat together."

What followed next might have shaken an American-born youngster, but to Erin it had become a tradition. She followed the tall man out to the cattle as he picked up a gourd with an open mouth. The two of them went out to where an enormous cow was standing chewing her cud peaceably. The Masai spoke to her and then patted her on the neck. Pulling out a sharp knife, he quickly and expertly slit the vein in her neck and caught the blood as it poured rich and crimson into the openmouthed vessel. When he had gotten enough, he reached down and picked up some cow dung and smeared it over the wound, holding it there until the blood coagulated. Then he squatted down and, holding the gourd in one hand, filled it with milk.

Erin watched all this, as she had done many times. Nbuta swirled the liquid around, tasted it, then said, "Good," and handed it to Erin. Erin could not remember the first time she had tasted this traditional Masai drink. Patrick could not stand it. It made him sick, but Erin drank until she was satisfied, then handed back the gourd. "Good, Nbuta."

Nbuta drank long and deeply, patted the cow on the back, then said, "Come. We will walk."

Nbuta carried the gourd back to the door of the house, handed it to his wife, then walked away. Erin walked beside him, and the tall man adjusted his stride. As they moved around, Nbuta began to talk. He knew that there was trouble in the child and that sooner or later it would come out. Finally it did. The two had stopped beside a baobab tree and were watching the multicolored cattle as they grazed languidly, tended by the young Masai boys, who all carried staffs that they pretended were spears. It was the job of every Masai boy to tend cattle until he became a warrior.

Finally Erin began to speak, and Nbuta listened gravely. He saw the pain in his young friend's face, and when she had finished, he said, "We all must bear our troubles."

"I know, Nbuta, but they call me names, and they say I'm stupid."

"But you know that you are not, and I know that you are not. And we are the ones who count. You and your friend."

Nbuta spoke for a long time. In his deep wisdom he recognized that she was more troubled than he had ever seen her.

"Come. We will go down to the river, and we will sit, and we will think, and we will ask the good God to tell us what to do."

"All right, Nbuta." Erin obediently walked beside him. She would have stuck her head in the fire for this man, for he had been her friend all of her life. As she walked slowly toward the river with the tall Masai warrior, her heart was aching.

★   ★   ★   ★

Nbuta stood before Barney Winslow, towering over him as he did over most men. "Do not be angry with her, my friend," he said. "She has a good heart."

Barney nodded at once. He and Katie had been greatly upset when Patrick had come home right after school to tell them what had happened. Barney had felt a moment's fear, for Africa was no place for a young girl to be wandering around. But when Erin had not come home, he had the strong feeling that she had gone to her best friend, and now he said to Nbuta, "Thank you for bringing her home, my friend."

"She is a fine daughter, but she has a different spirit in her than most of the white young people I have known."

"I know. She is different," Barney said. "Therefore, her mother and I must show much patience."

Nbuta smiled gravely. "That is wise, but you are always wise, Pastor Barney."

"Not always," Barney said, shaking his head at the thought of situations in the past he had handled badly. "Well, come inside, Nbuta."

"No, I will go home. I have told her she can come to my home, and we will hunt together tomorrow if you give permission."

"I think it might be a good break for her. She'll miss a day of school, but I'll take care of that."

Nbuta nodded and turned, moving away swiftly in the darkness. Barney stood for a long time and then turned and went back into the house. "Has she gone to bed?" he asked Katie.

"Yes. She didn't want to talk. She's very hurt. Patrick was right. When that Long boy called her stupid, it just seemed to tear her to pieces."

"I wish we could do more to help her. I just don't understand it," Barney said helplessly. He stood in the middle of the room with Katie in front of him and shook his head in despair. "She's so good at some things, but she just can't seem to get anything much out of books."

Katie came over and put her arm around him. "We'll pray. She'll find her way."

Barney Winslow took Katie in his arms, and the two clung together tightly. They felt a deep helplessness that all parents feel when they cannot find the key to handling their children's problems. Both of them knew that this problem was one only God could solve.

CHAPTER TWO

WOMAN OF THE MASAI

★ ★ ★ ★

1920

"Praise God for the blood of the bull, which brings strength to our loins, and for the milk of the cow, which gives warmth to the breasts of our lovers."

Erin stood before Nbuta and the other hunters and watched as he drank deeply of the gourd. It was the ritual of the hunt, and the entire group gathered around as Nbuta echoed his words: "Praise God for the blood of the bull."

Erin's heart beat faster, for this was the day she had awaited with excitement. Her sixteenth birthday had come, and though the Masai did not celebrate birthdays in the same way as whites, Nbuta had sensed that the day had a special meaning for the young woman. "When you are sixteen," he had said, "I will follow the white customs and give you a gift, for you will be a woman on that day. What gift would you have?"

The corners of Erin's lips turned up as she stood with the hunters, thinking of how Nbuta had been shocked when she had said, "Let me go on a hunt with you and the other warriors."

Nbuta had been shocked because Masai women did not hunt, but the humor of her request had caught his fancy. "I will have to talk long to convince the other men, but it will be even as you say. When you reach the sixteenth year, you will hunt with the Masai warriors."

Excitement raced through Erin as the men prepared themselves for the hunt. They all carried broad shields and straight spears. She herself was permitted to carry a spear, but Nbuta had made it clear that she was to be merely an observer and not a participant when the animal was slain.

"Come. We will go," Nbuta said.

Erin moved forward with the group of twelve warriors, and they left the village as the first light of the sun began warming the earth. They passed through the large herds of cattle, goats, and sheep moving along the trails until they reached the open country. The animals turned their eyes upon the hunters and made slobbering noises and tried to nuzzle them. Erin had been with the Masai so much she was only vaguely aware of the pungent stench of the bulls and cows.

The group moved silently in single file as they skirted the edge of the wooded country, then wheeled north toward the Mogai Valley. The rains had begun two months previously, and now the grass in the valley reached the top of Erin's knees. She was wearing khaki shorts, and her lower legs were scarred from brushing against thorns and sharp sticks. She had grown up to be a sturdily built young woman, her blond hair gleaming in the sun and her blue-green eyes that the Masai found so fascinating darting from point to point as the hunters moved. She had perfectly shaped eyebrows arching over slightly slanted eyes and a shadowed hollow between her cheekbones and jaw. The planes of her face made strong and pleasant contours, and she had clean-edged and beautifully curved lips.

The party traveled swiftly, and Nbuta glanced at Erin from time to time. She was aware of his scrutiny and made sure that she kept up. She followed Nbuta through a field of fresh-smelling leleshaw bushes and imitated him as he leaped over the stinging nettle and thornbushes. As they traveled along swiftly, Erin was aware of the life pulsing about her. A bevy of partridges rose out of the grass, exploding with a miniature thunder, then wheeled away as one and disappeared into the eastern sky.

The heat of the valley arose more intently with every step they took deeper into the bush. Erin loved the grating sound of the singing cicadas and the tingling feel of the butterflies that were swept by the wind against her body. She watched them hovering over the bushes, and as they fluttered about the tall grasses and vegetation, the blood coursed through Erin's veins. She had that special feeling of anticipation that always filled her when she was moving into any kind of action. She never felt it when she was in the schoolroom or working around the house with her mother, but whenever she was with the Masai or was hunting with her father, the feeling came, and she laughed softly now as she kept up easily with the hunters.

Suddenly she saw Nbuta halt abruptly, and his body bent as he drew back his spear. She had seen a flicker of movement ahead, but Nbuta's reaction to it was too swift to follow, the flight of his spear but a flash in the sunlight. A cry went up from the hunters, and she raced ahead with Nbuta to the reedbuck that had fallen. Rich crimson blood poured from the wound where the spear had pierced the animal's hide. The other hunters gathered around the fallen buck, their eyes gleaming with admiration, and a stocky, muscular man named Keintu cried out loudly, "The hand of our leader is quicker than the stroke of a leopard!"

The others echoed the praise, but Nbuta paid them no attention.

Erin studied Nbuta's arms, which seemed too slender to generate such immense strength. She had often marveled that the Masai did not have bulging, heavy muscles. They were lean like leopards, usually tall, and almost all of them strong. As Nbuta pulled the spear out of the animal, Erin was not in the least offended by the blood. She had been hunting with her father since she was twelve years old. Patrick had never cared for hunting, but she loved every minute of it. She watched as Nbuta carefully cleaned his spearhead. She understood that to every Masai warrior the spear was as much a part of himself as any muscle or organ of his body. She had heard Nbuta speak of this once, saying, *"Without the spear the Masai warrior can do nothing. There will be no honor until he is master of it."*

She watched as Nbuta ran his fingers over the spearhead, searching anxiously for a chip or nick, which happened occasionally when the spear struck bone. However, he smiled with relief.

"My spear is well. It struck no bones. By the will of God it is unbroken."

The buck was quickly dressed and the meat distributed among the men who would carry it, but the hunt was not over. As they continued on their way, Erin quietly observed the hunters in their splendor and felt she must look pale and colorless by comparison. They wore ocher-colored capes falling loose from a single knot at the shoulder. Erin had often thought their garments looked like the Roman togas she had seen pictured in her history book. As they moved along quickly, she admired the muscles in their backs rippling under their oiled skins. There was a beauty about the Masai she had never seen anywhere else, and she knew she would never forget them.

The hunt went on all morning. Another reedbuck was killed, and finally they stopped by a red salt lick. She was disappointed, as were the others, when they found no animals there. "Where are the animals?" Nbuta questioned. A murmur went around, for the lick was always crowded with impala, kongoni, eland, and dozens of many smaller species. Today, however, it was strangely empty.

"The good God has not brought the animals to our spears," Nbuta murmured.

"Why is there no game here?" Erin asked in a puzzled tone. She dropped the butt of her spear and watched as the men moved around, their nostrils distending as they listened carefully.

Suddenly Nbuta whispered in a hard voice, "Do not move, Erin."

Erin turned slightly and then froze. There, crouching in the tall grass, was a full-grown lion. He stared at the group and switched his tail angrily, as if to say, "So ... you are on my ground. If you want a battle, let it begin."

The lion did not move forward from his crouch, and Erin glanced at Nbuta. The warrior's face had taken on an exalted expression, and he stared at the lion almost with pleasure, it seemed, and his eyes shone with a joy she could not understand. His muscles swelled, and then he raised his shield slightly and let his spear arm drop to his side.

Erin knew enough about lion hunts to understand that even

if Nbuta killed the lion, some of the warriors would be mauled, for a lion is almost never brought down by a single spear. She remembered Nbuta saying, "*If you encounter a lion, watch him closely. Look into his eyes. You must show him that you are as fearless as he is. He has great courage and respects those who have the same.*"

Nbuta crept forward, placing one sinewy leg in front of the other. They all followed him, but for some reason the lion stayed where he was. As they filed past the watching beast, Nbuta whispered, "He is guarding his kill."

Erin understood that if she had not been with them, Nbuta and the hunters would have taken the lion then no matter what the cost. Now she was sad that she had come, for she was robbing them of the greatest thrill of the Masai warrior's life—killing a lion with a spear.

When they had passed out of range of the lion, Erin said, "I'm sorry I came. You would have killed him if I had not been along."

"Do not be sad," Nbuta said and dropped his hand on her shoulder. "There will be other lions and other days, but I could not risk my white daughter today."

Erin smiled up at Nbuta. She felt so at home and safe with these men and was simply glad to be alive. Falling into step once again with her friend as they made their way through the fragrant grasses, she put all other thoughts out of her mind.

★　★　★　★

The sun had begun its descent in the western sky when the party turned back. They had killed as much game as they could carry, and finally Nbuta had declared, "We must go home. You celebrate your womanhood tonight, my daughter. Is that not true?"

"Oh yes. There's a silly old party I have to go to."

Nbuta looked surprised. "You do not like to celebrate?"

"Parties are not as much fun as hunting with you, Nbuta."

The tall man smiled and would have spoken, but suddenly a sound rent the air. Every warrior turned to see an enormous warthog hurtling out of the bush, his maddened squeal followed by smaller ones as baby warthogs scurried everywhere, their tails held straight and erect. To Erin, they appeared to be doing some sort of dance.

The male warthog shot toward the group of hunters as straight as an arrow. Erin knew from her father's instruction that warthogs were courageous to a fault. Their curved tusks, sharp and deadly, were used for rooting as well as fighting. Now she saw the dust-covered animal, tough and clothed in bristles, his eyes, small and lightless, burning as he shot toward the invaders. This time it was one of the younger hunters who sent the first spear that caught the boar in the flank. It only slowed him down, but a hail of spears followed, piercing the boot-leather hide. The dust swirled, and the squeal of the maddened animal split the air.

The baby warthogs scattered into the grass as the adult animal collapsed and gasped in pain. When it was over, Erin stared down at the beast, lying still now, seeming almost at peace after his intense struggle. "He was courageous," she said quietly.

"Yes, he would fight anything—even a full-grown lion. He is not beautiful like the lion, but one must admire his courage." Nbuta put his hand again on her shoulder in a familiar gesture. "Always have courage, white sister."

"I will, Nbuta. I have learned that much from you."

"You are indeed a daughter of the Masai, Erin Winslow."

★   ★   ★   ★

"Where have you been?" Patrick demanded. At the age of eighteen, he was tall and beginning to fill out. He towered over his sister and glared down at her, irritation marking his features. His voice shook as he added, "Did you forget about your party?"

"No, I didn't forget."

"Well, you'd better watch out for Mom and Dad. They're on the warpath." Then his face suddenly relaxed and he put his arm around her in a brotherly embrace. "Happy birthday, Sis."

"Thank you, Patrick."

"You're all dirty and smelly. Don't go to the party like that. Nobody will dance with you."

"I don't care."

Patrick shook his head in wonder. "You really don't, do you? You'd rather be out killing something than putting on a party dress and having a good time. I'll never understand you, Erin. But happy birthday, anyway."

Erin gave him a peck on the cheek and moved quickly down the hallway, where she met her father.

"Do you know what time it is?" he demanded. "Your mother is going crazy!"

"I'm sorry, Daddy, but it was such a good hunt." As she began describing the day's experiences, Barney Winslow stared at this young woman before him, who had recently blossomed into a real beauty. Not only did she possess the gift of outward loveliness, but she exuded an inner strength as well that belied her youth and innocence.

He listened to her excited talk and then said, "Well, if you're going to the dance, you'd better go change. You can't go like that."

"Oh, all right, Daddy."

"Happy birthday, daughter. I'm proud of you."

His words disturbed her, for she did not really believe that he was proud of her. She was very aware of his disappointment over her performance at school, where she continued to have problems. She had never done well and knew now that she never would. Aware of the pain she had brought to her father by her lack of scholarship, she turned away from him with a feeling of regret and went to her room. She slipped out of her dusty clothes and put on her light cotton robe, grabbed a towel and soap, then went outside to the shower.

The outdoor shower was the only one Erin had ever known. It consisted of a bucket with holes in the bottom, suspended from a rope six and a half feet in the air. The hardwood floor also had holes for the water to run out. One of the servants had put three two-gallon buckets of water on a bench. Behind the privacy of a canvas curtain, Erin quickly took off her robe and picked up one of the buckets. She had to step up on a small stand to pour the water in; then she dropped the bucket and leaped under the water as it poured out of the holes. She lathered quickly with the soft soap and washed the dirt and grime from her hair. She soaped herself all over, rubbing briskly with a rough washrag, then filled the shower bucket again and rinsed herself off. When she had used all three buckets, she stepped to one side of the small structure and toweled herself down. Then she put her robe back on, as well as some moccasin-type shoes, and went back to her room. She dried her hair for a long time with towels and wished she had time to sit out in the sun, but it was too late for that.

She put on white cotton drawers and a cotton vest, then slipped on the new dress her mother had sewn for her birthday. Made out of light green cotton with Belgian lace at the neck and on the sleeves, it complemented her blue-green eyes and fair features nicely, and the full skirt swished delicately against her legs. She twirled about, enjoying the feel of the light fabric spinning out from the fitted waist. Then she sat down and studied her face in the mirror as she brushed her hair. She knew she was attractive, but her outward appearance meant little to her. Feelings were far more important to Erin than appearances. She put down her hairbrush and tried to get excited about the dance, but she simply could not. Her guests would be the same young people she had grown up with, mostly children of missionaries. The music would consist of scratchy old records played on an antiquated wind-up machine. They would dance to the ancient tunes and drink the nonalcoholic beverages supplied for the occasion.

She rose up just as her mother came in and said, "Why, you look beautiful, Erin!"

"Thank you, Mom. You did such a beautiful job on the dress. I love it. I couldn't have bought a better one in America."

"Here, let me fix your hair."

Erin sat down again while her mother brushed her hair until it shone, then tied it with a ribbon.

"Now we're all ready. It'll be a good party for you."

"I'm sure it will, Mom." But her heart was not in the words.

★　★　★　★

The party was no different from what Erin imagined it would be. The schoolroom had been decorated with crepe-paper streamers her father had bought in Nairobi. The furniture was all moved out except for tables along one side, where parents were handing out the refreshments. They were using the center of the room for games, which Erin found rather fun, and being good at games, she won a number of them.

When the dancing started, Todd Jennings made a beeline in her direction. He was eighteen and the son of a wealthy planter, not a missionary. He was a tall young man with closely cropped coarse brown hair and a bad sunburn. "Our dance, Erin."

Erin allowed him to take her hand and lead her to the center of the room, where they began dancing to the scratchy record. Although Erin had had few opportunities in her life to dance, she had a natural rhythm and enjoyed dancing. However, she was aware that Todd was holding her closer than necessary. "You're holding me too tight, Todd."

"That's impossible." He grinned down at her and spun her around, still holding on tightly.

"My dad will thrash you if you don't behave. He used to be a prizefighter, you know."

"Well, I'm sure he hugged your mother when they were courting. Don't you imagine?"

"We're just dancing, Todd—not courting!" She pushed the overly eager young man back a step and held him at arm's length. But she couldn't help smiling at him as they continued dancing. In truth she quite enjoyed his attentions and wound up dancing with him several times throughout the evening.

Later, after several dances together, Todd pulled her outside with a swift movement and said, "Let's get a breath of air."

Erin was not surprised. She had heard from one of the daughters of a missionary named Smitston that Todd liked the girls rather too much. Now as they stepped out onto the porch, he at once turned, pulled her into his arms, and kissed her squarely on the mouth.

In the past couple of years several boys had tried to sneak kisses from Erin, which usually landed on her nose or cheek, but she had always found it rather embarrassing. Now as Todd's lips touched hers, she found the sensation pleasant and made no move to stop him. But then his hand began to move along her body, and she pulled back, whispering, "Stop that, Todd!"

"Oh, come on. Be human, Erin." He put his hand on her again

and tried to wrestle her with his greater strength. Erin squirmed, more angry than embarrassed, and when he would not release her, she drew back her fist and struck him with a sharp blow right under the nose.

"Ow!" Todd yelped and stepped back just as Barney appeared at the door. "What's going on out here?" he demanded.

The two young people put their heads down and said nothing. It only took Barney a moment to assess the situation. "Todd, I think you'd better go inside."

Todd swallowed hard. "Yes, sir," he mumbled, then stepped back into the schoolroom without a backward glance at Erin.

Barney studied his daughter closely and asked, "Are you all right?"

"Of course I am, Daddy."

"He didn't behave himself, I take it. You have to be very careful about young men, Erin."

"I've already found out that some of them are beasts—like Todd."

"Well," Barney smiled, "there are some good ones out there, too. You'll find one."

Erin put her arms around him and hugged him. "Not as good as you, Daddy," she said.

"I hope you'll always think so—but you won't."

★ ★ ★ ★

Erin didn't think she would ever forget telling her father that there were no men as good as he was after he came out on the porch on her birthday and rescued her from Todd. She knew it would be one of those special memories that would stay with her forever.

A memory that would remain with her even more clearly, however, was the next hunting trip she took with Nbuta, a month after her birthday. Only this time, the hunt got completely out of hand.

The group had just killed an impala and were headed home when suddenly a whispered word came to Erin's ears.

"Simba—there!"

What happened then occurred impossibly fast. Erin only had time to look up and see that Nbuta had placed himself in front of her. Beyond him she saw the lion, a great black-maned creature, a lone hunter, his tail lashing back and forth. They were so close she could smell the lion's scent—meaty and pungent and almost indescribable.

The lion charged with such speed and ferocity that Erin could hardly take it in. She saw Nbuta's arm go back and then move forward with lightning-fast speed and strength. The spear flew through the air and struck the lion, but it was not a killing blow.

The world seemed to be full of its roaring, and the golden eyes of the lion blazed with fire. He was right in Erin's face, and without thought she threw her spear as Nbuta had taught her. She saw it strike the lion on the flank, and the great beast turned and snapped at it. As he did so, three other warriors rushed in and sank their spears into his flesh.

Erin watched the magnificent animal fight and snarl and finally die under the sharply honed weapons.

She turned to Nbuta, who was watching her carefully. He walked over and picked up her spear, which indeed had the tip bloodied. He smiled and said loudly, so that the others could hear, "The white Masai woman's spear is bloodied." A cheer went up from the others, and Nbuta said, "Get your image machine. We must have an image."

Erin had carried her camera on this trip in a light bag over her shoulder. Now with trembling hands she took it out. She had shown Nbuta how to look down at the little glass square and to hold it still and push a button. Now as she took her spear from him and knelt beside the lion, Nbuta positioned himself, and Erin stared into the lens. She held the bloodied spear in one hand and placed the other on the rough hide of the lion.

She knew that her spear had played no part in the lion's death, but she was proud to be there. When she rose Nbuta smiled and handed her the camera. "You are truly a woman of the Masai. You have the courage of a warrior," Nbuta said, clearly pleased with her.

Erin took the camera with unsteady hands. But when she looked down at the lion, a deep sadness overtook her. She murmured, "All that strength and all that courage, and now he's dead."

"He did what lions do, my daughter. He fought, and he showed no fear." Nbuta reached down, dipped his hands in the lion's blood, and marked Erin's cheeks with it. "You must be as brave as your brother the lion."

CHAPTER THREE

OUT OF THE SKY

★ ★ ★ ★

1921

As Erin entered the house from the front yard, her eyes went up to a framed picture mounted over the mantel in the living area. On an impulse she stopped, then turned and walked over to stare up at it. It was the photo that Nbuta had taken of her one year earlier with the lion. She was fascinated by the picture, which she had sent off to have enlarged, and she now considered it. Somehow, even though she was only a year older, the girl in the photograph looked much younger than sixteen. Her eyes were open wide, and she was staring into the lens with an intensity that was matched by the straightness of her body. To her right lay the dead lion, and her hand rested on its rough hide. As Erin studied the picture, she could almost feel the roughness of the fur and smell the rank odor of the dead beast, even as she had on that day. The head of the spear was dark, stained with the blood of the lion, and something in the whole tableau had always caused a pull inside of Erin Winslow. Perhaps it was grief over the dead lion, but more likely it was the fact that a year had passed and nothing eventful had happened since, nothing like that moment with the Masai on the grasslands.

Discontent seized Erin as she wheeled away from the picture and walked down to the study. She had struggled through school and hated every day of it. Somehow she had managed to win the coveted piece of paper stating that she was a high school graduate, but it meant nothing to her except a record of years of failure and painful discontent. Patrick had graduated with honors and was now working with a business firm in Nairobi. She was happy that he had done so well, but the only other happiness that came to her at the moment was the knowledge that she did not have to go to Mr. Simms's classroom again. Never again would she be forced to endure the humiliation of having much younger students rise above her.

At least I learned some humility—always being last at everything. Even as the thought passed through her, she knew it was a lie. She had not learned humility, but instead had become obstinate and determined to excel in those things she *was* good at. A satisfaction gripped her as she realized she had become an expert at things women were not supposed to excel in. She was a first-class hunter, a dead shot with the rifle that her father had given her on her fifteenth birthday. She understood cars and could strip down the engine of her family's ancient automobile and replace the rings in it quicker than anyone outside the professional garages in the big cities. She knew every square mile of the country surrounding their mission field. She was healthy and strong from long hikes across the veldt and from following the discipline imposed by Nbuta, so that he had often repeated what he had told her on the day the lion had died: *"You are a woman of the Masai."*

She turned into her father's study and found him standing at the wall staring at a map with red pins scattered randomly. "Going to start another mission station, Dad?"

Barney Winslow turned and smiled crookedly at her. "I'd like to."

"You'd like to have a mission station for every hundred square miles." Erin smiled and reached over to push a lock of his black hair off his brow. At the age of fifty-one her father's hair was as black as it had been as far back as she could remember. He needed no spectacles, and his light blue eyes, she had always thought, were the most attractive color in the world.

"Sit down. Time to have a talk."

Erin made a face. "That sounds ominous." She took a seat in the cane chair woven by one of the Masai and pulled her feet up under her.

Barney sat down and looked across at her and grinned. "You always did sit on your feet like that." He studied her for a moment, thinking about how she had matured in the past year. She looked older than her seventeen years. The African sun had given her a golden tan, and her hair was sun-streaked. He searched her countenance, looking for some trace of the small child who had come to bless his life, and he thought finally of her first years when she had been such a delight to both him and Katie. Now where was that child? She was gone except in memory and in a few snapshots; now a young woman with a mature build and beautiful features had taken her place. "So, you're all through with school—unless you want to go to college."

"Heaven forbid!" Erin shook her head so vigorously her blond hair swung from side to side. She usually tied it with a ribbon in the back, but now it fell loose about her shoulders. "I'll never go inside a schoolroom again!"

"What will you do?" Barney asked quickly.

Erin stared at him. "That's what you wanted to talk about, isn't it?"

"Well, you can't go on washing dishes around here for the rest of your life."

"No, I suppose not." She laughed suddenly. "I'm more fitted to be a Masai than I am a white girl."

"That's right. Not every seventeen-year-old has killed a lion with a spear."

"Oh, pooh!" Erin sniffed. "I didn't kill that lion. Nbuta did that." A smile touched her lips as a thought came to her. It brought out a dimple on her cheek and made her appear winsome indeed. "But *you* did once, Dad. 'The Lion Killer'—that's what the Masai call you."

Barney gave her a pained expression. "That was a long time ago. I still don't know how it happened."

Barney had indeed once killed a lion. It should have killed him, however. He had somehow gotten behind it and strangled the animal with his bare hands—something that had never happened in the memory of the Masai. Even though it had happened many years ago, the memory was still fresh in the minds of Nbuta and his fellow warriors, and they had always shown a deep respect for Barney Winslow. But right now Barney was not thinking of killing lions. "What would you *like* to do, Erin?"

Erin sat quietly for a moment, and as she did so Barney admired the way her face could express her thoughts. He knew she was filled with joy—that is, when not bound by a classroom! A love for life now seemed to lie impatiently behind her eyes. She looked up at him eagerly. "Maybe I'd like to train horses."

Barney blinked with surprise, but then he nodded quickly. "You're good with horses."

"Maybe I'll become a jockey." Her eyes sparkled with fun, and she saw her father shake his head quickly. "Of course, I won't be a jockey, but lots of the planters are breeding horses now. Maybe I could help with that."

"Well, if you're serious, we'll see about getting you a job as a trainer."

Erin thought for a moment, chewed on her lower lip, then said, "No, I don't think I'd want to do that." She suddenly laughed shortly. "You have a lot of trouble with me, don't you, Dad?"

"Not nearly as much as my parents had with me." He sat quietly in his chair, both of them aware of the affection that existed between them. It had been, perhaps, her inadequacies that had created the unique bond between father and daughter. He had quickly seen that Patrick was an excellent scholar, while for whatever reason, Erin was not good with books. It had reminded him of his youth when his own brother, Andrew, had been so brilliant, and he himself had been so slow. During those years he had always been in second place, which helped him to understand his daughter and caused him always to give his first allegiance to Erin rather than to his self-sufficient son—of whom he was also very proud.

"Don't worry about it. I'll tell you what," Barney said. "Why don't we make a trip home to the States next year? You need to spend some time with your relatives—especially your grandmother."

"Oh, could we really go, Dad?" Erin had only been in the States once, and that was when she was ten. It had been an exciting time for her, and she had never forgotten it. She had collected every book she had about America, and now she sat up straight and cried out, "I'd love to go to America! And I love my grandmother. She writes me the best letters!"

"She's very fond of you, Erin. Very fond indeed." Barney reflected slowly, "My folks are getting on in years now, and they've begged for you to come for a long time."

"Let's do it then, Dad."

"Well, my dad's offered to send the money often enough. We'll see what comes of it."

The two sat there talking for a long time until finally Katie came and stuck her head in the door. "What are you two up to? Plotting something, I'll bet."

"Plotting for supper," Barney said. "Are you going to starve me to death?"

Katie shook her head at him impatiently. "I don't think you're in any danger of that."

"I'll help with supper, Mom. Now that I'm out of school, I'll have lots of time to help you."

Erin left the room, giving her father an affectionate touch as she passed.

When she was gone, Katie asked, "What was that all about?"

Barney got up and went to stand beside her, a worried expression on his face. "Just talking about her future."

Katie knew this man well, and she put her arms around him and said, "Don't worry. We've prayed for her since the day she was born. God's going to give her something wonderful to do!"

★　★　★　★

Sitting astride her mare, Erin guided the horse carefully along the rough path, for she was farther from home than usual. When she spoke, her voice seemed very loud in the

silence. "Careful, Princess. If you break a leg, I can't carry you back." The mare snorted, tossed her head, and moved forward in a spirited trot.

A small peal of thunder set off a screeching of baboons that spread the length of the area. As Erin turned toward the sound, a blue monkey dropped from a lone tree in the savannah and scampered to the forest.

She rode on, knowing that the thunder was not a trustworthy harbinger of the weather, for it was the dry season, and no rain would fall for many weeks yet. She continued her ride across the wide grassland, and once in the distance she saw a herd of elephants making their way toward the north. The impulse came to get closer, but her father had made her promise to stay away from them. *"They're explosive as dynamite,"* he had warned her. *"Ordinarily they're quiet and peaceable, but when something sets them off, they'll charge anything!"*

She followed the bank of an almost dried-up riverbed, where several species of animals were still seeking the small trickle of water. She passed a herd of waterbuck, and later on she caught a glimpse of a leopard. It was unusual indeed to see one at this time of day, since they were nocturnal creatures. Half an hour later, she skirted an area of desert country, and far off in the distance she could see gazelles in quest of salt. They moved like ghosts across the white fields of alkali, and behind them a herd of jackals slunk, looking for anything that could be eaten.

She stopped to rest, ate half a sandwich, and drank sparingly from the large water bottle slung over the pommel of her saddle horn. She took off her sun helmet, partially filled it with water, and let Princess drink from it. The mare was thirsty, but on the hot grasslands it was better not to drink too much.

A great stillness lay about her, and she had the feeling that many eyes were watching her, although she saw nothing. This was the hunting ground of the lion, and though her heavy rifle rested in her boot, she did not want to shoot one.

Far in the distance the Mountain of God, as the natives called it, rose up, a mighty beacon in this flat land. She had been there once with her father on a mission trip, to a beautiful spot at the foot of the mountain. She could still remember the bed of lavender and yellow flowers and the clouds curling past the magnificent peak.

Finally she stepped into the saddle and touched Princess with her heels. The mare obediently moved along at a leisurely walk. The plains were bare and bony, with only a whisper of grass, yet the animals always kept to the ridges where the grass was shortest. She watched as a herd of wildebeest grazed, their black tail tassels sweeping behind them. A solitary bull, thin-ribbed and rag-tailed, his old beard showing, trailed along at a distance, and Erin knew that he soon would die a victim of a lion or of the prowling hyenas. She wondered if he felt his own death upon him as he moved along at a broken pace.

Not wanting to see the animal's demise, Erin pushed her horse into a gallop and soon was getting into a different kind of country. She avoided the low thorny scrubs and the toothbrush plants that grew prolifically here, and also the morari bush with its pink, fleshy flowers and rubbery limbs containing poison sap.

It was nearly one o'clock before she began to think of turning back home. She would have to ride steadily to get home before dark, and her father had strictly told her to be home before then.

She turned her mare around, but as she did, something bright caught her eye. At first she thought it was a small pond and would have gone on, but then the thought occurred to her, *That can't be a pond. It's the dry season. There's no water out here.* She turned Princess back, and her eyes searched the terrain ahead of her. As she moved her head, the sun reflected again on the silvery spot, and she shook her head and spoke aloud. "Well, Princess, that can't be water—but if it is, we need to know about it. We'll take one look—then we'll go home."

She nudged the mare into a slow trot, which was harder on Erin but easier on the horse. Winding her way around the rise, thirty minutes later she came up to the crest, and then she gasped with surprise.

There before her was a silver biplane, its tail up in the air!

Erin had seen planes before, since they flew over the area on occasion, but this one was obviously in deep trouble. "Come on, Princess," she said quickly. "Let's have a look." She drove the horse at a dead gallop, and when she came to the plane, she looked around for the pilot but saw none. Stepping down, she threw the reins to the ground, and Princess, trained to stay, did not move.

Erin ran to the plane. She knew practically nothing about aircraft, but out here in this wilderness the pilot had to be either dead or injured—or else he had walked out. She approached the plane and called out, "Hello! Is anybody here?"

A faint noise caught her attention, and she whirled to see a man who was lying under the shade of a shrub. There was not room enough for his whole body, but his head and shoulders, at least, were in the shade. Erin ran toward him and knelt by his side. She knew instantly that he was nearly dehydrated. His face was pale, and he had blond hair and a stubbled beard. His eyes were a ghostly blue, and he was badly sunburned.

"Are you all right?" she said quickly.

The man struggled to lift his head, and his lips were so cracked he could hardly speak. "Water!" he gasped.

"Oh, yes. Of course." Running back to the mare, Erin unstrapped the water jug, ran back, and knelt beside the injured man. She helped him sit up, and he sucked at the jug noisily, spilling some down his chest.

"That's enough for now," Erin said quickly. "You'll have to take it in small sips."

For the next fifteen minutes she nursed the water along, allowing him only small portions. She saw that the man was not tall and was rather small boned and trim. He had aristocratic features, with a narrow English nose and a sandy mustache. Finally he gasped, "Glad you . . . came along."

"How long have you been down?"

"I think two days—no. Three. I don't know. I don't know how long I was out."

"Are you hurt?"

"Something wrong . . . with my right leg."

Quickly Erin looked down. She didn't see any blood or anything obviously wrong with his leg. She touched it and saw him wince. "Can you move it?"

"I think I've done something to the knee. It took everything

I had to get out of that plane, and then I fell and hurt it again. I crawled over here. There was water up in the cockpit, but I couldn't get back to it."

"Well, you're all right now," Erin smiled. "It's a good thing I came along."

"Yes, I think it is. Could I have some more of that water?"

Erin gave him a somewhat longer drink and saw that his eyes were looking more alert. "What are you doing out here?" he asked. "Before I went down I couldn't see a town in any direction. I was pretty well lost anyhow."

"I come from a mission station over there. About a six-hour ride." She shook her head. "If you've been out here two or three nights, you're lucky that a lion or hyenas didn't get you."

"God loves a sinner, I expect. That's the only thing I know. I know I was pretty scared."

"I don't blame you. Night's not a very good time to be alone out here." She thought for a few seconds and then shook her head. "You can't stay here. I'll bring my horse up, and you'll have to get into the saddle. I may have to tie you on, but we've got to get you out of here."

"Whatever you say. My name's Stephen Charterhouse."

"I'm Erin Winslow. I'm very glad to meet you."

Charterhouse smiled at her. His lips were cracked, and he was in great discomfort, but his face still reflected some humor. "Not nearly as glad as I am to meet you, Miss Winslow. Well, bring the animal up, and we'll see what can be done."

Erin led Princess up to the injured man and said, "She's very steady. Here, hold on to me and see if you can stand up." She bent over, and Charterhouse put his arm around her neck and held on. She gave a sudden upright lunge, and he came to his feet.

"You're very strong," Charterhouse said, "to do that so easily."

"Getting you on is going to be hard." She studied his injured right leg and said, "Look, you hold on to the saddle horn. I know you can't put any weight on your right leg, so I'll hold you here as best I can. You've got to get your left foot up in that stirrup."

"Right." Charterhouse gritted his teeth, and then he put his weight on his good leg and gave a lunge. Erin shoved with all of her strength, and he went halfway over the saddle. She caught him and held him on, then shoved the injured leg over.

Charterhouse gritted his teeth together and uttered no sound. "Well, I'm on," he said finally in a short breath. "Are you going to get on behind me?"

"I think I'll just walk for a while. Princess isn't strong enough to carry our whole weight all the way back."

"Oh, I say—you can't do that!"

Erin looked up at him and smiled. He couldn't tell if her eyes were sea green or blue, but he was surprised to see excitement sparkling in them. He didn't quite know what to make of it.

"You just hang on, Mr. Charterhouse. I'll get you out of this."

"I suppose first names might be appropriate, seeing as how you've saved my life. Why don't you call me Stephen."

"Okay, Stephen, and you can call me Erin."

She took the reins and said, "You hold on to the horn. If you feel faint, just call out. We'll stop and rest. We'll stop anyway every fifteen minutes to get some water into you. You seem to be almost totally dehydrated."

The trip was hard on Charterhouse. Although Erin stopped three or four times an hour to give him a drink and eventually began giving him a few bites of food, he was very weak. From time to time he would actually pass out for a few seconds, yet he still held firmly on to the horn. Once he slumped forward, and she ran back to pull him up. "Here, this won't do." She swung on behind him and spoke to the mare. Charterhouse was aware that she was holding him in the saddle, and he did then pass out fully. When he came to, the horse was still moving along with a steady, even cadence, and he shook his head. "I'm quite a bother."

"Don't be silly."

"I thought I'd had it out there by myself," Charterhouse whispered. "Yesterday—or was it today? Anyway, a group of vultures started circling up in the sky. I think they were there until you found me."

"It must have been frightening."

Charterhouse was aware of her closeness as she held him tightly, one arm around him, the other holding on to the line. He could not guess her age, but she seemed very young. "You say we're headed for a mission station?"

"My father and mother are missionaries—Barney and Katie Winslow."

"What were you doing so far away from your home?"

"I often go on long rides like this. It's one thing I am good at."

Charterhouse, for the first time, laughed briefly. "It's a good thing for me. I've never believed in miracles, but I think I do now."

"You think God sent me to find you?"

"You looked like a golden angel to me when I opened my eyes. I've been an irreligious dog all my life, but I'll never forget to thank God for this day."

Erin felt the warmth of the man, who was so different from anyone she had ever known. He had an English accent, and there was an air of gentility about him, even in his present debilitated condition. "You'll be all right now," she said.

"I'm worried about the plane."

Erin laughed. "No one will steal it out there."

"I wasn't worried about that. I was worried about getting it flying again."

"The first thing is to get you in better shape. Then we'll worry about the plane."

★ ★ ★ ★

Erin pulled the weary mare up and slipped out of the saddle. Charterhouse was swaying. "We're here," she said. She saw that he was practically unconscious and said loudly, "Hang on, Stephen. Just a minute more." Then she lifted her voice and called out, "Dad—Dad, come and help me!"

Barney Winslow came out at once, took in the situation in one glance, and came hurrying over.

"This is Stephen Charterhouse, Dad. His plane wrecked. I found him out in the grasslands."

Barney asked, "Are you hurt bad?"

Stephen had awakened again as he realized they had reached Erin's home, and he managed to answer, "Just my . . . leg."

Barney heard the weakness in the man's voice. He reached up and with his prizefighter strength simply pulled the man out of the saddle. He carried him like a baby, and Charterhouse remembered little afterward. There was a flurry of activity, and soon he found himself stripped of his clothes and put between clean sheets. He looked up and saw his host, a sunburned man with black hair and light blue eyes. "If it hadn't been for the young woman, I would have died."

Barney said, "God is good, isn't He?"

"Yes," Charterhouse said. "I haven't acknowledged it before, I'm afraid—but I know now that He is."

Barney turned and went out to where his wife and daughter were waiting. "He's all right, just worn out. I'm pretty sure his leg's not broken, but he's not going to be using it much for a time."

"Should we send for David?" She spoke of Dr. David Burns, the doctor for their mission as well as half a dozen other mission stations.

"It's probably not a bad idea," Barney replied. "But my guess is that if we keep cold compresses on it, he'll be all right." He turned back to Erin and said, "You say his plane is wrecked?"

"It didn't look to be in bad condition, although I didn't examine it carefully."

"How long was he out there?" Katie asked.

"Two or three days. He wasn't sure."

"It's a wonder he's alive," Barney said. He reached over and put his arm around Erin and said, "You did fine, daughter. Just fine!"

Erin smiled. "He was nearly unconscious when I found him, and he said when he opened his eyes and saw me, I was like a golden angel."

"I bet he did. In his shape, if you had been as ugly as a warthog, you would have looked like an angel."

"Don't be silly!" Katie said. "But in truth, he was right. God clearly sent you to rescue him."

Erin thought for a moment. She was exhausted, but still her mind was filled with Charterhouse and the adventure. "I almost missed him," she murmured. "I was turning Princess around when I saw something glimmer. It looked like water, but I knew it couldn't be. It was the silver of his plane. If I hadn't seen it, I would have come home, and he would have died." She shook her head and said, "I think the Lord must indeed have been in it, and I'm glad."

"You go to bed now," Barney said. "You've worn yourself out."

"All right, Dad. Good night."

Erin went to her room, slipped off her clothes, and washed her face in the basin. She put on her gown and climbed into bed. Her last thought before drifting off to sleep was how strange it was, the way she and Stephen Charterhouse had met.

CHAPTER FOUR

THE AWAKENING

★ ★ ★ ★

Stephen Charterhouse awoke with a start out of a profound sleep. He jerked so violently that a stabbing pain caught his right leg and drew a sharp groan from him.

"Stephen, are you awake?"

The sound of a voice served to pull Charterhouse out of the last vestiges of sleep, and he opened his eyes to see Erin Winslow bending over him. Her golden hair was tied back with a green ribbon, and she was holding a tray as she looked down at him.

"Are you hurting?"

Charterhouse passed his hand in front of his face and tried to pull himself together. "Just got a bit of a start waking up," he admitted. He rubbed his eyes and then ran his hand through his hair. "What time is it?"

"It's almost noon. I would have let you sleep," Erin said, "but Mom says you need to eat something."

"That sounds wonderful. Here, let me get out of bed."

"Not on your life," Erin said firmly. "Just pull yourself up and put your back against the head of the bed there." She waited until Charterhouse had done so, then put the tray down on his lap. "You need to eat small portions at first, so I thought some porridge and a scrambled egg might be good with tea."

Charterhouse picked up the fork immediately and scooped up a portion of the golden yellow egg, chewed it for a moment, then swallowed it. "That's what I needed," he said with satisfaction.

"Do you like milk or sugar on your porridge?"

"Both, if you don't mind."

Charterhouse found himself ravenous and polished off the meal quickly. "I could eat twice as much or even more, but I suppose I'd better take it slowly."

"Drink your tea, and in an hour I'll give you something else." Erin pulled the chair up and sat down and watched as he drained the mug. "Don't drink so fast," she ordered him, laughing. "You'll founder. Here, let me pour you some more." As she poured the tea, she studied his face carefully. She had come in earlier to see if he was awake, and he had been lying on his side with his hand under his cheek. He looked very young then, much younger than he had the previous day. She had stood there watching him for a long time wondering what twist of fate had brought such a man into her world. Now she said, "We sent for Dr. Burns. He'll have a look at you."

"I think I'm all right. Leg's not broken." Charterhouse flexed his knee and winced. "Sore as the devil, though."

"We need to get some cool compresses on that leg. You lie there, and I'll go get some."

Charterhouse nodded and watched as the young woman picked the tray up and carried it out. He was, in fact, very weak, and the emotional stress of his brush with death had done something to him. Now that the danger was over, he found himself quite frightened at how close he had come to dying. He lay still until Erin came back with a basin of water and some towels over her shoulder. Putting the basin down, she moved the sheet back from his leg and looked at it. "It's all swollen," she said. "But I'm glad it's not broken." Dipping a small towel into the water, she draped it over his leg and said, "I wish we had some ice, but there's nothing like that out here."

"I would imagine not. That feels wonderful," Charterhouse said with a sigh of relief. "Do you have time to sit down and talk with me awhile?"

"Of course." Erin smiled. She came to the chair built by her father, sat down, and studied his face. "You look much better than you did yesterday."

"I don't imagine I could have looked much worse." Charterhouse shook his head in wonder. "I can't believe how it all turned out. When the engine quit I looked around trying to find a smack of civilization. Smoke from the village fires, a road, anything like that—but all I could see was a herd of impala."

"My father sent word by a runner to Nairobi. They won't be sending out search parties for you. It's a good thing you thought to tell him to send word. None of us would have thought of it."

"I say, that's very nice of you." Charterhouse smiled at her, and his patrician features were evident in the smooth planes of his jaw and the deep-set light blue eyes. He looked unmistakably English, and if he had not been, his accent would have given away his origin. "I'm sorry to be such a bother."

"How could you be that?"

"Well, crashing in here without any warning. It's not quite the thing, you know."

"It is out here. You haven't been in Africa long, have you?"

"No. Actually, only a couple of months."

"I've never lived anywhere but here, but I've heard visitors talk, and they all say that it's different. They all comment," Erin said, "on how we lean on each other."

"Lean on each other? In what way?"

A thoughtful expression crossed Erin's face, and her lips stirred with a pleasant thought. Her mouth curved in an attractive line, and Charterhouse noted the summer darkness of her skin. Her long hair fell below her shoulders, as golden and silky as anything he had ever seen. He had heard all of his life of golden hair, but never had he seen it like this.

"Out here people have to learn to serve one another," Erin explained. "They live on credit balances."

"Credit balances?"

"Yes, little favors that they give, and some they may have to have returned."

"I suppose that's because the country's so sparsely settled."

"That's right," Erin nodded. "Love thy neighbor is a rule for survival out here. If you meet someone in trouble, you stop. Another time he may have to stop for you."

"Well, I say, that's rather nice," Charterhouse nodded. "It's not like that in England."

"I don't think it's like that anyplace where there are a great many people—only out here where the land is open and we have to depend on each other."

The two sat there talking, and the sun put long fingers of light through the windows, touching the faded maroon carpet on the floor. Charterhouse grew sleepy, and Erin left the room for a minute, this time bringing back a bowl of rich, nourishing soup. She watched while he ate it, and he gave the bowl back, saying, "That was good. You're a fine cook."

"That's my mother, mostly. I'll leave now, and you can go to sleep."

Charterhouse carefully inched his body down the bed. He laid his head on the pillow with a sigh of relief and said, "I'm worried about the plane."

"No one will take it out there. If a group of Masai come upon it, they might take a souvenir."

"I'd hate to lose it. It's become a part of me, but I suppose there's no hope. I lost track of how far I traveled, but I know it was a long way."

"It really means a great deal to you?"

"Well, it does rather."

"I'll see what I can do."

Charterhouse stared at her with astonishment. He was very sleepy, and fatigue washed through him, pulling him toward sleep with a steady hand. "Do? There's nothing to do about that plane."

Erin's chin lifted, and she watched as the man's eyes closed in sleep. "Oh, I think something could be done," she said and, turning, left the room with determination in every line of her body.

★　★　★　★

Charterhouse sat at the table across from his host, Barney Winslow, and sipped scalding hot tea from the white mug that had become his. He had passed three days in the Winslow household and his leg had grown much stronger. Dr. Burns had appeared on the first day of his confinement and pronounced the leg bruised but no ligaments torn and no bones broken. "You'll be limping for a while, and I think you should stay off of it," the doctor said with a Scotch burr. "You're lucky, from what I hear, to be alive."

Now as Charterhouse studied Barney, he could see a faint resemblance to the young woman who had saved his life, but not in the color of the hair or of the eyes—more in the planes of the face. The daughter had the same strength and determination as the father.

"Do you think Erin will be back soon?" he asked.

"I expect so."

Erin had disappeared on the second day of Charterhouse's confinement. Katie Winslow had simply explained that she had business, and that she would be gone for two days or perhaps three. Charterhouse had been curious but had not felt it proper to question her further.

The two men had moved out to the verandah, and now the sun was going down quickly. Once Winslow left to go speak to a woman who had brought a child inside the gate. Charterhouse watched as the missionary put his hand on the child and appeared to pray for her. When Winslow returned, Charterhouse asked, "Sick child?"

"Nothing serious."

"Do they often bring their children to be prayed for?"

"Not as often as I'd like," Barney smiled. "Sometimes when they do, I can get them to see Dr. Burns. I've been here many years, but they're still a little bit suspicious of a medical doctor. Many of them still hold to the old ways."

The two men sat there enjoying the fresh air, and the time passed quickly. It was dusk now, and Barney suddenly said, "You haven't noticed anything?"

"Noticed anything? Like what, Mr. Winslow?"

"Like that."

Charterhouse had to twist his neck and look almost directly behind him. He squinted in the growing darkness and said, "What's that?"

"I think it's something that will please you."

When Winslow rose, Charterhouse got to his feet. He held tightly to the cane that Barney had provided for him and stood there. He could hear the faint sound of oxen bawling, and then suddenly he leaned forward, staring into the haze, and whispered, "My sainted aunt. . . !" He reached out and clutched one of the posts that held the roof to the verandah and shook his head in wonder. "I can't believe what I'm seeing!"

"You shouldn't have told Erin that nothing could be done about your airplane. She takes things like that as a direct challenge."

Barney smiled at the expression on the face of the Englishman, then he turned, and both of them stared at the team of oxen led by a Masai. Behind the man, on some sort of carriage with wheels, rested an airplane, its wings wobbling as the crude wagon moved forward. A group of men walked alongside. Beside them on her mare, Erin leaned over and spoke to the driver, then she shot forward as the horse obeyed her command. She pulled up and slid off the mare in one smooth movement. Dropping the reins, she walked forward, and Charterhouse could see that her eyes were laughing with pleasure and excitement. "There's your airplane, Stephen."

Charterhouse was aghast. He let go of the post and limped forward, putting his hand out. When the young woman came up and took it, he shook his head. "I can't believe it."

"Oh, it wasn't so much really," Erin said, very much aware of the pressure of his hand on hers. The look on his face gave her pleasure, and she let her hand remain in his.

"Let me see what you've done." Charterhouse hobbled out into the yard, and Barney went with them. When the oxen pulled up short, the Masai grinned and said something in Swahili. Erin answered and then turned to Charterhouse. "Making the wagon was the hardest thing, and then lugging the plane across the countryside, of course."

"How did you do it?" Barney asked.

"I had Mr. Williams make the cart. He had some old wheels and axles, and he fit it all together. I told him about the plane, then I got Nbuta here to go with me, along with some of his men. It was rather easy getting the plane on the cart. You remember the tail was up in the air?"

"I remember," Charterhouse said. He moved forward and, almost in reverence, put his hand on the side of the plane. He turned to her and said, "What did you do then?"

"Why, we just backed the wagon underneath it. Nbuta put a rope around the tail and pulled it down. We had plenty of help, so it wasn't too big a job to lift it up and lash it down."

"Well, I think it's a bloomin' miracle, and I can't ever thank you enough, Miss Winslow."

"It's Erin, remember? And you're very welcome."

Charterhouse began to examine the plane in greater detail. "I wasn't able to examine the damage when I went down, but it doesn't look too bad."

"The propeller's all bent out of shape, and it looks like that wing suffered some damage," Winslow observed.

"Yes, but it's *here*, and I can get parts in Nairobi. Oh, I say!" He turned and said, "I'm forgetting that I'm a guest here."

Winslow nodded. "We're used to guests, Mr. Charterhouse. You'll stay with us until your airplane is repaired."

Charterhouse nodded, and gratitude washed across his face. "Thank you so much, Mr. Winslow." He turned to Erin and said, "I'll bet when you woke up a few mornings ago you didn't know you'd have so much trouble on your hands."

Erin dropped her eyes, for she was proud of what she had done, and she knew that this man was grateful. "It's no trouble," she said. "But you'll have to let me help you. You won't be at your best for a while."

"And watch out or she'll take over your job, Charterhouse," Winslow laughed. He turned and walked away, and Charterhouse stepped closer to Erin. He put out his hand again, and when she took it, he squeezed it firmly. "I can't tell you how thankful I am. I was worried sick about the plane."

"I know you were. I could see it."

"I must make this right with you. Maybe," he said, "when I get it running, you'd like to go up."

Erin took a short breath. "Oh, I'd love it," she said. "We'll start in the morning. Any parts you have to have we can probably order, but it'll take a while."

"That will be all right with me." Charterhouse felt the firm, warm flesh of the young woman's hand and pressed it even harder. "It's a lucky thing for me that I went down where I did."

"I don't think it was luck," Erin said quickly. "I think it was God."

Charterhouse studied her, then released her hand. Nodding, he said, "You may be right. In any case I'm here, and you'll have to put up with me until I get airborne."

★   ★   ★   ★

"Hand me that wrench, Erin—no, not that one. The smaller one."

"This one?"

"Yes, that'll do it." Charterhouse was underneath the engine of the airplane with Erin at his side. The two had been working for three days, and the sun beat down upon the plane with considerable intensity.

Suddenly Charterhouse exclaimed, "Ow!" and dropped the wrench. He sat down and began slapping at his ankle when Erin reached out and pulled at his arm. "Get up! Those are army ants."

Quickly getting to his feet, Charterhouse held up an ant between his fingers and exclaimed, "That's the awfulest-looking ant I ever saw! I always thought ants were nice. Even the Bible speaks of them, doesn't it? 'Go to the ant, thou sluggard'—something like that?"

"I don't think this is the kind of ant you want to praise. These things don't just sting, they bite plugs out of you when they're on the march. Two years ago a horse was trapped in a stable when the ants went through. The poor animal was killed, and by the time the owner got there he was half-eaten."

"Not a nice thought! Are there more of them?"

Erin looked around carefully and stomped on the hard ground. "I think they're just strays, but even individual ants have a nasty bite."

"Let's take a break," Charterhouse said and took Erin's arm. They walked away from the plane, which was out behind the house, and onto the back porch. Erin said, "I'll get something to drink. You sit down and rest your leg."

"Almost well now," Charterhouse said. Nevertheless, he took her advice and sat down on an Adirondack-style chair that Barney had made out of teakwood. When she came back with two tall glasses, she said, "Not cool, but wet."

The two sat there drinking the tepid tea, and she listened as he spoke of his experiences during the war and since then.

"I never did see any combat in the Great War. I was a good airplane mechanic, so I completed my tour of duty on the ground making the planes ready for the fliers. My brother was a flier, though. Saw plenty of action. He shot down six enemy planes, but they got him at last."

It was one of the few times Stephen had mentioned his family. He was obviously proud of them, and now Erin asked impulsively, "Do you have a large family, Stephen?"

"There's only me and my sister now. My father's a barrister. We live in Dover. You've never been to England, have you?"

"No, I've read about it, though. It must be lovely, from the pictures I've seen."

"It's a pretty country all right in the summer and the spring. Nasty in the winter—cold, drizzly, and wet."

"I'd love to see it. I'd love to travel."

Stephen turned to her and studied her with a fond expression. "I hope you'll come and visit."

Erin was taken aback. He spoke as if England were only a few miles away. She had learned from their conversations that he had traveled greatly since the war. He had visited Australia and America and had even made one foray into the Far East, touching on the soil of China and Russia. "I doubt if I'll ever be in your neighborhood," she smiled.

"You never can tell. Life's sort of funny."

"What brought you to Africa?" she wanted to know.

"I have an uncle—my father's brother—who owns a cotton plantation between here and Mombasa. He came for a visit when he was a young man and just never left! Married a native woman and settled down here. He's been wanting me to come visit for years, so I finally came to meet him and spend a little time exploring this part of the world. I rather like it myself. . . ." He paused and gave her a winning smile. "Especially since you're here."

Erin felt herself blushing at his comment and the way his eyes explored hers. He clearly wanted to know her better. Suddenly she was aware of how closely she had been drawn to him during the few days he had been a visitor in her home. He was twenty-six, but still young enough so they could enjoy each other's company. She had taken him for a short horseback ride the day before around the mission station and had visited the Masai village. He had taken it all in eagerly. He was one of the most alive human beings she had ever met, Erin decided. He had told her enough about his life to know that he would always be moving on to a new challenge. Flying was the love of his life; he talked about flying as some men talk about heaven.

Working on the plane together had drawn them even closer together. They had sat out every night on the verandah speaking in quiet tones, and she felt she knew him very well indeed.

Suddenly Stephen looked over and said, "What about you? You let me talk all the time. You never say much about yourself."

"There's nothing much to say."

"Well, that's not right. You've led an adventurous life here. I don't know any other woman who can ride like you do—or who could go out into the African veldt, load an airplane onto a wagon, and drag it back to a beat-up aviator."

Erin laughed at that. When she turned to face him, her eyes were dancing with fun. "I didn't build the wagon all by myself. I couldn't have done it without Nbuta and his friends."

"But you got them together. You can shoot, and you even killed a leopard once, your father told me."

"That's true enough. I didn't like it, though."

"You don't like to shoot leopards?"

"He was an old leopard and would have died anyway, but he was preying on our calves, so somebody had to stop him."

"What are you going to do? You can't shoot leopards all your life. It's rather lonely out here, isn't it?"

"I never thought of it until—" Erin almost let the words slip out *until you came* but managed to bite them off. "I don't know. I'm really not fitted for anything but killing leopards," she smiled.

"Do you want to work?"

"Oh, I don't know, Stephen. I'll have to, I suppose."

"No handsome young man waiting for you somewhere in Nairobi or Mombasa?"

"No, nothing like that."

"I'm surprised." Stephen put his chin on his hand and studied her. "You're such a beautiful young woman—but then I suppose the pickings are pretty slim around here."

Erin was pleased with his compliment. "Pretty slim," she nodded. "I don't know what I'll do. I'm rather stupid."

"Oh, come, that's false modesty!"

"No, it's not. I never did well in school."

"But you're a genius with bringing airplanes off the plain, and you're quick at mechanical things."

"Maybe I could be a mechanic."

He laughed at that and said, "You'll find your niche, and I don't think it will be long."

"How long will it take to fix the plane?"

"As soon as we get the parts from Nairobi."

"There's a celebration at Nbuta's village tomorrow. Would you like to go? It might be interesting."

"Yes, I would. They're very fascinating people."

"All right. We'll go. I'll saddle up Fred for you. He's steady enough."

★　★　★　★

Nbuta nodded at the two. There was excitement in the air, and the dance was about to start. "It is good to have you here," the warrior said, nodding to Charterhouse.

"Jolly decent of you to have me, Nbuta."

"The lion killer did not come."

"No, he's off on mission work," Erin said.

"Lion killer?" Stephen asked. "What does that mean?"

"Oh, my father killed a lion a long time ago."

Charterhouse lifted his eyebrows. "Is that unusual?"

"This one was. He killed it with his bare hands."

Charterhouse stared at the girl, afraid that she was teasing him. "Is that true?" he demanded.

"Oh yes. He was clawed up, but it was a young lion, and he

got around and strangled it somehow or other. I think God must have done it."

"He is a brave man," Nbuta said. "He has the courage of a Masai. He understands lions." Nbuta looked rather fierce, standing tall and straight with his spear close to his body. "A lion will fight for what he has and for what he needs. He is never cowardly. You can always trust a lion to be what he is and nothing more, nothing less."

"That's rather a good thing to be said of any of us, Nbuta," Charterhouse said, interested in the tall ebony warrior.

"Oh, look, the dance is going to begin! Come along, Stephen."

Erin, of course, had seen the Masai dance on many occasions, but for Stephen it was all new. He took hold of Erin's arm and leaned forward to whisper, "Are we going to join them in this dance?"

Aware of the touch of his hand, she smiled. "I don't think so. Wait and see."

The moon was high in the sky, and its bright beams glinted off the smoothly shaved heads of the girls. The young men wore their hair in long plaits into which were woven colored feathers. Most of the men wore rattles of metal on their legs. They also wore black-and-white tails of the colobus monkey, and as they began to dance, Charterhouse saw that they were able to make them shake like snakes.

The voices of the dancers rose and blended with the veldt. The music had no tune but was one voice upon another, each of the same timbre.

Finally the young men and women made a circle and placed their arms around each other's shoulders. The moonlight, silver and glinting on the skin of the dancers, outlined them and made the shadows long. Soon a tall man came to stand in the center of the ring. He began to sing and then to sway. As the singing grew louder, the dancers stomped the ground with a rhythmic beat. The song grew faster, and suddenly the leader sprang up into the air. He had no sooner hit the ground than he sprang up again, holding his heels together, his head jerking back and forth on his neck.

"My word, I never saw anyone jump that high!" Charterhouse whispered.

"Some of them can jump higher than their heads," Erin said. "I used to do that when I was a girl, but I wouldn't care to try it now. I think you have to be Masai."

The dance went on for a long time, and when the leader became exhausted, another came and took his place. On and on it went, the dancers seemingly tireless. Finally the one who stayed in the circle the longest and leaped the highest was chosen, and a crown of woven branches was placed on his head.

"We'd better go. It's late, and this could last until morning," Erin said.

"I think you're right."

The two slipped away, mounted their horses, and rode out of the village. The sound faded behind them as Erin led the way. They spoke from time to time of the dance, and Erin kept her eyes alert for jackals, which were far more dangerous than lions.

When they reached the mission, Erin got down and opened the gate for them, then closed it again behind them. They took the horses to the open-sided barn, where they unsaddled them, brushed them down, fed and watered them, and left them in their stalls.

As they walked back to the house, Erin suddenly stopped and looked up at the clear night sky. "Look at all those stars. Just think how long they've been there. It makes me feel very young."

Charterhouse paused beside her. "You *are* very young," he said quietly. The music and the dance had stirred him, and he had been rather quiet on the way home. He said, "I've been thinking about the Masai celebration. They're an amazing people."

"Yes, I think so."

Erin turned to him, near enough to be touched, and Stephen was suddenly aware of her nearness. He reached forward and pulled her to him, and when he put his arms around her, she came to him with an innocence that touched him. He bent his head and put his lips on hers, and for a moment he sensed the wild sweetness that was in this young woman. He stepped back and said quickly, "I suppose that was gratitude." But then a moment of honesty came over him, and he had to admit, "But it turned out to be more than that. I'm sorry."

"Don't be sorry. It was . . . it was just a kiss."

She said good-night, then turned and went quickly into the house and to her room. As soon as she was alone, she discovered that she was trembling. She had never been kissed like that before—so tenderly—and not by a grown man. Somehow she knew she had come to a door that she must either enter or keep closed. She was a girl of deep emotions, and yet when Stephen had kissed her, it awakened feelings she barely knew existed until now. As she stood there in the darkness of her room, she knew she would never forget that kiss!

CHAPTER FIVE

AMONG THE CLOUDS

★ ★ ★ ★

Stephen Charterhouse stood in the shade beside the silver plane, which glimmered in the bright morning sun, then turned to rest his eyes on the mountains that lay to the east. It was a clear day, and he could make out the glitter of ice on the high rim of the Manegai Crater. By turning to his right, he could see the peak of Lagnga Mountain, which now delighted him with its delicate shade of purple. He was aware of the smell of fresh-cut mahogo, and from far away he heard the rhythmic song of some Masai workers. Turning again, he looked toward the corrals, where a colt's shiny coat gleamed like light on water as he frolicked, kicking up dust and lifting his head as he nickered into the air. Beyond the colt two stallions, sleek and steel muscled, stood almost immobile—only their tails alive and switching at the black flies that disturbed them.

"Your leg's almost completely well, isn't it, Stephen?"

Charterhouse turned to smile at Erin. "Yes, it is. You're a good nurse." She was wearing a close-fitting light blue shirt and exuded a sense of confidence as she smiled at him. For the past few days he had become more and more aware of the womanliness of this girl, and he enjoyed seeing her smile. Now as he admired her, an excitement stirred him, and he felt, somehow, that he was on the edge of a discovery. When he thought of the other women he had known, it struck him how rare she was: not only young and beautiful, but so very innocent. Being cut off from civilization—especially from the social world in which young men and women gravitate toward one another—had isolated her and made her into a woman who retained a great deal of youthful innocence. He knew she had courage, and many of her simple actions seemed almost primitive. He had also discovered she had a temper that could swing to extremes. She had a tremendous capacity for emotion, which fascinated Charterhouse.

Suddenly, without meaning to, he said, "Erin, I've become very fond of you, but—" He hesitated and noted that the slight breeze stirred her golden hair in a way that was most attractive. "But I think you might be a temptation to me. Perhaps we ought to keep some distance between us."

Erin grew solemn and studied him carefully before speaking. It was a way she had, at times, of considering her words slowly, as if she were meditating on them, her eyes careful and watchful. "I don't think that's necessary, Stephen."

"You may not, but I do." Charterhouse suddenly laughed aloud. "I sound like a wise old bird, don't I? But you're alone out here, or we're alone together, and things happen between men and women. Sometimes things that shouldn't."

"There's no need for me to be afraid of you, is there, Stephen?"

"No, there really isn't." He reached out and ran his hand over her hair as it hung down her back. It was a natural gesture, and he rested his hand on her shoulder, saying, "You've been very good for me, Erin."

"Good for you? How's that?"

"I'm afraid I've become a bit cynical about women."

"Have you known many women, Stephen?"

The directness of the question made Charterhouse blink. "Well, that's coming right out with it," he said wryly. "Not all that many really—but my experience hasn't been perfect."

"I don't think anyone's is. Did you love any of them?"

"Twice I thought I did, but both times it turned out I was mistaken." He picked up the cup of tea and stared down into it as if it were a crystal ball. "Life is a funny thing," he murmured.

There was economy in the straight lines of his face, and his light blue eyes seemed troubled. He hesitated for a moment, then added, "Life takes a different shape at times. At least mine does. It's like a tree. It puts out new branches, but the old branches die. I guess that's what my life has been, a constant pattern of discard and new growth. Old things pass away, and new things come." He was pensive for a moment, far away from her and absorbed in some deep-seated memory. He shook his shoulders and smiled. "I don't know why I'm mooning on like this. Life is fun, but it's also quiet when the goldfish die."

Erin suddenly laughed. "What in the world does that mean?"

"About the goldfish? I don't know. It's something a friend of mine used to say. It's rather silly, but one of those things that has stuck in my mind. I guess that's about the depth of my philosophy. Come on, let's sit down. We've done all we can to this plane anyhow." He slapped the side of the craft almost as one would slap the side of a favorite horse. They moved over and sat down in the shade of the aircraft, and she filled their cups of tea from the pot she had brought out with them. For a while they sat talking about the final repairs on the plane, and finally she said, "Do you ever think about God, Stephen?"

"I did when the plane was going down. You can bet on that." His tone grew serious, and he said, "Shakespeare said once, 'This fell sergeant, death, is strict in his arrest.'"

Erin said at once, "Shakespeare said a lot about death. I remember Caesar said to his wife, 'Death, a necessary end, will come when it will come.'"

"Right. And Edgar said to his father in *King Lear*, 'Men must endure their going hence, even as their coming hither; ripeness is all.'"

"I never liked *Lear*, but I remember in *Twelfth Night* there was a song. I forget who sang it. I don't know the tune, but I always loved the words:

"Come away, come away, death,
And in sad cypress let me be laid;
Fly away, fly away, breath;
I am slain by a fair cruel maid."

"How do you happen to know that? It must be a rather

obscure passage. I don't remember it at all."

"I don't know. My father used to read Shakespeare to us a lot, and some of the passages just stuck in my mind. That one did."

" 'I am slain by a fair cruel maid,' " Stephen echoed. He smiled then and reached out and pinched her arm. "Some day there's going to be a whole field full of corpses slain by the fair maid Erin Winslow."

"Oh, don't be silly! That doesn't happen anymore."

"I suppose not."

Erin studied him for a moment, then said, "You didn't answer my question really."

"About being afraid and thinking about God? Any man of sense does. When the plane was going down, I was pretty sure that was the end of it, and I thought of two things. One was another line from Shakespeare: 'A man can die but once; we owe God a death.' And the other was from the Bible: 'As it is appointed unto men once to die.' Well, at least I think it's from the Bible."

"Yes, it is. From the book of Hebrews, chapter nine, verse twenty-seven—and the last of it is, 'But after this the judgment.' "

"Well, I thought about death and the judgment a lot. It seemed I was in that dive for a long time, and all I could think of was 'This is the end of it.' "

Erin was watching the ground. An ant was trundling some kind of a burden along, striving to move it from one place to another. Its efforts seemed to have no purpose, for it was not food, as far as Erin could tell. She put her finger down in the ant's way, and it began trying to get around the obstacle. "The Masai have a myth about death—just a story, of course."

"What is it?"

"They say when the world began, every animal had a task to do, even the chameleon. When the first man was made he wandered alone, and he worried because he couldn't remember yesterday. Well, God saw this, and He sent the chameleon to him, saying there would never be such a thing as death—that there would always be a tomorrow and that the days would never stop. But after this God sent an egret with a different message, saying that a thing called death would come to man, and he said,

'Whichever message gets to the ears of man first will be the true one.' "

Erin looked up and her countenance was still as she spoke. There was an innate patience in her at times that intrigued Charterhouse. "But the chameleon was lazy. He lagged so much that the egret got there first. And the egret gave the message of death, and ever since then men have died."

"Fascinating story. You know so much about the Masai."

"I guess I do. They're such fine people. The most courageous I've ever known, and they never lie. They just tell the truth."

For some reason her words caught at Stephen Charterhouse. He grew very still and finally said in a voice no more than a whisper, "That's a fine thing—truth. We need more of it in this world."

★　★　★　★

Erin ran into the house closely followed by Charterhouse. She found her parents sitting at the kitchen table and burst out excitedly, "The plane's all fixed! It's ready to fly again, and Stephen says he'll take me up if you'll give your permission."

"Now, I didn't really say that, Erin," Charterhouse spoke up at once. He came to stand in front of the Winslows and smiled at the young woman's excitement. "What I said was I'll take the plane up and test it out thoroughly and then if it's in perfect running order, with your parents' permission, I'll take you up for a short flight. But I'll go first."

"Please, can I do it, Daddy?" Erin cried. "I want to so much!"

Barney cast a glance at his wife, who nodded slightly. "I never trust those things, but I suppose it's no more dangerous than being out in lion country."

"Not a bit of it," Charterhouse said. "I'll test my crate out well before I'll risk Erin in it. Come along, Erin. You can watch me take off anyway."

The two left at once, and as soon as they were gone, Katie said, "I'm afraid of that thing."

"So am I, to be truthful," Barney agreed. "I'd rather face a charging rhino than risk my life in that thing."

"We don't really know much about this man, do we?"

"Not much. He doesn't talk a great deal about his past. But I did talk to Giles Conboy in Nairobi. He says that Charterhouse is a careful pilot, that he avoids every risk. Not at all a daredevil."

"Well, that's something, I suppose." Katie shook her head and said quietly, "I worry about Erin."

"You think she's drawn to Stephen?"

"Why, of course she is! Why wouldn't she be?"

Barney shook his head and lifted his hands in a gesture of resignation. "How should I know? I'm not an expert on romance."

Leaning over, Katie took his hand. "Well, you were once— and you still are at times."

"Really?"

"Oh yes. You have your moments."

The two sat there holding hands thinking of old times, but gradually their thoughts returned to their daughter, who suddenly seemed very vulnerable. Both were aware that she had no experience at all with men, and they were equally aware that Charterhouse was an attractive man and, though he did not boast of it, must have known something about women by experience. They sat there quietly, in the way that happily married people have of knowing each other's thoughts without words being spoken.

★   ★   ★   ★

"Are you sure you want to go through with this? It can be dangerous."

"Oh, don't be silly, Stephen!" Erin's face glowed with excitement. They were standing beside the plane, and she had put on the extra helmet he had brought for her. The goggles were up on her head ready to be pulled down, and she was quivering with anticipation. "Come on, let's go. I can't wait."

"All right. You get in the front." He moved to help her, but she put her foot on the step and agilely mounted into the cockpit before he could get to her. He climbed in the back seat and looked at Tallboy, whom he had instructed how to turn the propeller to get the engine started. He waved his hand, and the tall black man gave the propeller a powerful spin.

Charterhouse's hands on the controls were sure, and the engine at once burst into action. Tallboy backed away abruptly, his eyes wide. Then he turned and ran away as the gust from the propeller stirred up clouds of pale dust. Charterhouse gently advanced the throttle, and the plane moved forward.

In the front seat Erin fastened her seat belt as Stephen had taught her and clenched her hands tightly together. She had looked forward to this flight all night long, after Stephen had told her the previous day that the plane appeared to be totally sound. Now as the craft picked up speed, her heart beat faster. She kept her eyes on the ground, which suddenly dropped away from beneath her. It fell farther and farther, and with delight she turned to watch her house as it grew smaller almost magically. Turning to the other side, she watched the fields below and was delighted to see the stables and the creek that held the homestead as if in the crook of an elbow, all lying beneath her. She had traversed every square foot of this ground many, many times, but now as the plane rose she could see all of it in one grand view. She saw the copse where the leopard had dragged the prize yearling three years earlier, and beyond that the bluff where she had shot her first game, a small deer called a dik-dik.

The plane rose higher and higher, and once Erin turned around in her seat and laughed at Stephen, shouting, "This is wonderful!" Everything was noise and movement, and there was a freshness to the air she had not experienced before. Her world was usually filled with odors of manure from the animals in the barn, the fresh scent of soil just turned over, the luxuriant green smell of the vegetation, and the acrid smell of dust. But here it was only fresh air, moist and almost sweet as the small plane rose quicker than any falcon.

When the plane banked, she went with the movement, delighting in the freedom of it. The plane still rose, and as they passed over the rolling plains, she saw little puffs of dust spring into the air as a herd of zebra ran in a panic at the sound of the engine. They were the most useless animals in Africa, as far as she was concerned, no use at all—except to the lions who fed on them. Ten minutes later she saw a huge herd of impala and wildebeest plunge into flight, and as the shadow of the plane passed over them, Erin laughed in delight. Stephen circled, throttled down, and lost altitude as the propeller bit into the air to give her a better view.

For over an hour Stephen sent the small plane in sweeping curves, steep climbs, and deep descents. Erin loved it all! She loved the sight of the impala leaping impossibly as they ran, and the wildebeest flaunting their brittle horns, sometimes throwing themselves on the ground in a comical fashion, almost like circus clowns. She had no idea why they did this, but she enjoyed watching their antics.

The zebras stirred up billowing clouds of dust, bucking like unbroken horses. They ran with their necks arched and their tails extended straight out behind them.

Finally Stephen slapped the fuselage right behind her head, and when she turned, he pointed downward. She shook her head, "No—more!" but he grinned and banked the plane. He brought it in to a perfect landing, and then when it rolled to a stop, he shut the engine off. He got out first and reached up for her. She jumped into his arms, and in her excitement held on to his forearms, her eyes dancing and her lips parted in a happy smile. "Oh, Stephen, it was wonderful!"

"You really liked it?"

"I never liked anything so much! I've always loved to ride horses, and I always will—but this is something else. When can we go up again?"

Stephen laughed and suddenly reached out and gave her a hug. She pressed herself against him and put her hands on his cheeks. "Please," she begged. "Take me up again."

"After lunch, if your parents agree."

"They'll agree," she said. "I know they will."

★　★　★　★

"I'm not sure it's such a good thing, this closeness between Stephen and Erin." Patrick Winslow was strolling along with his father. They had been out hunting, and now they returned with their game bag full of birds.

"You don't like him?" Barney asked, turning his gaze on his son. "I rather think he's a nice fellow."

"Oh, of course I *like* him, but what do we know about him?"

Patrick had come home on a few days leave from his job. He had been quick to see the relationship that had blossomed between his sister and Stephen Charterhouse. He had said nothing until now, for indeed, Charterhouse was charming and seemed a straightforward man. Now, however, Patrick lifted his eyes to the plane, where Erin was standing very close to the Englishman. He was speaking to her and moving his hands in expressive gestures. Even from this distance Patrick could see that Erin was totally absorbed in the man.

"I worry about Erin because she's innocent."

"Would you have her be otherwise?"

"Of course not, Dad! What I mean is she has no experience. She's never had a boyfriend. I don't think she's ever even shown any interest. That's not quite good for a seventeen-year-old girl."

Barney's eyes grew troubled, and he shook his head. "Your mother and I said about the same thing, but I don't think that there's much we can do about it."

"Charterhouse will be going soon, won't he?"

"Yes, later this week. The plane's all ready, and he has some contracts to do some flying out of Nairobi, I understand."

"Maybe I can see more of him while he's there."

"I think that would be a good thing, son. I guess parents always worry a lot about a young girl coming to this age. She's never given us any problems over boys."

"Erin's a strange girl, Dad. I don't think there's a sweeter girl in the world, but she's always felt—well, she's done so poorly in school, I think it's left a mark on her. And here comes this handsome, romantic fellow flying into her life. She saved his life—like something out of a romance novel. It's only natural she'd fall for him, but I think we need to look into it."

"He comes from a good family. I heard that much from Conboy in Nairobi."

"Yes, I've talked to Conboy. He has a good word for Charterhouse, but I'm just saying we need to be careful."

"We'll be as careful as we can, but when a young girl's in love for the first time, it's hard to reason with her."

★ ★ ★ ★

"Stephen, I want to ask a favor of you."

"I think I can safely say your favor is granted." Charterhouse turned to face Erin. They were walking together along a path that led beside the stream that bordered the mission station. It was late in the afternoon. The two had been flying twice that day, and then they had gone out for a walk before bedtime. The moon was a thin crescent overhead, and stars were scattered like frozen chips of light across the velvet darkness of the African sky. "What is it?" Charterhouse asked.

"I want you to teach me how to fly."

Charterhouse laughed. "I knew that was coming."

"You didn't!"

"Of course I did! All you've talked about is flying since the first time you went up. It's natural enough."

"Will you do it?" She reached out, took his arm, and drew him to a halt. He turned to face her, and she looked at him and pleaded. "Please, Stephen. I want it more than anything in the world."

"Some people can't learn to fly. They just *can't*. It takes something that not everybody has."

"I know I can do it. I've always been slow with books, but I can feel the life of the plane. It becomes like a part of you, doesn't it? I put my hands on the controls and followed your movements, and I know I can do it if you'll just give me a chance."

Indeed, Charterhouse had foreseen this, and now he said, "Of course I will, if your parents agree, but they may not. That's a little different from taking a ride with an experienced pilot."

"They'll let me. I know they will. Thank you, Stephen."

She reached up, pulled his head down, and kissed him on the lips. It was a gentle gesture, an expression of gratitude, but suddenly Charterhouse pulled her close and returned her kiss with a deep longing, his lips lingering on hers. When he lifted his head, he said huskily, "You're a sweet girl, Erin Winslow."

She reached up and touched his cheek, then put her head on his chest while he held her tight. "Thank you, Stephen, for coming into my life."

CHAPTER SIX

"PART OF YOU WILL DIE
SOON...."

★　★　★　★

June had come in splendor to the African continent, and now white clouds drifted across an azure sky like fluffy bundles of silk. Out of the distance a black dot appeared, and as Stephen Charterhouse stood watching, he smiled broadly. "Well, by George, she's done it quicker than anyone I ever saw!"

Four months had passed since Erin had persuaded Charterhouse to give her lessons. He had begun at once and several times had flown back to the mission station to continue her training. This had been far too slow for Erin, and she had moved to Nairobi to live with her uncle Andrew and aunt Dorothy and her cousins. The family had moved to the city two years earlier, when Andrew had been offered the position of senior pastor of a large church there.

It was the first time of any length Erin had spent away from her parents and her home, and it proved to be a period of discovery for the young woman. Charterhouse saw it—the excitement of independence—and he noted the intensity with which she threw herself into flight training.

The dot magnified itself against a huge mountain of clouds

and descended quickly. Charterhouse watched as the craft grew larger and made for the concrete strip. Critically he judged the approach and was satisfied as Erin brought the plane into a perfect landing. "She's got the knack," he murmured as he moved forward to greet her. "I've never known anyone so dead set on soloing." This was her maiden flight alone, and Charterhouse had been as concerned as he would have been about any student. But Erin was not just any student. Since she had moved to Nairobi they had been together almost constantly. At first this was merely at the airstrip and during flight training, but gradually they began spending more and more of their evenings together.

The silver plane came to a halt in front of him, and the engine shut off. Stephen watched as Erin scrambled out of the plane. She hit the ground and ran forward and threw herself into his arms.

"I did it, Stephen! I did it!" She pulled his head down and kissed him, and her eyes sparkled like diamonds. "I soloed! Wasn't I great?"

Stephen nodded and held her tightly. "Congratulations. You did it indeed."

Erin held on to him for a moment and then rather self-consciously backed away. There was an uncertainty in her, as her brother, Patrick, had known. She had never been around any young men who had attracted her, and Stephen was the first man she had ever felt so drawn to. She wasn't quite sure she could trust herself in his presence, and yet she also knew she loved him and wanted to be with him every waking moment. The weeks at Nairobi had been the happiest days of her life. Now as she smiled at him, she was so excited she could hardly speak. "You've got to take me out and celebrate."

"All right. We'll do the town tonight. You're going to be a great pilot, Erin."

"Do you really think so, Stephen?"

"I *know* so. You've got good hands, good eyes, and wonderful balance. And you've got that intuition that no great pilot is ever without. You're going to be wonderful."

Erin drank in the words. She had been thirsting for them all of her life. Her failure in academic subjects had scarred her deeply, and now to hear this man she had come to love say them meant more to her than she could ever have expressed. She squeezed his arm again and said, "I'm going to buy a new dress."

"Good. Spend a lot of money on it. I'm prepared to be impressed."

★ ★ ★ ★

When Stephen looked up to see Erin coming toward him, he was indeed impressed. "Well," he said, "you *did* buy a new dress."

She had on a sleeveless black-patterned silk dress with a low, square neckline. The skirt was gathered up on one side, with the extra fabric hanging down gracefully. The hemline brushed her ankles in front and the ground in back in one fluid line.

"Do you really like it, Stephen? I think I've lost my mind spending this much money on a mere dress."

"You ought to wear silks and diamonds every day of your life. Come along. I'm prepared to fight off the blighters who will try to cut in on me. I should have brought along a gun."

Erin laughed and clung to his arm. She turned to her aunt, who had entered the room, and said, "Aunt Dorothy, we'll be a little late coming in tonight. This is a celebration."

Dorothy smiled quickly. "Not too late, I hope."

"I shall take good care of her, Mrs. Winslow," Charterhouse said with a slight bow. "Don't worry for a minute."

Erin tugged on his arm and headed for the door. "Come along, Stephen. I'm anxious to start our celebration."

As soon as the two had left, Dorothy went to Andrew's study and spoke to her husband. "Well, they're gone. She looked beautiful in that new dress we bought her."

Andrew put down his pen and removed the glasses he had started using for close work. "I hope we're doing the right thing."

"I don't know how we could have prevented it. After all, she's a grown woman."

"She's still a child in some ways." Andrew frowned. "I'm not sure we did the wise thing. I'm not certain Barney and Katie did the right thing in sending her here. We're responsible for her. What time did she say she'd be in?"

"She said they'd be late."

"Well, I'll be up walking the floor just like I did for Amelia."

Amelia, their nineteen-year-old daughter, had been a severe trial to her parents. She had a rebellious streak, and now that she was out of her teens, she was even more willful. Phillip, their seventeen-year-old, would be leaving home the next year to begin his undergraduate work. "We went through some hard times waiting for them to grow up," Andrew recalled.

"Yes, but Erin's different. She's so . . . so innocent."

"That's true, of course. Well, if they're not in by eleven, I shall go looking in all the dens of iniquity for them." He gave his wife a teasing smile and put his arm around her. "But let's hope it doesn't come to that."

* * * *

The evening ended all too soon for Erin. Stephen had taken her to several nightclubs, where she had been somewhat shocked at the behavior she witnessed. Stephen had laughed at her. "You *are* an innocent one, aren't you? These nightclubs are pretty tame. I could take you to some *really* sinful ones!"

"This is sinful enough for me," Erin said, laughing. "Come along. Dance with me again."

While they danced, Erin talked on and on about her flying career. She had the feeling that her successful solo flight would mark a turning point in her life—the opening of a new door. Every new day that she had been in Nairobi had brought its own thrill, and she had grown and blossomed during this time.

Stephen listened to the excitement in her voice and smiled at the sparkle in her eyes as she talked. He was deeply touched by her exuberance for life and longed for a more intimate relationship with this special young woman.

Finally at a quarter of eleven, Erin said, "We'd better get home. My aunt and uncle will be worried about us."

"This early? Why, the night's just beginning."

"Not for me." Erin smiled up at him. "Can we do it again soon?"

"Of course. Whenever you say."

They went outside, and Stephen helped her into the car he had rented in Nairobi. He got in, started the engine, and then drove through the unusually quiet city streets. During the day the streets were crowded with hucksters, vendors of all sorts, stray dogs, and playing children, but now there were very few souls moving about.

Erin began talking about the next part of her flying program, but she suddenly looked up when the car stopped in front of a three-story brick building. "Why are we stopping here?"

Stephen turned to her and took her hand. He held it for a moment and kissed it, then reached out and stroked her hair. "I thought you might like to come in for a little while."

Erin stared at him. "Why, I can't come up to your room, Stephen! Not to your apartment. You know that."

"I wish you would, because—you see, Erin, I think I'm falling in love with you."

These were the words that Erin had longed to hear, and she willingly gave herself to him as he reached out, pulled her forward, and kissed her. She put her arms around his neck and pulled him even closer. She felt safe and secure in his arms, and whispered to him, "I think I'm falling in love with you, too, Stephen."

"Then come up with me. We'll just talk."

At his invitation, she pulled back and looked searchingly into his eyes. Erin was often described by her relatives as innocent, but she was not completely so. "I'd like to—I really would—but it wouldn't be a wise thing to do." She hesitated, then said, "I'm a good girl, Stephen."

The naïveté of her remark struck Stephen like a gentle blow. He recognized the truth of her words, and then he said quietly, "I know you are." He still had her in a half embrace and was aware of the delicate perfume she wore. He was also aware that she was intensely feminine as well as virtuous. He did not attempt to kiss her again but drew back to his side of the seat and released her. "I told you to stay away from wicked old men like me."

"You're not a wicked old man—but I should go home now. Thank you for a wonderful evening, but please take me home."

"All right, I will."

He drove her home in silence, and Erin found herself feeling anxious and disappointed. The question that kept running through her mind was *If he loves me, why didn't he ask me to marry him?*

★　★　★　★

That question never came. July passed and then August, and as Stephen continued teaching her to fly, he did not cease in his attempts to make their relationship more intimate.

Erin found herself physically more and more drawn to him. She had allowed him no more liberties than they had enjoyed up till now, yet he continually pressed on in his efforts to persuade her to give herself to him more fully. He never seemed to grow angry when she refused, but neither did he ever talk about marriage or their future together. Erin kept waiting and hoping for a promise of commitment to her. They declared their love for each other often, but nothing more ever came of it.

★　★　★　★

One Thursday afternoon Stephen and Erin were out on a sailboat he had borrowed from a friend. They had flown to Mombasa to enjoy a day in the tropical waters of the Indian Ocean. The two were far enough from land that it was but a distant line along the horizon. The breeze was light, and Erin had delighted in steering the tiller herself.

It had been a perfect day. They had enjoyed a picnic lunch, and now the gentle wind sent the small sailboat across the waters with a delightful motion. Stephen had kept her amused all afternoon with stories of his flying adventures. As the sun began to set, he tied the rudder off and lowered the sail. The small craft was bobbing slightly up and down, and Erin was reclining against his chest, half turned toward him. She was grateful for all this man had done for her in teaching her to fly. It was exciting to know that she would soon have her flying license. She had already planned to tell her parents she was going to make a living as a pilot. There were plenty of opportunities in this profession in Africa, for roads were few and those that existed were bad, and she knew she could get financing for a plane and pay the money back.

Erin was grateful to Stephen for far more than flying lessons, however. He had awakened in her a deep desire to experience life more fully, and she loved him dearly for that. Life could never again be the same, and she nestled closer to him as their conversation ceased and together, silently, they watched the changing colors of the sunset. He gently stroked her back through her light cotton shirt, and in response to his caresses she found herself longing to be with him forever, to love no other man. When he touched her chin and lifted her face to his, it seemed only natural to surrender to his kiss, the taste of salt on his lips increasing her desire for this man she loved so much.

He pulled her down beside him on the deck, and Erin felt lifted out of the world. Out here alone with only the endless sky above them, the green waters whispering in the waves, and the wind murmuring against the mast, she found herself yielding more and more to him. His caresses became more intimate, and though Erin knew she should stop him, she found instead that she was returning his kisses with a passion that at once surprised and disturbed her.

Suddenly she gasped and shook her head. "We must stop this, Stephen!"

"Why? We love each other, don't we?"

"Yes—but this is not right."

"If you love me and I love you, what could be more right?"

"I . . . I just can't do it, Stephen! Not here, not like this."

Stephen stared at her as she pulled back and sat up straight. He saw that her hands were trembling as she ran them through her hair. With a sigh, he slowly leaned up on one elbow and gave her a penetrating look. "Maybe you're not ready for this, Erin. You need some time to sort things out—decide what you really want in life."

His words frightened her. What was he saying? She couldn't

imagine wanting anything more than to be with Stephen—but not like this. She wanted a commitment of marriage before giving herself to him fully.

His next words hurt as much as if he had physically struck her. "I think we should stop seeing each other, Erin."

She answered in a rush, a feeling of panic rising up and choking her. "No, Stephen, I don't want to do that. I don't think I could live without you. We've just got to be more ... careful, that's all."

Stephen leaned forward. "I've been wanting to tell you something, Erin—"

She waited expectantly, hope gripping her that he was about to declare his feelings and commit himself to her alone. She waited for the words she so longed to hear—that he loved her, that he wanted to marry her and spend his life with her, but instead a shudder seemed to pass through him, and he pulled himself up and began to lift the sail. "Never mind. It's nothing," he muttered. "The wind's rising. We'd better get back before dark."

"All right, Stephen," she said almost in a whisper, not wanting to do or say anything to disappoint him further.

Erin sat quietly as they sailed back to shore, lifting her face to the wind, allowing it to dry the tears that stung her eyes, and trying to make sense of what had just happened between them. She could not bring herself to accept his suggestion that they should end their relationship. *No*, she thought, *I know he loves me. He just needs a little more time. I can wait—I will wait for him forever. One day he'll love me enough to marry me.*

★　★　★　★

The weeks that followed proved painful to Erin as she continued to work alongside Stephen, but without the tender closeness of their relationship. She steadfastly refused to believe that things were over between them, but the reality of their strained conversations was hard to ignore.

After completing her first commercial venture—delivering machine parts to a small village—she decided to stop on the way back to visit her family. To her delight Patrick was also there for a couple of days. Seeing her family again refreshed her spirits, and she enjoyed their company with hardly a thought of Stephen—until she lay in bed at night and thoughts of him crowded out all others. She made a valiant effort to hide her feelings of disappointment from her parents, but they could see that something was troubling her. At her father's encouragement, she decided to pay a visit to her dear friend Nbuta.

In the Masai village Nbuta sat listening as the young woman he loved so much spoke. The constant thread that ran through her conversation was the name of the pilot. Nbuta listened for a long time, and when she fell silent he said, "Something has come to me, daughter."

"What is it, Nbuta?"

Nbuta had a deep wisdom that Erin respected greatly. She said, "What is it? Tell me."

"It is not good. I do not know what it means. Perhaps it is nothing."

But Nbuta's insights before had always been truer than fact. She was frightened now, and she said, "What is it? I must know."

"Part of you," Nbuta said slowly, "will die soon." He saw her eyes narrow at the shock of his words, and he bent his shoulders, staring at the ground and remaining silent for a moment before speaking again. "We do not die all at once, but small pieces of us die. You will soon lose some small part of yourself."

Erin stared at her friend. Too afraid to speak, she got up at once and left. He had been cheerful enough until this last pronouncement, which had left her full of dread. Now as she walked away and mounted her mare, she was aware that he had seen something dark—something more than he was telling her, or perhaps more than even he could understand.

CHAPTER SEVEN

THE SKY IS FALLING!

★ ★ ★ ★

Erin looked down at the airstrip and gave a sigh of relief. It had been a long flight, and she was very tired. She had delivered a supply of oxygen to a remote mining camp for a dying miner and had been depressed by the experience. The camp itself was raw and unlovely in every respect. She had spent one sleepless night there, for the bed they assigned her in the small room was crawling with vermin. She had sat up all night and left at first light.

Now as she brought her plane around, she felt, despite her fatigue, a sense of accomplishment. She had gotten her pilot's license in early November and now at the end of that month she was keeping busy. There was, it seemed, a constant need for her services. She was the only woman pilot working in all of Africa, but she had learned to put up with the odd looks, the smirks, and the raw jokes that sometimes came her way.

Flying for her was something that had clicked into place. She felt now that her life would be incomplete without it. She banked the plane and lined up with a group of trees on the edge of the airstrip that seemed to be standing in disorganized ranks, like a regiment at ease. They laid their long shadows in lines, and as she came in and touched her wheels down gently, she uttered a sigh of relief. She taxied off the airstrip and cut the engine. As she got out, the mechanic, a short, squatty man named Roscoe Hayes, came forward at once.

"You have a good flight, Miss Erin?"

"I got back. That makes it a good one." She smiled at him wearily. "Give her a good going over, will you, Roscoe? I'll be leaving early in the morning."

"Where you going this time? Seems like you never stop."

"Taking a businessman to Mombasa."

"The engine run all right?"

"Seems to be fine. Just check everything if you will."

Shaking off her weariness, Erin began to feel better. She stopped and had a cup of coffee with the manager of the airfield, went over the flight for the next day, and then left.

She caught a taxi and rode to her uncle's house, where Andrew and Dorothy greeted her. They persuaded her to have a meal, even though she would rather have gone directly to bed.

"Did Stephen call while I was away?" she asked as they were finishing their meal.

"No, he didn't," Dorothy answered. "Were you expecting him to?"

"Well, I told him I'd be gone for another two days, but I finished quicker than I thought. I just thought he might call. I'll be leaving early in the morning."

Andrew and Dorothy exchanged guarded glances. They knew something had happened between the two young people during the summer, though exactly what they couldn't be sure. Erin still spoke of him occasionally but seemed anxious whenever she mentioned his name.

Andrew was happy to change the subject. "How long will this keep up, Erin?" he asked. "The flying, I mean. It seems you're awfully busy. Is there any end to it?"

"I hope not," Erin said, surprised that he should ask. "I'd like to keep flying for a long time. I enjoy it more than anything I've ever done."

Erin talked for a while to her uncle and aunt about her business plans, then showered and went to bed. She left quite early in the morning, allowing time to pay Stephen a surprise visit first. She was hoping he would be pleased to see her, and just maybe he would be willing to talk about their future. She got out of the taxi in front of his apartment, paid the driver, and hurried into the building. Finding the number of his apartment, she knocked on the door with anticipation, a smile on her lips as she waited.

The door opened, and a woman stood before her. "Yes? Can I help you?"

"I . . . is Stephen here?"

"Yes, he is. Do you want to see him?" The woman was in her late twenties or early thirties. She had black hair and wore more makeup than was customary in Africa. There was an attractiveness about her, but also a hard glint in her eyes as she stared at Erin.

Erin was confused, wondering who the woman was. She asked hesitantly, "If . . . if he's here, could I have a word with him?"

The woman turned and said, "Stephen, somebody to see you."

Not being asked in, Erin stood in the hallway. The woman did not move but turned and watched her with careful eyes. She was wearing a blue robe—and had apparently stayed for the night. Erin's heart sank, and then Stephen appeared before her. She saw his face suddenly go stiff, and at that instant she knew everything.

"This woman wants to see you, Stephen. Who is she?"

Erin's anger flared. "Who are *you*, I might ask?"

The hard light in the woman's eyes got even more intense, while her lips curled upward in a sardonic smile. "I'm his *wife*. Does that answer your question?"

"Stephen . . ." Erin tried to speak but could not. She saw the truth written on his face. There was no need for him to explain. The guilt was plainly there, along with pain and embarrassment.

"Erin, I wish you hadn't come," he whispered.

Erin knew all she needed to know. She turned and walked stiffly away down the hall. When she got to the lower part of the stairs, she heard footsteps and turned to see Stephen following her. "Erin, I didn't want it to be like this."

"Is she your wife?" Erin, by some miracle, kept her voice steady.

"Yes, she is, but I'm getting a divorce. We haven't lived together in two years now. She showed up yesterday and wants us to get back together again, but I've told her I can't do that."

"Why didn't you tell me you were married?"

"I don't know, Erin," he said, his face twisted. "I didn't want to hurt you, I guess. It didn't seem to matter, really—since I was getting a divorce anyway."

Erin stood watching him—not sure anymore that she could believe anything this man might say to her. She didn't even bother to wipe away the tears that coursed down her cheeks. Nbuta had indeed spoken truly. Something had died in her in these few brief moments, and she stared at Stephen as if he were a complete stranger. "You should have told me." She turned quickly and walked away, ignoring his protests and shutting his voice out. The taxi was gone when she stepped outside. Blindly she walked down the street, knowing that part of her would never forget him, and yet already that which had been in her was beginning to wither and die. She did not know how long it took love to die, but now she knew she would find out.

*   *   *   *

Erin made her flight and delivered the businessman to Mombasa. Following that she made three other flights, during which she performed mechanically. Her love of flying seemed to have died with her love for Stephen. Her mechanic, Roscoe, asked her once, looking carefully at her expression, "Don't you feel good, Miss Erin? You don't look so good."

"I'm fine, Roscoe." This had been her standard answer to anyone who asked how she was.

But it could not go on, and she knew it. During the hours in the air she could not get Stephen out of her mind. His betrayal was like a knife in her. Perhaps if she had had more experience with men, it might have been different, but he had been the only man she had ever cared for.

Finally she knew what she had to do. She made the trip back home again to the mission station and spent a day with her parents, trying to think of a way to tell them what had happened.

She went on long walks, and finally late one afternoon as she walked alone, burdened under the pressure of her emotions, she came to a decision. Her life had been hard, but nothing was harder than this. "I've got to get away," she said aloud. "I can't stay here anymore."

★　★　★　★

"You want to go to America? But, dear, why?"

Erin stared at her mother and knew that there was no way to make this any easier. In plain, blunt language she told them about Stephen and watched their eyes. It was obvious that they were both distressed. She knew they had been worried about her and her relationship with Stephen for some time. Finally she said, "It's all over. I'm putting it behind me."

"That's the wise thing to do," Barney said. "But why go to America?"

"I've got to get away for a while," Erin said almost desperately. "Please don't fight me on this—and please don't suggest that I go stay with Uncle Andrew and Aunt Dorothy. I've got to have a complete change of scene." After talking with her parents for some time, Erin finally agreed to wait a few days. The extra days would make no difference to her, and it was little enough to ask.

★　★　★　★

Two weeks had gone by, and now Erin Winslow stood on the deck of the *Queen Alice*. She had said good-bye to all of her relatives. There had been a small *bon voyage* party with Dr. Burns and his wife, Ruth, as well as Andrew and Dorothy and their two children. Annie and Jeb Winslow, her distant relatives, had been there as well, and, despite the circumstances, Erin had enjoyed herself.

Now standing on the deck of the ship, Erin reflected with satisfaction on her behavior. She had managed to hide her hurt from all except her parents. The others—even Patrick—were convinced that her desire to go to the States was just something she had to do. And indeed it was.

As she watched the coast of Africa grow smaller, a resolution came to her. *I can take care of myself. I can work—I can fly—and I can do it on my own*, she thought almost bitterly, *without the help of any man.*

PART TWO

QUAID

★ ★ ★ ★

1921–1922

CHAPTER EIGHT

ON HER OWN

★ ★ ★ ★

As the *Queen Alice* moved up to the New York dock and nudged at the slip, Erin stood at the rail, curiously unmoved by her new venture. On the entire voyage she had struggled to put thoughts of Stephen Charterhouse out of her mind, but without noticeable success. For hours she had walked the deck of the ship, despite the bitter cold weather and the freezing rain that sometimes swept the deck. All her efforts to erase the past had failed, and as she watched the stevedores attach the enormous ropes that tied the ship securely to the dock, it seemed to her that the past was tarnished and dull, like a cheap antique that was not worth saving or even looking at.

A ship that was departing about a half mile away down the harbor loosed a shrill blast that rocked the air. Snow was falling now in slanting lines, which covered the harbor in a pristine whiteness, making it almost beautiful. Erin watched as the flakes, some of them as large as quarters, came floating down, touched the water, and vanished. She thought of one of Robert Burns' poems with a sudden tinge of bitterness:

> But pleasures are like poppies spread,
> You seize the flower, its bloom is shed.

Or like the snow falls in the river,
A moment white—then melts forever.

The poet had known something of bitterness, and now as Erin stood there she summoned her thoughts before her as a king would summon his bodyguard—thoughts as clear as they were bitter. *If I have to leave the place I've lived in and loved, and I have to put behind me all the yesterdays, then I'll bury them deep! It's better to do it as quickly as I can. It's better never to turn back. I refuse to believe that an hour that's remembered is a better hour just because it's dead. Those old times seem safe, and even though I don't know where I'm going now, no matter what happens, I won't look back.*

The steward hurried down the walkway and stopped to say, "Miss Winslow, do you need help with your baggage?"

"Yes, please, Freddie, if you don't mind."

For the next hour all was noise and confusion, but Erin paid no heed. With Freddie's help she got her luggage safely down the gangplank and passed through customs. The customs officer looked at her passport carefully, then asked, "Are you here for a vacation, Miss Winslow?"

"No, I'm here to stay."

"Welcome to America." The official, a thin man with a sharp line of a mustache and careful gray eyes, stamped her passport and handed it back to her. "First time away from home?"

"Yes, it is—by myself, that is."

"Be careful. A young lady like you needs to watch her step."

Erin was confused by the crowd in the building, everyone talking and running about as if they were all late for an important appointment. She made her way through the door that said Exit and stepped outside. The snow was falling even harder now, and she turned to the black man who was helping her with her trunk and her bags. "I need to get to this address, but I have no idea where it is," she said.

Snow had already turned the man's black hair white. He had pulled off his cap and given her a friendly smile. "Yes, ma'am. Well, what you need to do is get in a taxicab and give the driver that address. These fellows who drive the cabs, they know every place in New York."

"Thank you very much." Erin had exchanged some Kenyan

money for American currency. She pulled the cash out of her purse and said, "I don't know what's right to give you."

The black man looked around with alarm and then leaned forward and whispered, "Ma'am, keep that money in your purse."

"What?"

"It ain't safe to show that much cash. And keep a good hold on your purse, too. There's men in this city that would snatch that purse, and you'd be left with nothin'."

Erin handed him a bill, and he protested, "That's too much!"

"No, I insist. Just help me get in a cab, and we'll call it square."

"Yes, ma'am, I'll do that."

The porter found her a cab and put her luggage inside. The driver was a short barrel-shaped man who wore a huge fur coat and heavy mittens. "Where to, lady?" he said when he'd settled back behind the wheel.

"This is the address. I don't know where it is or how far it is."

The driver took the slip of paper and whistled. "Lady, this is a long drive. It's gonna cost you."

"That'll be fine. Just get me there."

The trip seemed to last forever, as first trips to an unknown place usually do. Erin stared out the windows and asked questions from time to time, which the driver answered readily enough. She was aware finally that they had left the downtown area with the enormous, towering buildings and were driving through a residential section. "Is it far?" she asked.

"Maybe another forty minutes, miss."

Erin sat back and watched the snow as it collected into a downy blanket over the houses and streets. There were more trees now, sculpted by the heavy, wet snow into grotesque shapes. Long icicles hung like icy daggers from the eaves of the houses, and flights of small, bedraggled birds crossed in front of the cab as it made its way down the road.

Finally, after what seemed like a very long time, the driver stopped in front of a driveway that led back off the main road. "I think this is it, but the snow's covered the sign."

"The name is Winslow. Would you go up to the house and see if this is it?"

"There's a sign there. Lemme get out and knock the snow off of it."

Erin waited while the driver waded through the snow, which was more than eight inches deep now. She watched as he brushed it away from the sign, nodded, and came back. "That's what it says. Winslow."

"This is it, then," Erin said with a rush of relief. She sat there while the driver got in and drove down a broad drive edged on both sides with shrubs that had become round as balls. When she came in sight of the house, she took her breath in, for she had forgotten how grand the house was. There wasn't anything like this in Africa, even in the cities.

The Winslow house was a tall three-story structure made of red brick with four massive white pillars along the front and black wrought-iron railings surrounding balconies on the second and third floors. A long walkway lined with small evergreen bushes led up to six wide brick steps and onto the front porch, where a massive white door gave entrance to the house. Flanking the door were long, narrow stained-glass windows in the pattern of lilies in red, white, and green. The house looked very inviting to Erin.

The cabdriver pulled up in front of the door and said, "You want me to start carrying the luggage in?"

"Let me go in first," Erin said. "I'll pay you now, though. How much is it?"

The driver named the figure, and she fumbled in her purse with fingers numbed by the cold. She gave him what he asked, then added an extra five dollars. "You've been so kind. I appreciate it."

The cabdriver gave her a quick smile. The grin spread over his face like a ripple in a pond, expanding until there was no room for both the grin and his eyes, which disappeared almost completely. "I wish there were more folks in the world like you, lady. I'd get rich! You go see if your folks are here, and then I'll carry your trunk and your bags in."

Erin stepped out of the cab, walked down the walkway, then climbed up the steps to the porch. A brass knocker hung in the center of the massive door, and she struck it three times and waited. In less time than she would have imagined, the door opened, and a tall, thin black man stood there, dressed in black trousers and a white shirt. He said, "Yes, ma'am?"

"I'm here to see Mr. and Mrs. Winslow."

The man looked at the cab and said, "Come right in, ma'am. Do you intend to keep the cab waiting?"

"Just until I see my grandfather and grandmother."

"Oh." The man's face broke into a grin. "Yes, ma'am. You're a Winslow, then. Come right in."

Stepping inside, Erin glanced around the foyer, which was not ornate but carefully furnished. There was an air of ease and comfort and yet a taste of luxury in the thick carpets, the fixtures decorating the walls, and the heavy chandelier lighting the foyer. "I'll get Missus Winslow right now if you'll just wait here, miss."

"Yes, I will."

The man disappeared, and Erin took a deep breath. Ever since she was a child she had heard many stories about her grandparents—Mark Winslow and his wife, Lola. She knew the Winslows were fairly wealthy people, Mark having risen from working on the track of the Union Pacific to the vice-presidency of the company.

A woman came out, followed by the black man, and smiled at once as she came toward Erin. "Erin, my dear, it's so *good* to see you again!"

Lola Winslow was older than Erin remembered her, but she was still a very beautiful woman indeed. Her hair, which used to be coal black, was pure silver now, and there were lines in her face. But when she embraced Erin, the young woman remembered how gracious she had been when Erin had come on her only previous visit. She was but a child then, yet she still remembered the beauty and grace of this woman.

"Your grandfather isn't feeling well, but I'm sure he'll join us for breakfast tomorrow. James, will you help with the luggage?"

As the driver and James brought the luggage in, Lola took Erin to a room on the second floor of the house. It was a beautiful room with pale blue painted walls and a large mahogany canopy bed covered with a gauzy white-and-blue-striped fabric. A matching mahogany chest of drawers and a desk sat between the two long windows, which were draped with a sheer fabric in light blue. The floor was carpeted with a thick rug with a rose, blue, and white design.

Erin said, "This is the most beautiful room I've ever seen. I'll be afraid to touch anything."

Lola laughed. "Don't be afraid to do that. This house isn't a museum. It's here to be used. You get settled in and then come downstairs. We'll have a bite to eat and some tea or coffee."

★　★　★　★

Erin awoke early in the morning, as was her custom. She was buried under a pile of fragrant blankets and luxuriated in the softness of the featherbed. She hadn't experienced such physical comforts since her first visit to America. Lola had told her she had picked the down for the featherbed herself from ducks over the years.

Now Erin got out of bed and dressed quickly. She had not brought clothes warm enough for the American winter and knew she would have to buy flannel underwear and a heavier wardrobe all around. She finally picked out a light green dress but slipped a tan sweater over it, for it was chilly in the house. When she went outside the room, she found a maid coming down the hall, a short girl with merry blue eyes and yellow hair. "Miz Winslow says for you to come down to breakfast as soon as you get up. My name is Mary."

"Thank you, Mary."

"I'll show you to the dining room. You'll eat in the small dining room today."

Erin followed the maid downstairs, and as she entered the dining room, she thought, *If this is the small one, I'd like to see the large one.* It was a fourteen-by-sixteen-foot room with white walls and white furniture. Lola came in through another door and saw her. "Oh, you're here! Mary, will you bring the food in? Erin, go over by the fire and get yourself warm."

Erin stood before the fire and stretched her hands out toward it. "This feels good," she said.

"Did you sleep well last night?"

"Oh yes. That featherbed was *wonderful!* I'm not used to this cold weather, though. I'll have to buy some heavier clothes and some sturdier shoes, I'm afraid."

"Maybe we can go shopping, and I'll help you pick out some things."

The two women sat down, and Erin enjoyed her breakfast, which consisted of scrambled eggs, thick slices of ham, and something called grits, which, Lola explained, most northerners did not eat, but which Mark had developed a taste for in Virginia, where he had grown up.

They were almost finished when Mark came in and walked over to Erin. She stood up, and he reached out and pulled her into an embrace. Stepping back, he said, "Well, I must say. You've taken your good looks from your grandfather."

Erin laughed, for she remembered that Mark had always teased her on her last visit here. "Thank you, Grandfather."

"If your ego will allow it, why don't you sit down, Mark?" Lola smiled at the pair. "We just started. Could you eat some eggs?"

"I think maybe I could, and if Cora has any of those fresh biscuits, I could certainly eat one of those."

Erin noted that her grandfather still retained traces of his early good looks, but there was a frail look about him now. He had been a strong man all his life, her father had told her, but now he had the appearance of a chronically ill man. His eyes were tired, but he made an effort to speak with her and to find out all about her.

After breakfast was over, they sat at the table drinking coffee. Mark asked directly, "Well, what are you going to do with yourself here, Erin?"

"I've become a flier and have been working at it commercially in Africa. I'd like to do the same thing here—earn a living by flying."

"That might be a little bit difficult," Lola remarked. "Women don't do that in this country much."

"They didn't do it in Africa much, either. I think I was the only one."

Mark said, "Well, you can stay here with us while you look around."

"I knew you'd say that, Grandfather, but what I want to do is get a little place of my own."

Mark suddenly smiled, his eyes crinkling up. "You want to be an independent woman. Is that it?"

"It really is," Erin said quietly. "I've never had to make it completely on my own. There's always been family nearby to help, but now I think it's time to try it out."

"My, at the decrepit age of seventeen you've never had to make it on your own. Well," Mark smiled. "I think that will be good. But I want you to remember something, Erin. You'll always have family nearby. We're here now, and we're always ready to help."

Erin was warmed by the assurances of the tall, silver-haired man. "Thank you. I knew I could count on you, but this is something I have to do for myself."

★　★　★　★

Erin enjoyed the next week immensely. She was tired from her journey and emotionally drained from the disaster of Stephen Charterhouse. Her grandparents' house was like a haven for her. She rose early in the morning and went for long walks in the snow. She had long conversations with her grandparents, and she found herself growing very fond of them. But during this time an anxiety kept pushing at her, and finally after a week she set out to find an apartment in the city. She knew very little about New York City, but she got some good advice from her grandfather, who knew it very well. Finally she found a small apartment close to the airstrip. It was not a luxurious place, but it was in a respectable part of town, and for several days she took pleasure in settling in. She enjoyed stocking her larder and experimenting with different kinds of food she had never encountered before. She had always been a fine cook, and each night she prepared herself a different sort of meal.

One thing she quickly discovered was that men were interested in her. Some were brash and bold and came right up to her; this sort she handled without problems. Others were shy, but she could feel their eyes on her. None of them got anywhere, however, for she was determined to find her way in the world of aviation, and men were not part of her plan.

* * * *

"I'm sorry, Miss Winslow, but I don't think you're going to have much luck." Robert Jennings, the manager of the airstrip, had been kind to her when she had appeared asking for work. He had listened carefully as she explained her experience, then he had examined her license and shook his head with a look of regret. "You have to understand," he said, "it's not the best time of the year, and there are a great many experienced pilots who are out of work."

Erin felt a moment's disappointment, but then she said, "I thank you for being honest, Mr. Jennings, but it's only fair to warn you that you're going to get pretty sick of me."

"Oh, I doubt that, Miss Winslow!"

"You don't know how pesky I can be. I'll be coming back from time to time, and if you hear of anything, I'd appreciate it if you would call me at this number."

Jennings took the card, placed it in his desk drawer, and said, "I'll be happy to do that. I'll keep my ears to the ground, Miss Winslow. One thing I'd better mention: I'm not sure that your license will be good in this country. I expect you'd better check with the aeronautics people. They're getting rather strict. Anybody and everybody started flying after the war, and some pretty bad things happened."

"I'll do that, Mr. Jennings. Thank you very much for your time."

Erin made the rounds for the rest of the week, contacting and getting interviews with anybody who had anything whatsoever to do with flying in New York. There were not all that many, but she kept a list of their names, gave them her name and phone number, and promised each one of them that she would make a nuisance of herself.

Two weeks passed, and Erin began to grow somewhat fearful. She did not have a great deal of money, and it was going fast.

One Sunday she went to a large church in the center of New York. The building was impressive, almost like a cathedral, but the preaching was poor and no one even spoke to her, either going or coming. "I'll have to find something better than this," she said.

The next Sunday she found a small Baptist church off Broadway. The pastor's name was Harris Howell, a Welshman with a rich, warm baritone voice and excitement in his preaching. He met her at the door after the service and wrote down her name and address. He was a handsome man in his midforties with glowing blue eyes and a rich complexion. "You're from Africa!" he exclaimed. "How wonderful! I'll want to be hearing about that. Do you know any missionaries there?"

Erin smiled. "My parents are missionaries."

"Indeed! And their names?"

"My father's Barney Winslow."

"Why, I've heard him speak. Indeed, we *are* glad to have you! Perhaps you'd come and speak to those of us interested in mission work."

"Yes, I'd be happy to do that, Reverend Howell."

The church situation was solved, and Erin found herself looking forward to the services. She and Reverend Howell arranged a date for her to speak to a group of the congregation who were vitally interested in missions, and she found to her surprise that she did better than she had expected. The people were eager to hear about her father's work in Africa, and after it was over they surrounded her, wanting to know what they could do to help.

Reverend Howell said, "I believe you can be a big help to your parents and to other missionaries. People are anxious to hear firsthand about the work over there."

"I'll be glad to do all I can, Reverend."

★　★　★　★

January passed and February came; the snow, which had been so beautiful, was now dirty and covered with soot. Erin continued her pursuit of validating her license, which seemed to take forever, and she continued to pester Mr. Jennings and others who might know of available employment. She wrote faithfully to her parents and her other relatives in Africa, and she visited her grandparents three times during this period. Each time they had offered their help, but she simply smiled and said she did not need it. This was not exactly true, for she did need it desperately. She was almost down to the bottom of her purse and knew that something must be done.

The *something* turned out to be a job she had never thought she could handle. She had eaten out several times at a very small place called the Elite Café, which was operated by an elderly couple, Mattie and Silas Barnes, who lived in an apartment above the café. Silas did the cooking, and Mattie did the serving, along with the help of two girls who doubled as dishwashers and waitresses.

Erin had been eating her meal when Mattie Barnes came by to ask how she liked the food. Erin said, "It's just fine. Your husband's a very good cook, Mrs. Barnes."

"Well, I don't know what I'm going to do. Both of my girls quit yesterday. I'll have to find somebody."

Erin looked up and said, "Would you consider me? I need to work, Mrs. Barnes."

Mattie was surprised. The young woman was well dressed, and although she knew little about her, Mattie would never have thought she needed a job as a waitress. "It doesn't pay much," she said doubtfully. "And it's not real high-class work."

"Oh, I'm used to work," Erin assured her. "I think I could be of some help to you."

Mattie was somewhat doubtful, but when she saw that the young woman meant it, she said, "Well, it would be a godsend to me. When could you start?"

"Right now. Anytime."

"I need help right now."

Erin got up and said, "Show me what to do."

The job was not difficult. The Elite Café served three meals a day and had a regular clientele, mostly clerks and secretaries and others who worked in the nearby office buildings. Erin proved to be very efficient and surprised Silas by helping with the cooking.

Silas said later to his wife, "Mattie, that young woman is

something. Why, she can cook as well as I can or better."

"She's good at waiting tables, too. She remembers all the orders, and she's pleasant with the customers. But I'm afraid we won't keep her long."

"I expect not. A young lady like that, she wasn't born to be a waitress."

"Well, I just thank God she showed up when she did. We'll keep her as long as we can."

CHAPTER NINE

A THIEF IN THE NIGHT

★ ★ ★ ★

A warming March wind swept over the city, melting much of the snow and carrying a promise of spring. The grass began to turn from brown to green, and the leaves of the trees showed their first traces of gold. The city itself seemed to come alive, digging itself out from under the phenomenal amount of snow that the winter had brought, and now Erin looked forward eagerly to the warmth of summer. She missed the hot days under the blazing African sun and had learned to dress as warmly as she could.

As the weeks passed, Erin continued her weary round of chasing after bureaucrats, none of whom seemed terribly interested in validating her flying license. It was not that they were discourteous, but most of them seemed doubtful as to whether such a license would amount to anything. The unspoken criticism was always *You're a woman, and flying is a man's world.*

More than once Erin was strongly tempted to go to her grandparents and ask for help, but her pride stopped her. She had thrown herself out into the world with a strong declaration of independence, and now to go asking for help would reveal a weakness she did not want to admit.

Her job at the Elite Café was easy as far as the work was concerned. Silas Barnes suffered terribly with arthritis during the cold, damp weather, and as a result Erin had taken over most of the cooking. On those days when he was able, Silas was there doing all he could, but more often than not Erin would shoo him off, saying, "You go upstairs and rest. I'll take care of this."

It was natural enough that Erin would become fond of both Silas and Mattie. They were a kind couple, but they were worn down by time and worried about their future. Erin had to work as both cook and waitress as waitresses came and went, and there were days when she practically ran the café.

One of the things she discovered was that both Mattie and Silas yearned to leave New York. Their home had been in Arizona, and they had come to New York with a dream of making a great deal of money in a restaurant. The dream, of course, like many others, had faded, and now several times a day either Mattie or Silas would say, "Oh, if only we were back in Phoenix! Think about that warm weather there and that sunshine."

Mattie also would speak confidentially to Erin, saying, "We've got to do something about Silas. His arthritis has been getting worse for the past several years. This weather's no good for him."

"Do you have relatives in Phoenix?"

"Yes, what's left of our family is there. I have two sisters, and Silas has a brother. They have large families, and besides, our daughter is there. She's married and has four children, two of them married. We have four great-grandchildren now."

As winter turned to spring, Erin threw herself into the new life she had chosen. She wrote faithfully to her parents, downplaying her difficulties. She tried to sound lighthearted as she wrote about her quest to get a flying license and find employment as a pilot. But no matter how well she managed to disguise her real situation, when she lay down at night or walked in the parks for long hours, she grew discouraged, and to make matters worse, she was not able to pray.

She loved her pastor, Harris Howell, and her new church, but her prayer life seemed to be bogged down, and her spiritual walk was not what it should be. Deep down she knew it was because of the bitterness and resentment she still carried against Stephen Charterhouse. Over and over again she had struggled to forgive the man, but no matter how hard she tried, she could not accomplish it. Perhaps it was because she had been so stirred by his ardor and declarations of love for her. She was ashamed of that now, and she had to push away the thoughts that came to her at night of how he had kissed her and held her and how she had responded to him. She was almost as angry with herself as she was with Stephen, for she felt she had betrayed herself. She did thank God that their physical relationship had gone no further than it did, but she knew that if she had not found out about his real nature when she did, she might have found herself getting into a bad situation.

★ ★ ★ ★

Silas came down from their apartment one afternoon after lying down for a long time. He had helped with breakfast and managed to make it until noon, but it was obvious to Erin that he was in considerable pain, so she had insisted he go lie down. Now he sat down at a table near Erin as she cleaned up the last of the dirty dishes from dinner.

"I thought we ought to tell you this, Erin."

Erin stopped what she was doing and turned to look at him carefully.

Mattie had come in as Silas was speaking, and she went over to the table where he was sitting and brushed a lock back from his forehead. She remained beside him, placing her hand on his shoulder. "Did you tell her yet?" she asked, looking at Erin.

"I was just going to." Silas cleared his throat and said, "You ought to know that we're going to sell this place, Erin. We've got to get back to Arizona. I don't think I could stand another winter here."

"Oh, I think it's what you *should* do," Erin said quickly. She had thought of this often but had not felt qualified to give such an opinion. "It would be good for both of you. You'd be with your family there and get out of these awful winters. I hear the climate in Arizona is wonderful."

"It's dry as a bone. Even when it gets hot you don't notice it," Silas said eagerly. "I grew up there—Mattie and I both. I don't know why we left in the first place."

"I do," Mattie said, shaking her head with a rather grim expression on her lips. "We wanted to make a lot of money. Well, that wasn't in the Lord's plan. We see that now. We'll go home, and things will be better then." She patted his shoulder affectionately and then looked at Erin. "We thought we'd better tell you. You might want to find another job."

"I'll stay with you as long as you're here. It shouldn't be hard to find another job after this place sells."

"Of course not. You're the best cook I ever saw and strong and pretty, too."

"Pretty doesn't help wash dishes and cook," Erin smiled. "Do you think you'll have trouble selling the place?"

A worried look crossed Silas's wrinkled face. "We might," he admitted. "Times are bad. We've let the place here get run-down. Our regular customers, they don't care, but a prospective buyer would be put off, I reckon. "

"I'm sure the Lord will send just the right buyer along," Erin smiled.

Mattie laughed aloud. "You always have the most positive attitude, dearie. We're going to miss you when we get back to Arizona."

★　★　★　★

The next phase of Erin Winslow's life came in a manner she had never expected. The Barneses put a For Sale sign on the window of the café—but to no avail. Several prospective buyers came by, but none of them made an offer. Two weeks went by and then three. Finally April came and brought the spring with it, and Erin grew increasingly concerned about Mattie and Silas. They were terribly disappointed. Both of them were ready to leave, but they could not walk away until the place was sold.

Erin's concern for the Barneses helped get her thoughts off her own troubles, and she found herself able to pray again, this time for a buyer to come, but nothing happened. She could not understand why God would not answer prayers for this couple, who seemed so good to her and so in need of an answer. As her impatience grew, her prayers took the form of questioning God's purposes: "Lord, why don't you send a buyer? These are your people, and you know they need to get out of this cold weather back to their home and to their family. Just one buyer is all it would take. Why are you waiting, Lord?"

It was after a week of praying like this that Erin suddenly was struck by a thought that seemed to come from nowhere. She was mopping the floor at about ten o'clock one night. The dishes were all washed, and everything was ready for the morning meal. Actually, she was thinking about Nbuta and wishing that she could see him again. She missed his dark features and his warm smile, and she missed more than anything his advice and counsel.

In the midst of her thoughts of Nbuta, she suddenly, without knowing why, straightened up and looked around the café. The idea that came to her then was so clear it was almost like a spoken voice. *You could buy this café. . . .*

Nothing had been further from Erin's mind. She had not come to America to be a cook and certainly not to get into the business of running a café. She pushed the thought aside, but it persisted even while she was reading the Scriptures that night. She ran across a verse that said, "And thine ears shall hear a word behind thee, saying, This is the way, walk ye in it. . . . " She stared at the verse from the book of Isaiah in the Old Testament and finally closed the Bible and turned out the lamp beside her bed. She lay there for a long time, and the idea of buying the café along with the second-floor apartment kept nudging its way in— almost like a persistent wind trying to find its way through the crevices of a boarded-up house. "This is foolish!" she exclaimed aloud, breaking the silence. "I don't *want* to own a café. I want to be a pilot."

Turning over, she finally managed to go to sleep. But all the next day and the following day, she could not get away from the thought. She began thinking that it might be the guidance of God, yet she found herself arguing. "I don't want to be a café owner! And I don't have any money to buy a café. The Barneses couldn't sell it, and I'd be stuck with it the rest of my life. . . ."

Finally the impression that this was what she was supposed to do grew so strong that she began to consider it seriously. Someday she would fly—she knew that—but in the meantime she was having a hard time making ends meet. She was having difficulty paying her rent, yet she was determined not to ask for money from her family.

Taking a sheet of paper, she sat down one afternoon and went over the café's expenses and intake over the past few months. When she had finished she stared at the figures for a considerable amount of time and then took a deep breath. Shocked at her own decision, she rose with a new determination.

★　★　★　★

"Why, of course we'll lend you the money to take over the café, Erin." Lola Winslow and her husband had been surprised when Erin had sat down with them and explained what she wanted to do. Mark had looked over the profit-and-loss sheet Erin had made up and had nodded at once to Lola, who had spoken her approval.

"I know it seems like an odd thing," Erin said with some hesitation. "But it may be a long time before I get to fly. I think what I really want to do is take this business, build it up, and then sell it so I could get enough money to buy my own plane."

"That sounds like a good sound business venture to me," Mark replied. "When would you want to do this?"

"The Barneses are anxious to get back to their home in Arizona, so as quickly as possible."

"Well," Mark smiled, "I can give you a check right now."

"Oh, but I want you to make out a note, and I'll sign it and be responsible for it. I could go to a bank, but I doubt if any bank would lend me money. I don't have any credit history."

"Don't worry about that. You wait right here. I'll go to my office and be back in ten minutes. I'll have a note and a check and—" He stood up, went over, and kissed her on the cheek. "What's the use of having a wonderful granddaughter if a man can't spoil her once in a while? I'll be right back."

Erin turned to Lola and whispered, "He's such a good man."

"Yes, he is. He's a good businessman, too, and I can tell you right now, if he thought you couldn't do this, he wouldn't let you have the money." Lola beamed at her granddaughter. Lola looked especially attractive that day in a tan dress with a high neck and three-quarter-length sleeves edged in black brocade. The bodice was loose and decorated with tiny black buttons down the front to the waist, where the skirt, which fell to her ankles, was also edged in black brocade. "I just want you to find your way, Erin."

"Grandmother, nothing was further from my thoughts than buying a restaurant, but I can do the work. I can do it all—the cooking, the bookkeeping, waiting on tables. I'll have to hire someone to help me, but I think I can do that, too."

"Then do what you have to." Lola gave her a knowing look. "You've heard about what I did when I was stranded. I dealt blackjack at a saloon."

Erin was delighted with this story. She had always loved it, and now she said, "Tell me about it again, Grandmother."

"Oh my! You've heard that story before."

"Not since I was a little girl. I've heard Dad talk about it, but I want to hear it from you."

"Well, let's wait for your grandfather to come back. Then you'll stay for dinner. When he takes his nap, I'll tell you all about what it was like in those hell-on-wheels towns."

"Is that what they called them?"

"Yes, it was, and the title wasn't too far wrong. It was a rough time, and I didn't know what I was going to do, but God was with me all the way." Lola leaned forward and put her hand on Erin's. "And He'll be with you, too. I know it in my heart."

★　★　★　★

The next month passed so quickly that Erin was hardly conscious of the passing of time. She arose well before dawn, got to the café before first light to ready the tables and cook breakfast, and then she stayed until late at night. After the café closed, she threw herself into redecorating the place.

The first thing she did was paint everything that could be painted, especially the walls. The Barneses were not conscious of how dingy the place had become, but Erin was. Now she chose a nice off-white paint and set to it. The painting was not difficult, but scrubbing all the accumulated grease that had floated in from the kitchen was. Preparing the walls took her over a week before she was ready to paint, but for the next two nights she stayed up into the wee hours of the morning until the painting was finished. When her regular customers came in, most of them stopped and stared around, exclaiming, "Why, this is a different place, Miss Winslow. It's beautiful!"

Next, Erin set out to get new tables and chairs. She haunted the furniture stores and finally found a wholesaler who had been saddled with some tables and chairs he could not get rid of. They were painted an ugly shade of orange-brown, but they were sturdy and attractively styled. Erin bought the lot, and every night she would refinish one set, a table and four chairs. She painted some of them light blue, others light green, and others light yellow. Placed together in the café, they made a colorful and cheerful sight.

The next job was to do something about the floor. She had no idea what to do. The grease and dirt had so soaked into the hardwood floor that it would have been almost impossible to get off, so instead of even trying, she found a firm that installed tile floors. She argued and bargained with them for three days until the man finally gave up and, throwing his hands in the air, said, "All right, lady. All right. You can have 'em at your price, and my guys will work at night and give you a real bargain."

The men came the very next night, cleared everything out, and tore up the old floor, and by morning the tile was set in place. She had to close for a day to allow the adhesive to set, but the next morning the new cook, a treasure of an older woman named Lena, and the two waitresses, Dottie and Grace, were as proud as if they had done the work themselves.

"My stars, Miss Erin!" Lena exclaimed. "This looks like one of those fancy eating places over on Broadway. Why, John Jacob Astor himself could come in here and feel right at home!" Lena was given to overstatements, but she was a good soul, always on time, and she usually volunteered to help with the clean-up work.

The two waitresses were sisters, ages eighteen and nineteen, with identical light brown hair and brown eyes. Both of them were stagestruck and firmly intended to become stars on Broadway. They were so much alike that for a week Erin had trouble telling them apart, but she was pleased with their help.

All of this work consumed Erin's energy, but she was strong and determined. As soon as the dining area was complete with new walls, floors, furniture, and decorations, she started in on the kitchen. It was in sad shape, but she knew that sooner or later she would want to sell the place, so she used part of her capital to buy new equipment. She demanded that it not only be efficient but also attractive. She was fortunate to find a large café going out of business and managed to buy most of their kitchen appliances at a minimal cost. Then she threw herself into making the kitchen as spotless as the dining area. She also refurbished the large back room that had been used for storage into an office. Actually she only had a desk, a chair, a lamp, and a small cot there, but it gave her a sense of pride to have such an addition.

During this period she had done nothing to the apartment upstairs. She had bought all of the furniture from the Barneses, and they had charged her almost nothing for it. "Gracious, we couldn't haul it back to Arizona," Mattie had said. "And you've been such a godsend, Erin."

The apartment was a refuge for Erin. It could be entered one of two ways: one set of stairs led down to the street, and another set led down to the storeroom-turned-office. Silas had added those himself so they wouldn't have to go outside every time they wanted to go to their apartment.

And so the days passed, and Erin thought of little but work. Her only recreation was an occasional trip to the airfield to watch the planes land and take off. She still went by to see Robert Jennings and some of her other contacts every now and then, but they still had no flying jobs for her.

One thing, however, had been a help. All the time she had been working, as much as sixteen hours a day, she had not had time to think of Stephen Charterhouse. On Sundays she attended church services twice, and in between them she went to the airfield or to one of the parks to enjoy the spring weather.

During this time a strange sort of peace had come to her, and she was content for the moment. But always, at the back of her mind, she knew she would be flying one day.

* * * *

One night while she slept in her new apartment, a sound came to her ears as definitely as a touch on her arm. Erin was a light sleeper, and she sat up at once, staring into the darkness. For a few seconds she remained still, and then she heard it again. Her bedroom was directly over the café's kitchen, and she knew that the noise had come from that area.

Getting out of bed, she put on her robe, slipped on her house shoes, and without hesitation made her way to the stairs. She picked up the .38 revolver she had always carried in Africa when traveling across the countryside alone, and she quickly descended the stairs, her soft shoes making no sound. As soon as she reached the lower level, she heard a clatter emanate from the kitchen. Moving across the office, she put her hand on the door and pulled it back a crack. The light had been turned on, and she saw a man with his back to her. To her amazement he was eating something he had taken out of one of the cabinets. He was a very tall man wearing a nondescript light gray jacket and a pair of gray trousers.

"All right. You stop right where you are or I'll shoot!"

Erin held the revolver out at arm's length, pointed at the man's back. When he turned, she saw that he was very pale. He had a piece of bread in his hand and had just taken a bite out of it. The thought crossed her mind, *He's a strange sort of burglar, stealing bread.*

"You stand right where you are," Erin ordered. "I'm going to call the police." She expected him to protest, but instead the man simply stood there staring at her. He had a soft cap on, but his unruly black hair was exposed where it curled out from under the cap. His eyes, a strange gray-green color, were deep-set and sunken back in his head. He looked ill, Erin thought. He had high cheekbones, flat and ridged beneath his skin, and a rather long nose that looked like it had been broken. A scar on his forehead wandered down over his right eyebrow. He was a lean man, and for some reason she noticed that his fingers were long, extremely so.

"There's no money in here," she said.

He shrugged his shoulders, and a strange expression crossed his face. "I-I wasn't after money. I wanted something to eat." He reached into his pocket, pulled out two apples, and put them on the table. As he did so, he doubled over in a paroxysm of coughing that shook him like a tree in the wind. He reached out for the wall with one hand and grabbed his chest with the other.

Erin flinched, for the coughing was deep and raspy, as bad as anything she had ever heard.

"Are you sick?" she demanded.

But the burglar was past answering. The coughing grew worse, and when he suddenly slumped to the floor, she lowered the revolver. Helplessly she stood there and watched as he held both arms around his chest and tried in vain to calm his breathing. But as he drew in a breath, his whole body shook with a terrible rattling sound. Erin had been around the sick before in Africa, but she had never seen anyone struck down like this. She walked over to him, still holding the revolver, but the coughing continued unabated. Finally she stuck the revolver into her robe pocket and bent over. He was lying on his side holding his chest, and with some effort she pulled him to a sitting position. "You're sick," she said. "What's the matter with you?"

"Don't . . . know."

Erin could not think for a moment. She knelt beside him and held him steady. The coughing seemed to have drained all strength from him. Her eyes fell on the two apples he had taken from his pocket and the remains of the bread he had been eating. She knew she could not call the police on a sick, starving man.

"Here, see if you can get up."

The man was still holding his chest. His lips were white, and his eyes stared blankly at her. Getting to her feet, Erin tugged at him. "Come on," she urged. "You've got to get up. You can't sit here on the floor." She kept urging until he staggered upright, and then she turned him around. "Hold on to me. Just into the next room."

She helped the man as he took short, wavering steps into the office. She guided him to the cot and turned him around. When the back of his knees struck it, he sat down limply, and she pushed his upper body toward the top of the bed, then lifted his feet up. He lay there panting from the exertion, his eyelids fluttering. He began to cough again, and at once she got a blanket that she kept nearby and put it over him. When this was done, she sat down in her desk chair and stared at him. She was not afraid any longer, but now she knew she would have to do more than simply call the police.

★　★　★　★

"He's got pneumonia. A bad case of it." Dr. Robert Satterfield had come at Erin's request. Erin had gotten the name of Lena's doctor and had been relieved when he had agreed to come at once. She had sat beside the sick man until Lena arrived, too, and she explained to the astonished woman what had happened.

Dr. Satterfield was a short, muscular man with thick fingers and cool gray eyes. His hair was parted in the middle, and a pencil line of a mustache followed the line of his upper lip. "Look at the scars on his body. They look like bullet wounds to me. Do you know this man?"

Erin ignored the question. When the doctor had stripped the man's shirt off and listened to his chest, she had seen the scars and puckered white marks. There were three of them—one high on his chest and two lower down near his side.

"Will he die?" Erin asked.

"Probably," the doctor replied. "Who is he? A relative of yours?"

"No . . ." Erin said hesitantly. She avoided saying anything else for a moment, her mind working quickly. "He's just a friend who's fallen on hard times. Would it do any good to get him in the hospital?"

"I doubt it. The hospitals are pretty full. You've heard about this flu that's going around. It's hard to get a bed. If he has no money, that would make it harder."

Erin couldn't think clearly for a moment. Then she said, "Well, there are four of us women here. I suppose four women can take care of one sick man."

Dr. Satterfield considered the blond woman carefully. She was attractive and well spoken. Her demeanor indicated to the doctor that she had been brought up well, which caused him some surprise at finding her in a place like this. She had told him that she owned the café but had been evasive about the man. He was puzzled by her hesitation at answering some of his questions, and he wondered, therefore, who the man really was.

"Well, my office isn't far from here. I can tell you what to do. As a matter of fact, he'd probably be as well off here as he would be in a hospital. I think he's got pneumonia in both lungs, and if he does, it'll be a miracle if he lives."

"Thank you, Doctor. Now, tell me what to do."

CHAPTER TEN

A Hero in the Kitchen

★ ★ ★ ★

At first he was only aware of the soft darkness and the sense of being buried under some tremendous weight. Muffled sounds came filtering through, and from time to time voices would come to him. He soon learned to distinguish between the two voices he heard most often: one was loud and the other was soft.

Sometimes hands would touch him, and he would be vaguely aware that one pair of hands was rough and the other was firm but gentle.

In the darkness there was no sense of the passage of time. He might have been in this ebony cloud for a millennium, but perhaps it had only been weeks or even days or hours. Finally the darkness began to dissipate like a dark cloud that was breaking up. The voices also became clearer, and he felt that he had been rising from the bottom of a deep ocean and now was very near the surface. The blackness turned to gray and the gray to a lighter gray, and finally he came to the very top and opened his heavy lids.

"Well, so you've come back to us."

The woman he saw confused him, for he was certain he had never seen her before. A bare light bulb was behind her, and it made a halo out of the blond hair surrounding her face. Blinking his eyes, he opened them again and saw her bending over him with something in her hand. It was a damp cloth, and when she moved it across his face firmly, the sense of moisture made him aware of his raging thirst.

"Water—" This was all he was able to say. His lips were as dry as desert sand, and the inside of his mouth felt rough and parched. He watched as the woman put down the cloth. Then she was lifting him up, and he felt the touch of the glass she put to his lips. The water tasted so good, he grabbed her hand and spilled the water over his face. It ran down his neck and chest, but as the liquid touched his parched tissues, he gasped and almost strangled.

"That's enough for now." The woman pulled the glass back, and as he dropped his hand, he saw that she was studying him with an intentness in her eyes, which he noticed were deep-set and of a peculiar shade, neither blue nor green but a part of each. "What's your name?"

"Quaid. Quaid Merritt."

"Well, you fooled all of us. We didn't think you'd live."

Merritt licked his lips for the last remaining bit of water. "Could I have another drink, please?"

"All right, but just a sip." He did not grab at her hand this time, but he sipped slowly as she held his head up. When she laid his head back, he closed his eyes for a moment and enjoyed the sensation of the water as it seemed to go through his whole body. "That's good," he said. He lay there for a moment, then lifted his head and looked around. His voice was raspy from long disuse, and his throat hurt. "What is this place?"

"This is the Elite Café, the place you tried to rob."

His memory came back with a rush. He remembered entering the café after jimmying the simple lock, and he recalled eating something. Even that memory was faint, for he had been sick for days, and as he studied the woman, he saw that she was examining him carefully. "Who are you?"

"I'm Erin Winslow. This is my café." She lifted his head again and said, "Take just a sip or two. You think you could eat something?"

"Yes."

"All right. You lie there and be still. I'll be back in a moment. I'll go get you something."

Quaid Merritt felt like a character in a play. He had been sick for so long that his mind had been affected. Before he arrived at the café, he'd been moving around like a mechanical man going through the motions of living. He remembered the coughing spell that had nearly torn him apart and suddenly was aware that he had not coughed at all since he had awakened. Cautiously he took a deep breath and found that the pain was gone from his chest, and the fever that had clung to him for a long time seemed to be gone, as well.

His eyes swept the room, which was simple enough—a desk, a chair, a cot, and some shelves holding a few supplies. The naked bulb shed its light starkly over the bare room. He was covered with a sheet, and now he pushed it back to look at himself. He was wearing a nightshirt he had never seen before. He was trying to put the pieces together when the woman came back. She carried a steaming hot bowl of something that smelled wonderful. She sat down in the chair beside the bed, put the bowl down, then reached over and said, "You've got to sit up so you won't strangle."

Merritt pushed himself up, and she reached forward and turned the pillow lengthwise so he could rest against it. She asked, "Can you feed yourself?"

"I think so." He took the bowl, which rested on a plate, with his left hand, but his hand was so weak it trembled.

"Here, let me help you. You're going to spill this all over the bedcovers."

The woman took a spoonful of the broth and blew on it, then carefully extended it. Merritt tasted chicken, a salty flavor, and as she fed him steadily, he thought he could feel strength coming back into his body. It was, of course, impossible for the food to take hold that quickly, but his mind was clearing. And when the woman finished, he said, "I can't remember much."

"I guess not. You were nearly dead. The doctor said you had double pneumonia. He couldn't believe you were still alive."

Merritt felt his eyelids growing heavy. "I tried to rob you," he muttered.

"Well, you didn't do much of a job. You tried to make off with two apples and a piece of bread. That's not much to go to prison for."

He looked at her and saw there was no anger in her eyes. He wanted to apologize. The urge rose to do what he had not done for a long time, to explain his weaknesses and his failures, but sleep came on him like an armed man. He was aware that she was pulling him down in the bed and then lifting his head to arrange the pillow. All he could do was manage one word.

"Sorry..."

★ ★ ★ ★

He came out of sleep with a start, for the racket coming from the next room had shattered his rest. He opened his eyes and sat up for a moment, considering getting out of bed, but he found himself too weak to do so. Voices were coming from the next room, and suddenly the door opened and a tall, gaunt woman wearing a stained apron entered the room. She had iron gray hair and wore glasses. "Well, you're awake again. Could you eat something?"

"Yes, I could. What's your name?"

"I'm Lena. You've got a funny name. Erin told me, but I can't remember it."

"Quaid."

"Quaid? What kind of a name is that?"

"Just a name."

The unusual quality of his name caused her to sniff. "Well, I don't know what would possess a mother to call a baby *Quaid*. I'll get you something to eat."

She stepped back through the door and left it open, and he could see across the room a stove and a wooden table laden with cans and boxes and packages. Farther on there was another door, and even as he watched, it opened and the young blond-haired woman who had fed him the soup came through it. She was wearing a light green dress with a white apron trimmed in darker green, and her hair was tied up around her head. She saw him watching her and came straight into the room. "You're awake again."

"I've forgotten your name. I'm sorry."

"Erin Winslow."

The older woman came in bearing a dish. "Can you feed yourself?"

"I think so."

"This is chicken and dumplin's. It helped me to raise seven young'uns. Now you eat it, and I'll get you some milk to wash it down with."

Quaid took the bowl and sliced off a bit of the dumpling with the spoon she had given him, put it in his mouth, chewed, and nodded. "That's real good."

"I don't have time to watch you eat," Erin said. "Do you have any family we ought to notify? You've been out of it for over a week."

"No family. None that would care, anyway."

The answer, for some reason, displeased the woman. He saw it in her eyes but did not know how to make it any plainer. She turned and walked away, and the tall woman named Lena came back with a large glass of milk. "You eat all that, every bite, and drink all this milk."

"Yes, ma'am, I will."

He ate the chicken and dumplings, savoring the succulent bites of chicken that floated around, and then set the bowl on the table. He sipped the milk slowly and, when he finished, put the glass down. Reaching up, he touched his face and felt the bristles of his beard and then he folded his hands over his stomach and lay there wondering what would come next. *I wonder what the penalty for stealing two apples and a piece of bread is. Probably the same as if you held up a bank.* He was not overly concerned, however, and grim memories rushed in upon him as he lay in the bed and listened to the sounds around him—people talking, dishes clinking, and the sound of Lena singing a hymn in the kitchen just beyond. He had lived so long with such bleak disillusionment that he had no hope of anything better. Growing drowsy, he thought, *It would have been better if I'd died. I'm no good to anybody and never will be. . . .*

* * * *

"Where did he come from? How come a young man like that has to rob a café?"

"I don't know, Lena. I haven't asked him."

"What are you going to do with him?" Lena was washing a pot. She scrubbed it hard, going at it furiously, as she did everything else. "Looks like he ain't gonna die, so you're gonna have to do something with him. He can't stay back in that room the rest of his life."

"I'll talk to him."

"You gonna put him in jail?"

"Would you, Lena?"

"Don't reckon I would. After all, stealin' a couple of apples ain't the jail sort of thing. He tell you anything about himself?"

"Not yet. He's been pretty weak, but he's stronger today, I think."

"Would be a right nice-lookin' fella if he was cleaned up."

"I suppose so."

The two women finished the cleaning, and when Lena left for the night, she said, "Good thing we don't live in the town where I grew up back in Mississippi. A young woman keepin' a man in the back room—why, gossip would be all over the place."

"I think he's safe enough."

"Well, I been prayin' for him, but maybe you'd better give him this." Lena went over to her purse, fumbled through it, and found a small package of papers. She extracted one. It was printed on light green paper, and the bold-faced type said, "Have you ever been saved?"

"Yes, I'll give it to him, Lena. You go on home now. You've put in a long day."

Erin waited until the woman left and then read the tract. It was simple enough. It presented the plan of salvation, although it was printed on coarse paper and was not particularly attractive. She turned and opened the door and found Quaid Merritt sitting up in bed. Beside him were an empty plate and an empty milk glass. She walked over to the chair and sat down. It had been a long day and she was tired, and there was still cleaning up to do.

"How do you feel?" she asked rather tersely.

"Much better."

Erin studied the man, with his coarse black hair, gray-green eyes, and stubbled beard. He was roughly handsome—he didn't have the good looks that a matinee idol would have, but durable planes in his face and a suggestion of strength. He was far too thin, for the sickness had worn him down, but she suspected that at one time he had been much stronger, with the sort of lean strength some men have instead of bulky muscles.

"Lena said to give you this." She handed the tract over and watched Quaid as he studied it. He looked up and nodded and placed it on the table. "What comes now?"

"What do you mean?"

"Well, at this point you're going to have to call the police, aren't you?"

Erin grew curious. He did not seem particularly disturbed about her calling the police, and she wondered if he was sure that she wouldn't do it. There was an indifference about him she could not understand. "How old are you?" she asked.

"Twenty-six." He grinned suddenly, and it made him look much younger. "How old are you?"

"I'm eighteen." She shook her head and said, "Are you a criminal, Merritt?"

"I stole food, so I guess that makes me one."

"Don't be foolish! What do you do when you're not taking apples from a café? Don't you have any profession?"

"Just a natural failure, I think."

"I don't believe that. All of us have a chance."

"I guess I've had mine."

Suddenly she touched the tract. "Are you a Christian?"

"No."

She sat there studying his expression and then finally shook her head. "I'm not going to call the police. I'd hate to see anybody go to jail for a couple of apples."

She left the room and began cleaning up the place. She worked hard for two hours, and then when all was ready for the next morning's opening, she went back to the office and saw that he was lying down. "Do you want something to read?"

"That might pass the time."

"What sort of reading do you like?"

"Just about anything."

"I'll bring something down." She turned and went up the steps that led to her apartment and came back with a book. "I don't know if you'll like this or not. It's by Jack London."

"I like London." He took the book and read the title. "*Smoke Bellew*. Haven't read this one."

"Get all the rest you can."

She turned and moved toward the stairs when his voice caught her and turned her around. "I haven't said thank-you."

"No need for that."

"I guess there is, Miss Winslow. I'm pretty sure I would have died if you hadn't taken care of me. Lena's been tellin' me how much trouble I was, but she did it with a good heart. And she's right." He held the book in his hand and ran his fingers over the cover, then nodded. "For whatever it's worth, I'm in your debt. Not that I'll ever be able to pay it, but I thank you."

Erin was somehow touched by the simplicity of the statement. "You're welcome, Quaid. Don't stay up too late. You need your rest."

She went upstairs and prepared for bed, and when she lay down she was very much aware of the man on the cot just below her own bedroom. Who he was and *what* he was she had no idea, but something about him puzzled her. She had never known anyone that young who had not been able to make it in life, and as she fell asleep she wondered what lay ahead for such a man.

* * * *

Lena put the small package down beside Quaid, who had dressed and was sitting in the chair that Erin usually used for her deskwork. "These belonged to my second husband. I think you need to get out from behind that brush on your face." Turning to leave, she found Dottie trying to see in through the door. "Get on about your business, Dottie."

"I want to get a look at the robber."

"He's none of your business," Lena snapped, closing the door and turning back to Quaid.

On the other side of the door she could hear Dottie sniff and mutter under her breath, "Probably murder us all!"

Opening the package, Quaid found a razor and soap. "Well, that's nice of you, Lena. I would like a shave. I never feel clean unless I'm shaved."

"I'll get some hot water, and I'll bring you a little mirror."

Lena brought the mirror and hot water, then left Quaid alone. He sat down and fastened the mirror to a wall. Then standing, he put the basin on Erin's desk. He soaked his beard for quite a while in the steaming hot water, then lathered his face and let that soak in. He found the razor to be sharp and carefully shaved until his face began to burn. He rinsed his face, cleaned the razor, and put the shaving kit on the table next to his bed. He picked up the basin of water and, carefully balancing it, moved into the kitchen. Lena looked up from the wooden table where she was slicing beef into small strips. "Just pour the water in the sink over there." She studied him and said, "Now you look halfway human again, but you're too skinny."

"I appreciate the shave, Lena."

He dumped the water, washed the basin, and then noticed the pile of dirty dishes. He put the basin down, braced the front of his legs against the cabinet, and began washing the dishes in the pot of water that someone else had already filled. Lena glanced up at him and opened her mouth to speak but did not. She nodded as if she approved as the tall man stood there and slowly washed the dishes, then put them into a pan full of water to rinse them.

When Erin came in she stopped and blinked with surprise. "You shouldn't be doing that. You're not strong enough."

"Yes, I am. Feels good to be up and doing something."

Erin glanced at Lena, who shook her head. Erin did not say any more. She fixed three plates, put them on a tray along with drinks, and moved back out.

"How long has she had this place?" Quaid asked.

"Not too long. She bought it from an older couple who moved back to Phoenix. I ain't been here long myself."

Quaid worked steadily until all the dishes were washed and then found a towel and began drying them. "Where do these go?" he said.

"Right up on the shelf."

Quaid nodded, then put the stacks of clean dishes and bowls

in order. Feeling increasingly weak from being on his feet so long, he said, "I guess I'll go rest awhile."

He moved back into the small room and lay down gratefully. It had not been much, but at least he had done something, and he felt better about it.

*　*　*　*

Health came back to Quaid Merritt more quickly than he had thought possible. After the first dishwashing chore, he found he was able to work for an hour at a time and then later two or three. And finally, within four days, he was strong enough to last all day. Dottie and Grace, the two youthful waitresses, were somewhat leery of him, both of them warning Erin that no good would come of keeping a burglar. Quaid kept waiting for Erin to say something to him, to tell him to move on, but she said nothing. Dr. Satterfield stopped by once to examine him quickly, then said plainly, "Well, you lived through it, but I don't see how. You ought to be dead."

Quaid smiled at the doctor's words, which Erin, who was there during the examination, found strange.

"That's right, I should have been dead a long time ago," Quaid said.

"How'd you get those wounds?" the doctor asked, indicating some rather clean looking scars on Quaid's chest. "They look like bullet wounds."

"That's what they are."

The doctor stared at him, waiting for some explanation, but when the man gave none, he had said gruffly, "Well, don't get pneumonia again. I wouldn't advise it."

*　*　*　*

Erin was intensely aware of Merritt's activities. She saw him grow stronger by the day, and his cheeks began to take on a more natural color. More than once she had decided to tell him to move on, but he obviously had no place to go.

As she served customers one evening, her mind was on Merritt. She approached the table and put the plate down when suddenly a hand grasped her wrist. Startled, she turned her head to stare at the seated man who was holding her. He was a big, burly man with liquor on his breath. He had light blond hair and rather small blue eyes, and his mouth hung loosely. She tried to pull her hand away. "Let me go, please."

"Ah, come on, baby. Don't be so hard to get. What do you say you and me go out and see the town tonight?"

Erin tried to pull away, but his grip was strong. She jerked wildly, and the man came to his feet. He held on to her hand and suddenly leaned forward and whispered something vile into her ear. She slapped his face, and he turned ugly.

"You'll have to pay for that! How about a kiss?"

Erin looked around the café, seeing if there was anyone to help her, but there were only three elderly couples and four women. Not much help there. Grace, the younger of the two waitresses, had backed up against the wall, her eyes big with fright.

The man was laughing at Erin, enjoying himself. Suddenly, over the man's shoulder, she saw Quaid come through the door, his eyes fixed on the large man holding her. Quaid picked up a chair and in a wide, sweeping motion swung it up and brought it down, catching the man on the head with the edge of the seat. The man uttered a moan and went down. He started to get up, and then Quaid struck him again. This time he lay still.

Erin was breathing hard, but she saw that Quaid was no more concerned than if he had swatted a fly. "Better call the police on this one," he said calmly. "He might turn mean when he wakes up."

Erin went at once to the front door. There was usually a policeman somewhere close, and she saw one just a couple doors down. She called out, "Please, Officer Sullivan, can you help me?"

The patrolman turned at once and came to her at a heavy run. He was a large, bulky man with a red face.

"One of the customers tried to . . . tried to assault me."

"Did he now, Miss Erin? Well, we'll take care of him."

Officer Sullivan walked inside and saw the man stretched

out. His gaze lifted then to meet the gaze of Quaid. "You do this?"

"Yes, he was annoying Miss Winslow."

"Well, good for you." Sullivan smiled. "I don't think he'll die. His head's too hard for that." He leaned over and gave the man a jab. Blood was streaming down over his face, and Sullivan said roughly, "Come on, now. Don't bleed all over the floor." He turned to Erin and said, "I expect you'll have to swear out a complaint."

"I'll do that."

Erin looked around at the customers and said, "I'm sorry about all this. Go on with your meal. There won't be any more trouble." She saw Quaid go into the kitchen, and she followed him. "I'm glad you were there," she said quickly.

"So am I." He smiled and said, "I probably owe you for that chair. I don't know if it can be fixed or not."

She laughed and said, "Don't you worry about the chair."

Shyly Grace edged up to Quaid. "I'm glad you were here, mister."

It was the first time either of the two young women had spoken to Quaid, and he smiled at her. "If anyone bothers you, Grace, give me a call. There's plenty of chairs to take care of them."

★ ★ ★ ★

"Quaid, let's go get something to eat."

Quaid had just finished mopping the floor. It was late, and he was wearing an apron over the same clothes he had appeared in.

"What do you mean?" he asked mildly.

"I'm tired of my own cooking."

They had closed early, and Erin was restless. "Have you ever eaten Chinese food?"

"Once or twice."

"Come along, we'll try the Crimson Dragon."

"It'll have to be on you."

"That's all right."

She watched as Quaid removed his apron and folded it

neatly. She thought, not for the first time, that in some things he was very orderly. He had been a great help at the café, taking a load off of her, so she had postponed asking him to leave. Now as the two moved out, she locked the door behind her, and he remarked, "I'd change that lock if I were you. Easier for us burglars to get in than you might think."

"Yes, I should do that. Come along, now, I'm hungry."

The Crimson Dragon was only two blocks away, and as they walked along, Erin waited for Quaid to speak. When he did it was only about the weather. "I always liked the spring," he said. "But not in the city."

"Are you from the country?"

"I grew up in the country. I still miss things about it. It's such a simple life. I think there ought to be simplicities in every life, but they are usually crowded out by complicated things."

She thought about this until they reached the restaurant. When they went inside, a diminutive Chinese man gave them a quick bow and showed them to a table. Quaid pulled out the chair for Erin, which surprised her, and she sat down. When he sat down, too, the waiter said, "I bring tea."

"Apparently you can have either tea or tea." Quaid grinned. He looked at the menu and shook his head. "I don't know what most of this is."

"I don't either," Erin said. She studied the menu, and when the proprietor came back, she said, "We don't know what's good. Could you just bring us samples?"

"Yiss! I bring you samples, and you can share. If you like anything, you can have more."

Erin sipped the tea and found it surprisingly good. The two sat there without speaking much until the meal was brought.

"Here's some wonton soup, and this is fried rice. This is sesame chicken, and you try this sweet-and-sour pork."

The table was covered with small dishes and plates, and Erin said, "I've got a habit of asking a blessing over the food." She saw Quaid bow his head at once, and she said a quick prayer.

"My mother always did that," Quaid said.

"Where is she?"

"She died six years ago. My dad, too. The flu got them at the same time." He tasted the soup and nodded, "This is good."

Then a thought struck him. "I've always been glad they died together."

"Why's that?"

"Because they loved each other so much. The survivor would have been lost. Better they went together."

The two were enjoying the food, and somehow being away from the Elite Café gave them both a sense of freedom. They began to make jokes about the food, and the proprietor, Chi Ling, came often to urge more food upon them.

"What is this?" Erin asked Mr. Ling as he placed two more bowls of soup in front of them.

"Is bird's-nest soup. Velly good."

"Is it really made out of birds' nests?"

"Oh yiss! Velly good. Velly good."

"Are you game to eat a bird's nest?" Quaid said.

Erin laughed. "When I was in Africa one of my favorite foods was milk laced with the blood of a cow."

Quaid stared at her. "You really mean that?"

"Yes, it's a favorite food of the Masai. Not many white people like it, but I did."

"You grew up in Africa?"

"Yes, my parents are missionaries in Kenya."

"How did you get over here?"

Erin could not tell him the real reason, which was tied up with Stephen Charterhouse. She hesitated long enough for him to notice, then said, "I needed to try something different. I wanted to do something on my own. What about you?"

"I grew up in the Midwest on a farm. Worked at a lot of jobs and finally went into the army."

"You were in the war?"

"Yes."

His answer was short and clipped, and she saw that he was reluctant to speak. She was curious, however, and leaned forward. "Did you see action?"

Quaid tasted a bit of a tiny wafer, then put it down. When he spoke, his voice was even and almost without inflection. "I was a flier."

"Really! Tell me about it."

Erin listened as he spoke about how he had been tested and

found to have good reflexes, and how he had finally flown in a fighter plane. "Did you ever shoot down another plane?"

Quaid hesitated, then nodded. "Eleven," he said. "And then one of them shot me down. That's where I got the scars on my chest."

Erin stared at him. She did not think for one moment that he was lying. He was not boastful. Indeed, she was having to pry the information out of him, and finally she said quietly, "You must be very proud of that."

He did not answer, and his silence confused her. But seeing that he didn't want to talk about it, she added, "Well, what do you know? I've had a hero working with me all this time. Think of that!"

Quaid looked at her, and his lips drew together in a straight line. He shook his head and said, "There wasn't much heroics to it. I don't think about it any more than I have to."

"Will you ever fly again?"

"I don't think so. Who would trust a drunk?"

"Why, you haven't had a drop to drink since you've been with us at the café."

"No, that's because I have something to do—trying to pay back a favor. But I'm a drunk all right."

His words depressed Erin, but she shook it off and brought the conversation back to more pleasant things, entertaining him with stories about Africa.

When it was time to leave, she paid the bill but noticed that Quaid was uncomfortable with this.

When they were almost back to the café, he said, "I've been thinking I ought to leave."

"Do you have anyplace to go?"

"Not really."

Erin had been wanting to send him on his way, and here the opportunity was presented to her, but for some reason she found herself saying, "Stay for a while. You're such a big help to me. I'd pay you something. It wouldn't be much, but you could stay just until you're completely well."

He suddenly looked at her. "Why are you being so nice to me, Miss Winslow?"

"Oh, call me Erin. Don't be so formal. I don't know, I just like to help people—and I hate to see anyone wasting their life."

"Too late to pray about that in my case."

She looked at him and saw that his lips were twisted in a cynical line. "No, it's not too late."

When they got to the café, Erin stopped outside the front door for a moment and asked, "Are you married?"

"Would you believe me if I said that I wasn't? Men do lie about that sometimes, you know."

A shadow passed over Erin's face, but she asked again, "Well, are you?"

"No."

"What are you going to do with the rest of your life?"

Suddenly Quaid Merritt laughed as he answered, "Wash dishes at the Elite Café, I suppose."

Erin smiled with him. "That makes two of us," she said.

She said good-night and let him in the front door, then took the outside entrance up to her room. She kept the door locked on her side that led down to what had become Quaid's bedroom, and as she prepared for bed, she thought about what a strange evening it had been. *One thing I'm sure of. I'm not going to wash dishes at the Elite Café for the rest of my life! And I doubt if Quaid will, either. . . .*

CHAPTER ELEVEN

"MAYBE I SHOULD GO...."

★ ★ ★ ★

Erin had come to the Winslow house for lunch with her grandparents, but before they had sat down to eat she had shown them the financial records of the café. She was very proud of what she had done, and she could tell that her grandfather was pleased as well as he looked over the profit-and-loss statement.

"I guess you're just a natural-born businesswoman, Erin." He looked up, and his eyes were warm with approval. "You've done a wonderful job."

"And the café looks so nice. You've done a beautiful job of redecorating it." Lola saw that Erin was enjoying the praise, and she went on for some time talking about the improvements. She had been in twice to visit and had taken two meals there. "I didn't see the Elite before you took over, but I know it must have been fairly grim."

"It was just run-down," Erin said. "But I've done about all I can do now."

"This man you tell me about who's been a great help to you, this Quaid Merritt. Is that his name?"

"Yes, it is. I'm ashamed that I can't pay him more, but he

doesn't seem unhappy. I don't think he has any purpose at all in life."

Lola had met Quaid Merritt and had been interested in him. She had reported her findings to Mark, and Mark had been less than enthusiastic, saying, "A young single man living there doesn't seem the best idea in the world."

Lola, however, had been favorably impressed with the ex-flier. She had a heart for the many soldiers and airmen who had gone through the war, and especially for those who had not been able to pick up the patterns of their lives again. There were many of them, and work was scarce. Now she said, "What will Quaid do?"

"I've asked him if he would ever go back to flying again. He says that he probably never will."

All during her visit, Erin was aware of her grandfather's doubts concerning Merritt. She did not try to defend herself, nor did he make any accusations. Finally, before she left, she kissed him and said, "Don't worry about Quaid being there. He has his own room, and he's a big help. Once when the waitresses were both sick for a day, he filled in as a waiter. He laughed at himself, but he did a good job."

"Is he a Christian?"

"No, he's not. I've tried to talk to him, but he thinks he's a hopeless case."

"You should have seen me back when I was in jail down in Texas. I was a hopeless case, but Jesus specializes in hopeless cases, doesn't He, Lola?"

"Yes, He does."

Erin kissed her grandfather again, and as she left the house a sense of warmth came to her. *If everyone could be like my grand-parents, this would be a good world.*

★　★　★　★

The Elite was closed on Sunday, and Erin had stayed in her room in the morning before church, since all the work had been done below. She realized afresh how much work Quaid did. He did all the cleaning now, mopping the floors and getting the café ready for the next day's work. She had gone to church and come back to find him sitting at the table in the kitchen reading a newspaper. "They're having an air show out at the field today, Quaid. Why don't we go take it in?"

He looked up and said, "An air show?"

"Yes, it's supposed to be a really good one. There are posters all over town."

"Sounds like fun," Quaid said.

"I've never told you this, but I'm a flier myself. I just haven't been able to get a job here flying planes."

Interest quickened Quaid's gray-green eyes. He turned to face her, and putting the paper down, he leaned forward on the table, resting on his elbows. "How did all that happen?" He listened while she told him about taking lessons and getting her license in Africa.

"Who taught you?"

"A man I knew."

At her brief answer, Quaid looked up with surprise. He studied her for a moment, knowing that there was more to it than this, but he did not want to pry. "Well, what are we waiting for? Let's go to that air show."

"Good. I'll go get ready. We can take the trolley."

★ ★ ★ ★

The air show was a delight to Erin. She had never seen acrobatics, but this show gave her a full display.

"Looks like they'd tear those planes apart the way they twist and turn!" she exclaimed.

"Most of them are Spads. Tough little ships."

"Is that what you flew in the war?"

"For most of it." They were sitting in the stands watching as two biplanes approached each other head-on. Erin gasped and, without thinking, reached over and grabbed Quaid's arm. "That looks so dangerous!"

"It's not really. They've got it all worked out."

Erin watched as the two planes came within what seemed to be inches of each other, then broke off, one into a dive and the other into a steep upward climb. The one that came toward the earth suddenly flipped over, and the plane flashed across in front of the stands. The flier, with a yellow silk scarf attached to his helmet, waved at them as he sailed by, held in only by his safety belt.

Erin loved the acrobatics, but she was absolutely delighted at the wing-walking demonstration.

"Look at them, Quaid," she said. "They don't seem to have any fear at all." She was staring at a man with a red streamer of silk on his helmet as he walked almost casually from one wing tip to the other of a biplane. He got out a chair, set it down on the wing, and then sat down in it and read a newspaper, or seemed to.

"He's not even wearing a parachute," Erin said.

Quaid turned to smile at her. She was wearing an attractive light blue dress that went almost to her ankles. He could not help but notice the smooth roundness of her shoulders, the straight line of her body. The sunlight was kind to her, and he noted that she had a few freckles across her nose, but her complexion was flawless. Her hair was a rich gold, a color he had heard about but had never seen before. Her excitement at watching the planes and the daredevils sparkled in her blue-green eyes, and she made graceful gestures with her hands while smiling and laughing in surprise and delight, almost like a child.

Quaid was aware of the fragrance of her clothes and enjoyed the warmth of her body standing next to his. There was fire in Erin Winslow, and it made her even lovelier, drawing him in a way he had not been drawn to a woman in years. The excitement of the day had brought out the qualities of a rich spirit that was normally hidden behind a businesslike reserve.

The air show lasted for an hour and a half with intermissions, and finally when it was over, Erin sighed wistfully, "That was such fun."

"Would you like to meet one of the fliers?"

Erin turned to him, her eyes open, and her lips parted with astonishment. "We could do that?"

"Sure we could. One of them is a friend of mine, Hack Phillips. We flew together in France."

"Oh, I'd like to, and I'd like to look at the planes closer."

"Come along."

The two of them made their way out of the stands, and he led her to a short, rather rotund flier with electric blue eyes and a shock of blond hair. "Hello, Hack."

Hack Phillips stared at the tall man for a moment, then let out a sharp yelping sound. "Quaid, what are you doing here? Where have you been?"

Erin watched as the two men greeted each other with the roughness that men seemed to like, beating each other on the shoulders and punching each other in the ribs. Finally Quaid pulled back and said, "Hack, I want you to meet Erin Winslow. Erin, this is Hack Phillips."

Phillips grinned broadly and nodded toward Quaid. "You're in bad company, lady. Watch this one. He was a regular devil with the women in France. Put all the rest of us to shame."

"Watch your mouth, Hack!" Quaid said but was smiling as he spoke. "Erin is interested in anything that has wings."

"Is that so?" said Phillips. "Well, I always like to meet a fledgling aviator."

Quaid sketched Erin's background for Phillips, then he had a sudden thought. "You think I might take her up? See if she can really fly or if she's just putting me on."

"Be my guest. Come along. I'll get the crate gassed up."

★ ★ ★ ★

The next hour was even more delightful to Erin than the excitement of the air show. She had been so longing to get behind the controls of a plane again—and here she was finally! Seated in the front with Quaid in the rear cockpit, she found the controls quite easy to handle, and she took off smoothly. The power of the plane thrilled her after the underpowered plane she had flown in Africa. She climbed quickly and got the feel of the controls. Hearing a thumping noise, she turned to see Quaid knocking on the fuselage that separated them. "Let's try a loop-the-loop." He explained how to handle the controls and nodded. Erin pulled the stick back, went straight up in the air, turned the airplane over on its back and completed the loop with a long, sweeping dive. She had never done anything like this in her plane in Africa, but now she let out a whoop and said, "Let's do it again!"

For the next hour Quaid directed Erin as she went through loops, stalls, spins, and finally even an outside loop—diving down, turning the plane upside down, then climbing into the circle.

Finally Quaid tapped on the fuselage and pointed down, shouting, "Let's see if you can land it without killing us both."

Erin brought the plane in for a perfect landing and quickly released her safety belt. Turning, she scrambled out of the plane, arriving about the same time Quaid's feet touched the field. "Oh, that was such fun!" she said.

Hack Phillips came strolling up and nodded. "Was that you doing all those stunts?"

"Yes, it was." Erin smiled with excitement.

"Do you pass her, Quaid?"

"She's got good hands and good balance. Didn't have to teach her much."

"How long will you be here, Hack?" Erin asked. "I want to do that again."

"We'll be here for three days. You come back anytime. We war heroes have to stick together. How about we go out and get something to eat?"

"Fine," Quaid said. He turned to Erin and said, "But it'll be on you. I've never known Phillips to buy his own meal."

*　*　*　*

For the next three days Erin left the café at two o'clock, after the noon rush. She left Lena in charge, along with Dottie and Grace, and she and Quaid rushed to the airfield. She insisted on paying for the gasoline, even though Hack argued with her before giving in, then went up with Quaid. In those three days she became proficient at maneuvering the Spad.

On the third day Hack shook his head. "Afraid that's the last of it, Erin. We'll be moving on to Buffalo tomorrow."

"Oh, I wish I had the money! I'd love to do this for a living."

Hack shook his head ruefully. "It's not an easy job. You'd be better off trying to make a killing at the racetrack."

"Things pretty tough, huh?" Quaid murmured.

"Well, it's not so much that. There's money to be made, but . . ." Hack hesitated, then laughed. "You won't believe this, but I'm getting married."

Quaid smiled crookedly. "Good. I hope she'll take better care of you than I did."

"Fine woman, but she doesn't want me stunt flying. So I've got to find some kind of a dull job pretty soon."

★ ★ ★ ★

The next week passed slowly. Erin went about her work mechanically and without enthusiasm. Lena asked her once, "What's the matter with you? You're not sick, are you?"

"No," she had murmured. "Oh . . . oh, I don't know."

Each night, after the café closed, she joined Quaid in the final cleanup—washing the dishes, mopping the floor, wiping the tables, and throwing out the trash. She pumped him for tales of his experiences in the war, and the more she listened the more she was convinced that he was a talented man who could do anything he pleased with his life.

One Thursday evening after they had finished the cleaning, she fried up a couple of steaks, since both of them had skipped lunch and supper. He made a salad and some mashed potatoes. She scrounged about and came up with two candles to put on the table in the back.

He laughed, saying, "Why, this is as good as being in a fine restaurant in Paris. Candlelit café with a beautiful woman."

"Did you do that a lot?"

"Not as much as I wanted to. There at the last I was so drunk it didn't matter any." He shrugged his shoulders with that look of indifference that had by now become familiar to Erin.

She was troubled by the darkness she saw in this man and the memories that he clearly avoided talking about. But her heart went out to him, and she wanted to help him find peace with his past and move on to a better future. For now, however, she said no more as they sat down to eat. As usual she asked the blessing, but this time she put in at the end, "And, Lord, I pray that you would bless Quaid and give him a plan for his life. In Jesus' name. Amen."

Quaid looked up, a quizzical expression on his face. The light overhead brightened his eyes and built up the solid angles at the base of his ears and at the bridge of his nose. His face was getting tan, but there wasn't any fat on him even yet, and the edges of his jaws were sharp. He studied her, his long, full lips set firmly as always. "What's that all about? A plan? You don't think God's interested in a plan for me, do you?"

"I think God's interested in everyone."

Quaid began to cut up his steak methodically, filling his plate with uniform pieces before setting down his knife, while Erin cut off bites one at a time. He tasted the steak and nodded toward Erin with a look of appreciation. "This is good," he said.

"Anybody can cook steak," Erin said, shrugging off his compliment.

They sat there eating quietly, and finally he remarked, "What about the plan for *your* life? Are you serious about selling this place and getting into flying?"

"Yes, I am."

"I've got the feeling that you're thinking of getting a stunt plane and going into the air-show business."

"I want to do something different," Erin said.

"Well, that's different, all right. What would your parents say?"

"I . . . I haven't told them yet, but I'm going to in my next letter."

"And what about your grandparents? You've told me a lot about them. Do you think they'll be happy about that?"

"No, I don't, and I . . . I hate to hurt them, but I'm longing for some excitement in my life."

The look in her large eyes as she leaned across the table was that of a woman with a dream. He put down his fork and sipped at his coffee as she spoke with obvious longing.

"I never was good at books," she went on. "My brother, Patrick, could do anything. Now he's moving up in the world, but everyone's always made fun of me because I was stupid."

"Stupid? You're not stupid!"

"You don't know me. I always made the worst grades in school. I could do things with my hands, and I could figure things out by trial and error, but anything out of a book always threw me. It was very frustrating. So you see, I've got to do something in life with my hands—something I don't have to learn out of books, something physical."

The two sat there talking until the food was gone. Then they got up to clean the dishes. When Erin had put the last dish in the stack, she turned to him and said, "You don't know how it is always being the last in everything, but I think I'd be happy doing this one thing that I do really well."

Quaid was standing very close to her, looking at Erin. For him she made a vivid, real-life picture of an image he had encountered in his thoughts and dreams. It was a private image, one he had never shared with anyone. Neither had he ever expected to find any real woman who would come even close to the dream he had conjured for himself. He couldn't look at her without wondering what it would be like to hold her, to have her as his own. It was not a carnal thought, although he was very much aware of her feminine attributes. But here, he knew, was a woman he could not simply walk away from. As he looked at her standing in front of him, her eyes pleading for understanding, he bent to catch a better view of her face. He saw the heaviness of her expression, and something seemed to cut the cord that had been restraining him. He put his arms around her waist and drew her in tightly. He watched her face for a moment, waiting for resistance, but when there was none, he leaned down and kissed her lips gently.

His kiss created a powerful sensation in Erin. She had been lonely, lonelier than she knew, and she clung to him as he held her, enjoying the feeling of security she had been longing for. For just a moment she relaxed in his arms, sharing the warmth and closeness that both of them clearly wanted.

And then suddenly she drew back, ashamed and not knowing what had come over her. She stared at him and saw in his eyes a look she could not define, but it was one that had not been there before. It unsettled her, knowing that her response to him had brought the intimacy and familiarity that come between a man and a woman who share such a moment.

"You shouldn't have done that, Quaid."

"No, you're right, I shouldn't, but perhaps you don't know how you affect a man, Erin. You can pull a man's eyes all the way across the room."

"Any woman can do that to any man."

"No, not like that . . . but I'm sorry. I didn't mean to hurt you."

For one instant, Erin almost said, *You didn't hurt me*, but instead she found herself erecting a barrier between them. "This is wrong. I should never have let it come to this."

"It was only a kiss. I'll leave if you want me to. Perhaps that would be best."

"No, not unless *you* want to, but you must never do this again."

Quaid Merritt looked at her and said quietly, "I can't make a promise like that. You'd better let me go."

Erin suddenly felt reluctant to see him step out of her life. "No . . . don't go for a while. It was just a mistake, Quaid, and as much my fault as yours. I want you to stay."

When Erin left to go to her apartment, Quaid sat down at the table and for a long time did not move. The intimacy of their embrace had changed things completely. He wasn't sure now if he could stay in her presence without constantly thinking about it. He stared at his hands and thought of what had happened, then shook his head. "She'd be better off without me," he murmured.

CHAPTER TWELVE

A VISION FOR TOMORROW

★ ★ ★ ★

The park was marked with serpentine pathways that led through the towering trees and beside the ponds. A flight of swallows over Erin's head divided the air in evanescent shapes, and she admired the kaleidoscopic images as they made their way across the bright blue of the June sky. She had made Central Park a second home, and now as she stopped beside a pond, she watched as dragonflies hovered and darted and shook flakes of life from their clear wings.

The park was not yet crowded, for it was before ten in the morning. Erin had worked with Grace and Dottie serving the early-morning crowd, but without apology had left abruptly, saying to Lena, "I'll be back to help at noon."

Now as she stood beside the still blue water of a pond, for the moment at least, an illusion of peace was upon her. Looking high overhead, she watched a hawk turn on one wing in a geometric curve and then observed the sailing clouds, their cottony forms shifting gracefully on the air currents. Finally she turned and began walking along the edge of the pond.

She loved the smells and sounds of the park. This place reminded her, in a small way, of Africa. After the cement streets and the steel and brick buildings, feeling grass under her feet and hearing the sounds of birds and smelling the earth itself made her long for the land where she had been brought up. She thought often of Nbuta and his wife, Beti, then she would think of her parents and brother and long to see them all.

She passed a couple holding hands, oblivious to the world about them, lost in each other's eyes. The sight troubled her, and the memory of Quaid's kiss arose in her mind like a phantom. She shook her hair free from the collar of her dress, dissatisfied with her own inner world and angry with herself for not being able to forget his embrace.

I once cared deeply for Stephen, and now here's this man I hardly know, a petty thief and a drunk—and I'm falling in love with him. How stupid can I be? I'm not only stupid in books, I'm stupid in men!

She berated herself, knowing all the time that her anger was self-defeating. Abruptly she turned and made her way to the taxi zone. She hailed a cab and gave the driver her grandparents' address.

She made the trip in utter silence, staring out at the city, and then, finally, as the business district gave way to residential areas, she began to wonder what she would say. She did not know what to say to herself, much less to her grandparents.

When the cab pulled up in front of the house, the driver took the fare with the tip and said, "You want me to wait, lady?"

"No, I'll find a way back in."

"Okay."

Moving up the steps, she knocked on the door, and it was Lola herself who answered instead of the servant.

"Why, Erin, come in!" Lola came forward, kissed the girl's cheek, and then, with an arm around her, walked down the hall. "Your grandfather's in the study. He's having a good day today. Can you stay the night?"

"No, I have to be back pretty soon. I'm really playing truant today."

The two women went in, and Mark looked up. He was sitting at a table writing, but when he saw Erin he smiled and got up at once. His color was good, but as they hugged Erin could feel how thin he was. She thought suddenly of the strength that must have been his when he was the toughest man on the Union Pacific Railway, able to take on any of the thousands of workers and hold his own.

For a while she let the two make a fuss over her, until her grandmother went off and soon came back with coffee and cakes. She insisted that Erin eat some cake now and take the rest home with her.

After some enjoyable conversation, Lola said, "Is something troubling you, Erin?"

"I never could fool you, Grandmother," Erin smiled wanly. "Yes, something's bothering me. I don't have anybody else to talk to."

Her grandparents exchanged glances, then Mark said, "Well, I guess you know, Granddaughter, you can tell us anything, and we'll help if we can."

Erin took a deep breath and then plunged into the story of Stephen Charterhouse. She did not withhold any pertinent details but told the entire history of her relationship with Charterhouse. After getting it all out, she said bitterly, "I was a fool. It's only by God's mercy that I didn't get more involved with him than I did, but I was spared that. I found him out in time."

Lola put her hand on Erin's. "I've known since you came to America that something was bothering you. I'm sorry to see that this has been eating away at you."

"How can I help it, Grandmother? I made such a fool out of myself! I was always stupid in books, and now I find out I'm no better with people."

"That's not true," Mark said quickly. "From what you tell me, he was a very attractive man. You had no way of knowing his past. You were young, and there was nobody else around. We could tell from your letters that you were leading a lonely life. You mustn't blame yourself for things like this. Why, my word," Mark went on, summoning up a smile, "if you knew how many times I've made a fool out of myself, you'd feel you had a fool for a grandfather."

Lola's mind was working quickly as she listened to Mark comforting Erin. When silence finally fell among them, she ventured, "I think there's more to it than this matter of Stephen

Charterhouse. Does it have anything to do with Quaid Merritt?"

A rich flush suddenly colored Erin's cheeks. She put up her hands to cover her face and could not meet their eyes. "I . . . I found I was making the same mistake with Quaid that I made with Stephen."

"You think he's the same kind of man as Charterhouse?" Mark asked.

"I don't know. How *can* I know? How can I know whether or not to trust him? I thought Stephen was good, but he failed me."

Lola had always possessed a keen insight into people, and now she shook her head slightly at Mark as if to say, *We mustn't be harsh or judgmental.* Aloud she said, "I think it's good that you're cautious, Erin. Women have to be very careful these days, especially attractive young women like you. This man Merritt— you know so little about him."

"That's right. And what you do know isn't all that good," Mark added. "He was a war hero, but a lot of men who performed well in the army went sour afterward. We all expected that to be the war to end all wars, but I doubt that it will be. War simply hardens men's hearts even more toward one another— and the anger and bitterness leaves wounds that never heal."

Erin sat there as the two spoke quietly to her and felt a warmth toward them. She saw how careful they were being not to accuse her, which she appreciated. She finally rose to leave and kissed them both, saying, "I'll call a cab."

"No, I'll have James drive you home," Mark said. "What's the use of having a man working for you if he can't be a chauffeur once in a while?"

"I'm glad you could come see us," Lola said when Erin left to get in the car with James. "I hope you'll be back soon."

"I will, Grandmother—and thank you."

★ ★ ★ ★

Erin arrived back at the café after the noon rush and threw herself into her work, making up for lost time. Erin worked hard the rest of the day, and several times she passed Quaid, who gave her a strange look but only nodded at her. Erin knew he felt the barricade she had put between them. That evening when she said good-night and turned to go up to her apartment, he stopped her.

"I'll be leaving soon, Erin."

At his words she felt, strangely enough, not a sense of relief but one of emptiness. It was what she had decided must be done, but now that it was actually happening, she was unsure of her reaction. She knew she shouldn't ask him to stay, so she turned to face him, standing stiffly. "If that's what you want," she said, biting the words off.

"I'll stay until the weekend. I don't think I'll leave much of a vacancy. You've been very helpful, and I appreciate it."

Erin turned and walked away, fighting back tears at her feeling of loss.

For the next two days they maintained a guarded truce, and finally, on Saturday night, after he had cleaned up as usual, he went into the office that had served as his bedroom. He came out with a cheap suitcase he had bought for the few clothes and personal items he had collected, including the razor that had belonged to Lena's second husband. Erin asked, "Where will you be living?"

"I've got a job, of sorts. Hotel clerk over on Water Street." A wry smile briefly stirred the corners of his mouth, and he shook his head. "The name of it's the Royal, but it's not all that imperial, I'm afraid."

"Will you live there?"

"Yes, a room comes with the job." He was holding the suitcase loosely in his left hand, and for a moment she thought he might put his other hand out. But instead he simply nodded and said, "Well, I'll say good-bye now. I owe you a lot, Erin. Most people would have had me jailed."

"I've done nothing. You've earned everything back many times."

"Good-bye. I wish you well."

He left without offering to shake hands, and Erin stood

stock-still. She heard the door close and went out to lock it. As she did, the clicking sound gave a note of finality. She could see through the glass as he crossed the street and walked swiftly along, a tall shape appearing lonesome under the streetlights. She turned away, knowing that something had passed out of her life she had not wanted to lose.

★ ★ ★ ★

"Hey, Miss Erin, I'm lookin' for Quaid."

Erin looked up from the table where she was clearing the dishes. It was after the noon rush, and she was surprised to see Hack Phillips. "He's not here anymore, Hack."

"Not here! I thought he was workin' here."

"He . . . decided to take another job."

Phillips considered her for a moment and said, "You know where?"

"Yes, he's working at a hotel as a reception clerk—the Royal, over on the East Side. Are you here for an air show?"

Phillips grinned and shook his head. "No, it's worse than that. I'm leaving next week for Pennsylvania. Getting married. Tying the old knot."

Erin smiled and then came forward and took his thick, muscular hand. "Congratulations, Hack. Tell your bride I think she's getting a good husband."

"What do you know?" he grinned. "I'll probably be the world's worst husband."

"Don't you dare." A feeling of gratitude came to Erin as she remembered how he had offered his plane so freely. She leaned forward and, being almost as tall as he was, could reach his cheek to give him a kiss. "There. I won't be at the wedding, but there's the kiss for the bridegroom."

"I hope it brings me luck. This bridegroom may wind up in the poorhouse. I'm going to try to go into business."

"What sort of business?"

"Trucking business, if I can sell my planes. I need the cash to get into the business with my brother-in-law. He's a good guy, but we'll be starting out from scratch. I'm excited about it, though."

"You're going to sell both planes?" Erin knew Hack owned the plane he had let her use, as well as another one.

"I'll have to. I've got a couple guys interested, but nobody's come through with the cash yet."

"How much do you want for them, Hack?"

Phillips stared at her. "You mean for you? For you and Quaid?"

"Well—yes, for me." She listened as he named a figure, and her mind was working quickly. "Can you give me time to talk to someone?"

"Sure, Erin. You want to call me?" He pulled out a slip of paper and wrote a number on the back. "I'll be there for two days. If I don't sell 'em here, I'll have to fly 'em through and try to sell them in Pennsylvania. But it'd be a relief to leave here with the cash."

"I'll do my best, Hack."

As soon as Phillips left, Erin began making her plans. She went at once into the kitchen and said, "I need to take the rest of the day off. Can you take over, Lena?"

"Of course I can take over. I may have to take a switch to those trifling waitresses, but we can handle it. Where are you going?" she inquired.

"Just some business. I'll tell you when I get back."

She ran up the stairs and changed clothes. As she did so she found herself breathing more rapidly. She was stirred with excitement, but she calmed herself enough to kneel beside her bed and ask God's wisdom. "God, I've made so many foolish mistakes, and I'm not very smart. I want to do this, so I'm asking you to help me if it's your will." After praying briefly, she got up and left the apartment. She took a cab over to Water Street, to the Royal Hotel.

The driver turned to give her a doubtful expression as he stopped at the front door. "Are you sure you want to go in there? It's not fit for a lady, so I hear."

"I'll be all right." Erin smiled. "Will you wait for a few minutes?"

"Sure."

"I'll be right back."

Erin entered the hotel and saw that Quaid was not at the desk. She walked over and said to a young man who didn't look old enough to shave, "I'm looking for Quaid Merritt."

"He's on nights now. He's in room 220, and his key's here. I expect he's there." He winked at her decisively. "If you don't connect with him, I'm always here, baby."

"I'll keep that in mind," Erin said. He couldn't have been older than fifteen, if even that, and she shook her head at the thought of the world in front of him.

She ascended the stairs, found room 220, and hesitated. *Am I sure I want to do this? What will I say?* Thoughts rushed through her mind, but then she shook her head and drew her lips into a tight line. She had the same expression on her face that she had had when she had faced that lion out on the plains of Africa, along with Nbuta. "All he can do is say no," she muttered. Lifting her hand, she knocked on the door, and almost at once it opened. Quaid was standing there in his shirtsleeves and stocking feet. Surprise washed across his face, and he said, "Erin—come in. But maybe you'd better not."

"I want to talk to you, Quaid." She pushed past him, and he studied her, then shrugged his shoulders and closed the door.

"Hack came by looking for you. . . ." She rushed through her story and then said, "I know you think I'm crazy, but I'm going to my grandparents. I can sell the café for part of the money, and I think they'll lend me the rest. You know what I want to do."

In the silence that followed, Erin was afraid he would say no out of hand. She studied him carefully but saw no sign of drink on him, which was a relief. "We can do it together, Quaid. You're an excellent pilot, and you can teach me what I don't know. A woman needs a man in this business; I know that. Will you go with me to talk to my grandparents?"

Quaid stood there, his head tilted to one side. He studied her thoughtfully, then nodded. "I think you're crazy, and I think I'm crazy, too, for agreeing. But I'll go with you."

Relief rose in Erin. She had not known until that moment how desperately she wanted him with her in this venture. However, she had one thing to make plain. "We'll be partners, fifty-fifty, but no drinking, Quaid."

"I found out that's not so much of a problem anymore. If I have to drink, I'll tell you about it, and I'll leave."

A smile came to Erin, yet she hesitated. Finally she put her hand out, and when he took it, she said, "One other thing. This is just business. You understand that?"

Quaid's hand was warm, and she felt the power of his grasp. "I thought it might be that way," he said simply.

"You agree?"

"I agree to try."

Erin knew it was not a complete surrender, but she said, "All right. I may have to remind you of this. Can you come with me now?"

"Let me get my shoes on, and I'm ready to go."

★ ★ ★ ★

Mark and Lola listened carefully to Erin while Quaid sat quietly by her side. The Winslows could see that their granddaughter desperately wanted them to approve of the tall man. There was no time, really, for anything but a quick judgment— and Quaid spoke little—but he met their eyes with an honesty that impressed them both.

" . . . and so you see, I know I can sell the café for a profit. There was a couple in the other day from out of town. They were very nice, and they're here looking for a venture. They looked the place over, and they actually made a very good offer. I think I can actually get a little more. Here are the figures, Grandfather."

Mark looked at them quickly and said, "It seems like a good profit."

"It'll be enough to pay off what I owe you and some more besides, but this is what Phillips is asking for his planes. Then we'd need some capital to operate on until we can make some money."

Mark studied the sheet and said, "It's a very risky business, Erin." He turned to Quaid and said, "What do you think of all this?"

Quaid spoke slowly. "You said it right, sir. It is a very risky business."

"You mean dangerous?" Lola demanded quickly.

"Well, there's always some danger in flying, but I meant it might not work out economically. Most of these air shows operate on a shoestring."

"Will you be responsible for Erin's safety?" Mark asked.

"I'll make it as safe as I can, Mr. Winslow, but it's not like running a café. You know that. It's not as dangerous as flying over France in the war, but it's not the safest job in the world, either."

The conversation went on for some time, and in the end Quaid and Erin stayed for supper. They both knew that Erin's grandparents wished to find out more about him, and it was with relief that Erin saw that he was laying himself open. He told them about his experiences in the war and how afterward he had not done well. He made no excuses and ended by saying, "I'm a good flier, but I know there are others around who are probably better."

"But none of them would come in with me on this, would they, Quaid?" Erin put in.

"I don't know," Quaid shrugged. He suddenly smiled and said, "I think we're both crazy."

Mark Winslow suddenly laughed aloud, and as soon as he did, Erin's heart leaped, for she saw that her grandfather liked Quaid. She saw that her grandmother did, too, and things went easier after that. They spent more than an hour going over the figures, and finally Mark and Quaid went off to Mark's study to go further into the financial possibilities.

Lola said, "Are you sure this is what you want to do, Erin?"

"Oh yes! More than anything."

"I'm worried about all kinds of things. As Quaid said, it's a dangerous job. But there's one danger that you haven't mentioned."

Erin stared at her grandmother. "What do you mean?"

"The danger that you might fall in love with this man. You've already mentioned how you've struggled over your feelings for him."

"We have an agreement on that. It's just business."

"Maybe so. Time will tell."

Erin stared at her grandmother and shook her head firmly. "I won't fall in love with him."

Famous last words, Lola thought, but she enfolded her granddaughter in her arms and kissed her. "We both wish you well, dear. We want you to have a life that you can take joy in."

PART THREE

FORTUNE

★ ★ ★ ★

Summer 1922

CHAPTER THIRTEEN

PRACTICE, PRACTICE, PRACTICE!

★ ★ ★ ★

A series of tiny voices came faintly to Erin as she sat at the small desk in front of the single window. It was still dark outside, but a gray wash of antiseptic light threw shadows from the chestnut tree outside her window. She flexed her fingers, which ached from having written so long, and watched as a small war took place on the ground among a group of feisty sparrows. For a moment she wondered what collective noun to call them—a herd of sparrows?—a flock of sparrows?—a pride of sparrows? Smiling slightly at her own foolishness, she watched as the tiny birds fought over the bread and seed that she had put out for them the night before. Two of them were rolling and tumbling over each other in a furious battle. Erin shook her head and spoke aloud the first line of a poem: " 'If birds in their nest agree, why shouldn't we?' "

The sounds of the boardinghouse came to her faintly as people began to stir. From the next room she could hear a muted snoring, much like a miniature sawmill. She had been irritated by it at first but had eventually grown accustomed to it. From directly beneath her room came the faint sounds of Mrs. Foster already moving around the kitchen. She glanced around the room illuminated by a single bulb that burned steadily from the floor lamp beside the small desk and, for a moment, missed her apartment over the Elite Café, of which she had grown fond. When she and Quaid had taken rooms at Mrs. Foster's boardinghouse, her room had been like a prison for her. It was comfortable enough, though not at all ornate. The floor was adequately covered by a blue rug, worn thin by the passage of many footsteps. The wallpaper was old and faded, but tiny birds on it still chirped their eternal song. The massive walnut bed was strong enough to support the weight of a rhinoceros, but was comfortable enough, and the linens were clean.

Picking up her pen, Erin took up where she had left off in her letter to her parents:

> I sometimes miss the nice apartment over the café, but we're trying to make our money go as far as possible. It was wonderful of Grandfather and Grandmother to finance this wild scheme. Nobody else would have done it. My room at the boardinghouse is nice enough, and it doesn't matter much anyway because I don't spend much time in it.
>
> I thought that being a flier would be exciting, but it's nothing but practice, practice, practice! I always felt that you were a fairly demanding man, Dad, but Quaid Merritt is a slave driver.
>
> We leave the house every morning at dawn, usually before Mrs. Foster serves breakfast. We sometimes eat a doughnut and have a cup of coffee at a café near the landing strip, and then we work on the planes. Quaid is never satisfied! He's made me learn every part of both planes, which at first looked alike to me but are as different as Belle and Joe. You remember that team of oxen? They looked alike, but Joe was meek and mild, and Belle was a devil inside cowhide. The planes are that different to me. Mine, number one, tends to veer to the left a little on takeoff. It goes into a shuddering dance when I exceed the proper speed as if to complain with me about being misused.
>
> After we go over every inch of the planes and check everything that can be checked, we take them up, but first I have to listen to Quaid's lecture. Every day he goes over the same things so that I can say it backward, but I listen. He's a wonderful flier! I can't imagine anyone better. He has taught me so much, but as I said, he is a slave driver.
>
> We go up and practice, repeating things over and over again.

Quaid says I have to do it so often that it becomes automatic and I don't even have to think.

And he's right, of course. Our first show will be in four days. It will be right here in New York, and we're just a small part of it. Somehow Quaid talked the owner of the big air show into letting us do a few things. We'll get paid a little, but mostly Quaid says it's for experience. Since he doesn't need any, he means my *experience!*

Erin started when a knock broke the silence, and she capped her pen at once. "All right. I'm coming, Quaid." She got up and grabbed a light jacket. She was wearing jodhpurs, a man's cotton shirt with the top button unfastened, and shiny black boots. She opened the door and found Quaid waiting impatiently. "Let's go," he said. "We've got a lot to go over today."

Erin muttered her assent, and the two walked outside. They could not afford taxi fare, so they walked to the airfield, which took almost forty-five minutes. Quaid's legs were much longer, and at times, deep in thought, he would forget to shorten his stride to compensate for her shorter legs. As they forged ahead through the early-morning light, Erin thought, *He could even keep up with Nbuta. . . .* She noted that his face had color in it, and that his cheeks had filled out so that he no longer had any appearance of a sick man.

Reaching the airfield, they stopped at an all-night café. They took their seats in the café, which had only four other customers, all sitting at separate tables. A woman came over wearing a white uniform with a mustard stain on the pocket. She had black curly hair and sleepy-looking, rather sensual black eyes. Erin noted that the waitress looked at Quaid and not her. "Good morning, Quaid."

"Hello, Bessie. I guess I'll have a short stack. Same for you, Erin?" Receiving her nod, he smiled at the waitress, "And a gallon of black coffee."

"You gonna be in the show, Quaid?"

"That's right. Will you be there to watch us?"

"I wouldn't miss it." She lingered for a moment, her hands on the table and staring directly into Quaid's eyes. "Maybe you'd like to take me up sometime?"

"Sure, Bessie. You name the day."

Bessie laughed, reached out, and pinched his earlobe. "All right, big boy. Then maybe we could go out some night—and then we'll see where we go from there."

Bessie turned and left, and Erin saw that the encounter had not touched Quaid. She waited until the coffee came, and Bessie again had a smile for Quaid as she poured two cups. When the waitress left, Erin said, "I think you've made a conquest there."

Quaid looked up quickly. He picked up his coffee cup and stared down into it, then shrugged. "Not much of a conquest."

"She likes you, and she's rather pretty."

Quaid shook his head. "I don't have any time for Bessie. I'm thinking about that show."

His answer did not satisfy Erin. She knew so little about him, for he never spoke of his personal life. Finally she said, "Don't you like women?"

"Some of them."

"But not Bessie."

"I'll take her up in the plane. She seems lonesome."

"I didn't notice that. She probably isn't."

Quaid studied her and smiled, sipping the coffee. He lowered the cup and moved it in a circular motion. "Interested in my love life, are you?"

"Don't you ever want to get married and have a family?"

"Not to Bessie."

"I don't mean to *her!*" Erin said. "I mean to . . . well, somebody else."

"Not likely."

"Why not?"

"What do I have to offer a woman? No money, no future." He hesitated a moment and then put the full weight of his eyes upon her. "And no God."

Erin was surprised at the last qualification. "No God? Why is that?"

"I guess I've missed out on that, Erin. I remember Abraham Lincoln had taken a blow one time, and he told somebody he was too old to cry, and it hurt too much to laugh." He sipped the coffee again and said, "Sometimes I'm like that—an orphan. Too young to die and too old to play."

"You're not old," Erin said quickly. She leaned forward, and her voice was intense and had an earnest ring to it as she said, "You can do anything."

Quaid considered her words and studied her by the pale light in the café. He liked the way her eyes were set and the shape of them. Right now they looked blue, but he knew that in different lighting they would turn almost green—the color of the sea as he had imagined it. Now, however, he shrugged and said, "I don't understand God. Why does He let little children suffer and die? And what about people in places like Tibet? They've never even heard of Jesus. No Bible, no preacher, no church. What happens to them? I can't understand it."

Erin was disturbed by this, but she said quickly, "Quaid, if God could be completely understood, He wouldn't be God. As a matter of fact, I wouldn't want a God I could completely understand."

"Don't you ever get angry with Him?"

Erin's eyes blinked with surprise. She thought for a moment and nodded. "I suppose I do sometimes. But mostly it's myself I get mad at." She was disturbed by this cynical streak in Quaid and wished that he would be different. "Some people are never satisfied with God. I suppose when Moses struck the rock with a stick and brought the water forth in a miracle, some people thought he should have used a fancier stick. I don't look at the stick. I try to look at the God who brings forth the water."

At that moment Quaid seemed open, but Bessie arrived and put the two plates of pancakes down. She managed to brush against Quaid as she said, "Enjoy the pancakes." She put her eyes on Erin in a calculating fashion, and the smile she gave the younger woman was a challenge. "This is a good man. I may take him away from you."

Erin was confused and flushed. "Help yourself," she said tartly. "He's not mine."

Bessie laughed suddenly and shook her head in a taunting manner. She turned and left, and the two business partners applied themselves to their breakfast.

★ ★ ★ ★

The sunlight was bright as they stood under the wing of Erin's plane, Quaid going over the maneuver one more time. Erin kept her eyes on him, noting that the corners of his lips had a tough, sharp set to them. He had long fingers, and from time to time he punctuated a comment with a cutting motion through the air. He had a man's resilience and a rough humor that sometimes popped out—but he also had a temper hiding behind his quietness, which sometimes would flash forth as hot as fire.

"Here's what we'll do." He held up his two hands to illustrate. "We'll fly wing tip to wing tip, then we'll do a rollover just as we pass the stand. You'll be the pivot, Erin. Hold the plane as steady as you can, and when you roll over I'll take the big roll going over your ship, down beneath it, and up on the other side. I'll have to cover more air, so the timing will be tricky. The quicker we do it the better it'll look, but we won't worry about speed today. We'll go up, and we'll do it ten times."

"All right. I'll do the best I can," Erin said. At his curt nod, she adjusted her parachute and got into her plane. Quaid always wore a parachute and had insisted that Erin wear one, as well. As soon as her engine roared into life, she took off quickly, and they climbed to one thousand feet. She knew that when the stunt was done, they would be at about fifty feet, but she saw the wisdom of having plenty of altitude to begin with. She glanced over at Quaid, who had brought his ship to hers, wing tip to wing tip, and she felt a little nervous. She had done plenty of rollovers but never with another plane following her every motion. She saw his nod and moved the controls. The ship rolled over smoothly enough, and she was pleased to see that Quaid stayed on her wing tip so that the two made a unit. As soon as they had completed the roll, she smiled and gave him a thumbs-up. He nodded, returned the gesture, and then made a circular motion, meaning, "Do it again."

The time passed quickly, and when they finally came down, it was almost noon. "Let's get a snack," Quaid said, and they walked to a nearby newsstand that served coffee and snacks. The proprietor, Charlie Herendeen, operated his domain from a wheelchair. He had lost both legs in the war, and he grinned as the two greeted him. "How about some coffee and something sweet, Charlie?" Erin asked.

"Sure." He kept a coffeepot on a portable gas stove, the brew always black and hot and fresh. All the mechanics and pilots had learned to trust his coffee. He poured them two cups of the scalding black liquid, then said, "Got some new candy bars." He reached over and picked up one in each hand. "This is what they call a Mounds. This here one is an Oh Henry. Just came out."

"I'll try an Oh Henry, Charlie," Erin said. She took the candy bar and stripped the wrapping off as the two men stood talking. Quaid bought a copy of the *Times*, and the two sat down while they nibbled at the candy bars and drank the strong, rich brew.

Charlie asked Erin, "How's it going, lady?"

"Real good, Charlie."

"I wouldn't do what you two do for anything." Herendeen shook his head woefully. "I want to keep on good old terra firma. Back when I had two legs I was a little bit more daring. Now I've got to keep what I have left in good shape until Resurrection Day. Then I'll have my legs back again."

"Was it awful getting wounded, Charlie?" Erin had never asked him about losing his legs, but now she saw that it didn't bother him to talk about it.

"It was a mine. We roared out over the top, headed for the Krauts. I always went kind of crazy-like when we done that. Was almost up to 'em when somethin' went off." He shook his head in wonder and said, "It didn't make a big bang, you know? Sounded kind of like—well, an unhealthy cough. The next thing I knew I was fifty feet in the air turnin' over like a rag doll. When I lit in the mud, I looked down and saw I was gonna save money on shoes from then on."

"I'm sorry, Charlie," Erin said quietly.

"Ah, I can't be too unhappy. After all, I'm back home sellin' coffee and candy to good-looking girls like you, aren't I? Lotsa guys didn't make it."

Quaid had been listening to this, taking his eyes from the newspaper. He nodded slightly in agreement, then said, "Listen to this. The latest thing is marathon dances. 'In Houston after forty-five hours one couple was still dancing. They were twenty and nineteen years old, and they broke the world's record for continuous dancing by a twosome. Immediately after, the young man collapsed and was rushed to a Turkish bath. The winning girl's ankles were swollen to twice their size.' " He looked up and shook his head with distaste etched across his features. "How's *that* for stupidity?"

"Why did they do it?" Erin wondered aloud.

"For money, of course. That's the reason most people do things," Charlie said. "There's always a big prize. Most times they're poor kids who don't have much of a chance."

Charlie Herendeen was eating peanuts thoughtfully. "I thought the war was gonna make this country better. 'Save the world for democracy.' That's what Wilson said, but I don't see it that way. Things are gettin' worse."

Both Erin and Quaid listened as Herendeen went on in a mournful fashion. And, indeed, both of them could see what the postwar years were doing to America. The old notions of propriety had been weakened by the war in Europe, and now big businesses were encouraging consumers to pursue happiness through cars, clothes, cigarettes, and cosmetics. The new morality had rendered prohibition obsolete almost as soon as it had been ratified. Bent on pleasure, Americans were eagerly discovering speakeasies, jazz, and shorter skirts. In the battle for equality, women had gained the right to vote, and many were throwing off more traditional forms of dress and comportment and becoming "flappers" with their short hair, flattened breasts, and liberal use of profanity, tobacco, and alcohol. It was a different America for those who had grown up here and a puzzling one for newcomers like Erin.

After finishing their coffee, the two said good-bye to Charlie and then walked back to the field and practiced until four o'clock. When they finally landed, Erin climbed slowly from her plane and leaned back against it. When Quaid came over, she shook her head. "I thought I was fairly strong, but I'm worn out. I don't understand it. It's not hard work like I've done before at the café or back home in Africa."

"It's the close attention that does it," Quaid murmured. "You go home and get some sleep. I'll come along later."

"All right, I think I will."

"Maybe tonight we'll go out and sample some of Luigi's spaghetti."

"That sounds good."

★ ★ ★ ★

The spaghetti was indeed good, and what was more, it was cheap. As Luigi himself served them, a broad smile showed very white against his swarthy complexion. He had brought them two glasses of wine, which Quaid accepted but Erin did not. He drank hers also, and when he saw the concern in her eyes, he said, "Don't worry. I won't get drunk on two glasses of wine."

"I'm proud of you, Quaid. You haven't had a drink since we started practicing, have you?"

"When I have something to do, I don't need liquor."

"Are you worried about the show?"

"No, you've done fine, Erin. I never saw a quicker student."

The compliment warmed her, and she said, "You know what I'd like to do?"

Quaid was winding his spaghetti around his fork. When it was all balled up, he looked up at her and said, "What?" and then put it into his mouth.

"I'd like to do a wing walk."

Quaid stared at her, chewed the spaghetti, and swallowed it. "You can forget that."

"I could do it, Quaid—I know I could! I've always had good balance, and I'm not afraid of heights."

Quaid shook his head, picking up a piece of Italian bread and slathering it with butter. "Nothing doing," he said firmly. He put his fork down, reached over, and seized her arm. "You've got steady nerves, but I wouldn't risk it. It's just too dangerous." The light overhead struck against the solid regularity of his features. The scar on his forehead showed white, and his gray-green eyes seemed brighter. As he held her arm, time seemed to slow down, and Erin became acutely aware of his tough, masculine shape as he sat across from her.

Erin did not try to pull her arm back, but kept her eyes fixed on the intensity of his gaze. "Please let me try it," she pleaded. "We can't make it unless we've got something special."

Quaid released her arm and picked up the wineglass. He sipped the wine, then put it down and shook his head. "It doesn't matter. We'll make it with the stunts we have or not at all."

Erin desperately wanted to convince him. "You don't know how unhappy I've been all my life, Quaid. I've told you how stupid I am at books—" He started to protest, but she overrode him. "I've always done poorly at books. But if I can do this one thing well, I'll be happy."

"No, you won't."

His brusque words brought her up short. She was aware of the fatalistic streak that ran through this man, brought on not by the war but by his failure afterward. She leaned forward and spoke with her usual intensity. "Why do you say that? If we succeed, we're happy. It's failure that makes us bitter."

Quaid fell silent for a moment, and all that could be heard was the quiet stir of the restaurant—the tinkle of wine being poured at other tables, the soft laughter, the talk about them. But Quaid had shut all this out. "I had a friend," he said in a tone that was barely audible. "His name was Jamey Hunt—a fine pilot. He had a girl back in Texas. The war was almost over and everybody knew it. Jamey was talking about going home to marry his sweetheart. I was going to go with him for the wedding, and then three days before the armistice he got shot down. His plane caught on fire. None of us had chutes, so he burned up."

Shocked not only by the horror of the story but also by the raw pain she saw in Quaid's eyes, Erin could say nothing.

They finished their meal in silence, and Quaid suddenly said, "Let's don't end the evening like this. Every time I talk about the war I make everybody miserable. There's a new Harold Lloyd movie down the street. Let's go see it."

"All right, Quaid."

The two walked to the movie theater, and for an hour they watched the antics of Harold Lloyd. He had become even more popular than Charlie Chaplin, so they both surrendered themselves to the comedy and forgot any thoughts of the war.

They left the theater and walked slowly back toward Mrs. Foster's boardinghouse. Erin longed to ask him again about wing walking but knew that the time was not right. *I'm going to do something that will make people notice me*, she thought. *And if walking on the wing of an airplane will do it, then that's what I'll do!*

CHAPTER FOURTEEN

JO AND REV

★ ★ ★ ★

Despite her earlier confidence, Erin felt weak in the legs as she stood beside her plane looking at the grandstand. Quaid noticed this instantly and reached out and turned her toward him. "Are you scared?"

"No!" Erin was acutely conscious of the firm touch of his hands on her shoulders. When he dropped his hands, she said, "I'm a little nervous, all right, but I'm not afraid."

Quaid nodded shortly. "That's good," he said. "It's a bit like going into action, I guess. I was always shaky before I took off in France, but once we were in the thick of battle I didn't have time to think about it. That's what all the practice has been for, Erin, so that when we're actually flying you won't be thinking about the crowd or anything else—only about the plane. You become a part of it." He studied her carefully, then said, "You look nice."

Erin flushed slightly. She was wearing a pair of whipped-cord jodhpurs, over-the-calf black boots that were as shiny as she could make them, and an emerald green blouse with a light tan jacket over it. She carried her parachute in one arm and clutched her helmet and goggles in the other. The crowd roared, and both turned to look at a plane as it flashed by the grandstand upside down, the pilot nonchalantly waving at the crowd as if he were driving by in a car at ten miles an hour.

"Come on, we're next," Quaid said and turned to go to his own plane.

Erin strapped on her parachute, pulled on her helmet, and pulled down her goggles. She climbed into the cockpit, and when she nodded, the mechanic spun the propeller. The engine caught at once, breaking into a cacophonous roar. She felt the vibration through her whole body, and turning, she saw Quaid give the signal to take off. He grinned at her, and she smiled back as she pushed the throttle forward. The Spad answered obediently, and when she had taxied out to the airstrip, she looked in all directions to be sure the way was clear for takeoff. She was aware that Quaid was fifty yards behind her, and then the two climbed, gaining the necessary altitude.

Quaid pulled up beside her, wing tip to wing tip. The routine had been ground into Erin so firmly that it was as Quaid said— she did things automatically. She was concentrating on the plane, and she felt every quiver of the wings and every movement of the fuselage. She made tiny adjustments without having to think, and when Quaid gave the signal, they went into their routine. As the wind screamed through the wires, she felt exhilarated and knew that it was going to go exactly right. She seemed to hear Nbuta speaking, his deep voice repeating what he had told her back in Africa: *"Always have courage, my daughter. . . ."*

★ ★ ★ ★

Erin taxied up to Quaid's plane, and the area was filled with activity. She turned the engine off and climbed out of the airplane, noting that Quaid was also climbing out of his plane. When he stepped to the ground, she went to him at once.

"How did I do?" she asked.

Quaid saw from her sparkling eyes that she was in need of assurance. "You did fine. Couldn't have been better." He watched as she pulled her helmet off and the summer breeze ruffled her blond hair. "It was so much fun!" she exclaimed, almost ready to break into a cheer.

"Well, you're a stunt pilot. We just have to work on some new stunts now."

As the two turned away from one another, Erin was intercepted by a tall woman with red hair and green eyes. "You did a fine job, Miss Winslow."

"Why, thank you. It was my first time, you know."

"So I understand." The woman put her hand out and gave her a brilliant smile. "We have the same name. I am Jo Winslow. Some people still call me Josephine Hellinger—my maiden name."

"Oh, Mrs. Winslow, I've read so many of your stories! I'm so glad to meet you."

"I'm happy to hear it. I saw in the paper that you'd be here, and I decided to do a story on air shows and stunt flying. Would you be willing to let me interview you?"

"Why—yes, of course, but really you need to talk to my partner, Quaid Merritt."

"I want to talk to him, too." Jo started to speak, but then a tall man approached them, and she said quickly, "I want you to meet a good friend of mine. This is Revelation Brown—better know as Rev. Rev, I'd like for you to meet a member of the Winslow tribe, Miss Erin Winslow."

Erin found her hand swallowed by the man's enormous paw. He had merry blue eyes, and his face was squelched down with his nose almost touching his chin, it seemed. He was long and gangly and reminded her faintly of a spider.

"Proud to know you, Miss Winslow," he said, shaking her hand vigorously. "Are you saved by the blood of the Lamb?"

Startled, Erin could only stare at him, and then she nodded, "Yes, I am."

"That's good. Always glad to meet a fellow pilgrim."

Jo was amused at the girl's reaction. "Rev always asks the same question. I believe he'd ask the president of the United States that if he met him."

"Why, of course I would! The president needs savin' just like the rest of us sinners."

"Is your real name Revelation?" Erin asked.

"Sure is. Yes, ma'am, my dad was a nonconformist preacher back in England. That's where I was born. He loved the book of

Revelation, so he named me after it."

"I never met anybody with a name like that." Erin smiled.

Rev was accustomed to this response. "I had two brothers," he mentioned. "One named Dedication and one named Incarnation."

Erin shot a quick glance at Jo. "Is he making that up?"

"No, he's not, and he has three sisters. If you think his brothers' names are odd, wait until you hear his sisters' names."

"Yep. My three sisters were named Incense, Praise, and Blessing. I always liked them names myself."

Erin imagined that this tall man offended some people with his direct, evangelistic approach, yet she couldn't help liking him. At that moment Quaid came over, and she said quickly, "Quaid, this is Mrs. Jo Winslow, the famous journalist—and a member of my family, I might add. May I introduce Quaid Merritt, Mrs. Winslow?"

"I'm glad to know you, Quaid. Just call me Jo, if you don't mind. This is my friend Rev Brown."

Quaid took the hand that was offered him and opened his mouth, but before he could speak, Rev Brown said, "Pleased to know you, brother. Are you on the Glory Road?"

"Don't be embarrassed, Quaid," Erin said. "Rev asks everyone that question."

A strange expression had crossed Quaid's face at Brown's abrupt question, and he did not answer directly, saying only, "I'm glad to meet you."

"Mrs. Winslow, I mean Jo, wants to do a story on air shows. She wants to interview us."

Quaid turned to face the woman and nodded. "That would be fine," he said.

"I understand you flew a fighter plane in the war. I wonder if you ever met my husband. His name is Lance Winslow."

"No, I never had the pleasure of meeting Captain Winslow, but I heard a great deal about him." Quaid turned to Erin and said, "I had no idea that you were related to him, Erin. Seems like you have some famous people in your family." Then addressing Jo Winslow again, he said, "Fine pilot, your husband. Is he here?"

"No, he's in England. We make our home there for the most

part. I come back home fairly often to visit and do some writing."

"Your flyin' is plumb good, both of you," Rev smiled. "You got good airplanes there."

"Well, the one I'm flying has developed some kind of a glitch," said Quaid. "I don't know what it is, and the mechanic can't find it."

"Mind if I have a look at it?" Brown asked instantly.

"He was the best airplane mechanic there was during the war," Jo spoke up. "Now he's doing some flying of his own, but he's still a great mechanic."

"That's a good enough recommendation for me," Quaid said. "I'd appreciate it if you'd have a look, Rev."

"Let me take some pictures before you do that," Jo said quickly. "Wait right here while I get my camera."

For the next thirty minutes Jo snapped photographs of both fliers, but mostly of Erin. When she was through, Jo smiled. "Why don't you and I go someplace where we can have tea, Erin, and I can take notes?"

"Will that be all right, Quaid?" Erin asked.

"Go right along. We'll join you as soon as we look this ship over."

The two women left, and Quaid took Brown with him to listen to the engine. He explained the problem and then stood by while Brown listened intently, laying his hand on the plane and seeming to feel the operation of the aircraft. Finally he said, "I think maybe I can help you. If you'll shut her down, we'll see."

"All right." Quaid shut the airplane engine off, and Brown removed the cowling. His hands moved over the engine with an obvious love.

"Sure do love these airplanes," he murmured.

"Did you fly in the war, Rev?"

"Nope. Somethin' I picked up later. But I was a mechanic for another of the Winslow clan—a man related to them through marriage—Logan Smith."

"You mean Cowboy Smith?"

"Yep—that's him. Do you know him?"

"I never met him, but everybody's heard of him. He's a great pilot. I sure didn't know *he* was related to any Winslows!"

"Oh, they're one big clan, to be shore. Logan married a French girl—Danielle Laurent. Mighty sweet young lady."

Before long their discussion of the Winslow clan turned back to talking about planes. Quaid had been apprehensive that the gangling mechanic might pressure him about religion, but as Brown spoke cheerfully about plane engines, Quaid relaxed. "You knew Miss Hellinger—Mrs. Winslow, that is—during the war?"

"Shore did. We all went over together, me and Logan and her. Me and Logan joined the Foreign Legion. We were in a French flying unit of American volunteers called the Lafayette Escadrille. Jo went over to take pictures and write about the war."

"I read her stories. She was one correspondent who made sense."

"She does that, all right," Rev nodded. "Now, let's start her up again and see how she goes."

As the two men worked on the plane, Erin sat with Jo at a table in the café near the airfield. She found herself giving details of her life, and Jo wrote as fast as she could. "And you actually killed a lion with a spear!" she exclaimed, staring at the blond girl with something like awe.

"Not really. I've got a picture of it that I brought with me and some other things, but I didn't kill the lion. Nbuta and the other warriors did that. I just wounded him a little—made him mad."

Jo smiled and tapped her chin with her pen. "You're going to make good copy," she said. "The country's going airplane crazy now, and for a beautiful blond girl who's killed lions with spears to suddenly come out of Africa! This'll be an easy story to write."

"Oh, but that wouldn't be right!" Erin exclaimed. "It's Quaid who's done it all."

"Did he teach you to fly?"

"No. Another man I knew back in Africa did that. But Quaid taught me all I know about stunt flying. We couldn't be doing it if it wasn't for him. And he was a hero, too, like your husband and Logan Smith."

"Do you suppose we could go to your room and I could borrow that picture and any others you have of your past?"

"I suppose so, but what about Quaid?"

"Oh, I'll be interviewing him as soon as they get here. Now, tell me more about yourself, Erin. Anything you can think of . . ."

★　★　★　★

Jo stood in front of her editor, Ed Kovak, speaking with a great deal of animation. Kovak was a large, strongly built man with a square face, piercing brown eyes, and black hair that was thinning on the crown. A cigar grew from his mouth, and few people saw him without it. Clouds of purple smoke curled lazily toward the ceiling, and as he listened there was pride in his eyes for this young woman who had risen to the top of her profession. He felt partly responsible for that and often boasted that he had made Jo Hellinger what she was as a writer.

" . . . and it's going to be a *great* story, Ed," Jo said. She fished around in a folder and handed him a photo. "Look at that."

Ed took the picture and said, "A lion! Did *she* kill it?"

"She says she just helped, but we don't have to stress that too much," Jo said demurely. "Look how young she is. She told me a lot about her growing-up years. The Masai practically raised her. She even drank that awful drink of theirs—milk mixed with fresh cow's blood." She shuddered. "I don't see how she did it."

Ed just shook his head and looked at the photo again. "She's a good-looking woman."

"Much better looking now. Most beautiful blond hair you've ever seen. And look at this clipping, Ed," Jo added. She handed him a clipping she had run across from the *Peoria Star*. The headline said, "Golden Angel Rescues Downed Pilot."

The editor skimmed the story and said, "This will make great copy, all right."

"It's even better than that. Her partner is a man named Quaid Merritt. He was an ace in the war. Shot down eleven planes, I think it was, and a good-looking fellow. I took enough pictures to write ten stories."

Kovak chewed on the cigar and nodded. "Sounds like a winner. Nothing much else is happening right now. We'll do this up big."

★ ★ ★ ★

When Erin went to the airstrip the next day with Quaid to do the show, she found Rev Brown there. It was early, so she went with him to get a cup of coffee. They strolled over to Charlie Herendeen's stand, and when Herendeen took the money from Rev, he got the usual question. "I trust you're walkin' with the Lord today, brother."

"I'm not walkin' at all!" Charlie grinned up from his wheelchair, expecting the man to be embarrassed at such a gaffe.

However, Rev simply shook his head and smiled broadly. "Well, you can walk in the spirit. It doesn't take legs for that."

"That's right. Are you a preacher of some kind?"

"No, just a mechanic who loves Jesus."

"So do I," Herendeen said. "I lost faith when I lost my legs, but I found it again." He turned to get a paper and spread it out. "Seen this yet, Miss Erin? You and Quaid got quite a write-up."

"Mrs. Winslow did that. I'm sure she's made me much grander than I really am," Erin said, laughing.

"Yeah? Well, I think after people read this, the stands will be filled today."

Brown talked for some time with Herendeen while Erin read the article, and then he and Erin started back. She said, "I think it's wonderful the way you can just talk to anybody about the Lord. My dad's like that. His name's Barney Winslow. He's a missionary in Africa."

"Well, I'm plumb proud to be just a servant of the Lord. The joy just bubbles up," Rev said.

They were in sight of Quaid, who was standing beside the plane talking to one of the attendants. Brown said, "Your partner's kind of mixed up, ain't he?"

Quickly Erin shot a glance at him. "What do you mean by that, Rev?"

"Well, I mean he's runnin' from God. I seen it in him right off. A nice fellow, but he needs Jesus."

"Yes, I'm afraid you're right," Erin said quietly. "I've tried to talk to him, but he always builds a wall between us."

"That's the way folks do who are runnin' from God. Sometimes they get mad; sometimes they get embarrassed. But whatever it is, they just keep on runnin'. I have a favorite poem about how God chases people. It's called 'The Hound of Heaven.' " Rev slowed his pace, and Erin adjusted her steps as the mechanic went on. "It says God's like a big bloodhound, and He gets on some sinner's trail and He won't quit, not until He catches him."

"I suppose you can think of God like that," Erin said. "I'm worried about Quaid. He had a hard time after the war. He took to drinking and still has a problem with it."

"Well, he needs to give all that to Jesus. Can't overcome sin all by our lonesome. We need the healing power of God in our lives first."

Erin nodded in agreement, then pointed up ahead. "Look at the size of that crowd. There've never been that many people here before," she said.

When she got close she was suddenly approached by a group of men, some of them with note pads and pencils, some with cameras. "Hey, you're the Golden Angel, aren't you?"

Erin found herself surrounded by the reporters, who kept snapping her picture and popping questions at her. "Did you really kill that lion?" "How'd you take up flying?" "Do you ever get afraid up there?"

She fielded the questions as best she could, and then Quaid suddenly appeared, elbowing his way through the crowd of pushy journalists. "That's it, fellows. We've got to take off now. It's time for us to do our stuff."

"We want an interview after the show," one of the reporters called out. He lifted his camera and took a picture of Quaid and Erin.

"Come on," Quaid said to Erin, taking her arm and heading toward the planes. "We've got to hurry."

★　★　★　★

The reporters were waiting after Erin and Quaid had done their act. The fliers were no sooner out of the plane than the two were surrounded again. There was more picture-taking, and a great many questions were thrown at them.

During the entire interview Erin kept trying to bring Quaid into it, pointing out that he was the war hero and the one who had taught her to stunt fly. There was some interest, but basically they were interested in her.

Finally the two walked away, and they were met by Rev Brown, who grinned and said, "Can I get your autograph?"

"Oh, shut up, Rev!" Quaid said irritably.

"Don't bark at him, Quaid. It was kind of fun."

"I suppose so. It'll be good publicity, anyhow. It was by far the biggest crowd we've had."

Rev said abruptly, "I'd like to come and work with you two."

"Work with us? What do you mean?" Quaid demanded.

"Not much interested in money, but I can keep them planes in tip-top shape for you, and I fly myself. So if you ever decide that you need an extra pilot, maybe I can help with that, too."

"Oh, that would be wonderful, Rev!" Erin exclaimed. "But we can't pay much. Would it be all right, do you think, Quaid?"

"We do need help keeping those ships goin'."

"Well, don't worry about the money. Them reporters are loose now. You're gonna get offers you never even dreamed of. Don't worry about the money at all," he said confidently. "It'll come."

CHAPTER FIFTEEN

IN THE SPOTLIGHT

★ ★ ★ ★

Dusk had come, and a tawny hue had fallen over the African landscape. All day long the sun had been simply a white hole in the sky pouring down heat, but now the sun retired behind the hills, which seemed in their sullen haze to be brooding with some brutal thought. The earth cooled, and the night sounds began. Barney Winslow stood at the window staring at the moon, thinking how aged and scarred it was, and at a handful of pale stars. The odors of the animals and dust and vegetation growing close to the house wafted to him, and he seemed lost in thought.

The others gathered around the table included Barney's brother and sister-in-law, Andrew and Dorothy. Across from them sat their children. Amelia was now a beautiful girl of twenty with auburn hair and green eyes, and her brother, Phillip, two years younger, had the same coloring. At Katie's insistence Barney turned and left the window. Moving back to the table, he sat down and quietly listened as Amelia and Phillip talked excitedly about the pictures and the newspaper clippings. They had come in the mail two days earlier, and Barney had digested them thoroughly. He was aware that Amelia and Phillip were much more excited about their cousin Erin's success in her profession than were Andrew and Dorothy.

"Just look at this from the *Times*, no less," Phillip said. His eyes glowed as he picked up one of the clippings. "It's all about the Golden Angel. Imagine getting into the *New York Times*! Erin's really done well for herself."

"I don't see what the lion has to do with anything," Andrew sniffed. With his forefinger he touched the picture of Erin standing beside the dead lion. His eyes revealed his displeasure, and he shook his head, adding, "Newspapers don't make a great deal of sense."

"But look at this one!" Amelia exclaimed. "Imagine having your picture made with Douglas Fairbanks and Mary Pickford!" She stared at the picture excitedly. "I never get to meet anybody! Who would ever have thought Erin would get to run around with two famous movie stars?"

"It doesn't say she's running around with them," Barney protested. He was uncomfortable with all this publicity, and now he said, "The story says that the two just attended the air show and stopped by to give their congratulations."

"I don't care! I'd give anything to meet Douglas Fairbanks. He's so dreamy!"

Dorothy Winslow picked up one of the clippings and shook her head. "This one impresses me a little more. Imagine meeting General Pershing and President Harding."

Katie Winslow smiled. "I bet Erin was excited about it. I'd like to have seen her. She says in her letter that their mechanic and extra flier, Revelation Brown, asks all of them—movie stars, president, general, and all, if they know the Lord."

Barney slapped his leg and laughed aloud. "That's good!" he exclaimed. "That's what I'd like to have heard."

"Well, I would, too," Phillip said. He shook his head in envy. "Our Erin has really done herself proud."

"And I know you're proud of her," Amelia said, looking at Barney and Katie. "After she did so poorly in school all her life, now suddenly to be in the newspapers, and have everyone talking about her."

"Do you think she'll be coming home soon?" Phillip asked eagerly.

"I'll read you part of her letter," Katie said. She moved over to a side table and picked up an envelope. Extracting several sheets, she ran her eyes down and said, "Well, first of all, she sends her best to all of you."

"She's been very good about writing," Dorothy nodded. "We've had several letters from her."

"But not since she became famous," Phillip argued. "I'd like to get one now. Maybe her autograph will be worth a lot of money someday."

Katie smiled at him and then began reading:

"I can't really tell you how shocked I am at how things have exploded around here. It's all due to Jo Winslow, of course. Her story about Quaid and me started it all. That very day it appeared the reporters were at the air show, and they'd never been there before. She's a wonderful woman, and I'm anxious to meet her husband. He's coming over with their daughter for a visit soon, and I'll get the chance.

"We're getting offers now from everywhere—Chicago, Detroit, St. Louis, Little Rock. The big question is which invitations we can accept. Of course, having Rev Brown as a mechanic has made all the difference. Quaid never said so, but he was very nervous about the planes. He's a fair mechanic, as he says himself, but Rev is an expert.

"We've made enough money so that I was able to repay Grandfather for the airplanes, so we're in the black now. I'm sending a check along with this letter to help with the mission work. I know there are always needs.

"You might not believe it, but I miss home a great deal. During the act, of course, I can only think of one thing, and that's flying. But still at night, and even at times in the day, I get lonely for all of you. Tell Nbuta that I miss him dreadfully and all of my other friends there. I can't write to all of them because I just don't have time, but I'll do the best I can.

"A man named Joseph Harlin was here. He has something to do with making movies in Hollywood. He asked if we'd be interested in going there and maybe being in a movie. I thought it would be fun, but Quaid wasn't too excited about it, so I don't suppose anything will come of it."

Amelia spoke up with amazement. "You mean she's got a

chance to go to Hollywood and be an actress, and she's not going to take it?"

"I hope not!" Barney exclaimed. "I don't think Hollywood is a good place for a young woman to be."

"I'll agree to that," Andrew said. "After that episode with Fatty Arbuckle, I wouldn't think any young woman would be safe there." He referred to an actor named Roscoe Arbuckle, who had been tried for rape and manslaughter of a young Hollywood starlet at a wild party the previous year. It had been in newspapers not only in America but around the world. Barney shook his head grimly. "If the movie industry doesn't clean up its act, it's going to be the ruination of America."

"Well, I understand they're going to try," Dorothy said. "They've appointed a man named Will Hayes, who was the postmaster general at one time, to introduce moral qualities into movie contracts."

"I doubt if anything will come of it," Barney said moodily. "People want to see exactly the kind of thing they shouldn't."

"What else does Erin say?" Phillip asked.

"Nothing about coming home. You can read the letter if you want to." Katie handed it to Phillip, and Amelia came over at once, sitting close to him and scanning the contents eagerly.

Barney sat silently for a moment and then said, "I think the sort of thing that's happening to Erin right now can be dangerous."

"Why's that, Barney?" Katie asked quickly. There was a worried look in her eyes, and she trusted her husband's judgment. "What's the danger?"

"Well, Erin is a very unsophisticated young woman, and now all the spotlights are on her. Everybody wants to meet her. They're talking big money." Barney Winslow shook his head sadly. "That's a bad combination, Katie. It would be hard for anybody, even someone with more experience than Erin, but I just don't think it's a healthy thing for her."

"We can't tell her to quit," Barney said ruefully. "I always felt bad for her when she didn't do well in school, and now she's doing very well. At least the world would say so."

Amelia looked up at her father and said, "Dad, you've got to let us go to America!"

Immediately Andrew and Dorothy exchanged glances. This was not a new argument. Both of their children had been agitated for some time. Now they were old enough to do as they pleased, and it was obvious that they were going to get to America one way or another. Andrew and Dorothy were not concerned about Phillip, but Amelia was a different story. She was an impulsive young woman with a streak of rebelliousness. It had been difficult enough to keep her to a straight and narrow path while she was a teenager. Now she was a grown woman, and her parents knew she was headed for trouble unless she had a change in her life.

"We'll talk about it when we get home, dear," Dorothy said.

The women left to begin putting the meal together, but Barney sat talking for a while with his brother. "It looks like you're going to be losing Amelia and Phillip pretty soon," Barney said quietly.

"I know, and I dread it," Andrew said with a sigh. "Some bad things are happening in America. Some of the papers are calling it the 'Roaring Twenties.' Prohibition has been a flop. It hasn't been policed right, and all it's done is make some criminals into millionaires."

"Well, I hope our children have better sense than to get involved with something like that."

Andrew was moody. He stepped over to the window and stared outside. His eyes were fixed on a group of trees close to the house. They threw shadows like old sacks on the ground, and the moonlight touched their tops with a silver fire. He turned around then and shrugged his shoulders. "The world's changing, Barney. It's not the same one you and I grew up in."

"I'm afraid you're right." Barney dropped his head for a moment and then said, "We'll just have to keep praying."

★ ★ ★ ★

Later on, when they were alone, Katie and Barney talked more about Erin. Both had serious doubts about the life she was leading, and Barney said quietly, "Andy could be partly right. Erin's never had any real attention, and now she's a target for everyone. It would turn the heads of most young women."

"She's very strong in many ways, Barney. Growing up was hard for her, but it gave her a toughness, too." She hesitated, then said, "Do you suppose *we* could go to America? We've talked about going back a number of times, but we just never do. And it's been such a long time."

Barney turned to her and smiled. "I think we'll have to." He thought for a moment and said, "I wouldn't doubt but what Amelia and Phillip would go with us."

"That would be hard on Andy and Dorothy. They're worried about Amelia. She's a handful. "

"I'm grateful we never had to worry about Erin in that way. I can't say I blame them for worrying about Amelia. She seems bound and determined to go her own way. But that's what being a parent is all about—having the courage to turn your children loose sooner or later."

★　★　★　★

"Well, I've been to three county fairs and two snake stompin's," Rev Brown announced as he threw himself into a chair across from Quaid and Erin in the hotel room he and Quaid were sharing. "But I ain't never seen nothin' like this place."

The trio had arrived in Hollywood three days earlier. They had performed two shows and had been swarmed by reporters. One had even brought a movie camera to record an interview with the Golden Angel and Quaid.

"Do you like it here, Rev?" Erin asked innocently, winking at Quaid. She well knew the answer, for Brown's opinion of Hollywood and movies and actors was no secret.

"Why, it's got the whiff of brimstone about it! Sodom and Gomorrah, that's what it is!"

Quaid laughed. "Stop trying to hide your feelings, Rev. Just come right out and tell us what you think."

"I think it was less dangerous flying against Germans than bein' in this place."

"You don't really think that!" Erin protested. "It's such beautiful country."

"Nothin' wrong with the surroundings," Rev said defiantly. "It's the people here that bother me."

"What's wrong with 'em?"

"Why, they're as phony as a three-dollar bill. Ain't nothin' natural about 'em. Met one of them so-called starlets, and you know what that hussy done? Why, she kissed me right on the mouth!"

"I think kissing in Hollywood is just like shaking hands everywhere else," Erin said.

Rev stared at her and then demanded, "Do you like it here, Erin?"

"Well, we've only been here three days. The scenery is gorgeous, and the climate's wonderful."

"I agree with Rev," Quaid said. "The people here are pretty artificial." He was sipping a lemonade, and now he stared out at the hotel swimming pool. None of the three had ventured to try it, since it was usually quite crowded. The bunch gathered there now was getting increasingly rowdy, enjoying a great deal of laughter and horseplay. "Look at them," Quaid muttered, his face and tone suggesting annoyance at the antics of the poolside guests.

"Why, they're just having fun," Erin said. "I don't see why you two are so set against Hollywood and movies and the people here." Actually she did understand Rev's attitude. He was highly moralistic, and the subject matter of most of the movies would certainly cross a line for anyone who believed strongly in the Bible's admonition to keep one's thoughts pure at all times. Why, even the new Miss America pageant out East, which all the papers were talking about, horrified Rev—he couldn't quite fathom women going around in bathing suits that came up above the knee! He had prophesied doom for the nation if things like that weren't stopped. Quaid, however, she did not understand. He was, in his own way, sophisticated and had dabbled in the world enough not to be shocked by such things, but ever since they had been in Hollywood, he had been acting gloomy. Now she tried to figure out what was going on in his brain. "Didn't you like Mary Pickford, Quaid? I thought she was very sweet."

"How could you tell? She's sweet all the time," Quaid said.

"In all her pictures she's sweet. She's had lessons in how to be sweet. She makes millions of dollars being sweet!" He sipped the lemonade, then stirred it with his finger. "She may be the meanest woman in California. You'd never know it because she's always being 'Sweet Mary Pickford.'"

Quaid's mocking attitude disturbed Erin, and she whined at the two men, "I was hoping we'd have a good time while we were here, but you two are spoiling everything."

"Well, I'll tell you what we can do," Rev said. "Let's go to church tonight."

"Church? But this isn't Sunday," Quaid spoke up at once.

"No, but there's a revival going on right in the middle of town," Rev explained excitedly. "I saw an advertisement in the paper. I never heard of the evangelist, but if he don't preach the gospel, we'll go find another one."

In the end, Rev—by sheer energy—succeeded in getting Quaid and Erin to the revival meeting. It was in a tent on a vacant lot, and they got there barely in time to find a seat.

"The mosquitoes are probably going to carry us off," Quaid protested. He was sitting to Erin's right, with Rev to her left. Quaid sat silently waiting for the service to begin.

Rev, on the other hand, was in his element. He got up half a dozen times to greet people until the crowd thought that he was part of the evangelist's team. He greeted each one with the same question, "Are you saved, ma'am?" or "Are you saved, sir?" Most of them were indeed believers, and Brown was having a wonderful time.

Erin, too, enjoyed being at the meeting. The tent was full and there was a large choir that sang very well. During one of their numbers she noticed that Quaid was singing along quietly.

"You know these hymns, Quaid?"

"Some of them. My folks took me to church pretty regularly."

"It's so exciting to me. It takes me back home. I used to go out with Dad and Mom, and we'd have a meeting out in the bush. No tent, no nothing. Just black faces surrounding us."

"You miss that?" Quaid said abruptly.

"I do," Erin nodded. "How could I not?"

"I thought you had an unhappy life growing up."

"Just in the classroom. But with Dad or with the Masai everything was wonderful." She turned to him and said, "Maybe we could go there one day."

"I don't imagine there'd be too many places there for a flying act like ours."

"I mean just so you could meet my folks. I've tried to get them to come over here, but I don't think they'll ever leave."

"I'd like to meet them. They sound like wonderful people."

The preacher was beginning his message, so Erin and Quaid turned their attention back to him. The sermon was simple, and the evangelist was enthusiastic and appeared to have memorized the entire Bible. He was also a great storyteller, and Erin enjoyed it tremendously.

When the invitation came to give their lives to God, she looked at Quaid out of the corner of her eye and saw that he was staring at the songbook but not singing. She had an impulse to offer to go with him, but she was very much aware that such an offer would probably be rejected.

Rev moved among the crowd eager-eyed, looking for any who seemed as though they might be seeking God. He found one older man with white hair, and the next thing Erin and Quaid knew, Rev was by the man's side, escorting him to the altar for prayer. After the service was over and the three friends were heading back to their hotel, Rev gave a satisfied grin. "I'm comin' back every night. That fellow really preaches the gospel."

* * * *

The crowds at the air show the next day were enormous. Despite the early-August heat, the weather was beautiful, and the performers outdid themselves for the enthusiastic audience.

At the inevitable interview that now followed every performance, Erin consistently brought Quaid into the forefront. It was difficult to do, for he offered little to the reporters.

One of the reporters asked, "What are you going to do next? Do you have any new wrinkles in your act, Miss Erin?"

Erin shot a glance at Quaid, who didn't seem to be listening. They had been having a running argument for some time, and now she said loudly, "Yes, I'm going to do some wing walking."

The reporters all exclaimed at that, and Quaid's head snapped up. His eyes seemed to burn, and Erin knew that she would have some explaining to do. After the interview the first thing he did when he got her alone was to demand, "Why did you say a thing like that?"

"It would be so great for the act. You said so yourself."

"I also said you couldn't do it."

"But I can do it. I know I can. You can think of some way, Quaid, to minimize the danger. But we need to keep adding new things all the time."

The argument went on for some time, and finally Erin said, "I don't insist on many things, but I really want to do this. It can be very simple."

"The spotlight's getting to you, Erin," Quaid said shortly. "I hate to see it." He turned around and walked off without another word, and Erin was miffed.

"It seems like he'd be happy," she said to Brown later.

"I don't think your risking your neck will make any of us happy."

"Oh, I can do it! I've always had good balance, and I'm not afraid of heights."

Revelation Brown stared at the young woman and said, "Well, if I get a vote, I'm plumb against it."

★ ★ ★ ★

"Hello? Is this Miss Erin Winslow?"

"Yes, it is."

"This is an admirer of yours, Miss Winslow. I'd like to meet you if I could."

Erin was accustomed to this sort of thing. She had her answer down and said quickly, "I'm sorry, but you'll have to come to the show."

The voice was pleasant and full of confidence. "We haven't been introduced. I'm Derek Wells."

Derek Wells!

Erin knew that he was one of the biggest stars of Hollywood, some said even bigger than Douglas Fairbanks. He specialized in adventure movies and did his own stunts.

"Are you there, Miss Winslow?"

"Oh yes, Mr. Wells. I was just shocked that you would call."

"I don't see why you should be. Look, I know it's short notice, but could you possibly spare me a little time tonight? Go out to dinner perhaps?"

Erin's first thought was, *I could never face Amelia if I didn't go. Derek Wells is her idol.*

"Why, I think that would be very nice, Mr. Wells."

"Good. I'll pick you up at your hotel. I know where you're staying. Say seven o'clock?"

"That would be fine."

Erin put the phone down and started to call Quaid, but she knew he was upset with her about the wing walking. "I'll tell him about it when I get home," she said and immediately began thinking about what she could wear to go out with a Hollywood movie star.

CHAPTER SIXTEEN

DATE WITH A STAR

★ ★ ★ ★

Erin had been ready for over an hour. She was so excited about her date with Derek Wells that she couldn't conceal it. Nothing she had to wear seemed appropriate, so she had rushed to one of the big department stores and paid more money for a dress than she had ever imagined. Now she stood in front of the small hotel mirror and tried to see the entire outfit. That was impossible, but she saw enough of it to be pleased. She admired the shimmering light blue silk tubular dress with short sleeves and a low rounded neckline. It was covered with an overlay of black lace with black sequins and beads sewn in intricate patterns around the neckline and the hem. She had also purchased a pair of black satin shoes with a low heel and delicate crisscross straps over the top of the foot and a small black beaded bag.

Satisfied with the dress, she paced the floor nervously until she heard a car pull up outside. Running to the window, she stayed back, but looking down, she saw a car that glittered in the sunshine. It was painted the brightest yellow imaginable and was trimmed with chrome along the side and had a chrome radiator. The enormous headlights seemed to be big enough for a locomotive.

"He's here!" she whispered to herself, and she grabbed her

purse and ran out the door. She ran downstairs from her second floor hotel room and arrived at the door at the same moment Wells did. She caught a quick glimpse of two people who recognized him exiting the hotel. They stopped, gawked, and whispered to each other, but Wells paid no attention. He came forward and said, "I trust I'm not late, Miss Winslow."

"Not at all."

"You look lovely," he said.

Erin resisted the impulse to say *So do you*, for indeed Wells was a sight to behold. His features were perfect, and he was wearing a light gray suit consisting of a double-breasted jacket and matching trousers with wide legs and turned-up cuffs. His shirt was a crisp, clean white with a gray-and-red-striped tie knotted neatly at his neck, and his shoes were a two-tone black-and-white leather.

Erin took his arm as they walked out of the lobby. "That's a beautiful car," she said when they reached the street.

"Just got it. It's a Hupmobile. I'll put the top up so it won't blow your hair."

"Oh, it doesn't matter. Leave it down. It'll be fun."

Derek Wells turned to face her, somewhat surprised. "You're the only woman I've ever gone anywhere with who didn't worry about her hair."

"I spent most of my life out in the bush in Africa, and now I'm up in airplanes with my hair either flowing free or under a helmet. Are you afraid they won't let us in if my hair is mussed up?"

"Not a bit of it." He opened the door, and when she got in he walked around the car and got behind the wheel. He engaged the shift, and the car leaped forward abruptly with a loud roar.

"This is a wonderful car!" she said. Her hair was tied back, and she loved the wind in her face on the ground as much as in the air. "Where are we going?"

"I thought we'd go to the Brown Derby."

"The Brown Derby! That's a funny name. Is it a restaurant?"

"Oh yes. It's very famous. Made in the shape of a derby."

He continued to entertain her as they drove along, and when he pulled up to a stop, she found that the Brown Derby was indeed shaped like a derby. A tall man in a red uniform was at her door even as the car stopped. He opened it, helped her out, then nodded, "I'll take care of your car, Mr. Wells."

"Thanks, Harry. I appreciate it."

Erin once again took his arm, and they entered as another red-uniformed doorman opened the door and greeted Wells by name with a smile.

Inside they were met by a short man with a swarthy complexion and a pencil-thin mustache. "Ah, Monsieur Wells, it is good to see you again."

"Good to see you, Pierre. This is the famous flier, Miss Erin Winslow. You're honored tonight."

"Oh yes! I have read about the Golden Angel. We are indeed honored to have you. I will give you the best table in the house."

"He claims every table is the best table in the house," Derek whispered as they followed the diminutive maître d'.

The room was crowded, and the sound of laughter and talking rose as they made their way to a table near a small dance floor. They were seated, and the maître d' said, "I will have Veronica wait on you. She knows what you like."

"You've been here a lot, I suppose," Erin said after the maître d' left.

"Oh, it's popular right now, especially for movie people. Next year it'll be another place. These things don't usually last too long."

A waitress came up to the table with a smile. She was a young woman of no more than twenty with blond hair, who was dressed in a hoop skirt starched to resemble a derby hat. The uniform looked rather peculiar, but all the other waitresses were attired in the same costume.

"Would you like a menu, Mr. Wells?"

"I don't think so, Veronica. I'll have a steak. What would you like, Miss Winslow?"

"I don't know. I haven't eaten in places like this very much."

"Our lobsters are very good," Veronica said. "They're flown in fresh every day from Maine."

"All right. I'll have that."

Wells ordered wine, and then when the waitress left, he smiled at her. "I'm glad you could come," he said. "It's a break for me."

"Are you working on a picture right now?"

"Yes, and when this one's done there'll be another one."

"Don't you ever take a break?"

Wells leaned forward. His classic features were almost too perfect for a man, but there was a virile air about him, and his masculinity was undeniable. "In my business you never know what will happen next year. This year's star, next year's dud. So we have to make it while we can."

"It must be very exciting making pictures."

"It bores me to tears."

"Not really?"

"Well, no, not really. I like the action parts of it—the fights and the duels and the chases. Things like that."

Erin listened, fascinated by Derek Wells. He did not seem at all egotistical, which was what she had expected. His manners were easy and he smiled often, so that she found herself enjoying his company immensely. Suddenly she interrupted him and said, "Look. Isn't that Gloria Swanson over there?"

Wells turned to look. "Oh yes. That's Gloria. Would you like to meet her?"

"Oh, but that would be an inconvenience."

"I don't think she'd mind. After we eat I'll introduce you to some of the other stars. There's Buster Keaton over there—and look, you see that fellow over there with the dark-haired woman? That's George M. Cohan." He continued to point out celebrities until the meal came.

Erin looked at the enormous lobster on the platter before her and then lifted her eyes to Wells. "I don't have the faintest idea how to eat this thing. It looks like a big bug."

"Let me give you some help. I eat them myself pretty often. These are fine." He dismantled the lobster quickly with swift movements and showed her how to crack the claws with the nutcrackers that had been provided. "Now, you just put a bit on your fork, dip it in that melted butter, and you're in the lobster business."

Erin tried it and chewed thoughtfully for a moment. "It's very good," she said.

"I suppose you had all kinds of exotic dishes in Africa."

"Oh yes."

"Tell me about some of them." Wells listened as she spoke, and then finally when she mentioned the favorite food of the Masai, cow's blood and milk in a gourd, he stared at her. "You didn't actually drink that, did you?"

"Oh yes. It's very good."

Wells found this amusing. "I guess I sometimes get a little queasy. I couldn't eat snails when I was in France."

"Snails? They eat snails?"

"Well, not raw, of course. I couldn't even bring myself to taste one." He looked up at her, and she noticed how intense his brown eyes were. He had the habit of looking at whomever he was talking to, giving them his full attention. She had noticed that he had done the same with the waitress, with the maître d', and with the man who drove the car away. It was not the habit of an egotistical movie star.

As they continued the meal she found that he was tremendously interested in everything she had done. He asked question after question about Africa and then moved on to her career as a stunt pilot. Finally she said, "I've told you everything about me, but what about you?"

"What do you want to know?"

"Where were you born? What about your family?"

"I was born in Detroit, Michigan. My father was a bricklayer. I grew up with three sisters. I was the only boy, so they spoiled me rotten."

Erin listened as he continued to speak, telling her of the many jobs he had had before he became an actor. He had been a carpenter's helper, a roofer, and a salesman for funeral plots. "That was my best job," he said, "until I got into acting."

"I wouldn't think it would be a lot of fun selling funeral plots."

"It's better than being a carpenter's helper. My thumbs were always blue. I was hitting my thumbnail all the time. I wasn't very handy."

"How did you get into movies?"

"The usual way. I started out as an extra. Just one of the crowd, you know. The main job there was not to look at the camera. Finally I got a bit part, then another, and Fred Makin, the producer, saw me and gave me a juicy role. From then on I've been very fortunate."

"You never married?"

Wells had been about to put a bite of steak in his mouth, but he put the fork down and stared at her somewhat astounded. "You don't know?"

"No, I don't."

"Don't you read the magazines or the newspapers? They put out a pretty steady flood of details about the lives of us big stars."

"I suppose they don't come out very often in Africa."

"Well, you are unusual, Erin, I must say. You don't know how unusual." He grew thoughtful and said, "Yes, I was married once. I was only eighteen, and she was sixteen."

When he said no more, Erin saw that he was disturbed. "Did she die?" she asked softly.

"Die! No, she didn't die. She left me."

Something about the way Derek Wells pronounced the words struck at Erin. "Why did she leave you? Was it when you were poor and weren't making much money?"

"Not a bit of it. She was true blue all through that. I put her through some hard times, too. I'd just gotten into big money and was doing fine, but—" He halted and seemed to find trouble putting his words in order. He touched his chin thoughtfully and shook his head. "It's not a very happy story, Erin. I'm afraid I behaved very badly. She should have shot me instead of just leaving me. She got the divorce she wanted, but she didn't get much of a settlement. Any other woman would have taken me to the cleaners, but Helen didn't."

"Do you still care for her, Derek?"

Her question startled Wells, and he stared at her disconcertedly. "You *do* know how to ask rather pointed questions." He chewed thoughtfully on his lower lip and turned his head slightly to one side, a habit he had. "Most women, when they go out with me, don't want to talk about other women, and especially not my wife. They want to talk about themselves."

"That's not answering my question."

"No, it's not. All right. Yes, I loved her, and yes, I guess I still do. And yes, I guess I always will."

"I think that's very sweet of you. I think God could put you back together again."

"You don't know the kind of life I've led. Hollywood's a bad place for living a good life. That's the reason she left me. I got involved with other women, and I drank too much. I did a little bit of everything bad. I don't blame her for leaving me, and I don't think God himself could make her come back to me. She's a very strong young woman."

"Then maybe God will have to change you."

Throughout their conversation, the orchestra had been playing loudly, and they were having to speak up in order to hear each other. But now the music faded as the musicians began a soft waltz.

"They don't play waltzes very often. Would you dance with me?"

"I'm not very good."

"Probably better than I am. Come along."

He was an excellent dancer, and he complimented her often. But Erin saw that her questions concerning his wife had disturbed him. It was an enjoyable evening, but long before midnight she said, "I really must go, Derek."

"You mean—now?"

"Yes. I've got a great deal to do tomorrow. We'll be leaving in two days."

"Well, that gives us tomorrow. Why don't you come and watch me do my stuff? Have you ever seen a movie being made?"

"No. Never."

"It's rather interesting. I'd like for you to come."

Erin smiled at him. "I'll go with you in the morning, but if I do, you'll have to go with me, too."

"Where?"

"Up for a flight. I'll do some acrobatics and see if you're the hero you're made out to be."

A delighted look passed across Derek Wells's face. "Fine," he said. "I'll send a car to pick you up at eight in the morning. Then after we've done a little movie making we'll do some loop-the-loops."

He took her home then, and when they got to her door, she

turned and said, "I had a wonderful time."

"So did I." He put his arms around her and tried to kiss her, but she simply turned her cheek to him. He halted, somewhat surprised, then laughed. He kissed her cheek and said, "You smell good."

"Thank you. So do you."

Her answer delighted him, and suddenly he said, "Erin, are you a good girl?"

Erin stared at him, knowing exactly what he meant. "Yes, I am," she said simply.

Derek Wells was a sophisticated man. Women who would deny him nothing pursued him constantly. This young woman was something new to him. He had the feeling that she was stronger than most men he knew. The thought came to him that she was the kind of woman who, if necessary, could draw a revolver and shoot a man down and not go to pieces afterward. He loved courage and simplicity, but was intrigued by her virtue, which was obviously a very important thing to her.

"I'll see you tomorrow," he smiled. "Good night."

"Good night, Derek."

★ ★ ★ ★

"You have a seat right here by Bob, and you'll be able to see everything that goes on."

Derek Wells was wearing a dashing black outfit that was completed with a black neckerchief that was tied around his forehead. His belt was encircled with silver, he wore boots up over his calves, and a sword hung on his left side. He looked handsome indeed.

When Wells turned to go take his place on the set, Bob Hall, the director, smiled at Erin. He was a tall, thin man with sandy hair and black-blue eyes. "Just sit right down there, if you will, Miss Winslow."

"Thank you. I won't be in the way, will I?"

"Not a bit of it." Hall smiled at her and then turned and began shouting instructions.

The action that followed was almost amusing to Erin. She

had seen a few movies, but, of course, in the theater the action was always continuous. What she saw that morning was the same scene done time after time. Bob Hall would yell, "Action!" and people would start moving around. All during the scene Hall would say, "All right. Walk slower. Hey, you, get out of the way! You're going to be in view of the camera—smile just a little one, Stella. That's right."

The most exciting part was the sword fight. Erin had never seen a real duel, of course, and this was staged, but she found herself caught up with it. Hall mentioned to her, "Derek is a fine swordsman. He took lessons from the best, and he likes the action to seem real. I fully expect him to skewer somebody one day."

Indeed Wells did move gracefully. The villain, who was opposite him, Hall informed Erin, was the best instructor in the country. The two men moved back and forth, the steel blades slashing so quickly that she could hardly follow them. Wells, she saw, was enjoying it tremendously, and finally he lunged forward, and it appeared that he had punctured the breast of his opponent.

"Oh my! He's killed him!"

"No, he hasn't. George has a leather vest on under that fancy outfit he's wearing, and besides, the points are all blunted. But I'm glad you thought it looked real."

For two hours Erin enjoyed watching the action, and then Wells came and pulled his neckerchief away. He was dripping with sweat and shook his head. "Those lights are awful. Let me go change, and I'll keep my part of the bargain."

"You don't have to, Derek. I was only teasing."

"No, you're not getting off that easy. I won't be long."

★   ★   ★   ★

Erin pulled back on the stick, and the Spad moved suddenly from a horizontal position to a vertical. Kicking the aileron, she threw the plane into a roll. She watched Derek in front of her for some sign that he'd had enough, but he was beating on the side of the fuselage screaming something she could not hear. She had taken it easy at first, for some people grew deathly ill from acrobatics. He had not complained, however, but urged her to do more daring maneuvers.

Finally Erin slapped on the fuselage. When he turned around, she shouted, "Time to go down!"

She took the plane down and came in for a smooth landing. She started to get out, but Derek beat her to it. Hopping down to the ground first, he reached up and caught her around the waist and lifted her down.

"That was wonderful, Erin! No wonder you love it so."

"I'm glad you liked it, Derek. You ought to go up with Quaid. He could show you some real stuff. I'm really just an amateur."

"Well, if that was an amateur, I'd like to see the real thing."

At that moment Rev came up and nodded. "Hello, Erin."

"Oh, Rev, this is Derek Wells. You've probably seen his movies."

"Don't believe I have, but I'm mighty glad to meet you." Rev stuck his hand out, and when Derek took it, he smiled at him. "Are you washed in the blood of the Lamb, brother?"

Wells's face suddenly grew pale. Both Erin and Rev noticed it, and Erin said, "Don't be shocked, Derek. That's the way Rev greets everybody, even generals."

"It brought back some memories. My dad always did the same thing."

"Your dad? Was he a preacher?"

"Never was ordained. He was a bricklayer, but he preached on the streets. He'd ask everybody he met if they were converted. That's the clearest memory of my boyhood, I think."

"Sounds like a fine man, Mr. Wells."

"He was. I'm very proud of him. He never had a dime, but he took care of us the best he could, and he was very generous. He was the finest man I ever knew."

Quaid walked up, and his eyes were fixed on the actor. When Erin introduced him, Quaid said, "I've seen your pictures. I like some of them very much."

Wells laughed suddenly. "Do I dare ask which ones? No, don't tell me. Then I'd worry about the others." He grew serious then and studied Quaid. "I read in the papers about your service in France. Every time I meet someone who really did something over there, I feel like a heel."

"No need to feel that way," Quaid shrugged. "I read in the papers how you raised millions for the war effort selling Liberty bonds."

"Oh yes. I did that. I tried to enlist, but they wouldn't have it. The president himself asked me to go on tour selling Liberty bonds. I did it because he asked me to, but I always felt like a slacker."

"Oh, Derek," Erin spoke up. "You did what you were asked to do. That's all any man can do."

The four of them walked off the field and went to the café, where they had doughnuts and coffee. Although everyone recognized Derek, he seemed to pay no attention to it. And Erin didn't mind a bit that he paid almost no attention to her. He began pumping questions at Quaid, mostly about politics. He seemed keenly interested.

"Do you think the Germans will stay down? After all, you fought in the war to end all wars. That's what they called it anyway."

Quaid shook his head. "I don't think so. In this world there can always be another war."

"I've been thinking of doing a picture about the last war— especially the air war. Would you be available to work on it?"

"Why, I'm no actor."

"No, but you were there. You can be sure that if I do it, it's going to be done right. I'm not interested in prettifying it. I know men were killed. I read a lot of the stories about 'the knights of the air' and all that, but I doubt if it was all that glamorous."

"No, it wasn't." Quaid shook his head. "It was a bloody, brutal business, and toward the end they were sending up seventeen-year-old boys with no more than ten hours of training. There was nothing knightly or chivalrous about it."

"That's the kind of thing I want to show! I don't know that I'm going to do this, but if I do, can I count on you to at least be an advisor and perhaps do some of the flying?"

Quaid shrugged his shoulders. "It would have to work in with our schedule."

"Well, I know that's busy. How does it feel to be famous?"

Quaid suddenly laughed. "Me—famous? Here's the famous one—the Golden Angel."

Erin flushed. "That's not so. I tell everybody that you're the real secret of our success."

"But I don't have long blond hair and a nice figure, and I never killed a lion with a spear in Africa," Quaid teased.

"Oh, hush!"

The four had a fine time together, and when it was time for Wells to leave, he had a moment alone with Erin. "I've never had so much fun with a woman as I had today with you. I'd like to see you again."

"Why, I think that would be fine, Derek. I had fun, too."

"You're not afraid of me?"

Erin blinked with surprise. "Why, of course not."

"You know my reputation."

Erin suddenly laughed. "Well, now you know mine."

He reached out and took her hand, held it for a moment, and then kissed it. "Good-bye," he said. "One day you'll look up, and I'll be there. By the way," he said. "I talked to DeMille yesterday. He talked about you."

"About me? Why, I've never met him."

"He reads the papers, though. He asked me if I thought you'd be interested in being in a movie."

"Me! Why, that would be ridiculous. I'm no actress."

"DeMille doesn't make light statements. I wish you'd think about it. Maybe we could do one together. That would be fun."

"No, I don't think so, Derek. Hollywood's not for me."

"I thought you'd say that, but it was worth asking anyway. Well, good-bye, then, and thanks for a lovely flight."

When Erin walked to where Quaid was standing underneath the plane talking to Rev, she said, "Don't you two forget. We're going to take some time off and visit my grandparents in New York."

"It sounds good to me," Quaid said.

"And remember this, too. You promised to think about a way to work some wing walking in."

"I don't think I remember that." Quaid frowned.

"Well, I do, and I'm not going to forget it. You know how stubborn I am."

Quaid suddenly laughed. "I know that well enough. It'll be good to see your grandparents again."

"We'll all have a rest there. I think we need it."

CHAPTER SEVENTEEN

THE DOOR OPENS

★ ★ ★ ★

By the time they had arrived at the airfield in New York, Erin, Quaid, and Rev were exhausted, for the past days had been packed solid with performances. The trio had traveled across the entire country, giving performance after performance in state after state as they made their way east. Now the blistering heat of New York seemed heavy and oppressive after the dry heat of California.

Erin had obtained promises from both men to stay at her grandparents' house for at least a week, and now she watched Quaid as he drove the rented car. He looked tired and drawn. Part of this, she understood, was the responsibility of seeing that the act went well and that every safety device possible would be used. She realized how she leaned on him, and a wave of gratitude rose in her as she studied his face in profile. He had never told her how he had come by the scars on his forehead, but she assumed it had something to do with flying.

Suddenly Quaid turned and found her watching him. "What are you looking at?" he demanded.

"Oh, nothing." Erin quickly turned back to look at Rev, who was folded up in the back seat, his long, gangling arms and legs somehow arranging themselves as he curled into a ball like a spider. "Rev doesn't worry about a lot of things, does he?"

"Not that I know of."

"It must be nice to be like that."

Quaid swerved to miss a dog that had apparently been possessed by a suicide wish and tried to throw itself in front of the Marmon. "Stupid dog," he grunted. Then when he straightened the car out, he glanced at her. "Are you worried about something?"

"Oh, just the usual things. Not worried really, but we've been under a lot of pressure lately."

"Well, we'll be able to uncoil a bit now."

"I'm looking forward to it. We all need it."

Neither of them spoke for the next ten minutes, and then Erin said, "There's the house. Turn right there."

"I remember." As he turned, Quaid shrugged his shoulders somewhat impatiently. "I'm not sure this is such a good idea."

"What, Quaid?"

"Barging in on your grandparents like this."

"Don't be foolish! They're looking forward to it. I think they get a little bit lonesome out here."

Quaid was unconvinced, but he said no more. He steered the car down the road, which was flanked on both sides with flower beds, and stopped in front of the house. He shut the engine off, and the silence at once brought Rev out of his sound sleep. He pulled himself up, rubbed his eyes, and glanced around. "Are we here? Is this it?"

"This is it. Come on. We'll bring the luggage in later."

The trio got out of the car and walked up the steps. They were greeted at the top, not by Mark and Lola, whom Erin had expected, but by Amelia and Phillip Winslow. They burst out calling her name, and Phillip picked her up and spun her around while Amelia laughed, then she took her hug when Phillip set her down.

"What are you two doing here?" Erin asked. She was glad to see them, for they reminded her of home, and she asked, "Did Mom and Dad come with you?"

"No, they couldn't get away, but they'll be coming soon. We have a long letter for you."

"Well, what about you two?"

Amelia was radiant. "We finally persuaded our parents to let us come to the States. Phillip's going to school, and I'm going to get a job of some kind." She turned then to face Quaid and put her hand out, saying, "I'm Amelia Winslow, Erin's disreputable cousin."

Quaid found this amusing. He took her hand, noting she had a strong grip. "We ought to get along well. I'm her black-sheep partner."

"I'm sure we will," Amelia said. There was a directness in her gaze, and her grip was firmer than that of most women. Erin noticed that their handshake was lasting longer than normal and so did Phillip, who came forward and said, "Stop holding hands with him, Amelia." He took Quaid's hand and said, "I'm Phillip. I'm so glad to meet you. We read everything we could about your flying."

At this moment Lola came out wearing a light green dress, and she called, "Erin, come inside and bring your friends. Give your grandmother a hug."

Erin ran to Lola and hugged her and asked, "How's Grandfather?"

"Fairly well," Lola said noncommittally. She turned to meet Rev, who had said nothing. When Erin introduced her grandmother to the tall, spidery pilot, Lola smiled. "We're so glad to have you. I hope you'll enjoy your stay here."

"Why, I'm sure I will, Mrs. Winslow. Is there any chance you're a handmaiden of the Lord?"

Lola smiled, for Erin had mentioned Rev's peculiarity in her letters. "I like to think so," she said. "I've been a Christian for more years than you've been alive, Rev."

"Well, ain't that fine, now! And your husband, I expect he's a born-again believer, too."

"Certainly is. One of the finest Christians I've ever known."

Amelia was standing close to Quaid. When she was finally introduced to Brown, she said immediately, "Don't ask me if I'm a handmaiden of the Lord."

Revelation Brown took in the tall young woman and did not argue. He simply said, "I'm pleased to know you, Miss Amelia, and you, too, Phillip."

Lola herded them all inside and soon they were seated on

deep overstuffed chairs in the large drawing room. Though richly furnished like the rest of the house, it was, nonetheless, a comfortable room, where they did most of their entertaining. Framed paintings added a splash of color to the walls. Long windows on the east wall admitted pale shafts of sunlight, and the rich oriental carpet on the floor gave the room a regal feel.

"I can't believe you're here, Amelia, and you, Phillip," Erin said. "You've got to tell me everything."

Amelia had somehow seated herself close to Quaid on a love seat. She turned to him now and leaned over so that her shoulder brushed against his. "I've been anxious to meet you, Quaid. I've never met a real live war hero before."

"You haven't met one now! I just did my job over there."

"Oh, that's not true! I want to hear all about it."

Erin took this in with a swift glance, and her eyes then went to Phillip. She saw that her young cousin was disturbed, and when their eyes met, an understanding passed between them. Both were aware that Amelia was out of the will of God—in fact, she had clearly been ignoring Him for some years. Neither Erin nor Phillip felt they could trust her, and watching her flirt with Quaid was making them both very uncomfortable.

Mark came in just then, and after greeting everyone, he seated himself and took the tea that his wife poured for him. He inquired about the tour, and Erin gave him the particulars.

Amelia listened intently, and when Erin mentioned having gone out with Derek Wells, she screamed, "You don't mean it! Derek Wells in the flesh?"

"In the flesh."

"What's he like? I'll bet he's *something*, isn't he?"

"You know, he's not what I expected." She nodded to Quaid and said, "He could talk to Quaid about politics and to Rev about engines, and he wasn't at all stuck up or egotistical the way I thought Hollywood stars were."

Amelia was entranced. "I'd give anything to meet him."

"Well, you might get your chance," Quaid said. "He's supposed to get in touch with Erin again."

"You've *got* to introduce me, Erin! Why, he might help me get into the movies."

Erin smiled and shook her head. "I expect there are about

twenty million young women who would like to do that. I'm not sure it's a good idea, though."

Amelia opened her mouth to protest, but before she could launch into an argument with her cousin, Lola quickly interjected, "I'm sure you're all exhausted. Why don't you go take a shower and lie down? We'll have a fine dinner tonight, and then we can talk until midnight."

The gathering broke up and they all went to their respective rooms, except for Lola, who walked slowly with Erin to her room and went inside. She sat down on the bed and watched Erin unpack her suitcase. She inquired tactfully about the activities of the past few weeks and listened as Erin spoke.

"You've changed a little, Erin."

Erin turned quickly. She was holding a dress she had just put on a hanger and saw that her grandmother was serious. "What do you mean I've changed?"

"Well, of course, it was impossible that you would remain the same. You take a young girl who has been in the bush in Africa and throw her into the spotlight, put famous people around her and reporters and all that I've been reading about—well, it's bound to change you."

Slowly Erin ran her hand over the dress and studied her grandmother with a cautious look. "Do you think I've gotten a big head?"

"I'd be surprised if you didn't," she smiled, "but I don't think so. I just wanted to warn you that it could happen."

Erin turned and hung the dress up, then came back to sit down beside her grandmother. She picked up Lola's hand and held it with both of her own. "I don't want that to happen, Grandmother. God has been so good to me. You don't know how unhappy I was when I was growing up."

"I know. Because you did poorly in school." Lola suddenly squeezed her hand and smiled. "I have something I want you to do."

"Anything, Grandmother. What is it?"

"I want you to meet with a doctor."

"A doctor? But I'm not sick. I'm in wonderful health."

"He's not that kind of a doctor. He's doing some kind of special work with people who don't do well in school. He thinks he might have an answer. His name is Michael Oz. He's a professor at the university here and does a lot of work with patients in the charity hospitals."

"Oz? That's a peculiar name, but I don't see how he could help me. It's too late now."

"Just go see him. I think you'll like him. He's a member of our church. That's the way I got to know him. We got to talking about you one day, and I told him how poorly you'd done and how able you seemed in other ways. He at once showed interest and said he'd be glad to talk to you."

"I'll go if you say so, Grandmother, but I don't see that it will help."

"We never know what will help. Maybe God has put him in your way."

Erin suddenly laughed and threw her arms around the silver-haired woman. "I love you, Grandmother. You always blame everything on God, but I'll do it," she said as she released her. "I've always wanted to find out why I'm so stupid, and maybe he can tell me."

*   *   *   *

When Erin came down the next day, she noticed that Amelia and Quaid were not at the breakfast table. When she asked after them, her grandfather said, "She took him out to play tennis. She's very good, you know. I think she could do well in a major tournament if she wanted to dedicate her time to that."

For some reason the absence of the two disturbed Erin. She said little during breakfast, but afterward she went with Phillip to the sunroom, where they sat among the foliage of the exotic plants, enjoying the coolness. For a long time Erin plied Phillip with questions about things back home.

Finally she said, "I know you're happy to be here, and Amelia, too."

"I think Amelia would have driven our folks crazy if they hadn't let us come." He was a fine-looking young man of eighteen, and the sunlight caught his auburn hair, causing it to give off red tints. He turned his piercing green eyes on Erin. "Quite frankly, I've never been so worried about Amelia."

"I know. She's been a problem to your folks for a long time."

"She's just out of step with everything Mom and Dad have tried to teach her. She's got a rebellious streak in her. She got involved with a man back home after you left. It was pretty bad, Erin. He was a good-looking fellow—had lots of money—but everyone knew he was a woman chaser."

Erin shifted uneasily and put her eyes on Phillip. "I suppose you talked to her."

"Of course I did, but it's like talking to a stranger." Misery showed in Phillip's fine eyes, and he shook his head. "I love Amelia, but she's headed for trouble. Try to talk to her, Erin."

"I'll do what I can, but if she won't listen to you, I doubt if she'll listen to me."

★ ★ ★ ★

Mark Winslow walked slowly and carefully, seeming to plan each step as he moved along the gravel pathways that led between the flower beds. Quaid moved beside him, adjusting his long strides and listening as the older man spoke of how much pleasure his wife had gotten out of the flower garden.

"I've got a brown thumb, but Lola's always been able to make anything grow. Those roses are about gone now, but you see that bed over there?"

Quaid glanced at a full bed of roses, all bearing the most unusual pinkish yellow combination of color. "I've never seen anything like that. What are they?"

"She bred those herself. We call it the Lola Montez rose. That was her maiden name." Mark moved over, carefully took out his penknife, and snipped off a flower. He held it, smelled it, and then smiled. "It's almost as beautiful as Lola."

"She is a most attractive woman."

Mark glanced up and followed the flight of a hummingbird until it disappeared in the top of a chestnut tree. "I haven't told you, Quaid, but I'm very grateful for what you've been able to do for Erin."

"I think you've got that wrong, Mr. Winslow. She was the one who saved *my* life."

"Yes, I know about that. But you've helped her so much to find her way. She's just radiant now. We haven't seen her much since she was a girl, but even then she was . . . I don't know. Sort of beat down, I guess. She was always embarrassed about doing so poorly in school."

"I can't understand that. She's so able and smart in every way. Maybe she just didn't want to learn."

"No, it wasn't that. She just *couldn't* learn. Her grandmother and I have found a doctor who works with people who have trouble learning. He's a neurologist with some new theories about how the brain functions, and apparently he's helped a lot of people. He just might be able to help her. Erin's going to see him tomorrow."

"I hope he can. She's a fine young woman."

As the two continued their walk down the pathway, Mark was able to draw Quaid out and get him to talk about himself. Mark had dealt with men all of his life and knew them well. He wanted to find out all he could about Quaid Merritt, for he knew that despite what she said, Erin had a special feeling for him. Finally he said, "What do you think about Erin's success? Do you think it will spoil her?"

"It's spoiled a lot of good people," Quaid remarked. "Are you really worried about her?"

"Yes, I am. What about this actor fellow? What's his name?"

"Derek Wells. I don't know, Mr. Winslow. She only met him a few times. But you really don't think that she'd be attracted to a movie star?"

"I think she's generally got a barricade up between herself and the world. That fellow Charterhouse hurt her pretty badly."

"Charterhouse—the man whose life she saved?"

"Yes, you didn't know about him?"

"No, just that she saved his life."

"It was pretty bad. Erin fell in love with him. Barney said he had never seen a girl blossom so. You know how it is with a young girl who has had no social life and suddenly this handsome fellow shows up and gives her all this attention. Well, she fell for him, and it turned out that he was no good. Already had a wife he never told her about. But Barney says she was never the same after that. That's the real reason she came to America."

"I never knew all that, but it's too bad."

The two continued their walk, and the more Mark learned about Quaid, the more comfortable he became with the young man. He knew Quaid had been through some bad times and had made some poor choices in the past, but Mark became confident that at heart Quaid was a good man. He later told Lola, "I believe Erin's safe with him."

★　★　★　★

The next morning at breakfast, Quaid broached the subject of Erin's doctor visit. "Your grandfather tells me you're going to see a doctor today."

"Yes. His name is Dr. Oz. Michael Oz. I never knew anybody named that. I'm going to see him this afternoon."

"I hope he can help you."

"Oh, it doesn't seem to matter much now," Erin said carelessly. "I'm not going to be in a classroom ever again!"

Quaid knew this woman well enough by now to believe that she was bluffing, that it did indeed matter to her. Her failures had gone deep into her spirit, and despite her success and public acclaim, she was still hurt by two things. He had known about her poor record in school, but now he knew that Stephen Charterhouse had hurt her even worse.

Not wanting to press her further about the doctor visit, he changed the subject. "All right, you pressured me into this wingwalking thing, so we're going to do something about it."

Erin's eyes glowed, and she turned to him with excitement, tugging at his arm. "Oh, Quaid, really! What is it? Tell me about it."

"The problem has been making it safe for you, so I've tried to find something that would be foolproof, as much as things like that can be. So here's what we'll do. We'll modify the airplane. I'll be in the rear cockpit, and you'll be in the front. When we get aloft, you'll climb up out of the cockpit and get onto the center of the wing. But," he said almost sternly, "there'll be a metal cable attached to a safety belt. It'll be invisible from the ground, but it'll be there. If you slip, you can't fall more than five feet."

"Oh, Quaid, that sounds like cheating!"

"No, it's not. Performers in the circus have a safety net underneath, and nobody calls that cheating."

"What do I do then?"

"Rev and I will build two uprights about as high as your waist. At the bottom of them there'll be two built-in devices sort of like shoes. You'll slip your feet into them and fasten straps so that you'll be held by your ankles. You get the picture?"

Erin nodded. "I'll be held in place by my feet and a safety strap and leaning against two uprights. What then?"

"Then you take off your helmet, and the Golden Angel lets her golden locks fly in the breeze." He grinned at her and said, "That's about it."

"Well, that's nothing!"

"Well, there is one more thing. I'm afraid that the extra weight of the parachute pack may throw you off balance when you're fighting the wind out on the wing. So as much as I hate the idea, I think you'll have to perform without a parachute."

"That won't worry me," said Erin. "With all the other safety devices in place, I'll be plenty secure."

"Okay. If you're comfortable with that, then I thought that once you're in place I could do a slow rollover, or at least half a one. Then we'll fly over the field, and there you'll be upside down."

Erin was thinking about that. "I know what! You could do some acrobatics like a loop with me just standing there."

"That'd be all right. The main thing is for you to be safe." He reached out and touched her hair. "I couldn't have anything happen to my Golden Angel. You saved my life. I can't gamble with yours."

Quickly Erin looked up and smiled. "That's sweet, Quaid."

"Oh, I'm just a sweetie pie. Everyone knows that."

The two talked for some time about the wing walking, and Erin was full of suggestions, all of them more dangerous than Quaid was willing to undertake. Finally she said, "When can we do this?"

"Probably at the next show. But we'll go practice it after your appointment with Dr. Oz."

Erin was excited, but then suddenly a thought came to her. "Quaid, I want you to be careful about Amelia."

"What do you mean by that?"

"I mean she's not exactly what she seems."

"She seems like a very attractive, poised young woman."

"Oh, she is! She's very pretty, and that's part of the trouble. But, well . . . well, she's too easy with men."

Instantly Quaid's eyelids pulled down, and he stared at her narrowly. "I hadn't really caught that."

"Oh, I don't mean she's a flapper or anything like that, but her parents are very worried about her."

"And so are you, I see."

"Yes, she likes you a great deal. She likes any attractive man. So just don't give her any encouragement."

"You think I'd do that?"

Erin hesitated. "I think men can be pretty vulnerable where a beautiful woman's concerned."

Quaid studied her carefully. She was very serious, he saw, and he nodded. "I'll be watching for it, but you don't have to worry. I'm more worried about you doing wing walking than I am about anything else."

★　★　★　★

"But I don't understand, Dr. Oz. What do you call this problem that you're trying to pin down?"

Dr. Michael Oz was a rather small man, no more than five-eight. He had thick dark hair cut short, dark deep-set eyes, and a short, clipped black beard. He spoke with a slight accent that Erin could not place. Now his voice was soft as he said, "We call this particular problem 'dyslexia.' It comes to my attention that there are many people who do poorly in school but who do well in every other way. I began doing research and have found several doctors and social workers who have been aware of this."

"What is it? Is it dangerous?"

"Oh no, not at all," Dr. Oz said quickly. "Don't be alarmed.

What it means is that it has something to do with the process of seeing."

"But I have perfect eyesight."

"Not at all uncommon for people with dyslexia. It's a matter of *perception*, Miss Winslow. For instance, when people who don't have dyslexia look at a sentence, they see the words in perfect order. But a victim of dyslexia will not perceive it that way. They might, for example, see the last word coming first in the sentence. You've always had difficulty reading, I understand."

"Yes, I have." Erin thought back over the years. "I always did well with numbers and with things like geometry, but anything that required reading, like history or stories, was hard for me."

"I think we've hit on the source of your problem." Oz went on gently, "It's caused you a great deal of distress, hasn't it?"

"Well, yes, it has. I was always last in everything in school, anything that required reading, anyway."

"The tests I've given you have pretty well proven to me that this was your problem. It's not stupidity, Miss Winslow. It's just that you have this problem with perceiving words."

"Is there any cure?"

"Not exactly a cure. There are things that can be done to make life easier, but usually those things are for people who are still suffering. Young people in school, for the most part. But it ought to help you a great deal knowing at least that your problem isn't intellectual."

Erin smiled and said, "I do feel so much better knowing this, Dr. Oz. You have already helped me a great deal."

"Then," Oz said, "I feel that my purpose as a doctor has been fulfilled."

★　★　★　★

The engines were roaring after the mechanics had warmed them up. Rev came to Erin and said with a worried look, "I think we were doing fine without all this wing-walking stuff."

"It'll be all right, Rev." Erin patted his arm. "I'll be safer up there than I am in the cockpit. After all, when I'm in the cockpit, it's only the safety belt that keeps me in. But when I'm standing up on top of the wing, I'll be held in place by a safety cable, by those boots, and by those rods pressing against me."

Rev had given up arguing with her, and indeed they had gone over and over the routine. While still on the ground, Erin had attached the safety belt with a swivel to the steel cable, which in turn was attached to the fuselage. She had climbed up carefully, using handholds in the form of metal U-shaped bars; then when she had braced herself against the two uprights, she had bent over and put her feet into the restraints and tightened them as much as she could. They had worked long and hard on this contraption; they had even attached the boots upside down to a girder in a warehouse. Then they had hauled her up to the boots and thrown a rope over a girder. Quaid had held her while Rev pulled at the rope. She had risen in the air and swung there helplessly, laughing. "See," she had cried, "I can't fall."

She went over and found Quaid waiting for her by the plane. Rev had put her through this at least twenty times, but now it was time for the real thing. "Don't worry. It's going to be great."

"Don't forget that safety cable," he said. "And be sure you tighten the boots as tight as you can."

"All right, don't worry about me," she said. "You and Rev have done a wonderful job."

Quaid shook his head. "Let's go, then."

Erin climbed into the cockpit and fastened her safety belt, then they took off. When Quaid went up to two thousand feet, she turned around and nodded. "I'm ready," she shouted.

Reluctantly Quaid nodded, and Erin turned to face the propeller. She fastened the cable to the leather belt around her waist and then loosed her safety belt. Carefully she grasped the uprights in front of her and pulled herself out of the cockpit. The wind whistled over the surfaces of the wing with a sibilant whisper, and it caught at her as she stood up. She had been prepared for this, however, and moved very slowly. The uprights were placed no more than fourteen inches apart with the boots in the middle. Holding to the uprights, she bent over to avoid the full force of the wind. Quaid was flying as slowly as the airplane would operate as she stuck her right foot and then her left into the bootlike restraint. Bending over, she tightened the straps and felt them close around her feet and ankles. Carefully, still holding to the uprights, she tried to tug her feet out, but they held fast.

Now she straightened up and felt the braces against her calves. Reaching up, she unloosed her helmet and let her hair fly out behind her. She held the helmet in one hand, trying to remember that she'd have to find someplace to put it during the actual act. She kept her eyes almost shut, and holding her hands out and arching her body, she felt a sense of exhilaration. The plane flew steadily for a while, and then she felt it slowly begin to roll. It was no trouble at all for her. She was so fastened to the plane that all she had to do was keep her body stiff. Her legs were spread to give her better support, and as the plane rolled over and continued upside down, she gave a long cry of pure joy.

Twisting around, she held her hair away from her face and looked at Quaid. Actually she was looking up at him, and she saw that his gaze was fixed on her. She smiled and waved, and she saw relief come over his face. He completed the roll and then proceeded to do several other relatively mild stunts, including an outside loop.

Finally he called to her, and she freed herself from the straps and moved cautiously down into the cockpit. She fastened her safety belt and waited until he had brought the plane in for a landing. As soon as she was on the ground, she grabbed Rev, who had run anxiously to the plane. "It was wonderful, Rev! You ought to try it."

"Not me," Rev grinned. "But it sure did look good. It'll be a hit."

★　★　★　★

Indeed, the wing-walking act was a big hit. They performed the stunt at the next scheduled air show, which took place, once again, in New York.

The cameras were on the Golden Angel that day, with one photographer even coming alongside in another plane and filming the whole thing from the air.

After the show and an energetic interview with the reporters, Erin turned to go change her clothes. When she got to the dressing room, she was shocked to see a familiar figure.

"Derek!" she cried and ran over to him. She held out her hands, and he took them, smiling broadly.

"How's my Golden Angel? I don't have to ask, though. You were great."

"Did you just get in?"

"Came in yesterday. I've got to talk to you, Erin."

"Why, of course. Would you like to come out to my grandparents' place?"

"Let me ask you something first and then we'll see if there's any need for me to stay."

Erin was puzzled. "Why, of course I want you to stay. Everyone's eager to meet you."

"I don't know if they will be after they find out why I've come to New York."

Erin was completely baffled. "What do you mean?"

"I'm going to do a picture. I'll be the producer, the director, and the star. I want you to be in it—not the lead, just a bit part."

"Me! But, Derek—"

"I know. You're no actress. That's not a problem in Hollywood." He made a small grimace of disgust. "It's going to be about aviation in the air war over France. I want Quaid in it, too, and your friend Rev. I'm putting everything I have into this. If it flops, I'm broke with a flop on my hands." He studied her thoughtfully. "I know you can do it, but you have to want to."

"Derek, I can't answer right now."

"I know, but that's why I've come. I've got three days, and then I have to get back to California." He reached out again and held her hands tightly. "I think it would be lots of fun, Erin. Please consider it."

Erin Winslow could not think clearly. He seemed to be opening a door for her, but what that door led to she could not, for the moment, understand. She excused herself, then slipped into her dressing room. Once inside, she stood stock-still and wondered aloud, "What does all this mean?"

CHAPTER EIGHTEEN

THE HOUND OF HEAVEN

★ ★ ★ ★

"Quaid, I don't see why you're so upset about the offer I got from Derek."

Quaid turned from inspecting the rudder of his aircraft and put his eyes on Erin. He had kept to himself for two days, and now an expression of some emotion that Erin could not identify was in his eyes. He was holding an oily rag in one hand and a pair of pliers in the other. Slowly he worked the pliers as though he had not heard, but then he said, "I just don't like it."

"But *why* don't you like it?" Erin demanded. The entire two days since Wells had made his offer had been difficult for her. She felt she was being tugged in two directions at once, and now as she stood there, she found herself unable to express this in words. "It's a wonderful opportunity," she said. "Even the small part that Derek offered me would be great publicity, and you'd be involved in the flying scenes."

"We don't need publicity. We've got all the offers we can take care of."

"But Derek says I might have a real future in motion pictures."

"You're grown up, and you're going to do what you want to no matter what anyone says."

"That's not fair! I want to talk about it, but you've kept away from me for two days now. I want to know why."

"Did you talk to your grandparents about this?"

"Yes, I did."

"What did they say?"

Erin could not answer for a moment, and then she lifted her chin and said, "They didn't think it would be a good idea."

"What about your parents? What do you think they'll think about it?"

"I don't know. They haven't had time to answer my letter yet." Erin experienced a quick flash of guilt, for she knew very well what her parents would say. They were just barely reconciled to her flying a stunt plane, and she knew their opinion of Hollywood. Now she began to protest, saying, "You must not have a very high opinion of me to think I could be led astray."

"I've seen it happen before."

"Well, it wouldn't happen to me. It would just be a job."

Quaid shook his head, and his mouth was set in a determined line. "Look, Erin, you don't need all of this. We've done so well. You've got your picture in magazines and newspapers. You're not going to get rich at it, but you've told me many times that isn't what you want anyway. So what can Hollywood do for you?"

"I just think it would be good for the act."

"That's the first dishonest thing I've ever heard you say, Erin. You're not thinking of the act. I think you're stuck on Derek Wells."

A rich crimson crept up Erin's cheeks, and she clamped her lips together tightly. The wind ruffled the bright scarlet silk shirt she wore. She was angry that the people she most cared about didn't seem to understand her feelings in this. Her grandparents had made it clear to her they felt it would be a mistake for her to go to Hollywood with Derek Wells. Her grandfather had said, "I like the fellow well enough. He's a real charmer, but it's the world he lives in that bothers me. It would be a danger to any young woman. I don't think you ought to do it."

It had grieved Erin that she could not take her grandfather's advice wholeheartedly, but something in her wanted more. Her visit to see Dr. Oz had proven to be a significant boost to her self-esteem, and now she found herself wanting to pursue her dreams. Being able to explain the learning problems that had plagued her all her life—even being able to give them a name—encouraged her that she was not stupid after all. She was realizing for the first time that she could truly be as successful in life as anyone; it was just a matter of finding her own unique gifts. To some extent she had been doing that already with her business ventures and flying, but now she wanted more. Though she still had to contend with the dyslexia the doctor had described, she knew she could learn to overcome this obstacle, just as surely as she had many others in her life.

Now this offer to make a movie was before her, and she was determined not to let others deprive her of a golden opportunity. Who could say whether or not God himself might be leading her in this direction?

"I intend to go, Quaid—with or without you." With a determined sigh, she shrugged her shoulders and walked away.

Quaid watched her go, and a troubled frown showed itself in the creases around his eyes. *She's making a mistake, but she's not going to listen to me or anybody else.*

* * * *

The group gathered around the dinner table a few days later was unusually quiet. Erin had gone out with Derek for the second night in a row, and for some reason this had dampened the enthusiasm in the Winslow household, so that conversation became difficult. Amelia was the only one who seemed untouched by Erin's absence. She spoke brightly and cheerfully, mostly to Quaid, drawing from him stories of the war.

Finally Lola said, "Amelia, don't you see that Quaid doesn't like to talk about those times?"

"I don't see why not," Amelia said defensively. "I think it was a good thing."

"I suspect it might be best to let that time go by," Mark said. "There are some times in my life I'd just as soon not think about, certainly not talk about."

Amelia had no choice but to cease questioning him, but after the meal was over and Phillip and his grandfather had withdrawn to the study for their usual game of chess, she said, "Quaid, I'm bored to death. It's early. Why don't we go for a drive or something?"

Quaid shook his head. "I'm pretty tired, Amelia." But she went over to him, took his arm in both of hers, and smiled coyly up at him. Finally he said, "All right, I guess we could take a quick turn."

Amelia at once ran in to tell her grandmother. "Quaid's going to take me out for a drive."

Lola cocked an eyebrow. "All right, but don't stay out too late. Quaid has to be up early in the morning. They've got a show, you remember."

"Oh, we won't be late."

Lola watched with some apprehension as her granddaughter left the house. She went alone to the parlor to finish her letters, one of them to Andrew and Dorothy. She ran into difficulties as she tried to explain to them about Amelia. A frown crossed her face as she continued to write:

> *I know you've been concerned about Amelia. You've hinted at the fact that she has a rebelliousness in her that has given you grief. I think I have actually seen little of that on the outside, but there is a restless spirit in Amelia that troubles me. Mark and I have been so happy to have her and Phillip here with us, and we're going to do all we can to help them both. I wish you two could come and spend time with us, but until you get here, rest assured that we will do everything we can to see that the children are all right.*

★　★　★　★

In the half darkness of the theater, Quaid wondered how he had gotten there. The drive had turned out to be short enough, but Amelia had begged to go see a movie, and the one she had chosen starred Dolores Costello. The sensuous story was making him feel uncomfortable, and he wished he had not allowed Amelia to talk him into this.

Now he felt the pressure of her shoulder against his, and when she leaned closer to whisper something about the movie, he caught a heady whiff of her perfume. He distrusted his own opinions about Amelia Winslow. The rest of the family seemed to be straitlaced, and certainly Erin had taught him that the women of her family did not have loose morals. He could not bring himself to believe that Amelia was a loose woman, but he could also see how men could be led to that conclusion.

When the movie was over, Amelia jumped up and said, "That was wonderful!"

Slowly Quaid unfolded his long length and stood to his feet. "You really think it was?"

"Of course I did. Didn't you?"

"I think her parents should have taken a paddle to her."

"Oh, you're as bad as my parents! Come on." Taking his hand, Amelia practically hauled him down the aisle and out of the theater. When they got to the car, he opened the door for her, and she got in. When he was behind the wheel and started the car, she said, "It's too early to go back yet."

"Early! What are you talking about? It's after ten o'clock."

"Oh, don't be such an old man! Come on, let's go to a speak-easy."

Quaid laughed without meaning to. Quaid thought surely Amelia was teasing him. "What in the world makes you think I'd take you to one of those places?" The speakeasies were usually guarded, and people were permitted in only if the proprietors knew them. Liquor was served illegally, of course. "It's time to go home," he said firmly. He pulled the car out, and as they moved along, he said, "I'd have a hard time explaining to your grandparents if I took you to one of those places."

"Have you ever been?"

When Quaid did not respond, she reached over and tugged at his sleeve. "You see? You've been, so why can't I go?"

"That's different."

"I don't mean to do any harm. I just want to see what it's like."

"You wouldn't like it, Amelia. It's a bunch of people getting drunk. That's never exciting."

As they motored through the darkness Amelia pouted for a time. Finally he asked her, "What do you want to do while you're here in the States? Have you started looking for a job yet?"

"Not yet, but I'll find one. Right now I'm enjoying everything too much." She inched closer to him on the seat. "I'll tell you what I'd like to do. Erin's going to go to Hollywood to be in a movie. I'd like to go with her. Maybe Derek could find a part for me in the same picture."

Quaid was acutely aware of her leg against his, and when she turned, her body brushed his upper arm. He could not move any farther away and was distinctly uncomfortable. "She might change her mind about going," he argued, not really believing it himself.

Amelia laughed. "Don't be silly! Of course she's going. Any woman in America would snap at a chance like that."

"Your grandparents don't think so."

"Oh, they're wonderful grandparents, but they're a thousand years behind."

Quaid did not answer, but when they reached the house and got out of the car, he was thinking of what Amelia had said. They went up the steps together and suddenly she caught his arm. "I don't want to go in yet. It's too early. Sit down and talk for a while."

Quaid protested. "It's too late!" But she pulled him over to one of the wicker love seats and practically pushed him into it.

Amelia sat by him and said, "You act like an old man sometimes, Quaid. How old are you, anyway?"

"Twenty-six."

"My, what a young-looking face you have, Grandpa." As she said this, Amelia reached over and took Quaid's jaw, pulling at it playfully. She let her hand remain there and moved his face around so that she could look at him. The moonlight flooded the porch and filtered through the branches of the trees in a silver network on the ground. The air was rich with the smell of honeysuckle, but underlying that, to Quaid, was the perfume she was wearing. She was pressing against him, and she tilted her face up, smiling at him. She had a firm chin and there was an inviting smoothness to her lips. He was unprepared for what happened next. With her left hand still on his cheek, she suddenly put her other arm around him and threw herself fully against him. Caught by the beauty of the girl and stirred by the fragrance rising from her, he put his arms around her and held her tightly. Then he brought her around until her face was close to his and kissed her without restraint.

The kiss was not something he had planned, but his manly drives and emotions momentarily eclipsed his reason, and as she continued to press her lips against his, he lost himself in the moment. He was a decent man and never took advantage of a woman, but still he was a man, and her eager willingness had worn his restraint thin and taken him off guard.

Suddenly a sound broke through the moment, and he pushed her away and turned on the love seat. For a moment he could not see who it was, but then he came to his feet as the moonlight fell on Erin's face.

Her voice was as cold as the pale gleam of the moonlight. "I think you'd better go in the house, Amelia."

Amelia stood and shook her hair back. "Don't be silly, Erin. This is none of your business."

"I don't think your parents would be very pleased if I didn't say something."

Quaid had rarely felt so uncomfortable. He said quickly, "It was just a kiss."

"I could see that!" Erin's voice was as dry as dust, and she was holding herself stiffly.

The three stood there in a silent tableau, and then Amelia laughed, "You're nothing but a Puritan, Erin! Like Quaid said, it was nothing but a kiss." She moved away then, patting Quaid on the shoulder. "Thanks for the evening, Quaid. It was fun."

Erin did not speak until the noise of the closing door reached her, and then she said, "I'm sorry you did that, Quaid."

The impulse to explain rushed through Quaid, but he knew that no explanation would suffice. He had seen this stubborn expression on Erin's face before, and now, besides the stubbornness, he also saw her extreme disappointment in him. He remembered her warnings about Amelia and felt like a fool for his behavior.

Erin was shocked by her own anger at the sight of the two embracing. She was usually sweet-tempered, but this scene had stirred her ire.

Quaid shrugged, trying to make light of the situation. "I took her for a drive and to a movie, and we sat down here for a moment to talk."

"You weren't talking, Quaid."

Quaid felt his face grow warm. "It was my fault," he said, knowing all the time that was not true.

"I warned you she was an impressionable young woman. I'm disappointed in you."

"You want to get another pilot?"

"I might just do that."

"Fine! I think that might be best." He turned, brushed past her as he went inside, and left her standing in the moonlight.

She opened her mouth, intending to call him back, but pride got the best of her, and she stood there wishing she had not been so impulsive. *I'll apologize to him in the morning. If I know Amelia, she was the one who instigated that kiss, not Quaid.*

★ ★ ★ ★

In the morning when Erin came down to breakfast, she found that Quaid was gone. She asked her grandmother about it.

"He left very early this morning," Lola said. "I didn't talk to him. I assumed it was something to do with the show you're going to put on today."

Erin nodded. "Yes, I suppose he had to go see about the airplanes."

"He didn't say anything to me," Rev said, surprise in his eyes. "I think I'd better get over there and see if I can give him a hand."

Erin said nothing to Amelia during breakfast, but before she left to go to the airfield to get ready for the show, Amelia came to stand before her. "Well, I suppose you're happy. You've managed to run Quaid off."

"What are you talking about?"

"You had a quarrel with him after I left last night, didn't you?" Amelia challenged.

"We had a few words. We've had them before."

"You know what's wrong with you? You're jealous. You can't stand any competition."

Anger caused Erin to speak quickly and harshly. "Don't be foolish, Amelia! There's nothing between Quaid and me."

Amelia stared at her for a moment. "Is that so?"

"Why, of course it is."

"Then why did you get so angry last night? It was just a kiss."

Erin could not explain to her cousin that she feared the direction Amelia was taking. She said in a kinder tone, "I'm sorry, Amelia. Let's not quarrel. I was too hasty last night, and I'll tell Quaid so."

Amelia smiled at once. "I'm glad to hear you say that. Really, it was innocent. We just went for a drive and a movie. We were talking, and you know how it is in the moonlight and all. It just happened."

Erin forced herself to smile. "All right. I'll make up with him."

★　★　★　★

"What do you mean he's not here?" Erin demanded. She had gone to the airfield late, only half an hour before the performance, and had been shocked when Rev had asked her if she knew where Quaid was. "I thought he was here," Erin said, bewildered. "He hasn't been here at all?"

"Nobody's seen him," Rev said rather nervously. "We've only got twenty minutes. I wonder if he had an accident."

Erin did not think this was the case. She stood gnawing her lip for a moment and finally said, "Rev, do you think you can fly in Quaid's place today?"

"I can do some of the easy stuff, but not the hard things. Why don't you just cancel?"

"We can't do that. Everybody's come for the show. Well, let's revise our program, then. We'll have to tell the manager what's happened."

"I don't like this," Rev said. "I'm not that good a flier."

In the end they gave a performance after a fashion. The manager had been angry, for this was not what he was paying for, but Rev did a creditable job, although they did not try anything difficult. There was no wing walking that day, and the crowd was disappointed. Erin knew as they landed that the papers the next day would have something to say about this.

Rev turned to the planes to check them over, as he did after every performance. When Erin came to speak to him, he said, "Something's happened to Quaid. He's never missed a performance."

"We've got to try to find him."

"Find him! In New York? How would we do that, Erin? We can't go up and down the streets calling for him."

"We've got to try *something*! Maybe we ought to call the police. He might have had an accident."

Rev bowed his head. "I think you're right. If he is hurt somewhere, they might not know who to call. You get started on that and I'll put the planes to bed."

★　★　★　★

Night had fallen on the city as Quaid Merritt walked slowly down the streets of Manhattan's East Side. He had been like a man in a trance most of the day. He had hardly slept the previous night, for the quarrel with Erin had disturbed him greatly. All day long the thought of getting drunk had been on his mind. It came at first with a shock, and he had shrugged it off, but as the day had worn on and night had come, a sense of depression fell upon him.

What difference does it make whether I get drunk or not? I'm not going to fly with her ever again anyway.

The reasoning sounded weak even to him. At first he had been angry with himself for kissing Amelia, but he knew that it went deeper than that. It had something to do with his feelings for Erin. He had disappointed her and knew that he would have a difficult time forgetting the hurt expression in her eyes and the anger—along with another emotion he could not identify.

He wandered aimlessly, paying no attention to the crowds surrounding him. How much time passed he did not know. He was aware of an emptiness in his spirit, and somehow he knew that the confrontation with Erin was more than just a small quarrel. He had been relatively happy on the surface ever since he and Erin had started their careers together, but even during that time there had been moments of despair. The war had marked him more deeply than he knew, and lately the nightmares had been coming back—haunting images and sounds of young men going up out of the trenches and being slaughtered with the bullets of German fighters. He dreamed often of his best friend, killed so horrifically just a few days before the armistice. Along with the nightmares came a black depression that would stay with him even as he went about his daily tasks. He had not told anyone about these night terrors, but had struggled to keep them buried deep inside.

Now as he walked the dark city streets, more than once a woman would emerge from the shadows and approach him with a proposition. He was in that part of town where prostitutes were common. He had shaken them all off, taken their curses, and finally found himself standing in front of a liquor store. A struggle mounted within him, but in the end he muttered, "What does it matter?" He went inside, bought a bottle of whiskey, and came out. He wanted to get away from the crowds and get drunk, so deadly drunk he couldn't think. He had never been a social drinker, but was rather a solitary one, drinking only to forget.

He had gone a few blocks when suddenly he was aware of something going on just ahead. A building had been demolished, and on the vacant lot that was left a group of people had gathered on makeshift benches and odds and ends of chairs. In front of them a man stood and was speaking in a clear, powerful voice.

"Just what I need! A preacher," Quaid muttered. He would have gone by, but suddenly the preacher's words reached him and he could not ignore them.

" 'Behold the Lamb of God that taketh away the sin of the world.' "

Quaid never knew why it was that those words caught him almost with the impact of a bullet. He stopped as if he had run into a wall, and at that instant something took place within his heart—somewhere deep inside him. He could not move, but he turned slowly and fixed his eyes upon the tall preacher, who continued by saying, "The Jews all knew exactly what John the Baptist meant when he said those words. They all knew that for hundreds and even thousands of years the high priest had been putting a lamb on the altar and slitting its throat, and as the blood poured from that lamb, the priest would catch the blood and sprinkle it.

"But John must have told them that it was impossible for the blood of a lamb to cleanse anybody's sin. He was saying that all of those lambs, all of those animals slain on Jewish altars, were nothing but a *picture*. Not one sin was ever forgiven by their blood."

Against his will, Quaid moved forward. He held the bottle of whiskey in his hand, unaware of it, his eyes riveted on the speaker, and something in him gave a great wrench as the man continued.

"It is the blood of Jesus that covers our sin. The New Testament says that without shedding of blood there is no remission of sin." At this point the preacher's voice grew louder. "Put away your bankbooks. They will not bring remission. Put away your good works. They will not wash away your sins. Put away your church membership. It will not avail. Only those who come to Jesus and trust in His blood will ever enter heaven."

The preacher went on, and Quaid could not move. His feet seemed to be caught in the pavement. He wanted to turn and run away, to put his hands over his ears, but a more powerful force than he had ever encountered had come to him. He stood there until the preacher finished his message and lifted his hand, inviting his listeners with deep compassion, "If you want Jesus Christ to wash away your sins, come and He will give you rest."

An agonizing desire for peace and rest came to Quaid Merritt at that moment. He did not feel the bottle of whiskey slip from his hand and fall to the ground. Nor did he hear the glass smash on the sidewalk as he moved forward stiffly.

He was not aware of anything except his need for peace and rest, and when he reached the front of the small gathering, the preacher was there to greet him. He felt a comforting arm around his shoulders and a voice saying, "Let us kneel, brother, and Jesus will save you." Quaid fell to his knees, blinded by tears. He was aware that others were gathered around him praying. Such a thing would have embarrassed him beyond endurance at one time, but now he was caught by the mighty hand of God. He suddenly thought of Rev's description of God—that He was like a bloodhound pursuing its prey—and Quaid knew then that he had been chased and caught by God himself. It was not a fearful image, however. He was not the helpless victim of an all-powerful God, but rather the blessed recipient of a love that knew no bounds, a mercy that could not be understood. He began to weep and to call upon God, and he heard the joyful exclamations of those around him as they prayed. An indescribable peace washed through him, rolling over him in great waves, and Quaid Merritt knew at that moment the peace that only God can give to an individual. . . .

★   ★   ★   ★

Erin was not asleep. She had tossed restlessly for hours, it seemed, worrying about Quaid. She had called the police and the hospitals, but there was no word whatsoever.

She lifted her head suddenly at the sound of footsteps and a gentle tap at her door. She jumped out of bed, grabbed her robe, and threw it on. She belted it and opened the door, and when she saw Quaid, she murmured his name and, reaching out, grabbed his arm. "Come inside," she whispered.

When he stepped inside, she went over and turned on the lamp. She came back to him and found herself weak with relief. "Where have you been?" she asked. "We've looked everywhere."

Quaid was silent for a moment, and Erin saw that there was strain on his face, but that something about him had changed. She said, "I came to find you. I was wrong to be so judgmental about you and Amelia, but—"

"That doesn't matter, Erin. Something has happened to me." He saw her blink with surprise and said, "I couldn't wait until morning to tell you. When I left here I was angry and depressed, and I wandered around all day. Finally tonight I was down on the East Side. I had made up my mind to get drunk. I'd even bought a bottle of whiskey. . . ."

Erin listened, her eyes open wide, as Quaid continued to talk. He spoke of the sermon and how powerfully it had affected him.

Her lips trembled, and she said, "Oh, Quaid!" and took his hands in hers. She listened breathlessly about how he had given his heart to the Lord, and finally he said, "I don't know much about this business of living for God, but I'm going to find out. And I wanted to ask you if you'd help me."

"Of course I will, Quaid! Of course I will. Oh, I'm so happy!" She wanted to throw her arms around him but felt awkward. She still held his hands, and tears were brimming in her eyes.

Quaid looked at her with tears in his own eyes and said, "You've brought nothing but good to me, Erin."

"Have you told Rev?"

"I couldn't find him. I expect he's out looking for me."

"He didn't come back to the house. He'll be so happy. He's prayed for you every day since he met you, I think."

"He's a good man."

Erin suddenly felt very vulnerable. She was in her bare feet, and he seemed even taller than usual. He stood there silently, a small smile on his face, and she finally said, "I still want to go to Hollywood, Quaid. I know you're against it, but I wish you'd go with me. I . . ." She tried to speak but had to swallow to keep from crying. Finally she whispered, "I need you. I've just found that out."

"Why, sure I'll go with you. Who else would go?"

Erin Winslow stood there looking up at Quaid. She was astonished to discover how his return and his good news had made her heart soar with joy. "I'm so happy for you, Quaid."

"I knew you would be. I'll get out of here now." He reached out and touched her hair and smiled. "The Golden Angel. I don't know what other people make of that, but you've been an angel to me. Good night, Erin."

"Good night, Quaid." She waited until the door closed, then stood there for a moment, her knees feeling weak. She moved across the room, sat down on the single chair beside the window, bowed her head, and began to give thanks to God for saving her friend.

PART FOUR

ILLUSIONS

★ ★ ★ ★

Fall 1922

CHAPTER NINETEEN

A HOLLYWOOD PARTY

★ ★ ★ ★

As soon as Erin stepped down from the plane, she saw a lanky, sandy-haired man come forward. He was smiling, and when he reached her, he put out his hand and shouted over the engine noise of Quaid's plane, "Miss Winslow, isn't it? I'm Jerry Haskins. Mr. Wells sent me to pick you up."

Taking the hand that was offered to her, Erin smiled and nodded. "How nice of you. My friends will be ready in just a moment."

The two turned and waited until Quaid and Rev climbed out of the other airplane and came over. After Erin introduced them, Haskins spoke quickly. "I know you're worn out from your flight. As soon as you get your plane secured, I'll take you to a hotel. You can get a little rest."

"Sounds good to me," Quaid said. He stretched, arching his back, and nodded to Rev. "Let's go see about finding a place to stow these planes."

"Already taken care of," Haskins said cheerfully. "Just leave them there. The manager of the airfield is a friend of mine. Come along, I'll introduce you to him."

Haskins took them into the office, where they met the manager, a short, stubby man with hazel eyes and a bald, gleaming head. His name was Dent, and he assured them that the planes would be taken care of. "Mr. Wells himself called and said to take care of you folks. You go right on. I'll take care of your aircraft."

"Thanks, Dent," Haskins said. "You folks come along, and we'll get you bedded down."

He led them to a black car, seated them all, then drove toward the hotel, talking all the time. "We're so glad you're here. It's going to be great working with you folks."

"What's your job title, Mr. Haskins?"

"Oh, just call me Jerry. Technically I'm the assistant director." He turned and flashed a winning smile at Erin. "Which means I really do all the stuff nobody else wants to do."

"I've had that job quite a few times," Rev spoke up. He had waited as long as he could, and leaning forward, he stuck his head between Haskins and Erin and asked his favorite question. "Are you saved, brother?"

"Saved?" Astonishment swept over Haskins' face. "I don't understand you."

"He's asking you if you're a Christian, Jerry, but don't get scared and run off the road. He asks everybody the same question."

"Oh, I see! Well, I was baptized when I was a baby. Does that count?"

"Not for much," Rev said. "Me and you'll have to talk about this when I get the kinks out of my legs and arms."

"Fine, I'll look forward to it."

They arrived at a hotel, a tall pink structure with balconies. The driveway was lined with palm trees, and everybody that walked by seemed to have a tan. Haskins hustled them inside, got their keys, and took them to the sixth floor.

"Mr. Wells says for you to rest up, and then we'll start work tomorrow, if that's all right."

"That's fine," Erin said quickly. "Thank you so much, Jerry."

As soon as Haskins left to take Rev and Quaid to their room, Erin took a closer look at her accommodations. It was a large room with a sweeping view from the window, but as she walked toward it there was a knock at the door. She turned back and opened it to a bellboy who was standing there with a pitcher of orange juice and a glass. "Compliments of the house, Miss Winslow. I hope you enjoy your stay."

"Why, thank you." Erin let the boy set the tray down, then she tipped him and poured herself a glass of juice. She stepped out onto the balcony and looked over the sun-drenched landscape before her. "Here I am in Hollywood." She sipped the orange juice, which was delicious. After two glasses she headed for the shower, then put on her gown and lay down on the bed. She was asleep almost before her head hit the pillow.

★ ★ ★ ★

The sound of the phone brought Erin out of her sleep. She sat up startled and for a moment could not think where she was. Quickly she shook her head and then picked up the receiver. "Hello."

"Erin, is that you?"

"Yes."

"This is Derek. Did you get all settled in?"

"Oh yes. Jerry met us and brought us to this beautiful hotel. I took a shower and went right to sleep."

"Well, I hope you're rested up, because I want you to go to a party with me tonight."

Erin hesitated, then asked, "What kind of a party?"

"Oh, it's just a get-together of folks that are in the business. It'll be a good chance for you to meet the gang."

"What about Quaid and Rev?"

"Bring them along. I'll have you all picked up at eight o'clock."

"Isn't that kind of late for a party to begin?"

"Hey, you're in Hollywood now! Parties sometimes don't begin until midnight. I'm glad you're here, Erin."

"Thank you, Derek. I look forward to seeing you."

Erin hung up the phone, then got out of bed. She washed her face and noted that it was already after six. A thought came to her, and going to the phone, she asked for Quaid's room number and then called him. As soon as he answered, she said, "Derek just called. He wants us all to go to a party tonight."

"All of us?"

"Yes. You and Rev get ready."

"Don't have much to wear, Erin."

"He didn't say anything about formal dress, so just put on whatever you brought."

"All right. What time is it?"

"He'll send somebody by at eight o'clock."

"Okay. We'll be ready."

Erin put on a simple white dress she thought might be suitable, then wrote several letters. Finally, at ten till eight a knock came at her door. Getting up, she crossed the room and opened it. Haskins stood there smiling, and she said, "I'm all ready. What about Quaid and Rev?"

"We'll see. You look beautiful, Miss Winslow."

"Oh, please call me Erin."

"Fine. First names are pretty well the norm out here in Hollywood."

Rev and Quaid were ready. Both of them wore casual clothes, and as they went down the elevator, Rev said, "What kind of a party is this?"

Jerry grinned and shook his head. "I don't think it has any sort of a special meaning. There's a party every night somewhere. A lot of people spend their lives going from one party to the next. Some people I know haven't seen much daylight in the past five years. They party all night and sleep all day."

"Kind of like vampires?" Quaid grinned.

"Come to think of it, yes."

They got off the elevator, and Jerry led them outside and settled them all in the black car. When he pulled out and started down the street, he said, "The party will be at Eileen Day's house."

"Do you know her pretty well?" Erin asked.

Haskins shrugged his shoulders noncommittally. "I'm not sure anybody knows anybody well here in Hollywood. It's a strange place."

"What's she like?" Quaid asked curiously. "I've seen her movies. She's a beautiful woman, but what's she really like?"

Haskins swerved to avoid a large yellow cat that paced sedately across the street. When he brought the car back into the lane, he said, "She's spoiled, of course. Most stars are." He thought for a moment, then added, "She's real hard to handle."

Erin asked, "Do you mean in real life or in pictures?"

"Pretty much both of them, I think. I don't mean to be critical, you understand, but being a star does something to most people."

"I didn't think Derek was stuck up or conceited or anything like that."

"You know, I don't think he is—but he's an exception to the rule. Most stars of his caliber are temperamental, always demanding their own way and totally selfish. Derek's not like that, though, and I'm thankful. It'd be hard to work for him if he were."

Their journey ended after a twenty-minute drive. Haskins had been pointing out the homes of various movie stars, and finally when he pulled up in front of an enormous house set far back off the road, he nodded. "This is Eileen's place. It's not as big as the Taj Mahal—but then not a lot smaller, either."

After Jerry pulled the car up, he got out and a young man approached him, saying, "Hello, Mr. Haskins."

"Hello, Tim. How's it going?"

"Fine, sir. The party's already started."

"I can hear it." Haskins turned to his three friends and said, "Come along, I'll get you started."

Erin was filled with curiosity—and some uneasiness—for she had heard even in Africa about the immorality that went on at Hollywood parties. The Fatty Arbuckle case had been in newspapers all over the world, and the lurid details of the drunken orgy in which the young girl had been raped and then killed had disgusted her. When she stepped inside they passed through a foyer and walked down a long hallway. The raucous sound of a saxophone wailing like a soul in pain reached their ears, and when she stepped into an enormous room she was, for a moment, overwhelmed. Haskins must have sensed this, for he said, "A lot of folks here. I don't know most of them. They all gravitate to Eileen's parties. Free liquor and a chance to meet movie stars. You'll find all kinds here," he added. "Old washed-up stars trying to come back. Young starlets who'll do anything to get a part in a movie. Probably more ego in this room than in any comparable space in the universe."

An eight-piece band was blasting cacophonous music that seemed to swell and fill every part of the room. Much of the room was used as a dance floor. Erin watched as the couples were doing the Charleston. It was not the first time she had seen it, but she had always thought it was a vulgar dance. She loved waltzes, slow and sedate and smooth, but there was something animalistic and almost frightening about the way women, especially, flung themselves into this new dance.

Around the dance floor people were sitting on chairs or divans. Others were walking about, and all of them seemed to have a drink in their hand. Waiters dressed in white coats and navy blue trousers moved about carrying trays full of cocktails. Alcohol was illegal, of course, but Erin surmised that no one was going to be arrested at the home of Eileen Day.

As they crossed the room Erin glanced to her left and saw a woman sitting on the floor. Her hair was down in her face, and she was muttering something. A man was trying to get her to her feet, and when she refused he simply slumped down, put his head in her lap, and went to sleep.

"There's Eileen over there," Haskins said. He took them to the actress and said, "Eileen, I'd like for you to meet the people who will be working on the picture." He gave their names, and Eileen nodded. "Glad to see you," she said. She was a shapely platinum blonde with sultry eyes and pouting lips. For all of her beauty, there was a sharpness about her eyes, a strange predatory look. She at once fastened her attention on Quaid. "So you're the flier from the war. I love heroes." She suddenly laughed and took his arm. "Come on. Let's dance."

Quaid opened his mouth to protest. "I'm sorry, but I don't do that kind of dance."

"You don't? Well, we'll have another kind, then." Eileen suddenly yelled, "Let's have a waltz, Charlie!"

Instantly the bandleader nodded and spoke to the musicians. They went smoothly, without effort, into the "Blue Danube Waltz." Most of the dancers were caught off guard, but Eileen paid them no heed. "Is that old-fashioned enough for you, Quaid?"

Derek Wells suddenly appeared as the couple moved off across the dance floor. "Here you are, Erin. Hello, Rev." He took their greeting and said, "I see Eileen's already latched on to Quaid. Why does that not surprise me?" He laughed and shook his head. "Would you like to dance, Erin?"

"All right," Erin said.

"Make yourself at home, Rev." Wells suddenly thought of Rev's peculiarity. "You can start asking people if they're convert-ed. If you find one, let me know. I haven't run into anybody yet in that condition in this group."

Laughing heartily at his own joke, he turned and led Erin out onto the dance floor, and soon the two were moving about grace-fully to the waltz. There were very few couples waltzing, and Erin said, "You come to parties like this a lot?"

"It's more or less part of the business, Erin. Of course, a lot of people come just to get drunk. But a lot of business gets done here, too."

Erin looked at the woman scrunched over on the floor, and Derek's eyes followed hers. He shook his head. "Always some of that. Too bad." Quaid and Eileen passed by, and Erin noticed that the woman had plastered herself so close to Quaid that a playing card could not have been inserted between them.

Catching her glance, Derek smiled. "Eileen likes your friend."

"She's straightforward, isn't she?"

"That's a polite way of putting it. She's a star. We're all spoiled."

Erin managed a smile. She liked his honesty. "Good you rec-ognize it, Derek."

As they danced he spoke about films, but Erin was keeping her eye on Quaid.

As for Quaid, he had been taken aback by Eileen Day's bold approach. He tried his best to hold her at a respectable distance, but she insisted on pressing closer. She was a fine dancer, and he apologized for his own poor showing. "I'm not much of a dan-cer."

"You're doing fine." Eileen smiled up at him. "I like tall men. They make me feel small and feminine." She suddenly asked, "This Erin Winslow. Are you sleeping with her?"

Despite himself, Quaid let the shock of her question cause him to react strongly. He stared into Eileen's eyes and shook his head. "No, I'm not."

"Why aren't you?"

Quaid understood that this woman was accustomed to shocking people, that she rather liked it. He did not know exactly how to talk to a woman like this, so finally he shrugged and pushed her back slightly. "I respect her."

"So? You don't sleep with women you respect?"

"I'd rather talk about something else, if you don't mind."

Eileen laughed and pulled herself closer again. "I like you. You're pretty easily shocked. That surprises me for a man who went through a war."

When the music stopped and people applauded, Eileen said, "Come on. Let's go get a drink."

She led him to the table, picked up a champagne cocktail, and handed him one.

"No thanks," he said.

"What? You don't drink?"

"I've got a drinking problem."

"So do I." Eileen laughed. She drank both cocktails and then turned to him, her eyes amused. "You want to see my bedroom?"

By this time Quaid knew that this woman delighted in shocking people. "I don't think that would be a good idea, Eileen."

"You some kind of religious nut? I hope not. They're all hypocrites. Come on. Let's dance."

★ ★ ★ ★

"I've really got to go home and get some sleep, Derek," Erin said.

"But it's only eleven."

"I know, but I'm tired from the flight. I imagine we'll be up and at it early in the morning."

"That's right, we will. Come along, I'll get Jerry to drive you home."

Both Quaid and Rev were ready to go, and as they left, Eileen Day came over and stood beside Derek. "The holy rollers. They're all gone, are they?"

"Why do you call them that?"

"You can tell. That lanky one—all legs and arms—what's his name?"

"Revelation."

"He asked me if I was saved. Can you imagine?"

"He asked me the same thing," Derek smiled. "What did you tell him?"

"I told him to mind his own business, except I cussed him out a little bit."

"I think he's the real article."

"No, they're all hypocrites. That Erin! Sugar wouldn't melt in her mouth. It's just an act. Don't tell me, Derek. She's just like I am. Give her a chance, and she'll go along with the right guy."

"You've had a bit too much to drink, Eileen."

"Don't preach at me, Derek. I'll drink all I want!" She showed her defiance by plucking a beverage from a tray a waiter was carrying by and downing it in one gulp. "That Quaid. He's quite a man, I think."

"Better not try your wiles on him, Eileen."

"Why not?"

"Just not a good idea. There are plenty of fellows for you."

"I already gave him his chance. He turned me down, but I'll give him another chance, Derek." She laughed, then turned and wobbled across the room, weaving from side to side.

Derek watched her go and shook his head. "I wish she wouldn't do that. Quaid doesn't need that kind of trouble."

★　★　★　★

On the way back to the hotel, Erin asked, "Jerry, you say there are lots of parties like this?"

"Too many. That's all these people do. Drink and make movies."

"You don't drink, do you?"

"Not me. I need all the sense I've got."

When they arrived at the hotel, Jerry offered to go up, but Erin said, "You go ahead, Jerry."

"All right, I'll see you in the morning. I'll pick you up about eight. Derek wants you to have breakfast with him." He hesitated, then looked at Quaid. "You'd better watch out for Eileen Day. She's a man-eater."

Quaid did not answer, but as he and Erin got in the elevator, she said, "You were pretty thick with Eileen Day."

Quaid seemed disturbed by the comment. Rev had gone ahead and left them alone. Stopping, he turned and said, "You know, I think this is going to be a tough thing, Erin."

"What is?"

"Living in this kind of world. These people are destroying themselves, and they'll destroy anyone they touch."

Erin had felt the same thing, but she said stubbornly, "We don't have to do what they do."

Quaid was very thoughtful and seemed troubled. "I've been reading my Bible since I found the Lord. I came across a verse last week that has stuck with me. It says, 'Be ye not unequally yoked together with unbelievers.' But I think that's exactly what we've done."

"I know that verse, but I don't think it applies here."

Quaid did not argue. He said quietly, "Good night," then went to his room. He found Rev getting ready for bed and said, "Rev, I wish we hadn't come to this place."

Rev stopped, turned to him, and nodded. "Yeah, I think it was a big mistake."

"Erin doesn't think so."

Revelation Brown shook his head. "She's pretty taken with this life, but she's got good sense, and she knows the Lord. It'll come out all right."

Quaid was less certain. He said no more, but his thoughts went back to the party and to Eileen Day, and he could not help but wish that they were outside doing loops in the skies over Arizona, or anyplace other than Hollywood.

CHAPTER TWENTY

MAKING MOVIES

★   ★   ★   ★

Erin stood quietly beside Quaid, studying the scene that was unfolding before them. Derek Wells was wearing a flier's uniform, which included a dashing crimson scarf around his neck. Erin and Quaid had come in early in the morning for a meeting but found that they had to wait until the scene was shot to Derek's satisfaction. It never ceased to amaze Erin how the actors and actresses paid absolutely no attention to the racket and noise and talking that went on all the time they were acting. She was amused, too, by the exaggerated lip motions they used to speak their lines so the audience could read their lips. Of course, there would also be the printed words now and then on the movie screen, but the actors did everything they could to make the silent action exciting and understandable.

Suddenly she felt Quaid pressing against her side. Glancing at him quickly, she saw that his lips were turned upward in a smile, and she wondered what was amusing him.

The scene itself was simple enough. Eileen Day was dressed in a nurse's uniform, and the room was supposed to be a hospital. Several cots lined the wall, and wounded fliers lay on the cots, all of them apparently in comas, for none of them turned to look at the passionate love scene that was unfolding right in the middle of the room.

In this scene Derek was supposed to tell Eileen that he was leaving on a very dangerous mission, and she was begging him not to go. They had gone through it four times already, and now that Erin knew what to expect she waited for the final kiss. When Derek took Eileen in his arms, the camera focused on his eyes. They closed in exaggerated passion, and when his lips fell on Eileen's, they clung to each other desperately. When the embrace was over, Derek moved his lips distinctly to declare, "You are the love of my life! I would give anything if you could love me."

Eileen turned toward the camera, a look of helplessness replacing her usual harsh expression. Now her lips trembled, and her eyes filled with tears. She mouthed the words, more to the camera than to him, "I do love you. I always will."

Immediately Derek cried, "Cut!" And Eileen's face returned to normal as she spat, "I've got to have a drink, and I'm not shooting that stupid scene again!"

"I don't see how they can turn it on and off like that," Quaid said quietly.

"I don't either," Erin murmured.

At that moment Derek saw Erin and Quaid and approached them, with Eileen following right behind. She immediately sidled up to Quaid, draping herself on his arm, and winked at him. "Would you like to try that last love scene, Quaid?"

"Watch out," Derek warned. "She'll have you starring in the movie if she has her way about it."

"Is this one of the first scenes?" Erin asked.

"Oh no. This is almost the last scene in the movie," Derek said. "You've got to read the script."

"Let me get this straight," Quaid said with puzzlement in his eyes. "You're shooting one of the *last* scenes *first*?"

"Oh yes. That way the movie could be finished even if one of the actors died. It doesn't matter much whether we shoot from back to front or front to back. We take each scene as it is, and then it's more or less glued together."

"Kind of a backward sort of thing, isn't it?" Quaid grinned.

"This whole business is backward. Come on, I want to show you the planes."

"I'll see you later, Quaid," Eileen called out as they left. She laughed as Quaid simply smiled at her, and the group left the building.

"Let's go in the car. It's a little far to walk."

They all piled into the car, and Derek drove off the lot. He entertained them with stories about Hollywood until, five minutes later, he stopped in front of a large barnlike structure. "That's what we're using for the hangars. It used to be a barn, but it's big enough for some of the planes anyway."

Eagerly the three got out, and Derek led the way toward the planes that were lined up in front.

"What is that funny-looking plane?" Erin asked, stopping to point at one with three wings painted red.

"That's a Fokker triplane," Quaid answered. "It's the kind the Red Baron flew. I saw him in it once."

"Did you ever get in a dogfight with him?" Derek asked quickly.

"No, and that's probably a good thing. He was a deadly fighter. Many of his kills came when he dropped out of nowhere and shot his prey to pieces before the pilot even knew he was there."

"Did you ever fly one of these?"

"No, but it shouldn't be too hard," Quaid shrugged. "All these planes fly about the same way."

For the next hour Derek took them from plane to plane, including the famous Sopwith Camel, manufactured in Britain.

"Where in the world did you get all these airplanes, Derek?" Erin asked.

"Well, most of them are rented. Some are borrowed. We had to buy two. They cost a fortune, too."

"I'd like to have one of these just for fun, but they're getting pretty expensive. After the war they were cheap," Quaid nodded. "But now they're collectors' items."

"Come along, I'll introduce you to Harry Mapes. He's in charge of the planes."

"I'll be along pretty soon," Rev said. "I want to give this little hummer a once-over."

Derek led them inside the hangar and introduced them to Mapes, a strongly built man of thirty or so with calm gray eyes and a lantern jaw. He had strong, capable hands, and Erin felt the power of his grip, although he shook her hand gently.

"Quaid will be in charge of all the flying, Harry."

"Well, some of these crates are in pretty bad shape, Mr. Wells. They ain't really safe."

Erin spoke up at once. "Rev is a fine mechanic. The best I ever saw."

"I can use all the help I can get," Mapes said with some disgust. "These clowns I got working for me couldn't change the radiator cap on a Model-T Ford."

"Don't be shocked when you meet him, Harry," Erin said quickly. "He'll ask you if you're a Christian, but he asks everyone the same question."

"Well, we could use a Christian or two around here. There's enough heathens in here to start a mission."

"Come along inside. We're going to shoot a scene here. I've got a crew waiting, or they should be."

"They're in there," Harry Mapes said, nodding. "Just like a bunch of kids. I have to keep knocking them away from the aircraft."

Wells led them inside, and they were greeted by three men who had come over to speak to Wells. Wells introduced them and then said proudly, "Look, there's the mock-up we use for shooting close-ups."

Quaid and Erin followed him to where part of an airplane was sitting on sawhorses. It consisted merely of the fuselage with parts of the wings and the rear section, including the tail.

"I couldn't figure out any way to take close-up shots in the air. No place to put a cameraman, and those cameras are pretty bulky."

"We can shoot it now if you want, Mr. Wells."

"All right. Since I've already got the costume on, I think we will. You two make yourselves comfortable and just watch."

Erin and Quaid found a couple of director's chairs nearby and settled back to watch as Wells very carefully climbed up a small stepladder into the single cockpit. A platform was mounted on wheels, and on top of that a cameraman sat ready. Wells grinned. "There's no need for lights, as you see. We've got the best light in the world."

"I wondered why there was no ceiling on this part of the building," Erin said.

Indeed, part of the ceiling had been removed so that the full sunlight came down, illuminating the pilot's face.

"This scene's going to be shot in sunny weather, so show them how we arrange that, Larry."

Larry Tolmud, the cameraman, nodded at a screen and said, "We got a projector mounted right down here, and we can use any kind of background we want to. Right now I got nice sunny weather with bright clouds, so to the audience it'll look like Derek's flying in beautiful weather."

"Let's shoot it, Harry," Wells cried.

The cameraman said, "I'm ready," and Wells immediately put his helmet on and pulled his goggles down over his eyes. "Roll 'em!" he shouted.

Erin watched as Derek went through the motions of flying an airplane. "It looks sort of silly, doesn't it, Quaid?"

"He's right, though. There'd be no way to get this in the air. I'm curious about how they'll do a rainy scene."

The scene turned out to be quite simple. Derek had gone through several motions, pretending to wave to a wingman, turning his thumbs upward, and then down for another shot. Finally he called out, "Okay, let's have some nice stormy weather."

"Okay, boss."

The grip went over and changed the reel on the projector. Dark clouds appeared with lightning flashing on the large screen behind the mock-up.

"Draw the curtain!" he yelled, and Quaid and Erin looked up to see that a covering was being drawn over the open section of the roof.

"Get a shot of this and then give me a shower!" Derek called out.

The two watched as Derek Wells pretended to fly through stormy weather. One of the other grips rocked the airplane back and forth, giving the sensation of a plane being tossed by the wind. A water hose supplied the spray for the shower. Water flowed down over Derek's helmet and face and over his leather coat, and finally he yelled, "Okay, that's it!"

As soon as Wells crawled down from the mock-up, he took the helmet off and shook the water off of his coat. "What do you think, Quaid?"

"Well, there're only a few things wrong."

Derek looked disappointed. "What's wrong with it?"

"The machine gun is wrong. It should be a Lewis gun with that plane."

"A Lewis gun? What's this one?"

"That's a Spandau, a German gun. It'll be fine if you're going to do close-ups of German fighters."

"We'll do a lot of those."

"Then you should change the gun."

"Do you think anybody will notice?" Derek asked rather anxiously.

"Those who flew these planes will notice. But it's a small item. I don't know how technically correct you want to be."

"As correct as possible," Derek said.

"That's not all. Several times, when you fired the gun, you put both hands on the handle. Who was flying the plane while you were doing that? We had to fly with one hand and shoot with the other hand."

"Hmm—hadn't thought of that. Anything else wrong?" Derek demanded.

He listened as Quaid mentioned half a dozen other things, and finally he held up his hand in surrender. "I give up! You get together with Jerry this afternoon and make sure that all this stuff is right. Come to think of it, I guess you'd better read the script. No telling what kind of boners are in it from a technical point of view. Now, let's go have lunch."

"I think I'll skip lunch and go talk to Mapes a little bit," Quaid said. "I need to get to know these planes inside and out."

"Okay. I'll have a script sent to you, and to you too, Erin. Come on, Erin, unless you want to look at the planes. We can plan some of the other scenes."

"All right. I'll be back soon, Quaid."

★　★　★　★

After several days of filming, Derek took Erin out for their usual dinner date. He pulled over to a restaurant that said "Tony's" in big lights. "I'm starving," he said. "It's been a long day."

"I'm tired, too," Erin said. "I didn't know making movies was such hard work."

"That Quaid, he's a slave driver. He knows what he's talking about, though. Come on, let's eat."

They went inside and soon were seated at a table. They both ordered spaghetti and talked quietly about the day's activities until the food came. They fell to their meal with healthy appetites, and after a few bites, Derek asked her, "What do you think about making movies?"

"It's not what I thought it would be like. I don't have any sense of the story, since you don't shoot in sequence. That first day we saw the death of Lloyd Chandler first, and late in the afternoon you were shooting a scene about how he came into the squadron."

"I know. That takes some getting used to."

Derek took a sip of his wine and said, "Something bothering you, Erin?"

"Not really."

"I think there is. I'm getting to know you well enough I can spot things like that. What's the matter?"

"Oh, it's nothing."

Derek let the silence roll on for a while, and then he said seriously, "I know what it is."

"I don't think you do."

"You're bothered about Eileen coming on to Quaid, aren't you?" He smiled when she blinked her eyes with surprise. "You're not too good at hiding your emotions, Erin. Every time those two get together, I see warning lights go off in your eyes."

"All right, it does bother me. I know this doesn't mean a lot to you, but Quaid's just become a Christian recently. And now one of the most beautiful women in the country is practically begging him to—" She broke off in confusion, unable to complete the sentence.

"Trying to get him in bed with her. Yes, she is."

"Why does she want him? She could have almost any man she wanted."

"It's the old, old story, Erin."

"What story is that?"

"Eileen wants what she can't have."

Erin thought about that and said, "I remember a story our teacher in school read to us once about a very rich man. Somebody asked him what he wanted most in life, and I'll never forget his answer: 'If I can think of it, it's not what I want.' "

Derek smiled. "I'm not too swift, but even I get that one. Some things can't be put into words."

"It's asking a lot for a man to refuse a woman who's being that obvious, isn't it, Derek?"

"Yes, it is. Most men can't do it. Most men won't even try. I admire Quaid. I can see he's doing his best to fend her off. Would it be so terrible if he did have a fling with Eileen?"

"It would be terrible for him."

"I'm not talking about him. Would it be terrible for *you?*"

"You're asking me if I care for Quaid, but the answer's not so easy."

"It shouldn't be too hard. You either love him or you don't."

"No, because there are all kinds of love. I love my father one way, and I love Quaid another way."

"So you *do* love him?" Derek said.

"I think you've got a different idea about love than I have. You've been in Hollywood too long. To you love is always something physical, but I don't think it's like that."

"What else, then?" Derek asked, a puzzled expression on his face. "You're right, though. Hollywood's got some twisted ideas."

"I think a person's life is a bit like an arch made out of stone. You've seen arches like that, haven't you?"

"Oh yes. Many times in Europe."

"You remember the top is always called the keystone. It's that keystone that holds all the other stones in place. I watched them build one once in New York City. They had to first build a platform to hold all the stones up, but when they put the last stone in—the keystone—they could tear the platform down and the arch would hold together by itself. That keystone was what held it up. I remember," she smiled, a sweet expression touching her eyes, "that the mason who was building the arch turned to me after he put in the keystone and said, 'The keystone never sleeps.' I thought about that for a long time, and it's become kind of a rule of life to me."

Derek Wells was used to attractive women, but there was something different about Erin Winslow. She was as lovely as any starlet he had ever met, but he saw a depth in her that radiated out from her eyes and made her more beautiful than her mere physical attributes. Her features were so quick to express her emotions. She loved laughter, and the love of life lay in her eyes and in her lips. She was inwardly serene and confident, he had noted, with a composed mouth and a directness that could either charm a man or chill him to the bone. Now she was pensive, and he urged her, "What does all that have to do with what I asked you?"

"I think our lives have to have a keystone. If it's not there, everything falls down. Everything depends on that keystone."

"And yours is Jesus Christ."

Surprised at his perception, she said, "That's right, Derek. What's yours?"

"Money. Power. Success."

Erin studied his classic features. He was handsome to a fault, but now she saw a sadness that most people never saw in this man. "Those things all fail sooner or later, you know."

"You're right."

His words were abrupt, and Erin knew she had touched him. Perhaps uncomfortable with the direction their conversation had taken, he suddenly shifted to talking about the movie's story line and about her part in it. "You'll do fine in your role, Erin."

"I feel like an impostor. I'm no actress."

"You'll do all right. I'll help you."

"The story seems a little sappy to me."

"I know, but it'll pack 'em in."

"Quaid says that the script doesn't really reflect what it was like over there in France during the war."

"Nobody wants realism in a movie. They want illusion. A handsome hero overcomes all odds and defeats the evil Hun. He kisses the blond heroine, and they live happily ever after." He saw her shake her head slightly and said quietly, "It's Holly-wood, Erin—it may not be true, but it's what people want."

* * * *

When they reached Erin's hotel room after leaving the restaurant, Erin turned to Derek to speak, but before she could, he said, "Let me come in."

"No, Derek."

"Please." He tried to put his arm around her.

"Don't you ever give up?"

"I'm like Eileen. I'm not used to being rejected. May I kiss you?"

Erin hesitated just one fraction of a second too long. She had done so not deliberately but out of confusion. When he kissed her, which he did expertly, she found herself enjoying it and kissed him back, despite her better judgment.

Derek held her tightly, but when he lifted his lips from hers, he said, "You're a wonder, Erin. I don't like starlets. They're as phony as a wooden nickel, but I'm falling for you."

Erin felt guilty now for allowing him to kiss her. "You'll have to find someone else, Derek." She hesitated and then said, "I think you're still in love with your wife."

"No, I'm not," he protested.

"Your face changes when you mention her name. And several times you've talked about good times in your life, and all of them are connected with her."

Derek dropped his arms and stepped back. "It's too late. You can't go back again to something like that." His usually chipper tone became suddenly morose.

"Why not?"

"I don't know. You just can't."

"Don't be foolish!" Erin said quickly. She touched his arm lightly and said, "Of course you can. Why don't you try? Is she married again?"

"No."

"Maybe she still loves you."

"She couldn't!" he said bitterly. He gave her one unfathomable look and bit off the words. "I gave her too hard a time. But you wouldn't understand. Listen, I've got to go." And with that, he turned and left.

Erin watched him go and felt a great pity for him. He had received so much of what the world had to offer—and he had so much to give—and yet life for the famous Derek Wells was empty.

★　★　★　★

Erin was exhausted. They had worked hard for two weeks, and Quaid was trying to talk to her about the next scene. "It's going to be a little bit dangerous, Erin."

"I'll be careful. I always am, aren't I?"

For a moment Quaid stood there silently, and she knew him well enough to understand that he was about to say something unpleasant. She had learned to recognize this sign in him early in their relationship, and now she said quickly, "What is it, Quaid? Are you really worried about this maneuver?"

"It's not just the air scenes that are dangerous, Erin." He could not seem to come out with the words. In the sunlight his black hair glistened, and the brightness made him narrow his eyes. "I don't know how to say this, but I think you're seeing Wells too much."

Perhaps it was guilt that caused Erin to say, "That's none of your business, Quaid. I'll see anybody I like."

Her words seemed to strike him with more force than she had expected. He did not speak for a moment, and then when he did he only said, "I'm sorry," then turned and walked away.

Erin had the impulse to call after him, but she did not know what to say. *He's right*, she thought. *I am seeing Derek a lot, but why does Quaid care?* The question she asked herself stayed with her all afternoon, and when they parted that evening there was a wall between them that she regretted.

CHAPTER TWENTY-ONE

LOVE UNDER THE LIGHTS

★ ★ ★ ★

"I love you, Darlene. I'll love you forever!"

Erin lifted her arms and put them around Derek's neck. He clasped her firmly, and his lips came down on hers. She had her eyes closed but was aware that her response was too rigid. It was something she could not help, and she was not surprised when she heard Jerry Haskins call out, "Cut!"

Erin freed herself from Derek's embrace and shook her head. "I just can't do this, Derek."

"It's all right," Wells said quickly. "It's just new to you."

Jerry Haskins, standing over by the camera, did not speak, but he was an anxious man. They had shot this particular scene four times, and none of the takes had proven good enough to suit either Wells's or his own taste. Jerry shook his head almost imperceptibly, but his frustration with her was obvious.

Although Erin could not know what Haskins was thinking, she was embarrassed that she couldn't please him. Her part in the movie was no more than ten scenes, but two of those were love scenes, and every time Haskins and Wells tried to capture these particular moments on film, they all knew it wasn't working. The other scenes were accomplished easily enough, but Erin was well aware that she was slowing down production.

"Let's take a break, everybody," Derek shouted out. He turned and took Erin's arm, and the two walked away. The setting for the scene was an ornate drawing room, and Erin was wearing a beautiful satiny gown. She said nothing until Derek stepped into his makeshift office, converted from what had originally been a storeroom. A coffeepot sat on a small gas stove, and Derek, without asking, took down two mugs and poured them full. "Have some of this." He sipped the brew, then shook his head. "It's strong enough to stop a charging rhino, I think."

Erin was grateful for the break. Her nerves were wound up tight, but she could not sit down, even though Derek waved toward one of the chairs. She was trying to find some way to explain to Derek how difficult this all was for her, but he seemed to read her thoughts.

"I know it's tough, but it's really an impersonal thing." Derek leaned against the wall, stuck one hand in his pocket, and held the cup with the other. "Everybody asks about the love scenes, but as you see, in scenes such as the one we've been shooting, love is the last thing on anybody's mind. Everybody's thinking about position and lighting and expression and a thousand other things. But there's nothing personal in it."

Erin managed to summon up a faint smile. "I don't altogether agree, Derek."

Surprise washed across Derek's face. "You think it *is* personal?"

"I just can't relax. Kissing somebody just seems to be a very personal thing."

"I suppose you have to be brought up on it. Most actors and actresses start out very young, and they learn to disassociate themselves from emotions like you're having."

"Do you really feel nothing at all when you kiss me in these scenes?"

Derek's lips framed a no, but then he laughed shortly. "I confess that I do, Erin, but you're different."

"Why am I different from any other woman?"

"Because you can't help but make me conscious of your feminine side. Professional actresses—" Shrugging his shoulders, Derek made a face tinged with disgust. "None of the ones I've known have the qualities that you have."

"I don't understand."

"Why, it's simple. Most of them are doing this kind of scene for a living. It's just a job to them, like typing a letter or making a machine part in a factory. No more than that. But you're not like that, Erin."

"I know. I don't think I ever will be."

"Sure you will. We'll just have to practice harder."

Erin shook her head. "How can you say that? You and Jerry have done everything to help me through this. Everybody's been wonderful, but it's just not working."

"We'll make it work," Derek said. He set his coffee cup down on the desk, came over, and took her free hand. He held it firmly and looked into her eyes. There was a magnetism in him that attracted Erin. She had learned that he was a good-natured man, kind, not at all what she had expected from a world-famous actor. She had also discovered that, despite the atmosphere and the bad moral climate of Hollywood, there was a decency and a goodness in him.

Now she felt the power of his personality, but at the same time she knew she could never become what he wanted to make of her. "I'll try it again if you say so," she sighed.

"That's my girl!" Wells put his arms around her and squeezed her and smiled. "I've got some news for you."

Erin noticed that he did not immediately release her from his arms. She moved almost imperceptibly and then he let his arms drop. "Cecil B. DeMille called me today. He wanted to talk about you."

Erin blinked in surprise. "Me?"

"Yes. He's interested in using you in a film."

She laughed shortly. "He's not as smart as you make him out to be."

"Why do you say that?"

"Because I'm just no actress."

"Well, in DeMille's film you don't have to be much of an actress. He makes adventure films. Lots of scenes with thousands of extras all riding horses and things like that. He's not at all picky about great acting, but he does demand action, which is probably what drew him to you."

Despite herself, Erin was interested. She had met DeMille

twice and had liked him very much indeed. The qualities that DeMille demanded of an actress, according to Derek's description, would not be difficult. She was aware that Wells was watching her carefully and said, "I don't know, Derek. I'll have to pray about it."

Her remark amused Wells. He laughed softly and shook his head. "You are a wonder, Erin! Every actress in Hollywood would give an arm and a leg to work for DeMille, and you'll have to *pray* about it. But that's what makes you so different."

At that moment Haskins knocked on the door and asked, "Do you want to try it again?"

"What about it, Erin?" Derek asked.

"All right." Erin took a deep breath, and as she moved back toward the lights and the camera, she was thinking, *I've learned to do other things. I can do this, too.* A strange dichotomy had taken place within her, although she herself was not aware of it. She was repelled by much of what she saw in the world of motion pictures—yet at the same time there was something that attracted her to it. Without realizing it, she had been drawn by the excitement, the money, and the recognition that comes with stardom. She had tasted a little of it as a stunt pilot, but this opportunity was much greater. *I can do it! If I can spear a lion, then I can act a little!*

★ ★ ★ ★

The sound of the phone ringing jarred Erin from her intense scrutiny of the script she was reading. Since reading was so difficult for Erin, Quaid and Rev had helped her with her scenes earlier that day—taking turns reading the different parts out loud. But now she was trying to decipher them once again on her own to make sure she had them memorized for filming in the morning. Placing the manuscript on the bed, she leaned over and picked up the phone. "Hello?"

"Hello, Erin. This is your grandmother."

"Oh, Grandmother, I'm so glad you called! I tried to call you, but you were out."

"Yes, I heard that I missed your call. How are you, Erin? Are things going well?"

"Oh yes, very well. How are you and Grandfather getting along?"

A silence punctuated Erin's question, and suddenly she knew that all was not well. "What's the matter? Is something wrong with Grandfather?"

"I'm afraid so. He's not doing well at all."

"Oh, I'm so sorry to hear that! What's the trouble?"

"It's his heart. He had palpitations, and we had to rush him to the hospital. They called it fibrillation, and the tests they ran weren't at all encouraging."

As always when Erin received bad news, she did not know exactly how to handle it. Her heart went out to her grandparents, for she had learned to love them dearly during her time in America. "What does the doctor say?"

Again a brief silence, and then Lola's voice came to her quietly. "He doesn't offer a great deal of encouragement."

"But can't they do *something*? Can't they operate?"

"No, Dr. Williamson says not."

"I'll come home right away!"

"No, don't do that, although it's sweet of you to offer."

Erin listened, grasping the phone so tightly that her fingers ached. Lola explained more about her husband's illness and then finally said, "I'll call you if there's any change, and of course, I'm calling all the family to ask them to pray for your grandfather."

"I'll do that, too, Grandmother. I just know that God's going to heal him."

"I knew you'd say that, Erin. I must go now. I have several other calls to make."

"Good-bye, Grandmother. I love you."

"We love you, too."

Erin replaced the receiver in the cradle and stood uncertainly by the bed. Her nature was always to attack a problem head-on, for she had great determination and a strong will. But what could she do in a situation like this? She knew her grandmother would not have put the matter so strongly if there were not serious problems with her grandfather, and this frightened her. She sat down slowly on the bed and folded her hands, noticing that they were not quite steady. She had not realized before just how much she loved her grandfather. *Maybe we don't know how much we love someone until we're faced with the possibility of losing him.* The thought startled her and grieved her. She slipped to her knees beside the bed and began to pour her heart out to God.

★ ★ ★ ★

As Quaid walked along the edge of the airfield, something about the sky depressed him. Perhaps it was the hills over to the west, humped up on the horizon. They seemed to him to be sullen, and in the late September afternoon haze they shouldered their way upward, like wild animals with some brutal intent. He did not like California with its dryness and its relentless sunshine. But now the sun had gone into hiding with the approach of an unusual fall storm. The darkening sky was suddenly torn asunder with a brilliant bolt of lightning that spider-webbed down to the earth. He counted off the seconds, and when the low, moaning boom came to him, he realized the storm was too close to risk flying today.

Quaid turned and retraced his steps. A blue jay flew down ahead of him, spreading his wings as he landed and presenting the almost ferocious blue of his feathers. Defiantly he stood with his head turned, one bright beady eye on Quaid, as if determined to stay and endure whatever onslaught the man might give him. Quaid slapped his hands together sharply, and the jay flew up with a miniature thunder of wings. He circled twice, then flew off, uttering his raucous cry.

Quaid approached his plane and found Rev working on the engine. He stood quietly watching and noted that the lanky man had long, tapering fingers and that he handled a wrench as delicately as a surgeon would handle a scalpel.

Finally Rev took a final turn on a bolt, nodded with satisfaction, and turned around. "That ought to do it," he said. "This little hummer ought to do anything you've a mind to put it through!"

"You're a fine mechanic. I wish I knew as much about engines as you do."

"Well, to each his own, I guess. God's given different gifts to different folks."

Rev wiped his hands on a handkerchief, stuffed it back into his hip pocket, and said, "Let's go set a spell. Doesn't look like there's going to be any flying today or maybe tomorrow."

"I don't know," Quaid said as they found a comfortable spot under a tree. "Jerry says we need to get some shots in bad weather. Funny thing. Bad weather's hard to find here in California, but in France during the winters you didn't have much else."

The two men sat there talking idly about planes and about their experiences in France, and finally, as usual, Rev began speaking of the Bible. Quaid sat there quietly listening, for he had learned that there was a profound wisdom in this homely man. Rev was not widely read, except for one book, and that one—the Bible—he knew extremely well. Since becoming a Christian, Quaid had attended church with Rev, and every spare moment he pumped the other man for advice about living a Christian life.

"Rev, I want to ask you something," Quaid said tentatively.

"Shoot. Ask away," Rev said, putting his entire attention on the pilot. "Something bothering you?"

"In a way there is something. How do you know when God is telling you to do something?" Quaid ran his hand through his black hair and shook his head ruefully. "I've been trying so hard to find out how to listen to God. I remember you showed me where Jesus said, 'My sheep hear my voice.' Well, I'm not sure if what I'm hearing is the voice of Jesus or just some idea that came floating into my mind."

"Everybody I know has that trouble. All of us want help and guidance, and yet we've got a mind. I don't have much of one"—Rev grinned—"but it's busy enough. I know exactly what you're talking about. It can be bothersome."

"Well, how do you know?" Quaid asked insistently. He leaned forward and fixed his gaze on Rev, waiting expectantly.

"The first thing to remember is that God wants you to know His will. It's not like you're trying to figure out a secret and somebody's trying to keep it from you. He *wants* you to know His will, probably more than you want to *know* it yourself. Get that in your mind, Quaid. Secondly, God doesn't tell us everything all in one big vision. I know you've been studying Genesis, and you remember the other day you said you envied Abraham because God spoke to Him face-to-face."

"That's right," Quaid nodded eagerly. "That would be easy."

"Yes, it would, but did you ever stop to think that God, as far as we know, only spoke to Abraham in about fifteen-year intervals? Imagine going fifteen years waiting for God to speak! But Abraham did wait, and God did speak. So rule number two is don't get in a hurry."

"Is there any rule number three?"

"I think there is. When you have to move and you're not entirely sure of what God wants, then go ahead and make your play. If you've got two choices and you're not sure which one is right—and you've prayed about it and you're still not sure—then you finally have to take one road or the other. So you just pick one."

"What if it's the wrong one?"

"If it is, you'll get warning signs that tell you maybe you've made the wrong choice. You'll begin having some doubts about your decision. You just won't feel right inside. So you'll need to stop right there! You're on the wrong road. But on the other hand, if you make that choice and it feels good, it seems just right, keep going and trust God to turn you around if it's not right."

Rev pulled a New Testament from his pocket and thumbed through the well-worn pages. "Look at this. It's in the first chapter of James, verse five. It says, 'If any of you lack wisdom, let him ask of God, that giveth to all men liberally, and upbraideth not; and it shall be given him.' Now, ain't that plain enough? Just ask for wisdom, and God will give it to you."

Quaid sat quietly soaking this up and then smiled faintly. "I've got a big decision to make, Rev. I want you to pray that God will give me this wisdom."

"Why, shore! We'll pray together. I don't believe in puttin' prayin' off, so let's do it right now."

The two men bowed their heads, and Rev began to pray aloud, Quaid silently. Two mechanics wandered by, smoking cigarettes and jesting loudly. One of them saw the two men with their heads bowed, one holding a Bible, and he nudged the other. "Shut up, Bailey!" he said. "Church goin' on over there."

The man named Bailey looked over and grinned faintly. "It usually does, don't it, when that Rev is around."

★ ★ ★ ★

An unusually gloomy day descended on the coast and enveloped the city. Jerry Haskins had suggested that Erin take some time for herself. "Erin, there's really nothing for you to do. We've got all your scenes shot. Why don't you take the day off?"

Erin had found this a welcome suggestion. She had gone to her hotel room and spent the morning alone writing letters and relaxing. At eleven-thirty she was about ready to go get lunch when the phone rang.

"Hello?"

"Hello. Is this Miss Erin Winslow?" It was a woman's voice on the line.

"Yes, it is."

"You don't know me, Miss Winslow. My name is Helen Frazier. I attended one of your air shows once, and I thought you were wonderful."

Erin was used to these calls by now, along with all the fan mail she got. She said, "I'm glad you enjoyed it, Miss Frazier."

"I know you must be besieged with people asking you to do things, but I'm going to join the line."

Apprehensively Erin said, "Well, what is it exactly?"

"I do a great deal of work with handicapped children in a local hospital, Miss Winslow, and many of these children will never be able to go see you perform, but I've told them about you. I was wondering if you would have a half hour perhaps to come by and visit in the ward with some of the children."

Instantly Erin said, "Why, I could do that this afternoon, Miss Frazier. It's the only time I really have free."

"Oh, that would be wonderful!"

"Where is the hospital?" Erin took a pad and quickly wrote down the directions. "I'll meet you there at one-thirty, if that would be all right."

"It would be just fine. I so appreciate it, and the children will love it!"

* * * *

Helen Frazier proved to be a small woman, very attractive, with a wealth of light brown hair and a pleasing expression. She had large, well-shaped brown eyes and an expressive mouth. She put her hand out as Erin approached and said, "I thank you so much for coming, Miss Winslow."

"Why, I'm glad to do it. But I would imagine they would rather have a baseball player or a movie star, Miss Frazier."

"Call me Helen."

"Fine, and I'm Erin."

"Actually I've heard you are a movie star, of sorts, aren't you?"

"Oh, not really. I'm just now making a picture with Mr. Derek Wells, but it's a very small role. I think an actress is the furthest thing from what I really am."

The two were standing in the foyer of the hospital. There were people moving through, but Helen Frazier ignored them. "You don't know who I am, do you, Erin?"

"Why—"

"I was Derek's wife."

Erin reacted sharply to this. She had never seen a picture of Helen Frazier, but for some reason she was surprised at the woman's appearance. She did not look like the kind of woman that a famous movie star would marry. *But, of course,* she thought, *he wasn't a famous movie star when they married.* She remembered Derek telling her that they had had a hard time financially as a young couple, but they were close to each other then. It was only after money and fame came rolling in that their marital problems began.

"No, I didn't know that, but Derek has spoken of you."

"What did he say?"

Erin was taken by surprise at the direct question. She saw, however, that the woman was sincere, and she said, "Whenever he talks about you it's always in a very special way. I've met divorced men before who weren't this kind about their ex-wives, but he always speaks of you very highly."

Helen dropped her eyes for a moment. "We had something very good going for a while."

"Derek thinks so, too. He told me once that every time he thinks of anything good in his life, you're always involved with it."

Her words warmed Helen, and she said, "Thanks for telling me that."

"You've never remarried?"

"No, I don't think I ever will. You see, I became a Christian a few years ago, and if I understand the Scriptures correctly, a man and a woman are joined for life."

"I believe that, too," Erin said instantly.

"Do you really?"

"Oh yes! That's why I want to be so careful about choosing a husband."

"I thought I'd been careful. Of course, I wasn't a Christian when Derek and I married. That came afterward, but I loved him, and I know he loved me. But then when he became a star, it changed him." Sadness touched Helen's eyes, and she shook her head. "I stayed with him, but I couldn't become a part of the things that go with Hollywood and the life out here."

"What do you do now?"

"I'm a nurse, and I help these handicapped children as much as I can."

"I think that's wonderful," Erin said warmly. "Why don't we go see the children, and then afterward you and I can talk, if you have the time."

"Do *you* have time for that?"

"Oh yes. I've got all afternoon. I would enjoy it."

"Well, come along, and you can spend some time with the children. You'll find them very sweet, I'm sure. They'll break your heart, but you can't show it. Tell them stories. Try to make them laugh. Just be yourself."

As the two walked along the hall, Helen spoke of the children, but just before they entered the double doors that led to the children's ward, she turned to Erin. "The gossip columnists all say that you and Derek are having a romance."

Erin's cheeks burned. "They say a lot of things, but I want to tell you, Helen, that I am *not* having a romance with Derek."

"I imagine he's tried."

"I suppose you might say that, but I'm not interested in being any more than friends." She hesitated, then added, "I'm going to pray that you and Derek will get back together. Every time he's talked about you, I've had a very strong feeling that he still loves you. And I know you love him."

"It's too late for that, isn't it?"

"With God all things are possible!"

"Yes, they are. Well, come. Let's go see the children."

★   ★   ★   ★

During the next week Erin went back twice to visit with the children, and each time she had lunch with Helen Frazier. She genuinely admired the woman, who gave herself so unselfishly, and on Thursday Erin said to Derek, "I've been seeing Helen this week."

"Helen?"

"Yes. Your ex-wife, Helen."

Derek stared at her. "Why would you see her?"

"She called me and asked me to visit with the children at the hospital, and I went. We went out to lunch, and I've seen her several times."

Derek dropped his eyes and seemed sad. "What did you think of her?" he asked finally.

"I think she's a wonderful woman!"

Derek blinked. "Do you really?"

"Yes, I do. She's so honest and works so hard for those children. I admire her so much."

"So do I, Erin."

"Do you ever see her?"

"Not really."

"I think you should."

Derek stared at Erin. "Why do you say that?"

"I think you're still in love with her."

Erin's words seemed to strike Derek. He was usually a cheerful man, but now a cloud crossed his features. He did not answer but simply stared at her. Finally he turned and walked away without a word. Erin watched him go and thought, *He's so unhappy, and I think that Helen could change all that.*

★　★　★　★

Later that afternoon Erin got a phone call. When she picked up the phone and answered it, the voice came back, "Hello, this is your grandmother."

"Oh, Grandmother, how are you?"

"I'm fine, but I didn't call to talk about myself."

"Is it Grandfather? Is he worse?"

"He's about the same, but it's not about him, either. It's about Amelia."

"Amelia? What's wrong with Amelia?"

"She's left home, and all of us are terribly worried about her. She hasn't, by chance, contacted you, has she?"

"Why, I haven't heard a word from her. Did she say anything about coming here?"

"Not to me, but Phillip said she's mentioned California several times."

"She's not here yet, but if she comes, I'll call you at once."

"We're all terribly worried. She doesn't have much money, so we can't imagine where she is. Call us if she gets in touch with you."

"Of course I will. Right away."

Erin hung up the phone, and her brow contracted in a furrow. She had been worried about Amelia for longer than most people. They had grown up together, and Erin had seen Amelia's rebellious streak begin to develop when she became a teenager. Now she was in a strange country and vulnerable to all kinds of dangers.

Erin began to pace the floor and finally left her room and went down and knocked on Quaid's door. He opened it almost at once and, looking at her face, asked, "What's the matter?"

"May I come in?"

"Sure, come on in. Is something wrong? Is it your grand-father?"

"No," Erin said quickly. "He's about the same. But it's Amelia. She's run away from home. Grandmother just called me."

"Sit down," Quaid said. He waited until Erin sat down and then asked for the particulars. He listened while she spoke and then shook his head. "That's a bad one," he said finally.

"You could see how she wanted to experience everything life had to offer, Quaid. I'm worried to death about her."

"Tough when these things happen, and there's nothing you can do about it."

The two sat there talking quietly, and Erin was suddenly aware that there was a comforting quality in Quaid that she had never noticed before. Perhaps it had not been there before but had something to do with his becoming a Christian. He seemed so solid now, and he had a peace that had been lacking before. As he spoke quietly now, she was suddenly grateful that he was there for her to talk to.

Finally she said, "I've been seeing Helen Frazier, Derek's ex-wife." She went on to explain the circumstances and then said, "It would be wonderful if they were to find each other again. I know she's still in love with him, and I think he's still in love with her."

Quaid nodded his agreement. "I'd like to see that happen. I've been trying to learn a bit about how to live for the Lord, and everything I read about marriage says that it's forever, like geese."

Erin blinked. "What do you mean like geese?"

"Why, Canadian geese mate forever. Didn't you know that?"

"No."

"Well, it's true, from what I read. They find a mate and stay for life. If something happens to one of them, the other one grieves forever, I guess." He bowed his head and studied his fingers, which were locked together. "When people marry," he said quietly, "it should be for as long as they live."

Erin sat there silently for a moment. Then she whispered, "I think you're right. We should pray for Derek and Helen."

"For them and also for Amelia."

She looked up and saw a smile turning up the corners of his lips. "Sounds funny to hear myself say that. To talk about praying."

"It doesn't sound funny to me. It sounds wonderful!"

CHAPTER TWENTY-TWO

BETWEEN HEAVEN AND HELL

★　★　★　★

All but a few scenes of the movie had been shot, and Derek should have been happy, but Erin noticed that he did not seem to be particularly joyful. Whenever they went out to lunch or dinner, he talked little, and when they recently had gone to a concert he'd particularly wanted to hear, he had remained silent the whole time. He was not acting like the man she had first met.

Erin had been thinking a great deal about the handicapped children she had visited in the hospital. She had, in fact, gone back to make a fourth visit. While she was there a thought came to her that had slowly developed and ripened. Her heart had been touched by the children, some of them so young they could not even walk, and the desire to help them grew in her.

Finally she called Helen Frazier and asked to see her. The two met at the hospital cafeteria, where they got coffee and took seats in a corner. At ten o'clock in the morning the restaurant was not crowded, and the only sounds were the cooks talking in the kitchen amid the clatter of dishes.

"I've thought so much about the children you help, Helen," Erin said, "and I want to do something to help them myself."

"Well, you *have* helped them. You can't imagine how excited they've been about your visits. They all want pictures of you. Signed pictures."

"I'll have the studio make some, and I'll bring them back—but I want to do more than that."

"Well, what did you have in mind?" Helen asked curiously.

"I don't have much money, but while I was visiting in the ward last week an idea came to me. I'm wondering if it would be possible to put on a special benefit air show with all the profits going to the handicapped children you take care of here."

Helen exclaimed, "Why, Erin, that would be wonderful! Do you think it could be done?"

"It might be a very small air show, but Quaid and I have gotten to know quite a few of the stunt pilots. We could put out some feelers. At the very least, Quaid and Rev and I could put on a small show, but I'd rather it be bigger than that."

Helen's eyes suddenly filled with tears, and she bit her lower lip. "You know, Erin, I do this work day after day, and I see these children in such pitiful condition. Aside from a few doctors and nurses and relatives, no one seems to care. When someone does care—like you—it's like a light coming on in my spirit." Helen reached over and took Erin's hand and held it. "Whatever you could do would be so welcome!"

★　★　★　★

" . . . and so that's what I'm going to do, Derek, and I need some help." Erin had rushed into Derek's office and bombarded him with her idea for a benefit air show. Derek had listened at first with surprise, and then as Erin had gone on speaking rapidly, he had leaned forward, his face alight with interest.

"These are the children Helen works with?"

"Oh yes! That's how I got involved with it all, Derek. She's such a loving woman, and I do want to help."

Derek Wells rose and walked over to the window. He stared out silently for a while and was so still that Erin was afraid she might have crossed over some invisible line. She felt certain that Derek still loved Helen, but in Hollywood, it was virtually unheard of for a man to go back to a former wife.

Suddenly Derek turned and said, "I'd like to help you on this."

"You would? Oh, Derek, that would be wonderful!"

"Why don't you work on getting as many pilots to participate as you can? Put together a good show. And I'll work on the publicity. I'll make it sound like the greatest air show ever done, and we'll stress the fact that all the proceeds are going to handicapped children. And I'll get some stars to be there—that ought to help." His eyes grew bright, and he said, "I never would have thought of this, but I should have."

"Oh, Derek, I'm so excited!" An idea came to her mind, and she said almost casually, "Why don't you call Helen and tell her what our plan is? I'm sure she'd appreciate it."

"All right, I will. Now you get cracking on the nuts and bolts."

★ ★ ★ ★

Helen Frazier looked up, turned, and then stopped dead still. She had been helping Toby, a six-year-old, who was having great difficulty managing his new crutches. He was frightened, and the braces on his legs seemed to be part of his fear.

"Please, Miss Helen, I'm afraid."

Helen took her eyes off Derek Wells, who had entered through the double doors and was coming toward her rapidly. "It's all right, Toby. I will stay with you as long as you want." She looked up then and said quietly, "Hello, Derek."

"Hello, Helen. Who's this young fellow?"

"This is Toby."

Derek knelt down until he was on the boy's level and put his hand out. "Hello, Toby. How are you today?"

"I'm not so good."

"Well, I have those days myself. What seems to be the problem?"

"I can't make these things on my legs work, and I'm afraid to try to walk."

"Well, you're getting to be a big boy now, and I think you're going to make it. I'll tell you what. Suppose we help you a little bit—Miss Helen on one side and me on the other side."

"Would you do that?" Toby asked hopefully.

"Sure. Come on now. I'll get over here, and, Helen, you get over there, and we'll be running up and down these halls before you know it."

The walking lesson continued for fifteen minutes, and Helen was amazed at how Toby responded to Derek's jokes and smiles. She was very tired, for she had put in many hours this week working with the children.

After depositing Toby with another aide, Derek said, "Can you take ten minutes off for a break?"

"Of course. Would you like to go to my office?"

"That would be fine."

The two passed out of the large ward, walked down the hall, and stepped into Helen's small office that she shared with another nurse. Actually it was more of a nursery than it was an office, and it was cluttered with toys and a cot. Still, she had a desk, and now she said, "Would you like coffee or, perhaps, a cold drink?"

"Not really," Derek said. "I wanted to talk to you. Erin came to me with this idea of an air show with the benefits going to your children here. I'm very interested in it, Helen."

"You mean you'd like to help?"

"I'll do anything I can."

"You could do so much, Derek," Helen said, and suddenly she could not face him. She turned and looked out the single window, but he had seen her face.

"Hey, you're not crying, are you?" he asked.

"I guess I am," she said as tears gathered in her eyes. "You should have seen me when Erin offered to do the show. I blubbered like a baby."

"Well, there's nothing to cry about." Derek came over and hesitated, then put his hand on her shoulder and turned her around. Now tears were running down her cheeks, and she took a handkerchief out and dabbed at them. "Crying's okay. I do it myself sometimes."

"I don't believe you."

"It's true enough," he shrugged. A silence fell over them then, and Derek said, "I told Erin I would arrange all the publicity. It won't be advertisements. It'll be feature stories in all the big papers. I'm also going to arrange for some big stars to be there. People will come out stargazing as much as to see the air show. It'll be big, Helen."

"That—that's wonderful, Derek. I appreciate it, and the children will be so blessed."

"Here, sit down. I want to hear about what you've been doing."

Helen sat down and almost shyly began to talk about her work. As she did she saw that she had Derek's total attention, and that he did not take his eyes off of her. Finally she laughed nervously. "Here I am talking about myself and my work."

"You're doing a fine thing here, Helen. I'm proud of you." Derek reached over and took her hand, held it for a minute, then with a gesture that caught Helen completely off guard, he bent forward and kissed it. He looked up and said, "I'm *very* proud of you. I always have been."

"Oh, Derek—"

"I've been lonely, Helen. I think about the good times we used to have. Didn't have a dime, did we?"

"Not a dime."

"But we had fun. Do you remember going to the Crawfish Festival in Baton Rouge and dancing there?"

"I've never forgotten. It was such fun. We had such a good time there in Louisiana."

The two sat there talking, and Helen felt something stir in her heart. After a time Derek got up and said, "I know you have to get back to work, but maybe we could get together later. Maybe we could go out tonight and get some Chinese. There's a little place over on Sixth Avenue that makes the best fried rice you've ever had."

"If you really want to, Derek."

"I'll pick you up at six."

"All right, I'll be waiting."

As Derek left, Helen sat at the desk, and she recognized that the new sensation she was experiencing was hope, and she bowed her head and thanked God for His blessings.

* * * *

The grandstands that were assembled for the occasion were packed, and an enormous crowd had gathered, with standing room only along the side of the field. Erin reached up and grabbed Derek by the arm and said, "Look, Derek, there's Rudolph Valentino."

Derek Wells grinned down at her. "He'd better be here. I had to make him a lot of promises. And there's Bessie Smith and Al Jolson. They're going to do part of the entertainment before the air show starts."

Helen was standing on the other side of Derek, and she smiled at him, saying, "You've done so wonderfully well with all the publicity and getting all these stars to come. It was a great idea to have a little entertainment before the show."

"I don't know as I've ever enjoyed anything more," Derek smiled. A photographer suddenly approached, and he said, "Uh-oh, get ready to smile." He reached out and put his left arm around Erin, his right around Helen. "Smile now and try to look sweet. That'll be hard for me, but not for you two."

Several photographers converged on them, and all of them knew Derek, of course. One of them, however, a sharp-eyed man with a head of bushy black hair, said, "Hey, you stirring up an old romance, are you, Mr. Wells?"

Wells did not release his grip. "No comment. Just take pictures of these beautiful ladies."

"Are you going to do more pictures, Miss Winslow?" Another reporter shot the question and then flashed a bulb in Erin's face.

Blinking to regain her vision, Erin smiled. "I'd rather fly upside down over Madison Square Garden. Acting is too hard for me."

The three stood there answering questions as the musicians entertained the crowd. Finally Quaid appeared. He smiled as he saw the trio and then moved over and said quietly, "It looks like the music is about done. It's about time for the flying to start."

"All right, Quaid." Erin waved at the reporters, and the two pushed their way through the crowd. A wire fence held them back, and the attendant opened the gate. "Show 'em how it's done, Miss Winslow, and you, too, Mr. Merritt."

"We'll do our best, George."

As they walked quickly toward where the planes were being

prepared, they stopped, and Erin said a quick thank-you to all the pilots who had volunteered their services. They had actually put together a very respectable show, and for the next forty-five minutes they watched as some of the best stunt pilots in America went through their paces.

Quaid leaned against the fuselage of his plane, speaking quietly to Rev, and finally he looked up and said, "I guess it's time to go. You ready, Erin?"

"I'm ready."

Erin did not even put on her helmet, for she was going to do her wing walking for the crowd. They had practiced it for several days just to be sure that all was still fresh in her mind. Rev came over and put his arm around her and gave her a hug that made her gasp. "You be good now, and be careful."

"I will, Rev. We'll be back before you know it."

Five minutes later Erin was sitting in the front cockpit, and she knew that the announcer below was announcing her wing-walking act. Her hair was flying in the wind, and when she turned around to face Quaid, who was smiling at her, she had to hold it back. She shouted against the wind, "Let's do a good one for the kids!"

"Right, be sure that safety cable's good and tight."

"I did. It's okay."

The act had become very easy for Erin. She climbed up quickly and surely, slipped her feet into the boots, and then stood up, holding her arms out. She put her head back as the wind whistled through the wire of the wings, and a thrill rushed through her, as it always did during this stunt. She held this position as Quaid brought the plane down no more than twenty feet from the earth. He rolled the plane over slowly, and Erin felt the blood run to her head. She kept her arms out straight, but as she flashed by the grandstand, she waved, and she could actually hear the cheers of the crowd over the roar of the engine.

When they sailed past the end of the field, Quaid slowly rolled the plane into an upright position and then the nose rose, and they gained altitude. For the next ten minutes Quaid and Erin put on a real show. Quaid did acrobatics while Erin stood tall, her golden hair flying in the sunlight.

The last feature of their act was the most thrilling. They

would climb almost out of sight until the plane was a mere dot. Then Quaid would put the plane into a steep dive and actually turn into a spin. He would wait until they were only three or four hundred feet from the earth and then do a loop in front of the grandstand.

The sun was warm on Erin, and she was excited about the way the show had gone. She arched her back, for it was difficult to stand up against the constant wind. The wind pulled her hair across her face, and she reached up with both hands to move it. Just as she did the plane suddenly seemed to fall away beneath her, the nose dropping so rapidly that it jerked her upward. Fear shot through her, and she made a quick grab for the stays beside her legs, but the power of the sudden drop was too much. She felt her feet pull from the leather straps that held them, and before she could even think, she felt herself blown off of the wing by the force of the sudden lurch. As she flew over the rear cockpit, she actually caught a flashing glance of Quaid's face, which was filled with horror. The only thought she had was, *Thank God for the safety cable!* She hit the end of the cable when she was immediately behind Quaid's cockpit, and it brought her up with a tremendous jerk, but it did not completely stop her. She was thrown against the upright rudder, and she saw to her horror that the end of the cable was whipping around. It was still tied to the short piece of metal bar that had been the anchor, but the bar had been torn loose.

I'm going to die!

Now she felt the wind pulling her past the upright rudder, and she tried desperately to hang on, but the force of the wind tore at her.

Quaid had been caught off guard by the sudden downdraft that had yanked the plane downward. He had often hit downdrafts, but this time there had been absolutely no warning. He saw Erin's form as it flashed over his head, and he heard the wrenching of the metal as the bar tore loose. Twisting his body, he pulled back on the throttle until the plane was running at the lowest speed. When he turned, however, he saw Erin slowly sliding from the upright fin, and even as he watched, the wind pulled her loose. His heart seemed to stop as he saw her grab the leading edge of the horizontal tail section. Her body was stretched out, and he saw in one instant that her hands were white with the strain. His mind worked like lightning. *I'd never be able to get her back into the plane, even if I could grab her before she fell!*

His actions were almost automatic. He came up out of the cockpit and slid his body down the fuselage. He reached the tail section, but just when his hand was no more than a foot away from Erin's, the plane suddenly gave another lurch—this time with the nose upward, and he saw Erin slip and fall away toward the earth. Without hesitation, he launched himself past the tail and hurtled downward.

Erin had seen Quaid leave the cockpit and come toward her. She had tried to scream for him to stay where he was, but the wind was in her face stealing her breath. As her hands left the rudder, she suddenly was free and falling toward the earth, which looked like a green, patched counterpane below. At that instant, when she knew that death was nearer than she had ever imagined, everything suddenly seemed to move in slow motion. She remembered a conversation she had once heard among pilots who did parachute jumps. They had been talking about how the fall to the earth slows when a parachutist holds his body parallel to the earth and spreads his arms and legs; whereas, if he wants to go into a dive, he needs to fold his arms and pull his legs together.

Erin immediately threw her arms out. Her back was now toward the earth, and above her she could see the form of Quaid Merritt. She felt herself slow down almost imperceptibly, and she saw that Quaid, who was wearing his parachute as always, had his arms along his sides and his feet together and was descending straight down. He was no more than ten feet above her, but she guessed that the ground was very close. Most parachutists bailed out at a much higher altitude, she knew.

Oh, God, be our help! was her prayer.

Quaid approached closer and closer until finally he was only a few feet away. Still she did not move her hands, for she knew that every bit of resistance she gave to the air would help. She had no idea how close they were to the earth, but one thing she knew: Quaid would die with her before he would pull his ripcord.

Quaid's hand suddenly touched the front of her silken shirt. She grabbed desperately for his arm, and he came against her, holding her tightly. "Hold with everything you've got!" he shouted. And as she clung to him with every ounce of strength, he freed one hand and pulled the ripcord. As soon as he did, he threw both of his arms around her.

Erin was looking up and saw the chute open, and a tremendous jerk rattled her teeth.

And then . . . and then there was quietness. Erin had never known such quiet. He was holding her in his arms, and his face was inches from hers. She glanced down and saw the smoke and flames from their plane, which had crashed some distance from the crowd. She looked straight down and saw that they were over the landing strip, coming down very close to the stands. And then she could hear the crowd cheering and screaming.

"Erin, are you all right?"

"I am now, Quaid," she said.

He suddenly leaned forward and kissed her hard and then he laughed. "This is an odd time to say it, but I've got to."

They were descending rapidly now with the double weight, and the ground was rushing toward them, but Erin did not take her eyes from him. "What is it?"

"I love you."

A few seconds later, before she could even speak, he yelled, "Here's the ground! Double your knees up!"

Erin hit the ground with a tremendous blow that hurt her feet, and the two of them rolled over. But she knew even then that Quaid had pulled his body around to take the brunt of the blow, and she was cushioned by it. As they lay in their awkward embrace, she cried, "Are you all right?"

Quaid hugged her tighter and said, "I'm okay now."

And then there were people there pulling at them and shouting. Erin's whole body ached, and the sharp pain in her side told her she had injured a rib. But she struggled to her knees, and the first person she saw was Rev Brown. Right behind him were Derek Wells and Helen Frazier. The three knelt down, and Rev had tears in his eyes. "He gave you wings like an angel. This time the angel had black hair and was six-two."

"I never saw anything like it," Wells whispered. "You gave your life for her, Quaid."

Quaid slowly got to his feet and helped Erin up. He looked at the three and then at the mob that was coming, and then he looked down at Erin. "That's what a man's supposed to do for the woman he loves. Give his life for her."

Derek took a deep breath and put his arm around Helen and held her close, and then the crowd surrounded them, shouting and screaming.

CHAPTER TWENTY-THREE

"DO YOU REALLY LOVE ME?"

★　★　★　★

"Oh, come on, Rev, give us a break! You know where Quaid's hidin' out, and Erin, too."

Revelation Brown leaned against the fuselage and studied the four reporters who had converged around him. They had appeared shortly after he had managed to get rid of another group. Now he scratched his head thoughtfully and said, "Sorry, fellows. But truth be told, I don't know where they are."

One of the reporters, a short, thin man with a pair of penetrating blue eyes, shook his head and argued. "That can't be true. You and Quaid, at least, are always closer together than any two guys I ever saw. Now, come on, Rev, I've got a wife and three kids."

"Congratulations," Rev smiled. "I trust you're a follower of the Lamb?"

The small reporter scowled. "You can preach your sermon at me some other time, but right now Quaid Merritt is hot news. Did you see this morning's paper?"

Rev glanced casually at the newspaper the reporter pulled out of his hip pocket and spread before him. "Yeah, I seen it. It's right interesting reading."

"This country's starving to death for heroes, Brown." The

speaker was Charlie Handley, a short, pudgy man with a pasty face and a mustache, which was a mistake. Charlie Handley had worked for a number of newspapers during his career. He was noted for finding out things nobody could find out except him. Now he said, "Look, Rev, I know you two are friends, and if you are a friend of Merritt, you can do him a big favor. Right now he's hot news." Handley shook his head and gestured toward the paper held by the smaller man, whose name was Johnson. "Look at that story. America's starving to death for heroes, and we've got a real live one here."

Rev reached into his pocket and pulled out a pack of gum. He stripped the paper from one stick, rolled it up into a circular form, and popped it into his mouth. "Quaid's been a hero for a long time. Didn't you ever read what he done over in France?"

"I know that," Handley said, "and that's what makes this story so great. He saved the life of the Golden Angel. Everybody knows about it. Everybody wants to meet him."

"That's right," a third reporter interjected. He was a tall, lean man with a bushy head of red hair and pale blue eyes. His name was Dodge, and he worked for the Hearst papers. "The boss told me to find out all I can about this guy. I've got to have a personal interview, Brown, and I'm willing to pay for it." He reached into his pocket and pulled out a billfold, but stopped when Rev shook his head firmly.

"Nothin' doin', fellas. In the first place, I don't know where Quaid is. In the second place, I wouldn't tell you even if I did."

"Don't you want to see your boss make a pile of money?" Johnson demanded. "Why, he'll be more popular than Doug Fairbanks."

The reporters argued to no avail. Rev Brown simply stood there chewing his gum, his arms crossed, and from time to time inquired into the spiritual life of the reporters. Finally they gave up in disgust, and Rev shook his head as they turned and left. He had spoken the truth. He had no idea where Quaid was. After the air show Quaid had been pursued by almost everyone. Reporters wanted to talk to him, and young women were anxious to be seen with the hero. Writers wanted to write books about him, and businessmen wanted him to endorse their products. Quaid had put up with this for two days and then had finally hidden himself away.

All them people tryin' to make Quaid rich and famous, and he runs off and hides. Rev grinned at the thought and shook his head. *I think it's the right thing to do. He doesn't need all that stuff.*

★ ★ ★ ★

As Erin entered Derek's office accompanied by Quaid, she was pleased to see Helen by the actor's side. As Erin glanced curiously at the other man in the room, Helen came over and hugged her gently, for she knew Erin was sore from all the bumps and bruises she had acquired in the accident. "Where have you been? I've tried to call you a dozen times."

Erin took her embrace and smiled ruefully. "It's been a little hectic, Helen. The phone's been ringing off the hook." She turned and looked at Quaid. "Everyone's looking for the hero."

Quaid shot a look of disgust at Erin and shook his head. "Foolishness, that's what it is!"

"No, it's not," Derek said, "it's just natural. People want to meet a real hero. I know you don't like to be called that, so I'll lay off. But I've got a gentleman here I think you might be interested in meeting." He turned and said, "This is Mr. Harold Goldfine. Mr. Goldfine, I think you recognize Quaid Merritt and the Golden Angel, Erin Winslow."

"Of course I do." Goldfine came forward. He was a shorter man with an olive complexion who appeared to be in his late forties. He had coal black hair and a pair of piercing, dark eyes. "I would like to congratulate you on your rescue, Miss Winslow. And you, sir, on your daring feat."

Derek said quickly, "You may not know it, but Mr. Goldfine is a producer. He's one of the best in the business. He's come here with an offer for you two."

Erin felt Quaid stiffen, and when she shot a glance at him, she saw that he was not smiling. Quickly she said, "What kind of offer, Mr. Goldfine?"

"In this business you have to catch the tide, Miss Winslow," Goldfine said easily. He had a high tenor voice and used his hands a great deal as he spoke. "Someone asked me recently, 'How do you know, Goldfine, what kind of picture will be a hit?' You know what I told him?" Goldfine grinned and nodded enthusiastically. "I told him to go make a living at the racetrack betting on the horses. It's a lot safer than making movies!"

"Listen to the man, folks," Derek said quickly. "He knows what he's talking about. He's got a string of hits behind him that's the envy of Hollywood."

"In any case, nobody knows who producers are except the people in this town." Goldfine shrugged. "They know the stars. But somebody has to get things rolling, and that's what my job is. I hear a good idea or I think of something that would make a good movie, and I put it together."

Erin turned her head to one side and asked quickly, "You're not thinking of making a movie with Quaid and me, are you?"

"Of course I am!" Goldfine nodded enthusiastically. "Why not? Think of the possibilities. We have a genuine heroine, the Golden Angel—a daring young lady from Africa who kills lions with spears. We have a man who was a hero in France keeping his country safe shooting down Germans—a fine-looking man, I might add, who looks more like a hero than some who are taking money for it. Of course I'm thinking about this. Why wouldn't I be?"

Quaid shifted uneasily. "I may as well tell you right up front, Mr. Goldfine. I'm not interested in anything like that."

"Wait a minute, Mr. Merritt. You haven't listened to my proposal yet. I'm a good salesman. I don't know what your objections are, but I assure you that there's a fortune to be made in it. I was thinking of another movie featuring airplanes. Derek here's already done the war, but how about a movie starring a pair of stunt fliers such as you and Miss Winslow? Why, it would be a natural! Everybody in the country would pay to see you two. We can show how you saved her life—might even reenact it and put it on the screen."

"No, thanks. I don't want to go through that again," Erin said quickly. She turned to Quaid and saw that his face was set in a rather stubborn expression. She knew this streak ran in him, and she quickly said, "I really don't think it would be possible. In the first place, I'm not an actress." She laughed suddenly. "Derek can tell you about that."

"And I'm no actor," Quaid put in.

"Well, that really doesn't matter too much. Listen, just sit down and let me go over some figures with you, and then you can think it over. Some people say I like to push people around, but I can see you two have reservations. Just listen to my proposal, and then if you don't like it, I'll leave you alone."

"Yes, please do," Derek said. "You sit down with Mr. Goldfine. Helen and I will come back when you're finished."

Derek and Helen left the room, and both Quaid and Erin sat down and listened as Goldfine outlined his plan. He was enthusiastic and even eloquent as he presented his plan. When he spoke of the money, Erin's eyes opened wide at the figures he mentioned, but she was aware that Quaid was stolid and unmoved.

"Well, that's it. I'll let you two think it over, and I'd appreciate it if you'd get back to me as quickly as you can. I hope you decide to do it. It would be a great movie and maybe the beginning of a new career for both of you."

Goldfine rose, shook hands with both of them, and left. As soon as he left, Helen and Derek came in, their eyes bright.

"We were waiting outside the door," Helen said quietly. "What did you decide to do?"

"We didn't give him an answer," Erin said.

"I could have given him one," Quaid said. "I don't want anything to do with it."

Derek stared at the two and then laughed. "I can never get a handle on you two."

Erin saw that Helen was holding on to Derek's arm, and she smiled. "I take it you two are getting along well?"

Derek laughed and then put his arm around Helen and hugged her. "I asked her to marry me a week ago. She turned me down."

Helen Frazier was radiant. There was joy in her expression, and she said, "But something happened. We argued about getting married for two days, and then finally I told him that I couldn't marry a man who was running from God."

"That's what I've been doing. I see that now," Derek said quickly.

"So finally after a long discussion about our relationship and about God and about our future, Derek and I prayed together."

"That's right, and something happened to me. I don't know what it was, but it's been different ever since. I just told God I'd do anything if He'd have me."

Both Erin and Quaid were smiling then. They congratulated the couple, and when Erin hugged Helen, she asked, "When's the wedding to be?"

"We haven't set a date, but God is in it. I know He is."

"I'm a little concerned about being a Christian in Hollywood and making movies," Derek told the two before him. "Do you think I can do it?"

"God can use anybody anywhere. You just stand up for Jesus like Rev Brown does. Well, maybe not that blatantly. That may not be your style," Erin laughed. "But God will be with you. I'm so happy for both of you!"

★　★　★　★

Quaid stopped the car beside an orange grove, and Erin said, "Why are you stopping?"

"Just want to talk a little bit."

"All right." Erin turned to him and saw that he was very serious. She said quickly, "That was wonderful about Derek and Helen."

"Yes, it was. I'm glad for both of them. I think they're going to make it."

They sat there in silence for a moment, then Quaid turned more fully around to face her. "How are you feeling about all these things, Erin?"

"What things do you mean?"

"I mean all these offers to make movies—to be a star."

"I thought it was what I wanted," Erin said slowly. She leaned back against the seat and closed her eyes and thought. Finally she sat up and met his eyes. "I'm really confused. Anybody would want to make a lot of money and be a success, wouldn't they?"

Quaid did not answer her for a long moment. Instead, he seemed to change the subject. "I've been thinking about all the friends I lost in France. It comes back to me, and I don't know why. It was pretty rough, Erin. Young fellows would go over there sometimes, no more than seventeen years old, and they'd fly off on their first mission. Sometimes they wouldn't come back. A young blond-headed fellow named Terrence Stevens did that. He flew off on his first mission and never returned. We all knew he was dead. When that happened it reminded me of a story or a poem I read one time that talked about children who went off to pick flowers in a field—and just never came back."

"That must have been awful!"

"It was. I still don't like to think about it. Nobody who went through it does, but I can't help it, Erin." He reached over and ran his hand over her golden hair and did not speak for a moment. Then he said, "Those fellows who died over there will never be able to do what a man should do. They'll never find a girl to fall in love with or marry or have children. They'll never be able to do whatever it was God put them on this earth to do."

Erin's heart went out to Quaid. She took his hand and held it tightly and waited for him to continue.

"I've got to leave for a while, Erin."

Quaid's words caught Erin off guard. She swallowed hard, then said, "Leave? Where will you go?"

"It's just that I've got to be alone for a while. I've got to settle something about who I am and where I'm going."

Erin had determined that she would say nothing to Quaid about what he had said just before they had landed after her brush with death. But now she said, "Quaid, when we were falling, you told me you loved me."

He looked at her and squeezed her hand. "Yes, I did."

"Did you mean it?"

"I never meant anything more in my life, but—"

Erin waited for him to finish, but instead he reached forward, put his arm around her, and pulled her close. She knew he was going to kiss her, and when he did she surrendered to him completely. As the moment lengthened she felt her heart pounding.

When he raised his head, she whispered, "I love you, Quaid."

"I love you, too, but I've got to leave for a while."

"How long?" she cried, almost in anguish.

"I can't tell you. Until I get something straight between me and God." Quaid moved away from Erin, reached down, and started the engine. The car took off, and Erin sat back against the seat. She was stricken but knew that his mind was made up.

When they got to the hotel, he parked the car and helped her out. He said, "I'd like to use the new plane for a while if it's all right." Since losing their best plane in the accident, Erin had purchased a brand-new one and had hardly had a chance to fly it herself yet.

But they did have a backup, so she said, "Of course. Take it as long as you want."

"I'll say good-bye here, Erin. I've got to pack a few things and go."

Erin could not speak for a moment, and then she nodded. Her throat was tight as she said, "I'll miss you."

"I'll miss you, too."

Erin turned and walked away, and she felt, for that one moment, as if she were losing something very precious.

★ ★ ★ ★

During the days that followed, Erin Winslow spent much time with Helen Frazier in the hospital. She had grown to love the children there more each time she visited, and it took her mind off of Quaid Merritt.

When she was not at the hospital, she pushed her aching body on long walks and spent hours at the ocean just sitting and listening to the breakers crash in and watching the dolphins and the gulls.

Once during this time Helen asked her, "What are you going to do, Erin?"

Erin said, "I don't know. I'm a little confused, Helen, but I'm glad things are going well for you."

Things were going very well for Derek and Helen. It was a joy to watch them together. They were making wedding plans now, and the fan magazines were having a field day.

But more and more as the days passed, Erin found herself thinking of her home in Kenya. As she walked along the beach or sat in the quietness of her room, when she could get away from reporters, the scenes seemed to flash in her mind—the veldt, the animals, the smells, the sights and sounds of the bush—and this developed into a longing to see her homeland and her parents again.

During this time offers kept coming in from producers. She had told Harold Goldfine that there would be no picture with Quaid; she was at least sure of this much.

Businesses and firms and representatives of all sorts sought her out. One man offered her a large sum to have her advertise his piston rings.

"What do I know about piston rings?" she had demanded.

"Doesn't matter. If we can get your picture, that'll do it."

Erin had steadfastly refused, and more and more she withdrew into herself.

It was on a Friday night when she was alone in her room reading from the Psalms when the phone rang abruptly and caused her to start. She picked it up and said, "Hello."

"This is your grandmother."

"What is it, Grandmother?"

"It's your grandfather. He's very low. If you can, I wish you'd come home."

Even with the grief that came, Erin felt the impact of that word—*home*. "I'll leave as soon as I can."

Erin immediately called Rev and said, "I've got to go. My grandfather's very ill. Is the plane ready to fly?"

"I'll meet you at the airfield," Rev said. "I'll see that it's gassed up. Can you navigate by yourself, or do you want me to go with you?"

"Could you do that, Rev? I . . . I'd like for you to."

"You bet!"

Erin hung up the phone and stood for one moment. She wished that Quaid were here so he could go with her, but she was glad she would not be alone—not only because she was not a good navigator, but also because she needed Rev's steadfast faith at this time. She drew her shoulders back and prayed, *Lord, let him stay with us until I get there*, and then she started to pack.

CHAPTER TWENTY-FOUR

The Real Adventure

★　★　★　★

Erin glanced down and spotted the landing strip. She banked the plane and glanced back at Rev, who gave her a thumbs-up signal and a broad grin. "We made it!" he shouted.

Erin nodded and smiled faintly, then turned to bring the plane in for a landing.

The trip from California had been uneventful. It had taken three days, but there had been no engine trouble, and the weather had been beautiful. During most of the flight Erin's mind had been occupied with thoughts of Quaid and of his sudden disappearance. She knew his absence had made a greater impact on her than she had thought it would, and somewhere on the long flight she had made a peace with God about him. It had been a simple surrender as they were flying over the flat fields of Kansas. She had been worried and confused, and finally, shaking her head almost fiercely, she cried out, "God, do what you will with Quaid and me. Thy will be done. . . ."

She brought the plane in for a perfect landing and slowed to a stop. Rev climbed out first. He held up his hands, and she took them and leaped lightly to the ground, enjoying the sensation of the cool early-November air. "A good flight, Erin."

"Yes, it was an easy trip."

"I expect you'll want to be getting to your grandparents' house."

"Yes, as quick as we can. Let's make arrangements for leaving the plane."

They walked toward Robert Jennings's ramshackle office, but before they stepped inside the manager came out. He greeted Erin with a smile and shook her hand. "Well, we have a celebrity here."

"Not much of one, Mr. Jennings." Erin returned his smile and the pressure of his hand.

"Not like it was the *first* time I saw you. You were begging for any kind of a job. Now I guess the jobs are begging for you."

Erin nodded and then said directly, "We'd like to leave the plane here."

"Sure. You can put it right over by your other one."

"By our other one?"

Jennings nodded to his right. "Yeah. There it is right over there."

Both Rev and Erin turned to see the shiny new plane they had purchased in California. Erin quickly exchanged glances with Rev and then asked, "Mr. Jennings, has Quaid been here?"

"Why, sure! I thought you knew that. He's taken your father for a couple of flights. Speaking engagements, they said."

"My father!" Erin said, puzzled. "What do you mean?"

Jennings grinned and pulled off his cap. He ran his hand through his thinning blond hair and said, "It's funny for me to know more about your business than you do. Your folks are here in the States, staying with your grandparents. Quaid's staying there, too."

"Oh my, I hadn't heard! When did they get here? I'd better get there quickly!"

"I'll take care of that plane for you. Just leave it there."

"Thanks a lot, Mr. Jennings. Come along, Rev. We'll get a cab."

Rev pulled their small bags out of the plane, and ten minutes later they were in a cab headed north. The two made the ride without speaking, both engaged in their own thoughts. When the cab pulled up in front of the Winslow house, Erin got out and paid the driver while Rev got the bags. The cab pulled away, and they started for the house. When they reached the first step, Erin looked up to see her parents emerging, both of them smiling.

"Mom—Dad!" Erin exclaimed. She ran forward, hugged both of them, and then demanded, "Why didn't you tell me you'd be here?"

"We did, but I guess the letter got misplaced somewhere. Maybe the ship we were on traveled faster than the one that carried the letter." Barney smiled faintly.

Erin introduced Rev, and Rev at once said, "I usually ask folks if they're saved when I first meet 'em, but I've heard enough about you to know better."

"That's a good way to meet people, Revelation. I like that name."

Erin asked quickly, "How's Grandfather?"

She saw her answer before her parents spoke. "He's not doing well," Katie said.

"I'm afraid it's time for him to go home," Barney said soberly. "He's been waiting for you. He wants to see you."

"Come along," Katie said. "I'll take you to him. Barney, will you show Mr. Brown to a room?"

Erin turned and accompanied her mother as they went up the stairs to the master bedroom. As they entered, Erin saw her grandmother seated beside her grandfather, and she went to her grandmother at once. Lola rose, and the two exchanged embraces.

Lola said quietly, "He's been anxious to see you, Erin. I'm glad you were able to get here."

Erin took the seat Lola had been sitting in and reached over and put her hand on her grandfather's shoulder. "I'm here, Grandfather," she whispered as Lola and Katie quietly slipped from the room.

Mark Winslow was pale, and his cheeks were hollow. A pang came to Erin, for she had always remembered him as a strong, vibrant man filled with health and ready to tackle any task. Now the years had caught up with him. When he opened his eyes, however, she saw that they were clear, and his voice was surprisingly strong as he took her hand and said, "I'm glad you're here, Erin. I wanted to see you before I went home."

The simple sentence brought a thickness to Erin's throat, and she had to close her eyes, for the tears welled up. She held on to one of his hands with both of hers and leaned forward. "I'm glad I could get here."

"You flew?"

"Yes. I brought Rev with me."

Mark Winslow lay quietly studying the face of the young woman. Erin could see the irregular beating of his heart in one of the veins of his throat. She waited, not knowing what to say, and finally Mark sighed and gave her a smile. "How are you, Erin?"

"Why, I'm fine, Grandfather."

"Tell me what you've been doing. Quaid's been telling me some of the things, but I want to hear it from you."

"You've been talking with Quaid?"

"Yes. He's a fine man, Granddaughter. Now—tell me."

Erin spoke of how she had spent her time, for the old man seemed interested. He listened intently and said, "What are you going to do with your life?"

Erin lifted her head, for she understood well what her grandfather meant. She knew that he and Lola and her own parents were concerned about her connection with Hollywood and making movies. And now she said quickly and forcefully, "I'm not ever going to be in a movie again! It's not for me. It's not the kind of life I think God wants me to live."

When she said this, Mark's hand tightened on hers. He gave her a beautiful smile. "I've been praying that I would hear that before I left. I'm so proud of you, Erin."

Lola peeked her head in the door and asked if Mark needed anything, and he said, "See if you can find Quaid, sweetheart."

Lola nodded and went out at once. Mark let his hand remain in both of Erin's and said, "I've been praying a great deal lately for my children and grandchildren. I'm very concerned about Amelia. I want you to pray for her and help her all you can."

"What's she doing now?"

"She has a job and her own apartment. She was here yesterday, but I see a restless spirit in her." Mark Winslow squeezed Erin's hand and said, "You're going to have to stand by her. She's going to have a hard time."

The door opened, and Erin turned to see her grandmother come back into the room, followed by Quaid. Their eyes met, and he smiled and came over and stood beside the bed. He put his hand on her shoulder, and when Mark Winslow reached out his other hand, he knelt and reached out and took it.

"Lola and I saw something in you, Erin, when you were very small. God wants to do something very special with you." Mark's eyes went to Quaid, and he said, "Watch over her, my son. God has something very special for you, too."

Quaid's voice was thick as he whispered, "I'll do it, Mr. Winslow."

Mark seemed to be exhausted with this effort. He closed his eyes, and his grip relaxed. The two waited, and Erin was conscious of Quaid's left hand on her shoulder. They stayed there for some time, and finally Erin rose and said, "I think he needs rest." She left the room, followed by Quaid, and walked down the hall. She found Barney waiting for them, and he asked instantly, "Is he sinking?"

"I . . . I'm afraid he is, Dad."

Barney Winslow straightened his shoulders, but Erin could see he was grieving. "I've always loved him. I've always known he was there for me if I needed him."

Erin suddenly reached out blindly for her father. He took her in his arms and held her, and his eyes met those of Quaid, who was watching. Something passed between the two men, and finally when Erin straightened up and groped for a handkerchief and failed to find one, Quaid handed her one from his pocket.

The three walked slowly down the hall, and Barney said, "The family's gathering. I've canceled all my engagements." He turned to Erin and said, "Did you know Quaid has flown me to a couple of my speaking engagements? I always said I hated airplanes, but he's almost made me like them."

Erin could not speak, but at that moment she felt Quaid come and take her arm. "Come and sit down. You must be tired after your flight. Would you like to rest?"

"I think I'd like to lie down."

Actually she was not tired, but she needed to be alone. She turned and left the two men, saying, "I'll just rest a little, then I'll come back. Call me if—"

When she broke off, Barney said, "I'll call you."

Erin went to her old room and sat down on the bed. She had not wanted to break down in front of the men, but now she wept, for she knew that a great loss lay before her.

★   ★   ★   ★

Mark Winslow only lingered for two days after Erin arrived. Erin talked to him twice more, but when he passed from this life to the next, only Lola was with him, and she would not reveal her final good-byes with the man she loved so deeply.

The funeral was large, but Erin could remember little of it. She did know that Quaid stayed close to her, and when she began to weep silently during the service, he put his arm around her and held her. She had turned to him, and he had whispered words of consolation.

The next day the world seemed lonely to her. She spent the day alone, and the week passed slowly. Quaid flew Barney to a speaking engagement and brought him back the next day.

Erin prayed much and spent a great deal of time with her mother and her grandmother. The three women grew even closer together, and Lola demonstrated a peace that was difficult for Erin to understand. When she mentioned this to her mother, Katie said, "It's the peace that passeth understanding. God gives it to His children when they need it."

Rev spoke with Erin often, and the two became much closer. He spoke of the Scriptures and of the love of God and the power of Jesus in such a way that it filled Erin's spirit. He was a man who knew how to give comfort, and he gave it freely. Not one time did he ask what Erin was going to do, and this was a blessing, for Erin had no idea.

She rose early one morning, and after breakfast she and her mother tarried over coffee alone when the others left. They sat quietly for some time, and finally Katie said, "Do you mind if I ask you something, Erin?"

"Of course not."

"Do you love Quaid?"

Erin answered at once. "Yes, I do, Mother, but things are so complicated."

Katie put her hand on her daughter's and smiled. "Life is always complicated. It always will be."

"Do you like him, Mother?"

"Yes. Your father and I think he's a wonderful man."

"I'm glad." The two women sat there in silence, and somehow Erin felt a special bond with her mother and a peaceful spirit.

★   ★   ★   ★

Erin had been in her room reading the Scriptures for a time but had grown restless. She had just put her Bible down when a knock came at her door. "Come in," she said. When the door opened and Quaid walked in, she jumped to her feet. "Quaid, you're back!"

"I'm back," he said. There was strength in his voice as he asked, "Are you all right?"

Erin nodded. She looked up at him and saw some excitement in his eyes. "What is it? Has something happened?"

"When I left California I told you that I had to settle something. I've been talking to Rev a lot about what's been on my heart. I didn't know whether it was just me or whether it was God."

"What is it, Quaid? Can you tell me now?"

"Yes, I can. I would have told you earlier, but I wasn't sure. These days that I've been spending with your dad have been good for me, and I've decided to believe God." He reached out and took her hands and held them for a while, squeezing them and just smiling at her. "I don't know when it started, but somehow God began to tell me that I was going to use my skills as a pilot not to entertain people but for His glory."

Instantly something touched Erin's heart, and it was like the last piece of a puzzle coming together. "Is that what you've been talking to my father about?"

"Yes. When he goes back to Africa, we're going to take a plane. I'm going to use it for the missionary work there. Oh,

Erin, there's so much to do! Your father has told me about it, and I know that you already know what it's like there. But there are times when supplies need to be flown in. When missionaries need to be taken inland. And there are times when doctors and medicines have to be moved and moved quickly. I can do this, Erin. It's what my heart tells me that God has chosen me for."

"Oh, Quaid, how wonderful! Such a beautiful thing!" Erin's eyes were filled with tears, and she could not speak. She could only look up at him, and now she freed her hands and put them up on his shoulders. "I know it's not my place, but I've got to do this with you. You said you loved me once, so now I'm going to tell you. We're not in a parachute falling, but I feel like God has put us together. I love you, and I want to marry you and be your wife and have your children and fly planes with you in Africa. And—"

She got no further, for Quaid uttered a glad cry and pulled her forward. He kissed her, and to Erin it was like coming home from a dangerous voyage at sea into a quiet and peaceful harbor.

The two stood there embracing, and then she lifted her head and said, "Can you believe that God intended this from the very first?"

"Yes," Quaid said. He held her in his arms, looking down at her, and finally a great joy flashed out of his eyes. "Other men are thrilled with ordinary women, but God gave me the Golden Angel."

Erin put her cheek down on his chest and clung to him tightly. His arms closed about her, and she whispered, "Wait until Nbuta meets you."

The two stood there, and each of them knew that the future was in God's hands. But as they clung to each other, a melody seemed to be chiming, for this was right, and this was good, and this was the way God had planned it all.

EPILOGUE

★　★　★　★

Nbuta stood with his left heel against the inside of his right leg. He held his ever-present spear in his right hand and looked at the two who had come to visit him, and pride swelled his heart.

"So, my young pale hunter has come back home."

"Yes, Nbuta, and I'm so glad to see you." She held tightly to Quaid's hand and looked up at him and then back at Nbuta. "You'll have to call me by my married name now. I am Erin Merritt."

Nbuta nodded. "There is no need for titles. You will always be my daughter." His eyes went to Quaid, and his look seemed to pierce down to the heart of the tall man. "We must celebrate. We will eat now to celebrate the coming of the young lion hunter with her mate."

Suddenly Erin saw the glint of humor that was almost hidden in the tall Masai's dark eyes, and she knew what was coming. "I think that would be wonderful. We haven't eaten anything since breakfast. Would you like to eat a little, Quaid?"

"I'm starved to death," Quaid said.

They had been in Africa for only three days, but already he loved it. He had heard a great deal about Nbuta and was somewhat in awe of the tall, strong warrior with the classic features.

"Come. It would not do to offer old food. We will have a fresh meal."

Quaid glanced at Erin and saw that she was smiling. "Come along, husband," she said.

"All right, wife."

They followed Nbuta out to the herd. He had stopped to pick up a gourd with a large, open mouth. When they came to a big red cow, Nbuta put his hand on her and said, "Be still. You must honor our guest." He quickly filled the gourd with milk and then reached for his spear, which he had given to Erin to hold. Quaid watched carefully and with some apprehension. The tall warrior expertly sliced a large vein in the animal's neck and put the gourd under it. The rich crimson blood poured a steady stream, and finally Nbuta reached down and closed the artery with a blob of cow dung. He then shook the contents of the gourd, saying with a solemn air, "You are our guest, so you will go first." He handed the gourd to Quaid, who took it but stood there uncertainly.

"A happy marriage to both of you. We will eat and drink to that," Nbuta said, and a smile touched his lips as he waited.

Quaid Merritt knew that he was being put to a test. Even though Erin had told him of the Masai custom of drinking this unusual beverage, his stomach churned at the thought of what he had just seen. He did his best not to let his discomfort show on his face as he swirled the contents of the gourd, lifted it, and drank deeply. He blocked all thoughts from his mind, and when he lowered the gourd, he said steadily, "Thank you, Nbuta. Very good."

Erin threw her arms around him and cried, "I didn't think you could do it!"

Nbuta watched as the two embraced, and then he laughed. "You have a good man there. He would make a good Masai."

Quaid then said, "And I have a good woman." He looked down at her and lifted the gourd high in the air. "Here's to the Golden Angel!"

In Rugged Lands, These Women Found Hope

YUKON QUEST: A Series of Renewed Hope

Torn between her desire to obey her parents and her terror of the man they've arranged for her to marry, young Grace decides to escape to Alaska. With "gold fever" and the call of the wild drawing a host of characters to the frozen north, she encounters others who also believe they can build a future of hope and peace with the growing opportunities Alaska offers. But, can they ever truly escape the pasts that haunt them?

Treasures of the North
by Tracie Peterson

Page-turning Fiction From Kristen Heitzmann!

Driven by hope and vengeance, Carina Maria DeGratia sets out for a new life in Crystal, Colorado. She soon finds that the town nicknamed the Diamond of the Rockies is anything but luxurious. Realizing she can no longer depend on her family's reputation, she must instead learn to rely on others to help her. Two men vie for her trust, but both hide a secret. Will Carina learn the truth—and confront the secrets hidden in her heart—in time to prevent tragedy?

The Rose Legacy
by Kristen Heitzmann

⟐ BETHANYHOUSE

11400 Hampshire Ave. S. • Minneapolis, MN 55438 • 800-328-6109 • www.bethanyhouse.com